ATEST WARRIORS

GENGHIS KHAN

OWN

NAPOLEON BONAPARTE

MATTHEW REILLY

THE FIVE GREATEST WARRIORS

Also by Matthew Reilly

CONTEST
ICE STATION
TEMPLE
AREA 7
SCARECROW
HOVER CAR RACER
HELL ISLAND
SEVEN ANCIENT WONDERS
THE SIX SACRED STONES

MATTHEW REILLY

THE FIVE GREATEST WARRIORS

MACMILLAN
Pan Macmillan Australia

This is a work of fiction. Characters, institutions and organisations mentioned in this novel are either the product of the author's imagination or, if real, used fictitiously without any intent to describe actual conduct.

First published 2009 in Macmillan by Pan Macmillan Australia Pty Limited
1 Market Street, Sydney

National Library of Australia
Cataloguing-in-Publication data:

Reilly, Matthew, 1974–

The five greatest warriors / Matthew Reilly.

9781405039338 (hbk).
9781405039833 (pbk).

A823.3

Typeset in 11/14 pt Sabon by Post Pre-press Group
Printed in Australia by McPherson's Printing Group
Cartographic art and illustrations by Laurie Whiddon, Map Illustrations
Illustrations on pages 134, 188, 273, 306, 318, 408 and endpapers by Wayne Haag

Papers used by Pan Macmillan Australia Pty Ltd are natural, recyclable products made from wood grown in sustainable forests. The manufacturing processes conform to the environmental regulations of the country of origin.

*This book is dedicated to
all the men and women
who serve in the
Australian Defence Force*

The Mystery of the Circles

THE FIRST
SHALL BE THE NOBLEST, SCHOLAR AND SOLDIER BOTH.

THE SECOND
A NATURAL LEADER OF MEN,
NONE SHALL ACHIEVE GREATER FAME THAN HE.

THE THIRD
SHALL BE THE GREATEST WARLORD KNOWN TO HISTORY.

THE FOURTH
IS THE GREAT OBSESSOR, SEEKING ONLY GLORY,
BUT GLORY IS A LIE.

THE FIFTH
SHALL FACE THE GREATEST TEST AND DECIDE IF
ALL SHALL LIVE OR DIE.

5,000-YEAR-OLD INSCRIPTION FOUND ON
THE SPHINX STELE, GIZA, EGYPT, KNOWN
AS 'THE RHYME OF THE WARRIORS'.

A MORTAL BATTLE,
BETWEEN FATHER AND SON.
ONE FIGHTS FOR ALL,
AND THE OTHER FOR ONE.

3,000-YEAR-OLD INSCRIPTION FOUND ON A
CHINESE SHRINE IN THE WU GORGE, CENTRAL CHINA.

EVERYTHING IS CONNECTED TO EVERYTHING ELSE.

LENIN

THE STORY SO FAR . . .

The Five Greatest Warriors is the third part of the story begun with *Seven Ancient Wonders* and continued in *The Six Sacred Stones*.

In *Seven Ancient Wonders*, an intrepid international team led by **CAPTAIN JACK WEST JR** found the fabled Capstone of the Great Pyramid at Giza among the (widely scattered) remains of the Seven Wonders of the Ancient World.

After rescuing and raising a young girl named **LILY**—who along with her brother, **ALEXANDER**, was the latest in a long line of gifted Oracles from Siwa in Egypt—Jack managed to set the Capstone in place on the summit of the Great Pyramid before the occurrence of a rare solar event known as the Tartarus Rotation.

Jack's multi-national team was made up of soldiers from several of the world's smaller nations. It included: **ZOE KISSANE**, from Ireland; Sergeant Zahir al Anzar al Abbas from the United Arab Emirates who was renamed **POOH BEAR** by Lily; Lieutenant Benjamin Cohen from Israel, now known as **STRETCH**; a crazy pilot from New Zealand named **SKY MONSTER**; and a rogue American submariner named J.J. Wickham, a.k.a. the **SEA RANGER**.

Providing the team with research and expert knowledge was Jack's long-time mentor and friend, Professor Max T. Epper, call-sign **WIZARD**, and two young Scottish grad students, the red-headed twins **LACHLAN** and **JULIUS ADAMSON** (call-sign: the Cowboys).

As it happened, the Tartarus Rotation was actually the precursor to a far larger celestial event, the return of a 'Dark Star'—the opposite of our Sun, its dark twin. Known as a zero-point field, this Dark Star is a moving body of negative energy that will destroy all life on Earth when it returns to the edge of our solar system in March 2008.

In *The Six Sacred Stones*, it was discovered that this Dark Star was indeed returning to the outer reaches of our solar system. It was further discovered that a device built by a mysterious ancient civilisation and known as **THE MACHINE** exists on our planet and which, if rebuilt, will repel the negative energy of the Dark Star and save the world.

Rebuilding the Machine, however, meant first finding six magnificent underground 'temple-shrines' scattered around the Earth, each built in the shape of an inverted bronze pyramid and known as a **VERTEX**.

At each Vertex, a long-lost **PILLAR**—a dazzling rectangular diamond the size of a brick—must be set in place: the First Pillar at the First Vertex, the Second at the Second Vertex and so on. The locations of the six lost Pillars was another mystery that had to be solved.

It was this mission, the mission to rebuild the Machine, that was begun in *The Six Sacred Stones*.

During that quest, it was discovered that other parties were also seeking to rebuild the Machine: a powerful triple alliance of the Caldwell Group from America, China and Saudi Arabia.

The American side of this alliance was led by Jack's father, **JACK WEST SR** (known as **WOLF**), the Chinese by **COLONEL MAO GONGLI** and the Saudis by a Saudi spy named **VULTURE** who had worked for a time with Jack's team, only to betray them. Aiding Vulture was **SCIMITAR**, Pooh Bear's older brother, who joined Vulture in his betrayal of the team.

Through the influence of the shadowy Caldwell Group—a military-industrial organisation that had once held sway over the American president—Wolf still commanded a special forces branch of the US military, the Commander-in-Chief's In Extremis Force, or **THE CIEF**, which he used as his own private army.

Jack and his father had long been estranged, and at one point in the adventure, in a mysterious mine in Ethiopia, Wolf ruthlessly tried to kill Jack, but failed.

A further group aiding Wolf was a coalition of three European royal houses, those of Britain, Denmark and Russia. They were represented by the beautiful **IOLANTHE COMPTON-JONES** of the British Royal Family.

Finally, a sinister brotherhood of Japanese nationals, humiliated by Japan's defeat in World War II, entered the fray, only with a different agenda: *they did not want to see the Machine rebuilt at all.* Led by Wizard's one-time colleague **TANK TANAKA**, this Blood Brotherhood wanted to see the world destroyed by the Dark Star, to avenge their defeat in World War II. To achieve this end, they managed to infiltrate Wolf's team with one of their own men, a Japanese–American Marine codenamed **SWITCHBLADE**.

After many adventures, Jack ultimately managed to plant the First and Second Pillars at the First and Second Vertices (at Abu Simbel and Cape Town respectively), but not without loss, for *The Six Sacred Stones* ended with the team in desperate straits.

One of their number, Stretch, having been captured by Wolf, was taken back to Israel to face his angry former masters at the Mossad. Pooh Bear was last seen heading off to rescue his friend.

Zoe, Wizard and Lily—having survived a terrifying ordeal at the hands of the Neetha tribe in the jungles of the Congo—dashed to southern Africa in Jack's plane, the *Halicarnassus*, to help Jack at the Second Vertex.

They brought with them **DIANE CASSIDY**, an American archaeologist whom they had rescued from the Neetha. Unfortunately, before they could help Jack, they were forced to flee southern Africa in the *Halicarnassus*, with enemy fighters on their tail.

One unexpected witness to Jack's astonishing success at the Second Vertex was Lily's best friend, 12-year-old **ALBY CALVIN**, who had been brought there by Wolf as his captive. After Jack had laid the Pillar, Wolf left young Alby to die in the dark cavern containing the Second Vertex.

As for Jack himself, after laying the Second Pillar—and foiling Switchblade's plan—he was last seen falling into the fathomless abyss beneath the Second Vertex alongside the furious Switchblade.

The fates of Jack, Stretch, Pooh Bear, Lily and their team, and the search for the final four Vertices and the laying of the last four Pillars are the subject of *The Five Greatest Warriors* . . .

FIRST BATTLE

THE FALL
OF A HERO

Cape Town,
South Africa

SOUTH AFRICA
17 DECEMBER, 2007
THE DAY OF THE 2ND DEADLINE

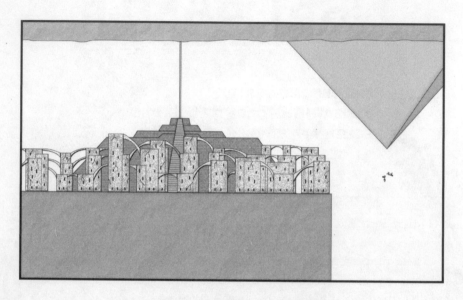

THE SECOND VERTEX

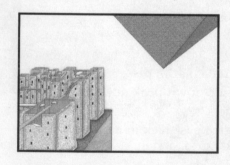

THE CITY AND THE PYRAMID

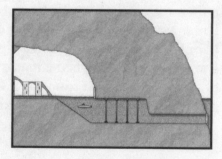

THE ENTRANCE TUNNEL

THE SECOND VERTEX
BENEATH THE CAPE OF GOOD HOPE
SOUTH AFRICA
17 DECEMBER, 2007, 0325 HOURS

Jack West fell.

Fast.

Down into the black abyss beneath the inverted pyramid that was the Second Vertex.

As he plummeted into the darkness, Jack looked up to see the gigantic pyramid receding into the distance, getting smaller and smaller, the jagged walls of the abyss crowding in around it.

Falling through the air beside him was Switchblade, the Japanese–American US Marine who moments earlier had betrayed Wolf and almost derailed his plan to insert the Second Pillar in its rightful place at the peak of the pyramid. It turned out that Switchblade's Japanese blood was more important to him than his American upbringing.

But after a last-ditch swing from Jack and a desperate struggle above the abyss, Jack had jammed the Pillar in place just as the two of them had dropped from the upside-down peak and commenced their fall into the bottomless darkness.

The rocky walls of the abyss rushed past Jack in a blur of speed. He fell with Switchblade in a tumbling ungainly way, their limbs still awkwardly entwined.

As they plummeted, Switchblade punched and scratched and lashed out at Jack, before grabbing his shirt and glaring at him with baleful eyes, screaming above the wind, '*You!* You did this! At least I know you'll die with me!'

Jack parried away the crazed Marine's blows as they fell.

'No, I won't . . .' he said grimly as he suddenly kicked Switchblade square in the chest, pushing himself away from the suicidal Marine—at the same time, grabbing something from a holster on Switchblade's back, something that every Force Recon Marine carried.

His Maghook.

Switchblade saw the device in Jack's hands and his eyes widened in horror. He tried to grab it, but now Jack was out of his reach.

'No! *No!!*'

Still falling, Jack pivoted in the air, turning his back on Switchblade to face the wall of the abyss.

He fired the Maghook.

Whump!

The high-tech grappling hook flew out from its gun-like launcher, its metal claws snapping outward as it did so, its 150-foot-long reinforced nylon cable wobbling like a tail behind it.

The grappling hook's claws hit the wall of the abyss, scraped against it, searching for a purchase before—*whack!*—they found an uneven section of rock and caught—and instantly Jack's cable went taut—and his fall was abruptly and violently arrested and it took all his might to keep a grip on the Maghook's launcher.

But hold on he did and as he swung in toward the vertical wall of the abyss, the last thing he saw behind him was the shocked, furious, powerless, horrified and *beaten* look on Switchblade's face as he fell into black nothingness, his evil mission a failure—a failure that was multiplied a hundredfold by the realisation that Jack West had got the better of him with one of his own weapons and that he was now going to die alone.

Jack swung into the wall of the abyss with a colossal thump that almost dislocated his left shoulder.

Silence.

For a moment, Jack hung there from the cable of Switchblade's

THE FIVE GREATEST WARRIORS   5

Maghook, dangling from the rocky vertical wall of the great abyss, high above the centre of the world and at least a thousand feet below the upside-down bronze pyramid of the Vertex. Despite its immense size, it now looked positively tiny.

Closing his eyes, Jack exhaled the biggest sigh of relief of his life.

'What the *hell* were you thinking, Jack?' he whispered to himself, catching his breath, letting the adrenalin rush subside.

A flutter of feathers made him spin and suddenly a small brown peregrine falcon alighted on his shoulder.

Horus.

His faithful bird pecked affectionately at his ear, nuzzling him.

Jack smiled wearily. 'Thanks, bird. I'm glad I survived, too.'

Distant shouts from up in the Vertex made him look upward— Wolf's people must have noticed that the Pillar had been set in place and were now sending men to get it.

Jack sighed. He could never hope to climb back up in time to catch them, let alone stop them. He might have saved the world and their lives *and* killed the traitor in their midst, but now the bad guys were going to get the booty: the Second Pillar's reward, the mysterious concept known only as *heat*.

But there was nothing Jack could do about that now.

He turned to Horus. 'You coming?'

And with that, he gazed up at the pyramid high above him and after a deep breath, reeled in the Maghook, grabbed a handhold on the rough surface of the abyss's wall, and began the long climb upward.

It took Jack almost an hour to scale the wall of the abyss—by firing the Maghook up it and then climbing up the hook's cable one hundred and fifty feet at a time.

It was slow going, since the rocky wall was largely sheer and slick, and sometimes the grappling hook found no purchase at all and just fell back down towards Jack.

But after about fifty minutes of such climbing, Jack slid over the edge of a stone rail and lay on his back on the precipice, his chest heaving, sucking in air. Horus landed lightly beside him.

When Jack sat up, he saw the magnificent underground city constructed in supplication to the inverted pyramid, with its hollow towers, its streets of inky black liquid and, through the forest of bridges and towers, the massive ziggurat rising in its centre; the whole scene lit by Wolf's dying amber flares.

Of course, the entire supercavern was now deserted, Wolf's force having long since departed.

Also gone, Jack noted sadly, were his companions, the Adamson twins and the Sea Ranger. Jack imagined that, thinking him dead, they had rightly hurried down the long underwater passageway that led back to the open ocean in the Sea Ranger's submarine—

Movement.

Jack spun, his eyes focusing on the summit of the ziggurat, just visible between all the towers.

'Oh my God . . .' he breathed, registering who it was.

There, sitting totally alone on top of the mighty ziggurat, his head bowed, one of his arms in a sling, was a small boy, his daughter's best friend, Alby Calvin.

★ ★ ★

Left alone in this enormous space, with his wounded shoulder aching and with Jack West Jr's battered FDNY fireman's helmet sitting in his lap, Alby had given up all hope of escape and was waiting for the last flares to fizzle out, when he heard the shouting voice.

'*Alby! Albeeee!*'

He snapped to look up—fresh tears still running down his cheeks—to see a tiny figure over by the edge of the abyss waving his arms.

Jack.

Alby's eyes nearly popped out of his head.

Jack negotiated his way across the underground mini-metropolis, over to the central ziggurat, using Wolf's plank bridges where he could and swinging across the wider thoroughfares with the Maghook where he had to.

The black ooze that filled the city's streets appeared to be a thick mud-like substance—semi-liquid and goopy. If you fell into it, you didn't get out.

As he traversed the avenues, he tried his radio. 'Sea Ranger, come in? Do you read me?'

No reply.

His small handheld radio didn't have the signal strength to reach the Sea Ranger in his submarine.

Moving in his unorthodox way, Jack hurried across the underground city.

At last, he came to the base of the ziggurat and bounded up its stairs, arriving at the roof, where he slid to Alby's side and embraced him as if he were his own son.

Likewise, Alby hurled his good arm around Jack, closing his eyes, tears streaming down his cheeks.

'I thought I was going to die here, by myself in the dark . . .' he whimpered.

'I wouldn't let that happen, Alby.' Jack released the boy from his bearhug. 'You're too good a friend to Lily . . . and to me. Plus, your mother would absolutely kill me.'

Alby stared at him. 'You just fell into a chasm with a guy who was trying to kill everyone in the whole world and you're afraid of my mom?'

'Hell yeah. When it comes to your well-being, your mom's scary.'

Alby smiled at that. Then he lifted Jack's fireman's helmet from his lap and offered it to Jack. 'I think this belongs to you.'

Jack took it, and placed it on his head, pulling the chin-strap tight. Just putting it on made him look and feel whole again. 'Thanks. I've been missing that.'

He nodded at Alby's sling. 'So what happened to you?'

'I got shot.'

'Jesus Christ, your mom's really gonna kill me. By who?'

'By that guy who fell into the chasm with you. Back in Africa, in the Neetha kingdom.'

'Maybe there is justice in the world,' Jack said. 'Come on, little buddy, this ain't over yet, we gotta move. We have to catch up with the Sea Ranger and the twins.'

He hefted Alby to his feet.

'How are we going to do that?' Alby asked.

'The old-fashioned way,' Jack said.

Jack and Alby hustled back across the city, heading for the north-east harbour, racing over bridges or swinging—with Alby piggybacking on Jack's back.

After twenty minutes of this kind of travel, they came to the hill of stone steps that descended into the enclosed harbour there.

'I just hope they haven't cleared the tunnel and got to the open sea yet,' Jack said, pulling off his helmet and stepping knee-deep into the water.

Then he began banging the metal helmet against the first stone step beneath the waterline.

Dull *clangs* rang out. Three short ones, three long ones, then three short ones again.

Morse code, Alby realised.

Jack clanged the helmet against the stone some more, punching out another code.

'Let's hope the sonar operator knows his Morse,' he said.

'How will they know it's you?' Alby said. 'They might think it's a trap, that it's Wolf trying to bring them back.'

'I'm signalling: "s.o.s. COWBOYS COME BACK." The twins only just got their nicknames, nicknames Wolf can't possibly know.'

'How will you know if they've heard you?'

Jack sat down on the top step, holding his helmet limply in his hand. 'I can't know. All we can do now is wait and hope they haven't already gone out of range.'

Jack and Alby waited, sitting on the top step of the hill of stairs rising out of the ancient walled harbour, in the dying yellow light of Wolf's flares.

The shadows lengthened as the flares began to sink and fizzle out. The majestic underground city and the pyramid lording over it, having existed in darkness for so many centuries, were about to be plunged back into blackness.

And as the last flare began to flicker and die, Jack put his arm around Alby. 'I'm sorry, kid.'

The flare went out.

Darkness engulfed them.

A moment later, a colossal whooshing noise filled the air, followed by splashing and the sound of water running off the flanks of a—

Bam!

A spotlight lanced out of the darkness, exposing Jack and Alby on their step, illuminating them in a circle of harsh white light. They had to shield their eyes, the light was so bright.

A Russian-made Kilo-class submarine loomed in the water in front of them, dark and immense.

A hatch opened beside the external spotlight and out of it stepped J.J. Wickham, the Sea Ranger, Jack's long-time friend and captain of the *Indian Raider*. With him were the Adamson twins, Lachlan and Julius, Jack's mathematical and historical experts.

'Jack!' the Sea Ranger said. 'And you must be Alby—Jack's told me all about you. Well, come on! Get in! We were in the middle of a perfectly good escape when you called us back. You can tell us all about how you escaped certain death when we're out of here. Now, move!'

Jack could only smile. He grabbed Alby's hand and they leapt down into the water and clambered aboard the submarine.

An hour later, the sub emerged from the ancient tunnel and powered out into the Indian Ocean, barely beating a South African Navy frigate sent to investigate the waters off the Cape of Good Hope.

Once they were safe and clear, the Sea Ranger sought Jack out in his quarters. He found him sitting with Alby, re-dressing the little boy's bullet wound.

'You're lucky the bullet went right through,' Jack was saying. 'Took a little chunk of your shoulder with it. You'll have full range of motion again in about six weeks.'

'What'll I tell my mom?' Alby asked.

Jack whispered conspiratorially, 'I was kinda hoping you'd let me put a cast on your arm and we'd tell your mum you broke your arm falling out of a tree.'

'Done.'

'Er, Jack,' Wickham interrupted. 'What do we do now?'

Jack looked up.

'We regroup. As soon as we're in safe radio-space, call the others on the *Halicarnassus* and tell them to rendezvous with us at World's End.'

'World's End? I thought it'd been abandoned.'

'It *was* abandoned, which is why it's perfect for us right now. Zoe and Wizard know the co-ordinates.'

'I'll get on it.' Wickham left.

Jack watched him go, lost in thought.

Alby was eyeing Jack. 'Mr West?'

'Yeah?' Jack came out of his reverie.

'That Wolf guy has the first two Pillars, fully charged, plus the Firestone and the Philosopher's Stone. That English lady, Iolanthe, has the Fourth Pillar. We have no sacred stones, no Pillars, no nothing. Have we lost this fight?'

Jack looked down at his feet. Then he replied, 'Alby, we're playing a different game to them: they want power and strength and riches. We just want to keep the world turning. And while we're still breathing, we're still in the game. No fight is over till the last punch is thrown.'

CAPE TOWN, SOUTH AFRICA
17 DECEMBER, 2007, 0600 HOURS

The South African Navy patrol boat came alongside a military dock in the shadow of Table Mountain.

As soon as its gangway hit the dock, Jack West Sr—Jack's father and bitter rival in this quest—strode off the boat and stepped straight into a waiting limousine. Known as Wolf, in his late fifties, he was burly and strong, and he looked just like Jack West Jr, with a creased face and ice-blue eyes, only twenty years older.

With Wolf was his five-person entourage, a mixed group that represented the coalition of nations and organisations backing Wolf's participation in the quest to lay the Six Pillars at the Six Vertices: China, Saudi Arabia, the royal families of Europe, and his own American military-industrial cabal, the Caldwell Group.

Representing China was Colonel Mao Gongli. Known as the Butcher of Tiananmen, he'd supplied Chinese weapons and man-power to the cause. His dead eyes hardly ever registered emotion, not even when he shot someone in the back of the head.

Representing the Caldwell Group along with Wolf was Wolf's second son, a cold-blooded CIEF operator, formerly of Delta, who went by the call-sign Rapier.

Representing Saudi Arabia was the man who had betrayed Jack West Jr's team earlier in the mission: thin and angular, with a long rat-like nose, he was an agent of the notorious Saudi Royal Intel-ligence Service, known as Vulture.

Accompanying Vulture was a handsome young captain from the United Arab Emirates named Scimitar. The first son of its chief sheik—and thus the older brother of Pooh Bear—Scimitar had joined Vulture in his betrayal of Jack and Pooh Bear, even going so far as to leave his younger brother to die in an Ethiopian mine.

The last member of Wolf's entourage was a woman, a beautiful and poised young lady in her thirties: Ms Iolanthe Compton-Jones, the Keeper of the Royal Records of the House of Windsor.

As the six of them sat in the limousine bound for Cape Town's military airstrip, Wolf pulled a glittering Pillar from his pack and handed it to Vulture.

'As per our bargain, Saudi,' Wolf said. 'Once I got the Second Pillar, fully charged, you became entitled to the First, also charged.'

Vulture took the First Pillar, charged at the First Vertex at Abu Simbel, eyeing it with barely concealed delight.

When he replied, his eyes scanned Wolf's closely. 'That was indeed our bargain, Colonel West. I thank you for honouring the agreement. I wish you good fortune in the remainder of your mission. Should you require any further assistance from the Kingdom of Saudi Arabia, you need only call.'

The limousine arrived at the military base. Passing the gatehouse without any checks, it arrived at two Gulfstream-IV private jets parked side-by-side.

Vulture and Scimitar boarded one and immediately departed.

Wolf, Rapier, Mao and Iolanthe watched them go.

Mao said, 'I don't trust the Saudis for a moment. They have money but they have all the honour of a gang of desert bandits.'

'They had their use,' Iolanthe shrugged. 'We used them.'

'And they came through,' Wolf said.

'So what now?' Mao asked.

'Now,' Wolf said, 'we get a reprieve of approximately three months, till March next year. And we'll need that time to research the locations of the remaining four Pillars and Vertices.'

Iolanthe said, 'I have the Fourth Pillar already. The Third Pillar is believed to be in the possession of the Japanese Imperial Family.

I understand that after the Second World War, a team of American agents was sent to find it but failed. Is this true?'

Wolf nodded. 'Hirohito hid it during the war. We never found it. We assume it's still somewhere in Japan.

'Which means we have in our possession the Second and Fourth Pillars,' he continued. 'The Third, Fifth and Sixth Pillars must still be found. Likewise, all four of the remaining Vertices need to be discovered before the return of the Dark Sun in March next year. I've had my scientific people working on the Stonehenge data while we've been traipsing around Africa, and I imagine our new African friend, the Neetha holy man, will have unique knowledge as well.'

'What about this coalition of minnow nations?' Mao growled. 'This group led by your first son, the Australian.'

'He doesn't lead them anymore,' Wolf said, thinking of Jack falling into the abyss. 'Without him, they're weakened but not destroyed. The Irish woman is formidable, as we discovered in Africa, and Professor Epper is resilient. In the short-term, pressure needs to be exerted on their masters.'

'And in the longer term? What if they cross our path again?'

'Then we crush them with overwhelming force,' Wolf said.

'Good,' Mao said. 'Finally.'

AIRSPACE OVER NAMIBIA
17 DECEMBER, 2007, 0645 HOURS

The *Halicarnassus* thundered through the sky, banking dramatically to evade the line of glowing tracer rounds that sizzled through the air all around it, tracers that had been unleashed by a pursuing South African Air Force F-15, the first of four fighters chasing it.

The big black 747 rocketed westward, crossing the boundary between the drab brown Namib Desert and the Atlantic Ocean, heading out over the vast expanse of blue.

It had been fleeing like this for almost an hour, since South Africa—all their expenses paid by the Saudis—had scrambled an air patrol to take it out: and in the last ten minutes, as the fighters had caught up with the big jet, it had become a running aerial gun-battle.

As the *Halicarnassus* flew, it returned fire at the lead F-15 from one of the 50mm gun turrets mounted on the inner sections of its wings.

Manning the starboard gun—facing backwards as the jumbo screamed forward through the air—was Zoe Kissane. She drew a bead on the trailing F-15 and assailed it with a withering blast of 50mm fire.

But the South African pilot was skilled and he barrel-rolled clear of the stream of gunfire.

'Sky Monster . . . !' Zoe called into her radio. 'This is like shooting at goddamn bumblebees! What's our plan!'

Sky Monster's voice came in from the cockpit: 'They might be smaller and faster than we are, but we can fly further than they can. They gotta be running low on fuel. So the plan is: you keep holding them off while I get us as far as possible over the ocean, till they decide they're too low on gas and have to turn back. We beat them with range.'

Sky Monster proved to be correct.

A few minutes later, the lead South African fighter loosed a single AIM-9 Sidewinder air-to-air missile and bugged out, heading back for the mainland with his buddies.

Zoe took care of the Sidewinder with a directed microwave burst that literally cooked the missile's dome-mounted infra-red targeting system and the missile ditched harmlessly into the ocean.

The aerial battle over, she wearily headed up to the 747's cockpit, where she found Wizard and Lily with Sky Monster.

Oddly, they were grinning, beaming even.

'Zoe,' Wizard said. 'We just got a call from the Sea Ranger. Jack's alive and he has Alby with him. The Sea Ranger has them both. They want us to rendezvous at World's End.'

Zoe sighed with relief. 'Thank God. Take us there.'

LITTLE McDONALD ISLAND
INDIAN OCEAN
20 DECEMBER, 2007
3 DAYS LATER

At the bottom of the Indian Ocean, in one of the most remote regions of the world, there can be found a cluster of barren rocky islands.

The Kerguélen Islands are administered by France, while the Prince Edward Islands are claimed by South Africa. But south of them all, battered all year round by icy Antarctic winds and the rolling waves of the southern seas, is the Heard group of islands. They are administered by Australia.

One of the Heard islands is Little McDonald Island. It has no wildlife and little flora. There is literally no reason to go there. Which is probably why it was used during World War II as a resupply base for the Australian Navy, complete with fuel dumps, storage warehouses and even a short landing strip.

By the 1990s, its use as a base was long obsolete and it was shut down in late 1991. Whole containers of canned food and diesel fuel had been left there and in sixteen years, not a single can had been stolen. It wasn't worth the effort to get there.

Thus no-one in the world noticed the Kilo-class submarine and the black Boeing 747 that arrived at Little McDonald Island two days after the high drama at the Second Vertex.

Of course, they knew the island by another name: World's End.

★ ★ ★

The reunion of Jack and the team was a joyous occasion.

Lily leapt into Jack's arms, hugged him tightly—then she ran over to Alby and hugged him even harder.

Zoe and Jack also embraced warmly, holding each other for a full minute.

'Alby told me all about what happened with the Neetha,' Jack said softly. 'You must have been incredible.'

Zoe didn't answer.

She just began sobbing on Jack's shoulder, burying her head in his neck, unleashing the pent-up stress and emotion that had been inside her since her bloody encounter with the lost tribe of African cannibals.

When at last she spoke, she said in a hoarse voice, 'Next time, let's let somebody else save the world.'

Jack laughed, stroking her hair gently.

As he held Zoe, he saw Wizard and, with him the archaeologist and Neetha expert Diane Cassidy, plus the Neetha youth, Ono, who had helped them during their escape from the remote tribe.

Wizard smiled. 'Clearly, it's not the fall that kills you, Jack.'

'Right,' Jack said.

'Hey,' Lily said, looking around, suddenly alarmed. 'Where's Pooh Bear? And where's Stretch?'

Once the reunion was complete and introductions made, the team went inside a decrepit old warehouse beside the island's airstrip. Water was heated for showers; canned food was opened and eaten; and Jack explained to the others what had happened to him before he'd arrived at Cape Town.

He told them what had happened at the mine in Ethiopia, including the betrayal of Vulture and Scimitar, his own gruesome crucifixion, his and Pooh Bear's bloody escape and the parting gift they'd received from the Ethiopian slave-force there: the fabled Twin Tablets of Thuthmosis.

Jack pulled the two stone tablets from his rucksack, which had been kept on the submarine during the events at the Second Vertex.

Wizard audibly gasped at the sight of them.

'If Thuthmosis was actually Moses,' he said, 'then that would make these the Ten Comm—'

'Yes,' Jack said.

'Goodness-gracious-Mother-of . . .'

'As for Stretch,' Jack went on, 'Wolf didn't bring him to the mine. Instead, he took him back to the Mossad in Israel, to claim the sixteen-million-dollar bounty on Stretch's head.'

'Oh no . . .' Lily breathed.

Jack said, 'After Pooh Bear and I escaped from that mine in Ethiopia, we headed south to the old farm in Kenya. But when I set out for Zanzibar to find the Sea Ranger, Pooh Bear didn't come with me. He went off to rescue Stretch from the Mossad's dungeons. That was nine days ago. I haven't heard from him since.'

A solemn silence descended on the group.

Lily broke it.

'When we were in the Hanging Gardens,' she said, 'Stretch defied an Israeli Army squad and saved my life. He chose us over them and now they're making him pay.'

She recalled the scene vividly: trapped in a filling pool of quicksand, she had stood on Stretch's shoulders to poke her nose and mouth above the surface, while he had breathed through his sniper rifle's gun-barrel, using it as a snorkel.

Alby asked, 'What does the Mossad do to Israeli soldiers who switch sides and fight against them?'

Jack threw a glance at Zoe and Wizard. Zoe nodded silently. Wizard just bowed his head.

When he finally answered, Jack spoke in a low voice, his face serious. 'The Mossad isn't known for showing mercy to its enemies. Traitors like Stretch receive the harshest punishment of all. There are stories of maximum-security desert prisons, their locations kept strictly secret, where high-grade prisoners are kept under twenty-four-hour guard and . . . mistreated . . . for years.'

'Mistreated?' Lily said.

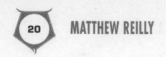

'For *years?*' Alby said.

Jack said, 'If Pooh Bear even manages to discover where they're keeping Stretch, getting in and busting him out will be an all-but-impossible task. It'd be like breaking into Guantanamo Bay and running off with a terrorist.'

Lily said, 'You did that once, Daddy. Can't we go and help Pooh Bear?'

Jack looked at her sadly. 'Lily. Honey. There are some operations that even I wouldn't dare attempt, and this is one of them. I'm sorry, I really am, but we have to leave that to Pooh Bear and keep our eyes on the larger mission. It's a hard decision for me to make, really hard, believe me, but weighing up the possibilities and probabilities of success, I have to make it this way. I'm sorry.'

Jack bowed his head, but not before he saw the look Lily gave him—a look he'd never seen on her face before. It was a look of the most profound disappointment, and in that moment, he hated himself.

'So what *are* we going to do now then?' Lily asked in a sour tone.

'First of all,' Jack said, 'Alby is going back to his mother in Perth; she'll be beside herself when she sees his arm. And after Christmas, I'll be sending you to join him. Keep you two out of harm's way for a while.'

'*What!*' Lily protested. 'What about the rest of you?'

'We're going to try to find the remaining Pillars and Vertices before the world ends in March next year.'

A PRIVATE
MISSION

THE DESERT
DUNGEON

Negev Desert, Israel

Lalibela, Ethiopia

ETHIOPIA – ISRAEL
DECEMBER 2007
BEFORE AND AFTER THE 2ND DEADLINE

WOLF'S MINE
LALIBELA, ETHIOPIA
11 DECEMBER, 2007
ONE WEEK EARLIER

Wolf and Mao Gongli emerged from the mine, stepping out into bright sunshine.

It was six days before the events at the Second Vertex.

Wolf had just seen his son Jack West Jr crushed underneath a massive stone slab, seemingly killed. He'd also left Pooh Bear down there to be sacrificed by the mine's zealous religious guards.

Waiting calmly and casually up here was the British woman, Iolanthe. Waiting less casually—hogtied hand and foot with handcuffs, bleeding from a beating, his eyes blindfolded by a filthy rag, and lying face-down in the bed of a pick-up truck—was Stretch.

Arriving at the pick-up, Wolf stood over Stretch for a long moment, as if assessing him.

'Lieutenant Benjamin Cohen,' Wolf mused. 'Once of the Sayaret Matkal, the famed Israeli sniper force, where you attained the call-sign *Archer*. Transferred to the Mossad in 2003 and soon after assigned to infiltrate the multi-national team led by Jack West Jr and monitor its attempts to locate the pieces of the Golden Capstone of the Great Pyramid. But you went native and you *joined* West and his team, culminating in a terrible Solomonic Choice where you had to choose between your new friends and your old masters.'

Wolf paused. 'And you chose your new friends.'

Beside him, Mao grunted in disgust.

'Which is why your old bosses at the Mossad made you a Category 5 Enemy of the State of Israel—a category usually reserved only for ex-Nazis and terrorist leaders. They put a price on your head, sixteen million dollars, which I will be only too happy to collect. You chose wrong, Lieutenant Cohen.'

With his head pressed against the hard steel bed of the pick-up, beneath his blindfold, Stretch closed his eyes in dismay.

A single tear appeared from underneath his blindfold and trickled down his cheek.

Curiously, Wolf himself took Stretch to Israel.

Of course Stretch was kept blindfolded for the duration of the short journey—during which time he heard Wolf occasionally speak on a satellite phone with his team in Africa, the team pursuing Wizard, Zoe, Lily and Alby through Rwanda and the Congo.

But for the final leg of his journey to his former masters, Stretch was drugged and his world went black.

When he awoke, he found—to his horror—that he was suspended upright inside a reinforced glass tank of some sort, his hands and feet spreadeagled, star-like, manacled to chains at the four corners of the phone-booth-sized tank.

He was naked.

He noticed an IV drip stuck into his right arm—its tiny clear tube rose up and out the open top of his rectangular glass coffin. A catheter-like excretion unit covering his groin area took away waste.

Beyond the confines of his tank, Stretch saw Wolf talking with an older man whom Stretch had met only once in his time at the Mossad: Mordechai Muniz, the ruthless former head of the Mossad, now its 'official advisor'.

Bald, fat and pale, with pitiless black eyes, Muniz had been on the team that abducted Adolf Eichmann from Argentina in 1960.

He had also captured the Black September mastermind behind the Munich Olympics massacre—alive. The terrorist had not been seen since. In the world of spy agencies, Muniz was a legend and his nickname, 'the Old Master', was well deserved.

The Old Master turned to appraise Stretch, surveying his manacled and exposed body like a hunter assessing a captured lion.

Muniz smiled thinly, revealing a set of uneven yellow teeth. 'Lieutenant Cohen. Welcome back to your homeland. You know, there are some who believe that traitors like you should simply be executed for their crimes. But in the higher echelons of the Mossad, we believe that as a punishment death is too easy, too quick, for one such as you: you the wrongdoer suffer no *consequence* for your actions, you don't get to really think about what you've done.'

As Muniz spoke, Stretch saw two technicians climb up a pair of stepladders on either side of his nine-foot-tall glass tank. One of them reached in the open top of the tank and jammed a nose-and-mouth scuba-diving regulator over Stretch's mouth and nose, securing it firmly to Stretch's head so he couldn't dislodge it. The regulator's oxygen tube snaked up and out of the big tank to an air canister attached to its rear flank.

The second technician did something far more frightening.

He angled a wide-bore firehose into Stretch's tank and pulled a lever, unloading gallon after gallon of a stinking green liquid into the tank. The liquid swelled around Stretch's feet, sloshing wildly, quickly rising to his knees . . . then his waist . . . then his chest . . .

Bang!

The two technicians slammed a thick glass lid down onto the tank's open top and started welding it into place with blowtorches.

Welding it . . .

His mouth covered by the breathing apparatus, Stretch's eyes boggled.

They were welding him inside this tank!

The sickly green liquid rose ever higher, reaching his throat.

Muniz's voice sounded hollow now, distant. He said, 'No, Lieutenant Cohen, death is far too good a sentence for you. Your crime deserves more than that; it requires substantial suffering. This is where I come in. Trust me, after several years down here with me, you'll wish we'd executed you.'

And with that the foul green liquid sloshed over Stretch's face and he began to breathe quickly, desperately, through his scuba mouthpiece.

The world around him became blurred, veiled in pale green.

Stretch could just make out Muniz and Wolf shaking hands, and Muniz handing Wolf a suitcase of some kind.

Then Wolf left.

Muniz returned, alone.

And he stood before Stretch's tank, arms folded, just staring up at Stretch—naked and spreadeagled, submerged in the foul green liquid, encased in the welded-shut reinforced glass tank.

Unable to move, and hearing only the sound of his own breathing inside his head, Stretch watched the blurred figure of Muniz standing there gazing at him.

Then Muniz went over to his desk and casually sat down to make a phone call, and in a moment of the purest horror, Stretch suddenly saw how he was destined to spend the rest of his natural life.

RIO DE JANEIRO, BRAZIL
31 DECEMBER, 2007, 2358 HOURS

It had taken Pooh Bear almost three weeks and two million dollars to find him.

Money certainly made things move more quickly, he thought. The Israelis had spent sixty years trying to capture Wolfgang Linstricht, but to no avail. Once, in Buenos Aires, a Mossad assassin had found him, but Linstricht had killed the man with a bread-knife through the ribs, having stalked his stalker through the grimy alleyways of the Argentine capital.

A lifetime ago Linstricht had been the sergeant-at-arms at the notorious Nazi concentration camp Treblinka. He had been Franz Stangl's enforcer: when the commandant ordered that someone be shot, it was Linstricht, a towering six-foot-four brute, who'd carried out the order.

But when World War II ended and top Nazis like Stangl scattered, Linstricht also slipped the net and fled to South America, and had not been seen since.

As Pooh Bear had discovered, Linstricht moved constantly between South American countries to avoid capture: from Brazil to Argentina to Chile. The Israeli abduction of Adolph Eichmann must have scared the shit out of him. But as the episode with the Mossad stalker showed, even at age 86 and constantly hunched to disguise his height, Linstricht was still lethal.

And now here he was, Pooh Bear saw, right there across the street, an old man chatting up a long-legged Brazilian prostitute amid the fireworks and festival atmosphere of New Year's Eve in Rio.

Pooh Bear watched them from the shadows, watched them head back to Linstricht's hotel.

After Pooh Bear and Jack had parted ways at Nairobi airport three weeks earlier, Pooh Bear had headed back to his home country of the United Arab Emirates, his primary goal: to discover where the Israeli Secret Service, the Mossad, was keeping his friend Stretch.

He also wanted to inform his father, the Emirates' chief sheik, Anzar al Abbas, of his brother Scimitar's heinous betrayal.

But en route to Dubai, Pooh Bear had discovered from a friend in the Intelligence Service that only a day before, his father had abruptly disappeared. The old sheik, he was told, had been summoned by Scimitar to join him in Riyadh. Shortly after, all contact with him had been lost.

Dubai, Pooh Bear's friend told him, was now in the hands of his brother's cronies. It was not safe for him to return.

Despite the state of affairs back home, being the second son of the Emirates' chief sheik still had its advantages. Pooh Bear had contacts in the international intelligence community and large amounts of his own trust-fund money—a couple of million dollars—to throw around.

For a week, Pooh Bear made calls, did research, paid bribes and spoke with Mossad watchers both legitimate and not-so-legitimate. For a quarter of a million dollars, he acquired a collection of CIA intercepts of phone conversations between the highest ranked Mossad officials.

After all that, his key discovery about Benjamin Cohen—once known as Archer, but known to Pooh by the name Lily had given him, Stretch—was that he 'had been designated a Category 5 Enemy of the State of Israel for the crime of treason.'

Israel's 'Category 5 List' was an elite one, reserved for the worst of Israel's enemies.

But despite his intelligence contacts, intercepts and money, Pooh Bear could not discover where captured Category 5 enemies were jailed. No-one knew. Lesser targets were placed in military prisons or supermax jails. But not Category Fivers. If they were jailed, no-one knew where, and if they were executed no-one knew where or how such executions were carried out.

The only thing that Pooh knew for sure was that if Israel captured a Category 5 enemy, that man disappeared from the face of the Earth.

And so he formed a plan.

He would find a Category 5 Enemy of the State of Israel and turn him in to the Mossad—but not before doing one last thing.

The target he chose was Wolfgang Linstricht.

Fireworks exploded in the sky above Rio.

Ten minutes after the New Year was rung in and with the last fireworks still flaring above the city, Pooh Bear kicked in the door of Room 6 of a run-down hotel on the waterfront.

Wolfgang Linstricht leapt out of bed, naked, hurling the woman off him, reaching for a pistol among his clothes—but Pooh Bear was faster, bounding across the room. He must have looked fearsome to the ageing German: a burly, dark-eyed, big-bearded, olive-skinned Arab, charging across the dingy room. Pooh kicked Linstricht to the ground before he could grab the gun and jammed a handheld taser into the German's ribs.

Linstricht convulsed violently and then slumped to the floor. The prostitute screamed.

'Get out,' Pooh Bear growled.

She scuttled out, clutching her clothes, leaving Pooh Bear standing over the unconscious Linstricht in the damp little room.

Pooh Bear pulled a capsule from his pocket—it was the size of a standard headache pill—slid it into Linstricht's mouth and pinched the man's nose, forcing him to swallow it.

Then Pooh Bear called the Mossad.

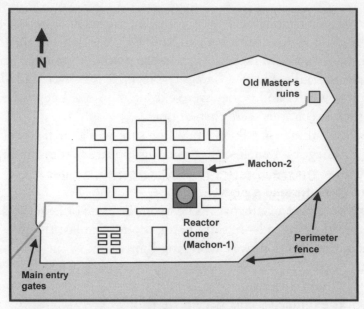

DIMONA NUCLEAR RESEARCH CENTRE
NEGEV DESERT, ISRAEL

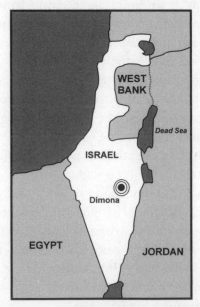

ISRAEL AND SURROUNDS

DIMONA NUCLEAR RESEARCH CENTRE
NEGEV DESERT, ISRAEL
10 JANUARY, 2008, 0530 HOURS

Ten days later, Pooh Bear lay flat on his belly in the hills of the Negev Desert in the barren core of Israel.

Two hundred metres ahead of him stood an enormous military facility, the centrepiece of which was a sixty-foot-high shiny silver dome. Arrayed around the dome were a dozen warehouse-sized buildings, two concrete smokestacks and a cluster of satellite dishes and radio antennas. Anti-aircraft gun emplacements marked every corner of the base—emplacements, Pooh had noticed, that were manned twenty-four hours a day.

It was the Dimona Nuclear Research Centre, the beating heart of the Israeli nuclear weapons programme, a programme whose very existence Israel has neither confirmed nor denied since the 1960s.

As Pooh Bear well knew, Israel possessed nuclear weapons—about two hundred of them, in fact—and they built them here at Dimona, making it the most heavily guarded installation in the country.

It was curious then, Pooh thought, that the capsule-sized GPS transponder that he'd slipped down Wolfgang Linstricht's throat had led him here. After the Mossad had picked up Linstricht—based on Pooh's tip-off—they had taken a circuitous three-day journey halfway around the world that had ended here at Dimona.

And according to Pooh's GPS monitor, Linstrict had been taken to a small bunker-like building half-buried in the earth in the isolated north-eastern corner of the base.

★ ★ ★

The Negev Desert is one of the most desolate places on Earth.

The ruins of ancient waystations, stopping points on the spice route, can be found among its rocky hills and valleys. Likewise, Roman-era quarries and mines are common: King Herod's vast salt mine, Baqaba, lies forty kilometres south of Dimona, not far from its smaller sister mine, Uqaba. Crumbling mesas and craters provide the only sights. It is a dead land: vast, empty and of little interest to anyone. Nothing grows in the Negev.

It had taken Pooh Bear four days to get into position close to the fenceline.

Four days of careful slow crawling, so as not to set off any motion sensors; sleeping under a camouflaged thermal blanket so as not to betray a heat signature; and lying still during the day so as not to catch the eye of the sentries who periodically patrolled the perimeter of the complex.

He'd spent half of one day locating some kind of weak-point in the fence—and found it in a small eroded crevice of crumbled rock that straddled the base of the fence on the eastern side of the complex. The second half of that day had been spent chipping away at the crevice, making it wide enough for him to slip through under the fence.

After that, he'd backed off and waited till this morning to make his move.

The reason: according to his intel, the previous night Dimona was to receive a large shipment of enriched uranium, during which security would be upgraded.

His intel proved to be correct: that night the whole base had lit up like a football stadium, with floodlights blazing and extra guards patrolling the fences. Around midnight, over at the main gates on the western side of the complex, a large semi-trailer rig— with a lead-lined shipping container on its back and flanked by escort jeeps equipped with .50 calibre machine guns—had rumbled into the complex and headed for the base's storage and enrichment facility, Machon-2.

This morning, with the operation safely over, the extra guards were let go and—Pooh wagered—the base guards would be unwinding, glad it had gone off without a hitch. They would be looser. They would be careless.

Pooh Bear gazed up at the massive silver dome rising above the base before him—the main reactor, known as Machon-1.

Game time, he said to himself.

Dawn came and Pooh Bear made his move.

He slipped under the fence and crouch-ran toward the isolated bunker. A small explosive blasted open the lock on its heavy steel door and Pooh Bear was in.

Dark concrete corridors, a darker concrete stairwell plunging down into the bowels of the Earth, and suddenly a strange pungent odour that made his nose crinkle, an odour that smelled like formaldehyde.

Moving fast and low with his MP-7 gripped tightly and guided by his blinking GPS receiver, Pooh Bear emerged from the stairwell into a wider space . . .

. . . and his mouth fell open.

'Allah in Heaven save me . . .' he breathed in horror.

Pooh Bear found himself standing in an ancient subterranean room built by Roman engineers over two thousand years ago: multiple sandstone arches and ornate columns dominated each side of the square three-storey-high space. A small pool, empty of water, lay to one side, once a Roman bath.

A large desk and a high-backed leather chair sat at one end of the chamber, facing the source of Pooh's horror.

On the opposite side of the room, arrayed in three horizontal rows of four so that they were positioned within the Roman arches, stood twelve massive water tanks, each the size of a large telephone booth.

Each tank was filled to the brim with a pale green liquid and encased in them, hovering in the liquid, arms and legs outstretched in humiliating star shapes, were *men*—naked men wearing half-face scuba breathing masks and plugged into IV and excretion tubes.

Pooh Bear found he couldn't breathe.

It was a wall of human trophies.

Living human trophies.

They looked like a dozen Harry Houdinis, all having failed the same water-tank escape trick. Lines of bubbles rose from their mouthpieces. Some of them blinked, alert and awake in their liquid hells.

So this is what happens to Israel's most reviled enemies, Pooh thought.

And in an instant the meaning of the pungent odour became clear: the green liquid was formaldehyde or a watered-down form of it, and formaldehyde was an excellent preservative. These men were being kept alive and *preserved* in their tanks.

Pooh Bear began to feel ill.

He shook the thought away and began searching the tanks for his friend.

In the first tank he came to, he saw Wolfgang Linstricht suspended in the green haze, eyes closed, asleep. In the next tank, Pooh saw another elderly white man whom he couldn't place, then in the third, a younger man with the distinctive long beard of an Islamic extremist, and then in the fourth . . .

. . . Stretch.

Pooh Bear gasped as he saw his friend spreadeagled in the green liquid, his head bowed, his eyes closed.

Pooh banged on the glass wall of the tank and Stretch's eyes opened. At first they squinted in the green gloom but then Stretch seemed to realise that the person standing in front of his tank was not the usual person.

His eyes sprang open when he saw that it was Pooh Bear. A burst of bubbles exploded from his scuba mouthpiece.

'Hang on,' Pooh Bear said, even though Stretch couldn't possibly hear him. 'I'm gonna get you out of there—'

It was at that exact moment that Pooh Bear felt a stinging stab on the nape of his neck. He reached up and felt a small dart there.

Then his arm fell suddenly limp and a wave of terror shot through him as he realised he couldn't move his limbs.

Pooh slumped to the floor in front of Stretch's tank, his entire body going slack.

He heard a voice.

'One shouldn't enter a spider's web unless he is truly sure the spider won't return while he is there.'

A figure stepped into Pooh Bear's field of vision: he was an older man, bald, fat and pale, and he smiled meanly. With him was an Israeli soldier, holding a tranquilliser gun.

'Hello, Zahir al Anzar al Abbas,' the older man said brightly. 'My name is Mordechai Muniz. We've been watching you on our thermal imagers for two days now. You've been a source of immense amusement to me and to the guards at this base. You really are a tenacious son of a whore. That you got this far at all is very impressive. Foolish, but impressive.'

The Old Master grinned. 'You like my living human decorations? The diluted formaldehyde mixture works well—it's a marvellous preservative, although after a decade or so, its carcinogenic properties seep through the skin to produce very painful cancers in my guests. I learned this technique of "live-imprisonment" from a Russian friend of mine, an ex-Soviet general who has a collection of his own. We have a friendly competition going, he and I, to see who can amass the most impressive collection of human beings.'

Pooh Bear still couldn't move.

Muniz shrugged. 'Considering the long silent life your friend has ahead of him, today you have brought him a rare gift: an event. Congratulations, Lieutenant Cohen will get to watch you die in front of him.'

Pooh Bear could only lie there, helpless on the floor, his eyes wide, his limbs useless.

But then in a sudden moment of realisation, he saw his watch— the watch Jack had given him on the tarmac at Nairobi Airport when they had parted; the watch which Jack had said was fitted with an emergency GPS beacon that Pooh could press if he were ever captured or in danger.

With all his might, Pooh Bear willed his right hand toward his left wrist, toward the watch, but no matter how hard he tried or how desperately he focused his mind on it, his right hand wouldn't—couldn't—move.

The watch, his only means of letting anyone know where he was, remained tantalisingly out of reach.

Pooh slumped his head against the hard marble floor, devastated, and in that moment, he knew this rescue was over, a valiant but foolhardy failure.

He closed his eyes in disgust . . .

. . . just as from somewhere outside there came a dull shuddering boom that took both Pooh Bear and Mordechai Muniz by surprise.

Sirens wailed and emergency lights flashed all over the Dimona Nuclear Research Centre.

A great plume of black smoke rose up from one end of Machon-2, the uranium storage warehouse next to the main reactor dome, Machon-1. The charred remains of the giant semi-trailer rig that had delivered the uranium shipment the night before now lay in a smoking heap at the building's docking bay.

People in uniforms and civilian clothing ran as fast as they could away from the rising column of smoke while, a few minutes later, two firetrucks and three jeeps carrying soldiers in full-body yellow biohazard suits hurried *toward* the disaster.

Despite its relative plainness, Machon-2 was actually the most important structure in the whole complex. During a series of now-infamous inspection visits by US nuclear weapons inspectors between 1962 and 1969, the Israelis had built a false wall and an entirely fake control room to conceal the four underground levels *beneath* the surface structure, levels on which the Israelis built their nuclear devices.

For an accident to occur in or near it was catastrophic.

Inside the Old Master's bunker, Mordechai Muniz snatched up his phone: 'What's going on!'

'*We have a Level-4 situation, sir,*' the voice at the other end of the line replied anxiously. '*All personnel must evacuate the base immediately. Please report to your rendezvous point for head-count.*'

Muniz hung up, glancing over at Pooh Bear on the floor of his private chamber.

No, he thought. *The Arab was passionate, sure, but not nearly clever enough to engineer this.*

Muniz nodded to his private guard, 'Let's go.'

The two of them hustled out of Muniz's trophy-lined office, clambered up the stairwell and threw open the heavy steel door to the Old Master's lair, only for the guard to be blown away by two shots from a Desert Eagle pistol held by Jack West Jr.

He wore a bright yellow full-body biohazard uniform, with the hood slung back over his shoulder.

Quick as a whip, Muniz drew his own pistol, but Jack shot him in the forearm and the gun went skittering away. Muniz roared and clutched his arm, his teeth clenched more in anger than in pain.

'Morning, General. I'm Jack West Jr and I'm here to take back my friends.'

Handcuffed and gagged, Muniz was thrown across the floor of his subterranean lair as Jack stepped down into it.

'Well, this is just a little creepy . . .' he said on seeing the array of tanks containing Israel's enemies.

He went straight to Pooh Bear's side, slid to the floor beside his fallen Arab friend. Pooh Bear was only just breathing, paralysis setting in.

'Jack . . . ?' Pooh gasped. 'How . . . ?'

'Tell you later,' Jack said, extracting a hypodermic syringe from the combat webbing beneath his biohazard suit before quickly and precisely jabbing it directly into Pooh's heart.

Pooh Bear came leaping up into a sitting position, gasping deep hoarse breaths, his eyes bulging.

Jack said, 'That'll wake you up in the morning.'

As Pooh regathered himself, Jack was already moving toward Stretch's tank. He paused in front of the big tank—it was only for a moment but it felt like an eternity—and beheld his friend suspended in the green solution, in womb-like silence, kept alive by the intravenous drip, a living, breathing trophy.

Then he raised his Desert Eagle and fired two shots into the thick glass of the tank, angling the shots away from Stretch's body.

The front panel of the tank shattered and then quickly collapsed under the weight of liquid pressing against it. A waterfall of green fluid came blasting out of the tank, sloshing around Jack until all that remained was the empty tank with its front section completely open and Stretch dangling there, still cuffed, the scuba regulator strapped to his face.

Through bleary, heavy eyes, Stretch looked up to see Jack standing before him.

Jack nodded curtly. 'Welcome to your own rescue. This is the halfway point. Time to start the second half.'

Reaching up, Jack removed the mouthpiece first—Stretch coughed and gagged, sucking air into his dry throat. Then Jack extracted the IV drip and, painfully, the excretion catheter from Stretch's body. After that Jack used his gun to shoot through the chains of Stretch's four manacles and Stretch fell out of the tank, free, the manacles still looped around his wrists and ankles like macabre bracelets.

Jack leaned forward, allowed Stretch to fall onto his shoulders in a fireman's carry.

Pooh Bear joined them as Jack raced for the stairs, gun in one hand, Stretch on his shoulders.

'What about those others?' Pooh Bear said. 'In the tanks.'

'I'm only concerned about one guy today,' Jack said grimly. 'Unlike Stretch, those other men did terrible things. I say, if they've still got any, we leave it to their friends to rescue them. Come on. We gotta hustle.'

'How did you find me?' Pooh Bear asked as they bounded up the stairwell. 'I never pressed the SOS button on the watch you gave me.'

Jack spoke as he ran. 'The button triggers an active alarm, but the watch sends out a constant passive GPS signal, plus a pulse rate. I kinda didn't tell you about that.'

'It was transmitting all along . . .'

'You've covered many miles this past month, my friend,' Jack threw a quick look back at Pooh Bear. 'Tel Aviv, Haifa, Buenos Aires. And Rio for the New Year, although I can't imagine you were there for the fireworks. You became a Nazi hunter.

'When I saw you turn up here in the Negev outside Israel's most important nuclear weapons centre and stay here for a few days, I knew you'd found him. We hung back, waiting to see how you did. But when we saw your pulse rate start to plummet a short while ago, we made the call and figured you needed a hand.'

'We?' Pooh asked. 'Who's here with you?'

As he said this, they burst out into sunlight, just as an Israeli military ambulance came to a skidding halt right in front of them, with Zoe at the wheel. She also wore a yellow biohazard suit with the hood swept back.

'*Everyone's* here,' Jack said, and Pooh felt his heart soar.

'How on Earth did you get inside this base?' Pooh Bear asked as they arrived at the ambulance.

'How else?' Jack gave Pooh another enigmatic look. 'We came inside last night's uranium shipment. Where do you think Israel gets its high-grade uranium ore from?'

'Where?'

'Biggest uranium producer in the world: Australia.'

Of course, it was a little more complicated than that.

What Jack had said about the wristwatch was true. Observing first from Little McDonald Island and later from SAS headquarters in Fremantle, Jack had tracked Pooh Bear's progress around the world.

When he saw Pooh head into the Negev and stop for several days in this area—an area that every military organisation in the world knew about: Dimona—he knew Pooh had discovered where the Mossad was keeping Stretch.

The question was whether Pooh could bust Stretch out by himself.

Some calls were made, and Jack discovered that a shipment of uranium was on its way to Dimona from Australia. It was already halfway across the Indian Ocean, heading for Israel's Red Sea port of Elat.

Arrangements were made for Jack and Zoe to rendezvous with the freighter carrying the uranium, and they helicoptered onto the ship in the dead of night three nights ago, along with two trusted military engineers and one lieutenant-general whose orders could not be overruled by anyone.

Some hasty engineering work was carried out on the lead-lined shipping container holding the uranium—it was a 90-foot container on the outside, but after some quick reconfiguring, it was only 85 feet long on the inside: a small gap had been inserted at one end with enough space for Jack and Zoe to stow aboard.

The irony that they might get past the Israelis' defences at Dimona by using the same trick the Israelis themselves had used on the US inspectors in the '60s was not lost on Jack.

Other precautions were taken: the Sea Ranger was getting into position; and Sky Monster had been dispatched to meet up with some Australian SAS troops in western Iraq, some of them former colleagues of Jack's. Lily and Alby stayed at Alby's home in Perth—this mission was far too dangerous to bring them along.

And so Jack and Zoe had entered Dimona, hidden inside the uranium container, watching Pooh's pulse rate and waiting. If Pooh got in and out of there alive, they would simply leave inside the empty container when it was picked up a day later. If on the other hand, Pooh's pulse rate took a sudden dive, then . . .

That morning, Pooh's pulse rate had plunged dramatically and Jack and Zoe had sprung into action.

'Have you got 'em?!' Jack called to Zoe as he placed Stretch into the back of the military ambulance, lying him on its wheeled gurney.

In the driver's seat, Zoe turned to answer him, but caught herself when she saw Stretch—naked save for Pooh's jacket, deathly pale and shivering, dripping all over with glistening green wetness.

'Jesus . . .' she breathed. Then, snapping out of it, 'Yeah! Got a pair of them!' She patted two chunky silver suitcases on the seat beside her.

'Then let's get the hell out of here!' Jack said, slamming the rear doors shut behind him.

The ambulance shot off the mark.

★ ★ ★

Pandemonium reigned all over Dimona.

Firetrucks roared through the streets of the base. Sirens wailed. Men in biohazard suits rushed toward the smoking hulk of Machon-2. Medical crews loaded coughing people into ambulances and sped away.

As three such ambulances sped toward the main gates of Dimona, a fourth military ambulance whipped out of a side street and joined the little convoy.

All four vehicles were stopped at the gates by the guards: Pooh was hidden beneath Stretch's gurney while Jack and Zoe now put on the yellow hoods of their biosuits, revealing only their eyes through Perspex visors.

The guard who saw Stretch—strapped down, still wet and pale and sickly to look at, with an oxygen mask over his mouth—screwed up his face in disgust and yelled, 'Go! Go!' and Zoe floored it and the ambulance sped out of the Dimona Nuclear Research Centre.

'I reckon we have about twenty minutes till they figure out who we are and what we've taken,' Jack said to Zoe as they sped west away from the base, tailing the other three military ambulances.

'Which means thirty minutes till they find us with chase choppers,' Zoe said.

'Where are we going?' Pooh Bear asked, kneeling beside Stretch in the back. 'You *do* have an escape plan, don't you?'

'Yeah, but it's not as imaginative as our entry plan was,' Jack said. 'How were *you* going to get out?'

'The same way I got in. Slowly and with patience.'

'Okay, our plan is definitely not like that.'

'So where are we going?' Pooh asked.

'Those ambulances are going west to Beersheba, in accordance with Dimona's Radiation Emergency Evacuation Plan. We're going to cut south and make for a place called Aroham near Uqaba.'

'How far is it?'

'About forty klicks,' Jack said. 'Which means it's going to be close.'

About five kilometres later, the ambulance convoy came to a fork in the road and the three lead ambulances took the right-hand route, heading for Beersheba. Jack's ambulance, however, swung left and immediately sped up, zooming down the desert highway, the vast emptiness of the Negev rushing by on either side of it.

Exactly fifteen minutes later, the first chase helicopters appeared on the horizon behind it: four American-made Apache gunships.

Attack choppers.

Jack saw them in his side mirror, then looked forward: to see a rise in the road ahead on which stood the dusty ruins of Aroham, ruins he wanted to reach before the choppers caught up with—

—their ambulance crested the rise and Jack's spirits rose at what he saw beyond it: a beautiful black Boeing 747, standing alone on the empty desert highway, beside a smaller set of ruins, wings swept back, tail raised high; a black plane that could only be the *Halicarna*—

—but just then one of the Apaches swooped in from the right and swung into a low hover over the road *right in front of* their ambulance, all its guns pointed right at them, cutting them off from the escape plane!

There was a dirt side-road to the left and Jack yelled to Zoe, 'Go left!'

The ambulance fishtailed as it swung left, zooming onto the dirt road, kicking up a cloud of dust that swirled around the hovering Apache.

A short way down the dirt road was a sorry collection of half-crumbled sandstone ruins: the Roman ruins of Aroham.

Seeing the ambulance take the sudden turn, the other three Apaches leapt forward and caught up, pulling into a wide circular formation around the ambulance and the ancient ruins.

Zoe brought the ambulance to a skidding halt, a dustcloud billowing up all around it as she did so.

The ambulance's radio squawked.

An Israeli voice came over it, speaking in English: '*Attention in the ambulance! We know who you are, Captain West! There's no way out of here. Step out of the vehicle, with your hands raised or you will be fired upon!*'

'Jack . . .' Zoe said.

'On it.' Jack turned, grabbing the radio. He pressed the TALK button. 'Israeli helicopter patrol. I hear you, but I suggest you pull back to a distance of two kilometres and hold that radius.'

'*You have to be fucking joking,*' came the reply.

In reply, Jack grabbed one of the two silver briefcases on the seat between him and Zoe and took one step out of the ambulance, holding it high above his head for the encircling helicopters to see.

'Recognise this?' Jack said into the radio. 'I said two kilometres and not an inch closer. Do it now.'

There was silence on the airwaves, followed by, *That's a—holy fuck. Copy, Captain. We will comply.*

Pooh Bear watched the exchange first with curiosity and then with amazement.

'What's in the case, Huntsman?' he asked.

'Zoe and I didn't spend *all* night in that shipping container, Pooh. When you're left inside Machon-2 for twelve hours, there are other things to find that can aid your escape. This case,' Jack said, 'is an Israeli suitcase nuclear bomb.'

'A suitcase nuke!' Pooh Bear exclaimed.

Jack said, 'They say there are Israeli suitcase bombs at secret locations in all the major capitals of the world—New York, Washington, London, Moscow, Paris—and in the major cities of Israel's key enemies: Damascus, Tehran, Cairo. They're Israel's ultimate insurance policy. Small nuclear devices. Fifty-kiloton yield, blast radius of two kilometres, minimal fallout—but everything within that radius will be vaporised. Nice thing to mention in passing to your enemies.'

'So what do we do?' Pooh said. 'We can't get to the *Halicarnassus*. It's a stand-off.'

'It is,' Jack said. 'Which is exactly what I want.'

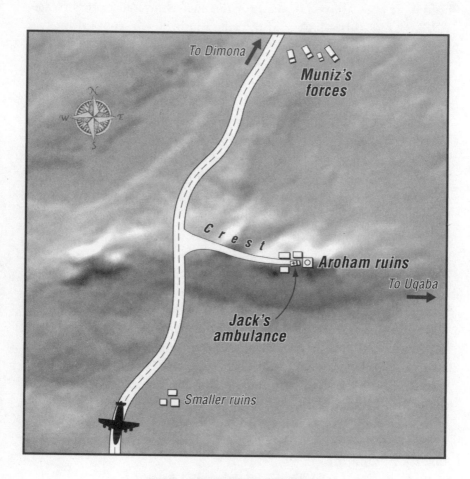

To Dimona

Muniz's forces

Crest

Aroham ruins

To Uqaba

Jack's ambulance

Smaller ruins

THE AROHAM RUINS

It was indeed a stand-off, a stand-off in the middle of the desert.

The Roman ruins at Aroham were once an ancient spice-route waystation. Their only claim to fame: their deepwater well. Now not even tourists bothered to stop there.

Twenty minutes ticked by and the rest of the Israeli chase force arrived on the scene.

Six more choppers, plus a convoy of vehicles on the highway: command vans, troop trucks, anti-aircraft jeeps.

Inside the main command van, his face red with fury, was Mordechai Muniz.

Of course by now it was known that the blast at Dimona had not caused any radiation leak. Jack's detonation had only blown the outer wall of Machon-2, but at a facility like Dimona, in the event of *any* blast, full emergency procedures had to be observed.

But now the Israelis were pleased—they'd managed to cut Jack off from his escape plane. And sieges like this always came out in favour of the force with time and food on their side, and the Israelis had all the time in the world.

General Mordechai Muniz raised his binoculars.

He saw the big black 747 in the distance, just visible about four hundred yards beyond the ruins on the low hilltop. The scene had not changed for thirty minutes now. Occasionally, movement could be spotted within the ruins, a figure crossing a doorway, a head bobbing up.

'What about their plane?' a lieutenant asked. 'Choppers are awaiting instructions.'

'Don't destroy it yet,' Muniz said calmly. 'They need to think they have a chance of escape.'

He brought his radio to his lips. 'Captain West. Captain Jack West Jr. Come in. Let's talk.'

Silence.

After a moment, Jack's voice came in, crackly and grainy over the speaker. '*You offering a deal, General?*'

Muniz rolled his eyes. 'This is unpleasant, Captain. What do you honestly hope to achieve here? Your rescue attempt, while loyal and inventive, has failed. You cannot escape from this situation.'

'*Don't even think of storming these ruins. If I see anyone come within the two-klick perimeter, I'll detonate the nuke.*'

'What do you want?' Muniz demanded flatly.

'*I want access to our plane and safe passage to Syrian airspace. I can't imagine you'll shoot a nuclear-loaded plane down over Israeli population centres, nor would you like to have one of your nukes go off over Syria.*'

'Not going to happen.'

'*You going to wait us out, General?*'

'Captain West, be serious, even if you did board that plane, I'd still shoot you out of the sky as soon as you took off. Then your suitcase merely becomes a dirty bomb, and dirty bombs mean little out here in the desert.'

'*How about I just detonate the suitcase bomb right here, right now and we all die together. The concussion wave from the blast is easily enough to take you with us.*'

'You're not like that, West,' Muniz said. 'I've seen your profile: you wouldn't kill those you love. On the contrary, you prefer to risk your own life for theirs.'

'*And I know this about you, Old Master. You don't want to die. Let's see who blinks first.*'

'I don't bluff, Captain.'

'*Neither do I.*'

And at precisely that moment, an hour after the siege had begun, several things happened at once.

★ ★ ★

'Sir!' an Israeli corporal called from a radio console. 'Aerial Two just called in! They've been watching the plane over in the next valley—someone just ran over to it from a *second* cluster of ruins over there! The plane is starting to taxi down the highway . . .'

'It's doing what—?' Muniz turned, frowning.

'Sir!' another Israeli trooper ran into the command van, holding some plans. 'Those ruins they're holed up in! They're an ancient entrance to Uqaba, the salt mine that runs underneath this plateau.'

'A salt mine . . .' Muniz's mind began to race.

There was a salt mine underneath this plateau?

'Where are the other entrances and exits to this salt mine?'

'It's huge, sir. There are over a dozen entrances, some as far as ten miles away. The *nearest* one is in the next valley, right near their plane,' the corporal said. 'That second set of ruins is another entrance to the mine.'

Muniz's eyes widened as suddenly he saw Jack's plan.

Jack hadn't been holed up here at Aroham by chance. He'd *wanted* to get here, to these exact ruins. He'd *wanted* the chase helicopters to catch up to him when they did. He'd *wanted* to stage a stand-off here and then slip through the mine tunnels to his plane while they wasted time negotiating . . .

Muniz thundered: 'Stop that plane, now—'

'*Sir!*' a third soldier called urgently. This trooper was manning a radiation console. 'Sir! Geiger counters and passive radiation meters just went off the charts! The suitcase bomb has gone into the primary stage! He just activated the nuke . . .'

'Can we get to it in time?' Muniz asked.

'No, the primary ignition phase is five minutes, we can't get to it *and* disarm it in that space of time. That thing's going to go off. Our friend Captain West just initiated the detonation of a nuclear device.'

'Get everybody back!' Muniz roared. 'As far back as possible. The blast won't reach us, but the shock wave will. Go! Go! Go! The man is insane.'

The Israeli force leapt into action, retreating back north as fast as their vehicles could carry them.

At the same time, the big black 747 that had been pinned down in the next valley lifted off into the sky and banked round, heading west, cutting a bee-line for the nearest border, that of Egypt.

Five minutes after that, the small-yield suitcase-borne nuclear bomb went off.

The flash was blinding.

A colossal boom followed, the ground shook, and then a great towering mushroom cloud rose high into the sky above the Negev Desert, like some kind of unearthly force released from captivity.

In the five minutes they'd had, Muniz and his force had managed to get twelve kilometres away from the blast. To them, the mushroom cloud looked like a skyscraper looming on the southern horizon. Thanks to the compact size of the device, at this distance the electromagnetic pulse from the blast only served to disrupt their communications mildly.

For a long moment, Mordechai Muniz just stared at the eighty-storey-high cloud growing into the sky.

His lieutenant came alongside him. 'Sir. What should we do now?'

Muniz ground his teeth. 'Scramble some F-15s. Tell them to acquire that 747 and blast it out of the fucking sky.'

Two F-15 fighters were launched from a nearby base and within twenty minutes they had acquired the *Halicarnassus*, fleeing over the Sinai Peninsula, well into Egyptian airspace.

Maybe West figured he'd be safe once he'd crossed the border, Muniz thought. *Maybe he thought our fighters would pull back once he was over sovereign Egyptian territory.*

They didn't.

The Israeli F-15s just flew straight into Egypt and the lead plane unleashed two Sidewinder missiles at the fleeing jumbo jet.

Both missiles hit their mark.

And the big black 747 simply *exploded* in the sky, cracking in the middle, bucking in mid-air, orange flames spewing all around it and a long thin line of black smoke trailing it as it rushed downward at outrageous speed and crashed into the side of a rocky mountain in the Sinai.

The *Halicarnassus* was no more.

Egyptian Air Force personnel monitoring the area would later report that three illegal aerial signatures had entered Egyptian airspace that morning: two F-15 fighter signatures and one civilian airliner.

The two fighters left the area soon after they'd entered it, while the airliner signature had simply disappeared from their screens. A check was made, but no commercial airliners had been reported missing.

Curiously, however, just before the two fighters had caught up with the airliner, the Egyptians had noticed a minuscule signature soaring down through the air *beneath* the airliner.

It was a very small signature, too faint to be an aircraft of any kind, more like the ghost-like trace signal one saw when a paratrooper did a drop. The Egyptian Air Force personnel dismissed it as a software glitch.

Back in the Negev Desert, about ten miles to the *east* of the towering black mushroom cloud that stood above what had once been the Aroham ruins, Zoe, Pooh Bear and Stretch drove toward the Jordanian border.

They travelled in an old WWII-era jeep that Jack and Zoe had left here earlier, one without electronics that could be affected by the EMP emitted by the blast.

The labyrinthine salt mine beneath the ruins had indeed been vast, with tunnels running in every direction—including the one that had headed south toward the valley containing the black 747, and another running eastward. While Jack had gone south to be seen boarding the plane—talking to Muniz on his radio as he did so—the others had long before entered the mine and hurried east, getting nearly an hour's headstart.

The only things that had been in the Aroham ruins when the nuke had gone off were their escape ambulance, some crudely strung-up human-shaped dummies that would move every few minutes to create the illusion of their presence, and of course the suitcase bomb.

After a few hours, the jeep crossed the border into Jordan where it beheld a sea of sand dunes. As it crested the first dune, both Stretch and Pooh Bear's jaws dropped, as they saw what lay before them.

The *Halicarnassus*.

Jack's big black 747 stood proudly on a blacktop road, flanked by giant sand dunes, its black-armoured sides and wing-mounted guns giving it a particularly fearsome look. Beside it, standing equally proudly, was Sky Monster.

'Hello, folks,' he said jovially.

'But how . . .' Pooh Bear said. 'I thought . . .'

'That other plane you saw, it was a black 747, sure,' Sky Monster said, 'but did it have guns like this one? Or stealth panels? Or was it just black?'

'But where did you get a—' Stretch said, his voice husky and dry.

Sky Monster grinned. 'Remember how Jack got the *Halicarnassus* in the first place: it was one of several escape planes Saddam Hussein had stashed around Iraq. *One of several*. Jack's SAS buddies in western Iraq had found one of the others a while back and Jack called 'em to say he needed it.'

Sky Monster held out a portable radio handset. 'Here.'

Pooh and Stretch took the radio. 'Hello?'

'*You got away? Good,*' Jack's voice said. '*Now, if you don't mind, would someone please come and get me? I parachuted into the middle of goddamn nowhere! I'm in the Sinai somewhere . . .*'

'Quit your whining, West, it was your stupid plan,' Sky Monster grinned. 'We'll meet you at the rendezvous point as intended. You'll have to get there under your own steam.'

'*Copy that*,' Jack said. '*Oh, Pooh and Stretch . . . it's good to have you back.*'

Stretch and Pooh Bear smiled.

'Hey, Jack,' Stretch croaked.

'*Yeah?*'

'Thanks.'

Four days later, Jack rejoined the group, meeting them at the Sea Ranger's hideaway buried within the eastern coast of Zanzibar, underneath a long-dead lighthouse.

By the time Jack arrived there, Stretch had been cleaned up and had slept for almost twenty-six hours straight. He was sitting up in bed with a notebook computer on his lap when Jack walked in.

'I wasn't sure you'd come for me,' Stretch said.

'Had a gap in my schedule,' Jack said. 'And really it was Pooh Bear who did all the legwork.'

'*Is that Daddy?*' a voice said from the laptop.

Stretch swivelled the computer so Jack could see Lily on its screen. She was still at Alby's place in Australia, and until now had been unaware of the mission to save Stretch.

'*You could've told me what you were doing,*' she said.

'No, I couldn't,' Jack said. 'It was too dangerous even for you to know. I'm sorry about that.'

'*But . . .*' she hesitated. '*I was awful. I'm sorry, Daddy.*'

'Don't be sorry, kiddo. You were *right*,' Jack said, 'and your instincts were right, too. We don't leave any of our friends behind. We bust 'em out or we die trying. I'm just sorry I had to keep it from you and make you so upset.'

Lily smiled. '*I'm proud of you, Daddy.*'

'I like making you proud. Thanks.' He turned to Stretch. 'It's

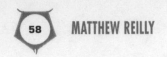

great to have you back, buddy. Eat up and get some strength, because things are about to get hectic.'

'Why? What happens now?'

'Now we figure out where the other Pillars and Vertices are, and we go after them.'

A MEETING OF MINDS

THE FIVE GREATEST WARRIORS

Zanzibar

ZANZIBAR
JANUARY – FEBRUARY 2008

Jack's team assembled around a long table in a glass-windowed office inside the Sea Ranger's underground submarine dock. The dark grey conning tower of the Ranger's stolen Kilo-class submarine loomed outside the office's windows.

Jack sat at the head of the table, with Wizard and Zoe beside him. Pooh Bear and Stretch sat with the twins, Lachlan and Julius Adamson. Sky Monster lounged on a couch under the window, dozing, while J.J. Wickham watched from the doorway.

Also there was the newest member of the group, the archaeologist Diane Cassidy. While Jack's team had gone to Israel, she'd taken the African youth, Ono, to an orphanage in Mombasa that helped dislocated African tribesfolk adapt to the modern world. Cassidy had also used that time to return to the States and contact family and friends, to let them know she was alive. Eager to repay her rescuers with any information she could provide, she had returned the day before.

Lastly, Lily and Alby were present via videolink, patched in from Perth.

Strewn over the table were numerous sheets of paper—the random notes of Wizard, Jack and the twins, photos of Stonehenge, maps with notations scribbled on them, plus Wizard's summary sheet:

REWARDS
(according to Rameses II at Abydos)

1. KNOWLEDGE
2. HEAT
3. SIGHT
4. LIFE
5. DEATH
6. POWER

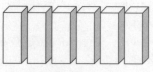

THE SIX PILLARS

- Oblong uncut diamonds;
- Must be '_cleansed_' by the Ph's Stone before they can be placed in the Machine;
- Whereabouts? The Great Houses of Europe; Perhaps the 'Five Warriors'???

THE GREAT MACHINE

Pillars???

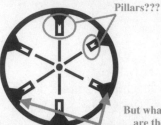

But what are the **TRIANGLES** then?

MUST HAVE BOTH THE SA-BENBEN **AND** THE PHILOSOPHER'S STONE! THEY ARE CENTRAL TO EVERYTHING!!

The Sa-Benben (a.k.a. 'The Firestone')

Interacts uniquely with each of the Six Ramesean Stones:

1. <u>Philosopher's</u>: cleanses Pillars.
2. <u>Stonehenge</u>: gives location of vertices of the Great Machine.
3. <u>Delphi</u>: allows one to see the Dark Sun.
4. <u>Tablets</u>: contain the final incantation.
5. <u>Killing</u>: gives dates by which Pillars must be laid.
6. <u>Basin</u>: unknown.

Rate of approach must be calculated. Call the Twins!

16,467 X 365.25
Mean v ≡ 125,445 km/s
Max output in 1962 was 10.57
But in 1991 was 10.72. Growing.

TITANIC SINKING & RISING (DEC 2007) CONNECTION? POSSIBLE SIGHTING OPPORTUNITY?

WRONG!

Faberge Egg - Newton's alchemical work
The Ness spring...??
Equinox/Easter '08

'All right,' Jack said. 'While we've been breaking into high-security bases, Wizard's been working on the next phase of our mission. Max, the dates.'

Wizard stood and wrote on a whiteboard:

3RD PILLAR – MARCH 11
4TH PILLAR – MARCH 18
5TH PILLAR – MARCH 18
6TH PILLAR – MARCH 20 (DUAL EQUINOX)

'For your benefit, Diane,' Wizard said as he wrote, 'allow me to summarise. Late last year, at a secret base off the coast of England, we placed the Firestone atop the Mayan Killing Stone—one of the Six Sacred Stones—and thus discovered these crucial dates. They are the dates on which the remaining four Pillars must be laid at the last four Vertices. As you can see, they are clustered within March of this year.'

'The Fourth and Fifth Pillars have the same date,' Pooh Bear said. 'Can that be right?'

'It's right,' Wizard said. 'I triple-checked it.'

'Which means?' Stretch queried.

'It means that Pillars Four and Five must be set in place *at the same time*.'

'But those vertices could be on different sides of the world . . .'

'We know,' Jack said. 'But we'll come to that later. Wizard informs me that March 11 and March 18 are both dates for the celestial event we know as the Titanic Rising, an event that coincided with the first two Pillar placings at Abu Simbel and Table Mountain. The last date, March 20, is *not* a Titanic Rising.'

'What is it, then?' the Sea Ranger asked.

'It's the big one. On all the other occasions, Jupiter, Saturn and Saturn's largest moon, Titan, serve to bend the light of the Dark Star. That bending of the light also weakens it somewhat. But on March 20, it'll be different. Wizard?'

Wizard explained. 'March 20, 2008, is a rare event, one that has not occurred in thousands of years. It is a *dual* equinox, a time when both our Sun and its twin, this Dark Star, are aligned on opposite sides of the Earth. Only on that date, Jupiter and Saturn will *not* shield us from the Dark Star's rays. On that date, the Dark Star will emerge fully from behind them and shine its deadly light directly onto our planet.'

'By which time, the Machine must be ready, all its Pillars set in place,' Jack said.

'Or what?' the Sea Ranger asked.

'Or we all get to witness the end of the world,' Wizard said.

'And what exactly will the end of the world look like?'

Wizard paused. 'Hit by the Dark Sun's fearsome energy, our planet will spasm from within, causing it to go wild on the surface.

'Imagine every volcano on Earth erupting at the same time. Imagine tsunamis crashing onto every shore. Imagine earthquakes at every fault-line. And all this will go on *for years*.

'Undersea eruptions will heat the oceans, turning them into boiling nightmares. The sky will go dark with ash and the atmosphere will quickly be filled by sulphurous gases escaping from the planet core. The air will become poisonous to breathe.

'Our planet is very robust, but life on it is not. Humans can survive only on the Earth's surface, and after March 20 that surface will become a hellish environment totally hostile to life—a landscape of black cloud, raging seas, endless fire and choking gas.

'Spectacular, gruesome and total. That is what the end of the world looks like.'

'Right, well . . .' the Sea Ranger said. 'That puts it all in perspective.'

'If it makes you feel better, this has probably happened several times before over the eons,' Wizard said.

'No, that doesn't make me feel any better.'

At that point, Jack took over.

For Wickham's and Diane Cassidy's sake, he went over what they knew about the Machine, the Pillars and the Vertices: how the Saudis had possessed the First Pillar for many generations; the Neetha, the Second; and the British Royal Family, the Fourth.

As for the other three Pillars, they had only very scant information about their whereabouts: apparently, the Japanese Imperial Family, the oldest royal line in the world, possessed a Pillar—and according to the British royal, Iolanthe Compton-Jones, they'd managed to conceal it from the Americans at the end of World War II.

Iolanthe had also told Jack that the pre-eminence of three European royal households—the British Royal Family, the Danish Royal Family and the Romanovs of Russia—had been due solely to their possession of Pillars.

Beyond that, Jack knew nothing of the whereabouts of the remaining three Pillars.

The all-important Firestone and Philosopher's Stone—needed to cleanse the Pillars—were currently in Wolf's hands, taken during the battle with the Neetha tribe in Africa. Where Wolf was getting his information from, apart from his researcher, Felix Bonaventura, Jack didn't know.

As for the locations of the remaining *Vertices*, Jack's team still had their photos of the trilithons of Stonehenge, lit by the light of the Dark Star, pin-pointing the locations of the six great temple-shrines on ancient maps of the world, maps that—unfortunately—depicted global coastlines long before the oceans had risen to their current levels. This had made deducing the exact locations of the Vertices extremely difficult.

Despite this, the twins had spent every day of the past month knuckling down to the immense task, comparing the ancient coastlines to modern ones, looking for matches.

'And what have you found?' Diane Cassidy asked them.

'Because it's the next one to happen,' Lachlan said, 'we've been focusing on the third light-shaft that struck Stonehenge. This one.' He spun his laptop around so Cassidy could see the image on its screen:

'The coastline featuring the point marked "3" is a tough one to deduce,' Julius said. 'It could be the east coast of *any* continent, country or landmass: Africa, India, Argentina, Sweden, even somewhere up among the islands of northern Canada. Even the scale is misleading, because it isn't drawn to the same scale the African one was.'

Lachlan said, 'We've checked every book we could find on ocean-level rises and ante-diluvian coastlines . . .'

'And?' Jack asked.

'And we're no closer to finding it,' Lachlan said sadly.

Julius said, 'Put simply, we need more to go on, Jack, we need more information.'

A silence descended over the table.

It was Diane who broke it.

'I might have something that could help.'

Diane lifted up her backpack, the only thing she'd taken with her during their escape from the Neetha, and extracted from it a battered leatherbound notebook.

Flicking the notebook open, she revealed page after page of hand-drawn images and densely packed notes.

She held the notebook open to a page on which was written:

THE RHYME OF THE WARRIORS
(Sphinx, Giza)

The First
shall be the noblest, scholar and soldier both.
The Second
a natural leader of men, none shall achieve greater fame than he.
The Third
shall be the greatest warlord known to history.
The Fourth
is the great obsessor, seeking only glory, but glory is a lie.
The Fifth
shall face the greatest test and decide if all shall live or die.

Below the poem were images of hieroglyphs and maps, plus scribbled notes.

Diane looked at Wizard. 'You've never asked me *why* I went in search of the Neetha in Africa, Max.'

'I . . . well . . . I guess I assumed that you simply had gone in search of them, to see if this fabled lost tribe actually existed.'

'While I became something of an expert on the Neetha, I wasn't searching *for* the Neetha. I also know of the Six Sacred Stones and the Pillars. My expertise in the Neetha was purely the result of my larger search: to discover if these fabled sacred stones and diamond bricks actually existed.

'I figured that the Neetha, as the original owners of one of the Six Sacred Stones—the Delphic Orb—might have information about the others, which they certainly did. My quest is the same as yours, it's just that my key reference point—this poem, *The Rhyme of the Warriors*—was different.' She turned to Jack. 'You know it?'

'I do,' Wizard answered for him. 'It was found carved on a tablet between the front paws of the Sphinx. Napoleon's men unearthed it.'

'That's correct. And that tablet now resides in the British Museum.'

'So what's the poem's significance?' Jack asked.

'Max suspected it had significance, didn't you, Max?' Diane said.

'For a time, but I couldn't make it fit.'

Diane nodded at Wizard's summary sheet. 'You even mention "Five Warriors" on your sheet as possible holders of the Pillars.'

'He does?' Jack checked the sheet and to his surprise discovered she was right.

There it was, under the heading 'THE SIX PILLARS':

Whereabouts? The Great Houses of Europe;
Perhaps the 'Five Warriors'???

'I believe,' Diane said, 'that this poem is directly related to our mutual quest. I believe it tells of the five people who over the course of history have most affected the fates of the Firestone, the Six Sacred Stones, the Pillars and the Vertices.'

Diane projected the poem onto the whiteboard and with a marker began circling various words and adding notes in the margins.

As she wrote, she spoke confidently and expertly: 'As we all know, the Great Pyramid was built by Khufu. The Sphinx, however, sits in front of the *second* pyramid at Giza—built by Khufu's son, Khafre—so for a long time archaeologists simply assumed it had also been built by Khafre. Today, however, many Egyptologists believe that *Khufu*, the builder of the Great Pyramid, actually built the Sphinx, too.'

'We've had some experience with the Great Pyramid,' Jack said kindly.

'But perhaps you haven't yet realised the monumental importance of its builder,' Diane said. 'I mean, the Great Pyramid, the Golden Capstone, the Firestone: *all three* of them have been integral to your mission. And it was Khufu who erected all three of them. It was Khufu who had all of them in his possession. Doesn't it make sense that Khufu might have had some knowledge—a very high level of knowledge—about your Machine?'

'It does when you put it that way,' Jack said, eyeing Wizard.

The old professor just shrugged bashfully. 'We concentrated on Rameses and the Six Ramesean Stones.'

'Understandably,' Diane said, finishing her writing on the whiteboard. 'But did you ever ask yourself, where did those Six Sacred Stones *come from*? And where did the six oblong diamond pillars *come from*?

'At some point in time, they must have all been together, right? And the first time we find them together is with Khufu—this is why in some texts, the Firestone, the Six Sacred Stones and the Six Pillars are collectively referred to as "Khufu's Treasure" or "Khufu's Wisdom". And the answer to what became of Khufu's Treasure lies in this poem, written over 4,000 years ago.'

With a flourish, she stepped away from the whiteboard, revealing her handiwork:

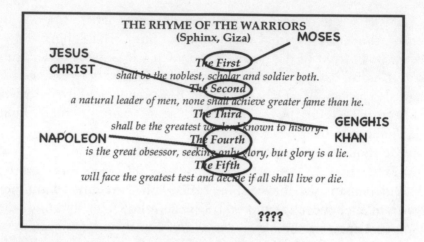

THE RHYME OF THE WARRIORS
(Sphinx, Giza)

MOSES

JESUS CHRIST

The First
shall be the noblest, scholar and soldier both.

The Second
a natural leader of men, none shall achieve greater fame than he.

The Third
shall be the greatest warlord known to history.

GENGHIS KHAN

NAPOLEON

The Fourth
is the great obsessor, seeking only glory, but glory is a lie.

The Fifth
will face the greatest test and decide if all shall live or die.

????

'Genghis Khan . . . Napoleon . . .' Wizard said.

'Jesus Christ . . .' Zoe breathed, 'a warrior?'

Julius jerked his chin at the whiteboard. 'I think you meant to say "Lachlan Adamson" for the fourth warrior. He's the great obsessor. Geez, you should see him combing his hair in the morning. That's obsessive . . .'

'Hah-de-ha-ha,' Lachlan replied.

'*This* is what I was studying,' Diane said. 'This is what led me to the Neetha—to see what information they might possess about the rhyme. I just never expected to be captured and enslaved by them.'

Jack remained silent for a long moment, gazing at the whiteboard.

Then at last he said softly, 'It's a *prophecy* . . .'

Diane nodded, impressed. 'Yes, Captain. Yes, it is. A foretelling, an insight into the five individuals who over the centuries will most affect the fate of Khufu's Treasure: the Firestone, the Six Sacred Stones and the Six Pillars.'

Jack said, 'So you're thinking that if we follow the trail of these five great warriors, follow their lives and histories, we'll find the Pillars and maybe also some clues to the locations of the remaining Vertices.'

Diane Cassidy pointed at him. 'That's exactly what I'm thinking.'

'Okay,' Jack said. 'So how'd you figure out that *these* guys are the warriors mentioned in the Sphinx tablet? I mean, what about other great military types like Raleigh or Nelson—'

'—or Caesar or Hannibal—' Zoe added.

'—Saladin or Alexander—' Pooh Bear said.

'—Hitler, Patton or Rommel—' Julius said.

Diane held up her hands. 'I know, I know. Believe me, I looked into all those figures and more before I settled on these ones. It took years of work.'

'Sorry. So how'd you decide on these ones?'

'Right. Well. Let's start with Moses. Now remember, the historical and biblical figure we know as Moses was actually an Egyptian priest named Thuthmosis. Moses or Mosis simply means "son of", so *Thuth*mosis means "son of Thoth", the Egyptian god of wisdom. So Moses the man is the namesake of one of the Ramesean Stones: the Twin Tablets of Thuthmosis.'

'Otherwise known as the Ten Commandments,' Pooh Bear said. 'We're aware of this.' He threw a look across the room at the Twin Tablets of Thuthmosis.

'Oh, yes, right,' Diane said.

Jack asked, 'So how did you figure that Moses was the first warrior in the rhyme?'

'The rhyme is not the only ancient text mentioning five fabled warriors,' Diane said. 'There are two others, one from the Wu Gorge in China, which is generally attributed to the philosopher Laozi; and a second from the ruins of Karakorum in Mongolia. This is the first one.'

She turned to a very old sepia-toned photograph stapled into her notebook. It showed a stone pedestal engraved with ancient Chinese calligraphy. She'd translated it:

The Five

1. A humble priest, son of the great god of wisdom, will flee his home, and a great king's hatred.

2. A seer, a healer, a man all would be, will die atop a hideous tree.

3. A lord of war but a ruler most wise, from the barren plateau his kingdom will rise.

4. He shall seek empire but find only tears, his empire shall last not one score of years.

5. A mortal battle, between father and son, one fights for all, and the other for one.

Wizard said, 'I saw this pedestal when I was at the Wu Gorge. It's still there, only it's ten feet underwater now.'

Diane turned to a second photograph, this one showing a large cast-iron door covered with studs and symbols that looked like a variety of ancient Chinese writing.

'The language is Mongolian,' she explained. 'This door is one of the gates of Karakorum, the Black City, the capital of the Khanate. This is from the time of Genghis Khan.'

Everyone read Cassidy's translation of it:

The Five Greatest Warriors

The First, the Warrior-Priest, will bring the treasure out of the ancient land and found the great lineage.

The Second, the Warrior-King, will join two royal lines and thus continue the God King line. He will break the treasure in two and leave his mark on the world forever.

The Third, the Horse-Warrior, will loyally guard the treasure in his halls of iron and pass it to those he deems worthy.

The Fourth, the Emperor-Warrior, will pursue the treasure for his own glory and succeed only in scattering it further. It shall forever remain out of his reach.

The Fifth, the Brilliant Warrior, will be there at the Second Coming and will decide the fate of all.

Diane said, 'This is how I settled on Moses, Jesus, Genghis and Napoleon. When you cross-reference all three sources—and numerous other historical clues—you can see how they all fit. I don't yet know the last warrior, the fifth one—the Black City text says the fifth warrior will be at the "Second Coming", which is the return of the Dark Star in March.'

Lachlan Adamson turned to Jack. 'A mortal battle between a father and son, Jack. Could be you and your asshole dad, fighting it out to the end.'

Jack gave Lachlan a sideways look. 'I seriously doubt that I am the subject of an ancient prophecy. Besides, these texts don't specify whether the fifth warrior is actually the father *or* the son. The warrior could be my father or Pooh Bear's father or even someone we haven't encountered yet.'

Zoe still looked unconvinced. 'Jesus Christ is not commonly called a warrior. He was a man of peace.'

'He carried a sword,' Wizard countered, 'and at one famous point in the Gospel of Luke, he urged his followers to go and buy swords.'

'And many of those followers were revolutionaries urging insurrection against Rome,' Julius said.

'And Napoleon?' Zoe said. 'The emperor–warrior? The guy failed more than he succeeded.'

Jack answered that. 'True, but he did have himself proclaimed Emperor of France. He was also an Egypt nut. It's because of him that we have the Rosetta Stone and deciphered hieroglyphics. And he was famously initiated into Freemasonry *inside* the Great Pyramid. There's no Western leader in history with closer links to Egypt.'

Jack turned back to Diane Cassidy.

'This is very helpful, you might be on to something here. Let's assume for the moment that you're right and chase up these four historical figures a bit further: Moses, Jesus, Genghis and Napoleon.

'Everybody, it's time to hit the books. I want you to cross-reference these four warriors with everything we know about the Machine, the Pillars and the Vertices.

'Cover everything, from astronomy and Egyptology to ancient mythology; from the sites of Vertices we've been to—Abu Simbel and Cape Town—to Aristotle, Rameses, Khufu, Hieronymus, the Neetha and the Great Houses of Europe. Anything and everything. Look for connections, crossed-paths, any kind of common denominator that will lead us to the remaining Pillars and Vertices.

'And just for you, Zoe, look for any other contenders for the title of "Great Warrior", in case Dr Cassidy here has got it wrong.

'All right, folks, let's move.'

ZANZIBAR
FEBRUARY 2008
THE MONTH BEFORE THE 3RD DEADLINE

Over the next few weeks, the team immersed themselves in research, reading anything and everything they could about the four known 'Greatest Warriors'—Moses, Jesus, Genghis Khan and Napoleon—noting journeys they had taken, texts they had written or books that had been written about them.

They read the Bible, plus the other known gospels; they read *The Secret History of the Mongols*, the great work recording the achievements of Genghis Khan, searching for any mention of ancient knowledge, 'wisdom' or 'treasure'.

Every two days they would convene for a meeting, at which Jack would write up key points on the whiteboard at the front of the room.

Sure enough, over the course of their research, curious connections came up.

The Great Houses of Europe, for instance, called themselves the 'Deus Rex'—the God Kings—the name used in the Mongolian Black City text to describe the line of Jesus Christ.

It went up on the whiteboard.

Likewise, it was found that Napoleon had shown an inordinate amount of interest in Rameses II. During his famous expeditions to Egypt, Napoleon had given explicit orders that all discoveries connected to Rameses the Great be brought directly to him.

One inscription found inside Rameses's palace ruins at Luxor had consumed him. It had read:

A LONE BEKHEN SENTINEL STANDS GUARD
OVER THE ENTRANCE TO THE GREATEST SHRINE.

The Greatest Shrine was a reference, of course, to the Sixth and last Vertex. And 'bekhen' was a rare variety of brownish-black basalt.

And so Napoleon had ordered his scientists to scour Egypt for monuments made of bekhen stone. Their most famous discovery was the Rosetta Stone, but beyond that only a few small obelisks were found and none of them stood over the entrance to any underground shrine.

In addition to his obsession with Egypt, it was discovered that Napoleon also had an unusual fascination with astronomy—including a particular interest in Saturn and Jupiter.

The French emperor was intrigued as to why the orbits of these two planets sometimes lagged behind their predicted positions. It was as if, he observed, some *outside force* were acting on their celestial movements.

'In artillery school, Napoleon was taught by the scholar Pierre Simon de Laplace—' Zoe reported to the group at one of their meetings.

'Laplace?' Wizard looked up. 'He was one of the greatest mathematicians of all time. He came up with the concept of the metre. He was also a leading figure in astronomy, some say superior even to Isaac Newton in the field of celestial mechanics.'

Zoe said, 'Well, when Napoleon became emperor of France, he brought Laplace to his court to consult on matters astronomical, in particular, to investigate the cause of the lag in Saturn's and Jupiter's orbits.'

Jack said, 'So Napoleon knew a lot about Egypt *and* about the orbits of Saturn and Jupiter. We can probably assume then that he knew about the Dark Sun.'

That too went up on the whiteboard.

At the mention of Isaac Newton, Stretch chimed in.

'I've been following up on Wizard's reference to Newton's alchemical work. Newton was a fanatic about alchemy, the "science" of turning lead into gold. It was his obsession. He wrote more about it than on any other subject.'

'And?'

'It's very dense and complicated and a lot of the time it just doesn't make sense at all. Call me crazy, but sometimes I felt Newton was using the term "alchemy" as a codeword for something else.'

Wizard said, 'Isaac Newton was notoriously secretive, and even in his time alchemy was a debunked notion. It wouldn't surprise me at all if Newton's "alchemy" was actually a cipher for some other kind of transformation.'

'Does any of his work refer to the Dark Sun?' Jack asked.

'Not that I've found,' Stretch said. 'No direct references, anyway.'

Jack said, 'So is he relevant?'

Wizard answered for Stretch: 'Oh, most assuredly. Even today, Sir Isaac Newton remains one of the world's greatest experts on planetary motion. He was, after all, the first person to accurately predict the Titanic Rising. Given Newton's proclivities toward the esoteric and the vast amount of work that he *didn't* publish, it's possible he discovered the Dark Sun and kept it to himself. We ignore Newton at our peril.'

It went on the whiteboard.

One quiet afternoon, Jack took Wizard into an office to chat privately. He wanted to discuss something that had been troubling him.

'Max, the reward for laying the First Pillar, *knowledge*, was highly advanced knowledge. The second reward, *heat,* was the secret of perpetual motion. Do you have any idea what the last four rewards are?'

Wizard shrugged. 'Guesses mostly. Information on the nature of the rewards is fragmentary at best. Take the third reward: *sight*. Is it seeing the future? The past? Or the ability to see into the hearts of men? I once read about an Egyptian blood ritual in which a priest slashed his own palm and then gripped a sacred gem in his bloody hand—it was said that he would then have visions.

'Why, our Chinese philosopher friend, Laozi, once postulated that the greatest thing of all to see would be the time of one's own death, so one could be prepared for it. Considering Laozi's connection with our quest, this might be an allusion to the reward known as *sight*.'

'What about the others?' Jack read from Wizard's summary sheet: '*Life, death* and *power*?'

Wizard said, 'Remember what Stretch said about Isaac Newton the other day? That he might have used the word "alchemy" as a code for something other than the transformation of lead into gold? I've often wondered if Newton's alchemical quest was actually an attempt to transform the ordinary human lifespan into a longer one.'

'You think the reward, *life,* is long life . . .'

'I like Newton's metaphor,' Wizard said. 'That our ordinary lifespan is lead, while an extended one would be golden.'

'What about the fifth reward then, *death*?'

'Piecing together some Egyptian references—the Pyramid Texts, the Book of the Dead—my guess is this reward is a weapon of some kind. The ability to deal out death to one's enemies.'

Jack thought for a moment. 'Is it possible that the two rewards *life* and *death* are somehow connected? *Death* might be some kind of power to kill, but *life* might be an antidote to *death*? After all, those two Pillars are the only two that have to be laid at the same time.'

'Mmmm, I hadn't thought of that,' Wizard mused. 'That could definitely be a possibility.'

'And what about the last reward?' Jack asked. '*Power*?'

Wizard spread his hands wide. 'It's the reward of rewards:

absolute Earthly power to the one who repels the Dark Star. But what form that power takes, no-one knows—'

There was a knock at the door.

Zoe poked her head in. 'Hey. Lily just called from Australia. She says she's got something big to report.'

The group gathered in the meeting room, facing a projector screen and the whiteboard.

Wizard stood at the front of the room. Lily's face was on a computer monitor, coming in via videolink from Perth.

Wizard projected a digital photo onto the screen. It depicted the golden plaque he and Zoe had photographed at the First Vertex at Abu Simbel, the one containing the descriptions of all six of the Vertices:

'So what's up?' Zoe asked.

Lily said, 'I can't believe I didn't see it before. Look closely at the left-hand side of this plaque and you will see the Thoth numerals for each Vertex listed as horizontal lines. Underneath each Thoth numeral, however, you will see a V-shaped marking. This is the Thoth symbol for *cleansing*.'

Zoe shrugged. 'Sure. The cleansing of each Pillar by the Philosopher's Stone.'

'Partly,' Lily said. 'Look more closely. The numerals for the last three Vertices have *two* Vs underneath them.'

'Oh yeah . . .' Lachlan said.

'Huh . . .' Julius said, seeing it for the first time.

Jack frowned. 'What does that mean? Some sort of *double* cleansing?'

'Yes,' Lily said.

Wizard said, 'I've just been checking my database for references to a second form of cleansing. It seems that because the Dark Sun will be a lot closer to Earth in late March and thus emitting more power, the Machine requires an *extra* form of cleansing for the last three Pillars. The key source I've found is this.'

He projected another image onto the screen, one of an ancient Egyptian wall, filled with hieroglyphs.

'This is from a chamber at Saqqara south of Giza,' Wizard said. 'The hieroglyphs read:

> *Cleanse the last three also in my basin,*
> *In the pure waters of the Spring of the Black Poplar.*
> *Do this and Ra's Twin will be satisfied and*
> *Upon you he will confer their bounties.*

'Their bounties?' Stretch said. 'The last three rewards?'

'That's right,' Wizard said.

'So to stop the Dark Sun at the last three Vertices,' Jack said, 'we need to cleanse the last three Pillars not only in the Philosopher's Stone, but also in the waters of this "Spring of the Black Poplar" . . .'

'. . . *and* this must be done "in my basin", in Rameses II's Basin, the last of the Six Sacred Stones,' Wizard said.

'And the only one we've been completely unable to locate,' Jack said. 'This is going to be a problem. Lily, Alby, Wizard: I want you guys to stick solely with this from now on. Find out what happened to that Basin and figure out where this poplar spring is.'

The research continued.

In between group meetings and reading sessions, Jack and the other soldiers in the team would go outside to exercise or maintain their weapons skills.

Jack and Zoe would go for morning runs along the remote coast. Pooh Bear created a man-sized mannequin out of sandbags into which he threw knives, and Stretch, now almost back to full fitness, fired long-distance sniper rounds.

One day, at Lily's urging on the videophone, he drew a smiling, bespectacled face on it. Lily then christened the mannequin 'George'. After that, when anyone went out to train, they'd leave with the words: 'I'm just going outside to kill George a few times.' When the battered mannequin was brought back in—leaking sand, sometimes decapitated, usually missing a limb—someone would invariably say, 'Poor George.'

The research went on.

More links between the great warriors were discovered and the whiteboard filled up. But it soon became apparent that some of the most startling—and most important—connections revolved around one particular warrior.

Jesus the Nazarene.

'No single individual has had a greater impact on the world than Jesus Christ.' Lachlan was giving the group a presentation with his brother, Julius. (As they often did, today the twins were wearing competing T-shirts—Lachlan's read 'Stewie Griffin for President' while Julius's countered 'Stewie Griffin is an Evil Genius'.)

'We'll leave for another time the question as to whether Jesus was the son of a divine being,' Lachan said. 'What all agree on, believers and atheists alike, is that Jesus was a man who lived in the Judea region about 2000 years ago.

'His teachings are promulgated by the organisation we know as the Catholic Church, but questions remain as to whether this organisation is really just a revived version of an Egyptian sun-cult—'

'We've had dealings with them on this issue,' Jack said.

'—yes, but are you aware of the critical importance to the Church of *Easter* this year, in 2008? Wizard even mentions this at the bottom of his summary sheet.'

'Enlighten me.'

'Well, as you're probably aware, the date for Easter changes every year, but do you know *how* the date for Easter is calculated?'

'How?' Pooh Bear asked.

Julius said, 'It was originally calculated this way: Easter Sunday shall fall on the first Sunday *after the first full moon* following the northern vernal equinox.'

'The Sunday after the first full moon of spring,' Lachlan simplified.

'Sun-cult,' Stretch said.

Lachlan said, 'But this year, in 2008, something very special happens. This year, Easter falls right *on* the equinox. Our day of reckoning is March 20 and this year, March 20 is Holy Thursday, the beginning of the Easter celebration that commemorates Jesus's death and supposed resurrection.'

'The sun at equinox and the return of the Dark Star,' Jack said. 'It's a religious perfect storm.'

'Too right. For the Catholic Church, March 20, 2008, is the *ultimate* holy date,' Lachlan said, 'when everything they believe in comes together.'

'You think they're still in this game?'

'The Church might have gone silent since your battle with its agents at the Great Pyramid, but it would be dangerous to mistake silence for inactivity. I'd proceed on the assumption they will be observing our mission very closely come the 20th of March.'

'Getting back to Jesus himself,' Julius went on. 'As most of you will know, he was called the "Messiah", a moniker that has acquired religious meaning over the years but which actually is a term connected with *lineage*.

'Much has been made of Jesus's paternal ancestry, his father, Joseph, being from the royal line of David. On his father's side, Jesus was from very wealthy stock. He wasn't a poor carpenter. Indeed, nowhere in the Bible is it said that Jesus ever actually worked at all.'

Lachlan took over: 'But on his mother's side, the story becomes even more interesting. Mary was from the line of Aaron, another royal line. Who was Aaron, you ask?'

Lachlan grinned. 'Aaron *was Moses's brother*. Jesus, our Second Warrior, was a very, very distant descendant of the family of Moses, our First Warrior.'

Julius said, 'Jesus was thus *monumentally* important even before he said a word. He was the living breathing union of two powerful royal lines: the lines of David and Aaron. The linking of these two great lines had even been prophesied and the one who joined them would be known as the Messiah.

'It makes sense, then, that a sacred family heirloom such as the "treasure" that Moses spirited out of Egypt would have been passed down through the generations until it came to Jesus. What Jesus did with that treasure is then the big question.'

'According to one of Dr Cassidy's poems,' Julius went on, 'the Second Great Warrior—Jesus—would "break the treasure in two and leave his mark on the world forever."

'Well, we know Jesus left his mark on the world. "To break the treasure in two", we take that to mean dividing the Six Pillars into two sets of three.

'Now, after a lot of research and a little bit of gap-filling, Lachie and I have come up with the following diagram, which summarises our best guesses as to the whereabouts of the Six Pillars:

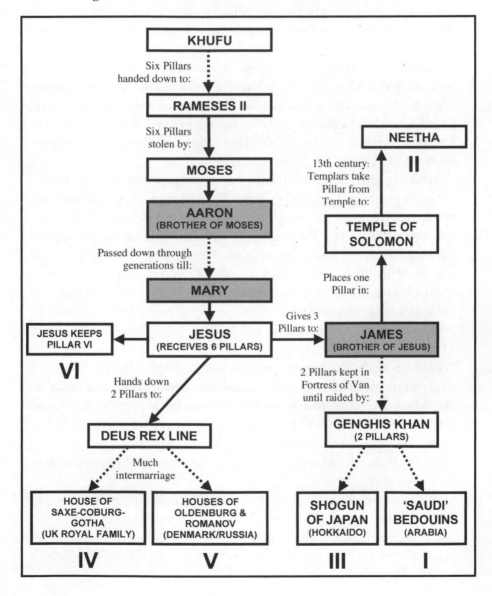

Julius said, 'It looks complicated, so allow us to explain. First, we need to work backwards from what we know now: that the Saudis had the First Pillar, the Neetha had the Second and the Brits have the Fourth. They're marked **I**, **II** and **IV** on the diagram.'

'So knowing those end-points, let's go back to Jesus,' Lachlan said. 'How does he split the Six Pillars in two? Well, they are valuable heirlooms, so he probably wanted to keep them within his family . . .'

Julius continued '. . . so again, working with what we know now, we think that Jesus kept three Pillars within his own immediate family, the now famous family born of himself and Mary Magdalene that popped up in France soon after Jesus's crucifixion. It is this holy-royal lineage, the Deus Rex, that certain European royal families claim as their birthright.

'And the British Royal Family, as we know, has one such Pillar in their possession, the Fourth. We believe that another Pillar, thanks to centuries of royal intermarriage and warfare, has been held equally between the Danish Royal Family and the Romanov descendants of the last Russian Tsar, Nicholas II.'

Jack said, 'You said Jesus kept *three* Pillars. That's only two. What do you think happened to the third one?'

Lachlan glanced at Julius.

Julius glanced at Lachlan.

Then they both shrugged.

Lachlan said, 'We have no reason to believe the third Pillar travelled out of Judea after Jesus's crucifixion. While historians are sure that Mary Magdalene went to France, no-one is certain that Jesus left Judea at all. We think he stayed and he kept his Pillar with him.'

'*What?*' Wizard exclaimed.

'So what happened to it, then?' Zoe asked carefully, considering the implications.

'Well,' Lachlan hesitated. 'We think Jesus had it buried with him.'

★ ★ ★

'You're saying that we have to find the tomb of Jesus Christ . . . !'
Zoe said in disbelief.

'More or less,' Julius said apologetically.

Lachlan said, 'Whether or not he rose from the dead, no-one's
ever actually found *the tomb* where he was laid to rest, either in
Jerusalem or elsewhere.'

'So how do we go about finding it?' Zoe asked.

Lachlan said, 'We've only found one ancient document concerning Jesus that mentions both a resting place and his "wisdom": a
letter in Aramaic discovered in a church in southern France, purported to be from Jesus's brother, James, to Mary Magdalene. It's
pretty vague but it translates as follows:

> *He lies in peace,*
> *In a place where even the mighty Romans fear to tread.*
> *In a kingdom of white*
> *He does not grow old.*
> *His wisdom lies with him still,*
> *Protected by a twin who meets all thieves first.'*

'No names, no locations,' Zoe said. 'Typical.'

'But a clear reference to "his wisdom",' Diane observed.

Zoe sighed. 'That letter could have been written by anybody—'

'What about the other three Pillars Jesus possessed?' Jack said
gently, moving on. 'Where did they go?'

Lachlan nodded. 'Right, right. In the Gospel of Peter, there is
mention of Jesus giving "three pieces of wisdom" to James shortly
before he himself was detained in the Garden of Gethsemane.
We've interpreted this as a reference to the three remaining Pillars.
Remember, family heirlooms, and James was an heir as well. Jesus
also trusted James greatly.'

'Again, working backwards from what we know—that the
Knights Templar ransacked the Temple and stole a Pillar which
ended up with the Neetha—we can postulate that it was probably James who hid that Pillar in the Temple,' Julius said. 'As a

member of the Line of David, he had privileged access to the inner sanctum of the Temple.'

Lachlan said, 'As for the other two Pillars, James ended his days at the Fortress of Van, a great hilltop city in modern-day Turkey, situated between the Black and Caspian seas. The route he took to get there is given in great detail, town by town, in the same Gospel of Peter.'

Lachlan opened a nearby book to a photo of an ancient parchment, on which was a long handwritten list:

Jerusalem	Dibon
Ephraim	Medeba
Jericho	Rabbath Ammon
Gilgal	Damascus
Masada	Aleppo
Ein Gedi	Diyar Bakir
Ein Bokek	Erzurum
Mountain of Sodom	Mountain of Ararat
Ein Aradhim	Yerevan
Kir Moab	Van
Aroer	

Julius said, 'James went to Van and a thousand years later, guess who sacked Van with his armies? *Genghis Khan.* Another link between the Five Warriors.'

'Interesting,' Jack said. 'Did Genghis attack Van just to get the Pillars?'

'That's not known, but it is possible. Either way, Genghis got his hands on the two Pillars kept at Van and one of those Pillars—the First—ended up with the Saudi Royal Family.

'How it got to them is unknown, but we do know that, as thanks for helping his army approach the Kwarezmi Empire in secret from the west, Genghis gave a Bedouin chief a "brick-like stone of tremendous beauty the likes of which none had ever seen". Hundreds of years later, that Bedouin tribe became the House of Saud.'

★ ★ ★

'And the last Pillar?' Jack asked. 'Genghis's other Pillar?'

Julius flashed a 13th century portrait of Genghis Khan onto the projector screen.

A stern-looking Mongolian with a long grey beard glared out at them. He was dressed in leather-and-bronze armour and a sturdy helmet, and he held in one hand a pentagonal shield, covered in studs and raised images. Even in painted form, the man's eyes cast a spell. They blazed with authority.

'"Attack with aggression, but always have a plan of retreat,"' Julius said. 'Genghis Khan's famous military axiom, and also the central thesis of countless business self-help books in the 1980s.'

Lachlan said, 'Did you know that Genghis conquered all of China and half of Europe?'

'More or less,' Jack said.

'But he never conquered Japan,' Lachlan said, 'and it was a lot closer than Europe. Ever wondered why?'

'Should I have?'

Julius said, 'Around 1220 AD, Genghis made a secret voyage to the northernmost island of Japan, Hokkaido, where it is said he met with the Japanese Emperor and his most senior commander, the Shogun.

'Genghis liked the Emperor, but he was even more impressed by the Shogun, who wielded the real power in Japan. Genghis figured, correctly, that it was the Shogun who was responsible for the orderly and dignified running of Japanese society. Given the unruly state of his own empire and the quarrels among his sons over succession, Genghis later wrote that he left with the Shogun "the wisdom of my life".'

'A Pillar . . .' Wizard said.

'We think it was the Third Pillar. The Shogun in question, Hojo Yoshitoki, had a unique carving hewn into his burial headstone: a white oblong with three horizontal lines inscribed on it.'

Lachlan said, 'The Shoguns would rule Japan for the next hundred years as a military junta, with a series of puppet emperors, but eventually the Imperial Family regained control of the country and presumably the Pillar.'

'That supports Iolanthe's story of the Japanese Imperial Family hiding their Pillar from the US at the end of World War II,' Jack said.

'The Americans weren't the only ones to make a play for it,' Julius said. 'One of Genghis Khan's *grandsons*, Kublai Khan, tried to invade Japan on two occasions, and failed both times, repelled by the Shogun's forces. We found a Mongolian record of his campaigns: curiously, Kublai was attacking the remote north-western coast of Hokkaido, a region known for its high cliffs and violent seas. It has no strategic value at all, yet Kublai attacked it *twice*.'

'You're thinking Kublai Khan wanted to get his grand-daddy's Pillar back,' the Sea Ranger said.

'That's right.'

Jack leaned back in his chair, glanced at Wizard. 'It's good, but . . .'

'One more thing.' Lachlan projected one of their photos of Stonehenge onto the screen:

'You see the coastline with "3" marked on it? Inspired by Genghis's secret journey and Kublai's failed attacks, we think we might know where the Third Vertex is.'

Jack leaned forward. So did the others.

'Where?'

'This coastline's changed considerably over the millennia, which is why it was so hard to deduce.' Lachlan flashed up two new images. 'On the left is a close-up of the upright at Stonehenge; on the right is a map from today.

'As you can see, whole seas have flooded into hollows in the landmass, megafloods that created Korea and all the islands of Japan. And right there is the Third Vertex: situated on the north-western coast of Hokkaido in Japan.'

'This is splendid work, boys,' Wizard said. 'But—'

'But a Vertex without a Pillar is useless,' Jack said.

Lachlan said, 'It is indeed. We're not done.'

'My humble apologies.'

Lachlan went on: 'Soon after Genghis Khan died, messengers from the Shogun came to see him. They found his son, Ogedei, on the throne. According to a scroll in the Shanghai Museum, it's said that they gave Ogedei a most peculiar gift: a beautiful glass orb, cloudy-white in colour, the size of a football, *and covered with intricately painted pictures.*

'With the gift came a message from the Shogun intended for Genghis:

> **Great Khan, after nine long years, the works are complete. A maze of our own devising—a match for the one already there—has been constructed within the temple-shrine to protect your glorious gift to my people.**
>
> **It is our honour to present to you this Wingless Dragon's Egg, found at the temple-shrine during our excavations. It portrays the glorious cliffs above the shrine's entrance, plus images of five other most beautiful landscapes. Its artistry is beyond compare.'**

Wizard said, 'So Genghis gave the Japanese the Third Pillar as a gift and the Japanese hid it within the Third Vertex itself. The Pillar is *inside* the Vertex . . .'

Lachlan turned to Jack. 'A Vertex without a Pillar might indeed be useless, but I'd say one with its matching Pillar inside it is pretty frickin' awesome.'

'Touché.' Jack bowed his head in acknowledgement.

'A Wingless Dragon?' Pooh Bear said. 'What is that?'

'The term "Wingless Dragon's Egg" is very peculiar,' Julius said. 'But think about it. What would a wingless dragon look like?'

'*Like a dinosaur . . .*' Lily said over the videolink.

'That's just what we think,' Lachlan nodded. 'We figure this Wingless Dragon's Egg is actually some kind of petrified dinosaur egg, or a glass version of one, that was decorated with painted images.'

Jack turned to Wizard. 'Max? Any famous eggs we should know about?'

Wizard said, 'Only the most famous. In the late 19th century, the Russian tsars commissioned fabulous jewelled artworks in the shape of eggs from the master craftsman Peter Carl Fabergé. I mention them in my summary sheet.

'Fabergé Eggs are beautiful, rare and practically priceless. One such Fabergé Egg—made of gold and lost during the Bolshevik revolution—apparently depicted landscapes such as the twins describe. Given the Russian Royal Family's links to the Machine, I have often wondered if that Fabergé Egg was created as a replica of this or perhaps another Dragon's Egg. If there was an Egg found at this Vertex, there might be other Eggs at other venues, Eggs that the royals already possess.'

'If the royals have one, it would explain some of Iolanthe's superior knowledge,' Jack said.

'It certainly would.'

Jack said, 'Well, whatever it is, this Dragon's Egg is central to everything. If it depicts the landscapes around the entrances to this and all five of the other Vertices, we have to get it.'

At that point, Diane Cassidy chimed in. 'There were pictures of a sacred orb such as you describe among the carvings of the Neetha tribe. If Jack's father is still travelling with the Neetha warlock then it's likely he knows about this Egg, too.'

'We have to assume Wolf is doing exactly what we're doing,' Wizard said, 'researching and planning. Likewise the royals, especially if they have the Fabergé replica.'

'I've got someone keeping track of my father,' Jack said, somewhat enigmatically. 'According to my guy, Wolf's been hunkered down at the American base at Diego Garcia for the last two weeks. If he knows about this, he hasn't gone after it yet.'

Alby said over the videolink: '*According to the Shogun's message, this Dragon's Egg was found* inside *the Vertex, which would mean the ancient builders of the Machine left it there.*'

'Which means we're going to need Lily to decipher it.' Jack turned to the computer. 'Looks like you're back in the game, kiddo.'

'*Yay,*' Lily squealed over the videolink.

Jack turned to the twins: 'Don't tell me, no large intact dinosaur egg has ever been found, either in Japan or Mongolia?'

Julius shook his head. 'No. Never.'

'So let me get this straight,' Zoe said. 'You're saying that if we find this Egg, and combine the images on it with the knowledge we have of the Hokkaido coast, we can find the Third Vertex *and* the Third Pillar?'

'Yes,' Julius said.

'Yes,' Lachlan said.

'So we find it,' Jack said resolutely. He turned to the twins: 'Okay, my Mongolian experts, where did it go? Where do you think this Wingless Dragon's Egg ended up?'

SECOND BATTLE

THE KHAN'S ARSENAL

MONGOLIA
28 FEBRUARY, 2008
12 DAYS BEFORE THE 3RD DEADLINE

AIRSPACE OVER WESTERN CHINA
28 FEBRUARY, 2008, 0800 HOURS
12 DAYS BEFORE THE 3RD DEADLINE
(2008 BEING A LEAP YEAR)

'*Genghis Khan's Arsenal*,' Lachlan's voice said over the speaker-phone in the main cabin of the *Halicarnassus*. '*That's where the Dragon's Egg ended up.*'

'His arsenal?' Jack said.

Jack, Lily, Zoe and Wizard were soaring over central Asia, heading towards Mongolia. Guessing that the Egg lay somewhere in Genghis's former empire, they'd headed here while the twins had researched the matter further.

On the way, they had picked up Lily in Perth. When they'd collected her, however, Alby had mentioned something about a discovery he'd made regarding the Basin of Rameses II—and so Pooh Bear, Stretch and the twins had been dispatched to, of all places, England. Diane Cassidy had gone home to America, to rebuild the pieces of her life and put together all her research so she could help from there.

Sadly for Lily, Alby couldn't come on this trip. After he'd arrived home from their last adventure with his arm in a sling, his mother Lois wasn't letting him out of her sight.

Julius's voice said, '*While reading* The Secret History of the Mongols, *we found a few odd references to something called "the Lost Arsenal of the Khan". Apparently, it was a secret redoubt of Genghis's, a last refuge, and also the place where he kept all the treasures he'd acquired on his many conquests. Not even his sons* knew where it was, which pissed them off immensely. Its location is one of history's greatest mysteries.'

'Of course it is,' Jack said drily.

'It was reputedly built by 25,000 Kwarezmi slaves—only when it was finished, they were all executed, so they couldn't reveal its location,' Lachlan said.

'Effective way to keep a secret,' Wizard said.

'So how are we supposed to find it?' Zoe asked.

Lachlan said, 'Artefact thieves have been searching for the Lost Arsenal for years. All we can do is what we've been doing: connect some otherwise random dots and hopefully get an idea where to look. For instance, there are reports in Mongol literature that after a long campaign, Genghis would go off to the distant village of Unjin in the lands of the Uyghurs to meditate and recuperate—'

'Or to go and deposit extra special booty,' Jack finished for him. 'Like the Egg.'

'Exactly,' Lachlan said. 'Now, Unjin still exists and the ancient lands of the Uyghurs correspond to the modern Mongolian province of Bayanhongor; it's in the south-west of the country and incorporates a large section of the Gobi Desert. It's remote, hard to get to, and the northern half of the province is perpetually covered in permafrost.'

Julius added, 'There's also a curious land feature about twenty miles to the west of Unjin: a desert plain at the base of the Altay Mountains that's pock-marked with meteor craters, some big, some small, about thirty in total. Dotted all around these craters are burial mounds, dozens of them, some as small as haystacks, others almost as big as the pyramids.'

'Sounds like a good place to start looking,' Jack said. 'Keep at it, Cowboys.'

'Jack.' Sky Monster emerged from the cockpit and handed Jack a printout. 'Just came in from Pine Gap.'

Pine Gap was an ultra-secure communications station in outback Australia, not far from Alice Springs. Jointly owned and operated by the Australian and US militaries, the facility was used by the US to co-ordinate its satellite communications in Asia and the Middle

East. What the Americans didn't know today, however, was that an Australian operator at Pine Gap was surreptitiously monitoring *their* transmissions.

'What is it?' Zoe asked.

'My guy keeping track of Wolf.' Jack scanned the printout. 'Thirty minutes ago, Pine Gap picked up some encrypted radio chatter on a US Navy satellite frequency. My man didn't have authorisation to decrypt exactly what they were saying but he could see *where* the signal came from: south-western Mongolia, got the GPS co-ordinates here.'

Jack punched the co-ordinates into a plotting computer.

'Son of a bitch, he left Diego Garcia.' A map came up on the screen. 'And he's now in Bayanhongor Province, Mongolia, ten miles west of the village of Unjin. Damn it!'

Zoe said, 'The twins were right . . .'

'They were,' Jack said. 'Only we were too slow. We're behind. Wolf is following the same lead and he's already there.'

'Jack, there's more,' Sky Monster said, holding up a second printout and handing it to him.

Jack read it quickly . . .

. . . and this time his face went pale.

'Oh, no . . . *no* . . .'

'What is it?'

Jack looked up. 'Pine Gap just picked up a *second* cluster of encrypted transmissions coming from the exact same area an hour *after* the US Navy signal. Only these transmissions could be decrypted, because they weren't American.'

'And?'

'The encryption algorithms matched those currently used by the special forces section of the Japanese Defence Force,' Jack said. 'Two messages were decoded. The first:

TELL THE GARRISON FORCE AT YOMI
TO MAINTAIN THEIR POSITION INSIDE
THE HALL OF OROCHI.

'Yomi?' Jack looked to Zoe. 'My Japanese geography is kinda rusty.'

'You're not going to find Yomi on any map,' she said. 'Yomi is the name given to the underworld in Japanese mythology, like Hades or Tartarus . . .'

'And the Hall of Orochi?'

'Orochi is a gigantic eight-headed serpent, also from Japanese mythology. But I've never heard of a hall dedicated to him.'

Jack nodded. 'Okay. The second message is less cryptic:

OUR ENEMIES HAVE FOUND THE
ARSENAL OF THE KHAN.
IMPERATIVE THAT THEY DO NOT
ACQUIRE THE EGG.

DO WHATEVER IS REQUIRED.

'Tank and the Blood Brotherhood are going for the Arsenal,' Jack said. 'Damn, this could get very crowded.'

Zoe said, 'Jack, you said these messages were encrypted with systems used by Japanese special forces. You think Tank might be getting some unofficial help from inside the Japanese military establishment?'

Jack gave her a look. 'I don't know. It's a possibility. Either way, once again we're bringing up the rear. Sky Monster, get us there, *now*.'

The *Halicarnassus* rolled to a halt on a windswept plateau twenty miles north of the remote Mongolian town of Unjin. Stretching away to the south of the plateau was the vast emptiness of the Gobi Desert.

For most of the year, the Gobi was a land hostile to human existence—desolate, dry and brutally cold—but in late February, hostile was an understatement.

Snow fell. A layer of permafrost blanketed the landscape in grey. Biting winds swept across the plain, penetrating to the bone, lowering the daytime temperature to –22 degrees. The combination of temperature and altitude prevented any kind of helicopter activity—rotor blades could not get any lift in the thin, cold air. Without ultralong landing strips, jets like the *Hali* struggled; indeed, this was why they'd had to land so far away.

As the big black 747 stood parked on the remote clifftop, two small dots sped away from it, racing out across the desert floor: a pair of all-terrain quad-bikes.

Jack drove one of them, with Wizard riding pillion and Lily sitting on his lap. Zoe drove the second bike, with Sky Monster as her passenger. Not used to travelling under someone else's command, the big hairy-faced Kiwi pilot was terrified and he rode with his hands gripping Zoe's waist tightly. Zoe grinned at his discomfort. All of them wore heavy-duty snow gear—parkas, hoods, goggles, gloves.

As they crested a low hill, Jack scanned the terrain through some digital binoculars.

They were in the foothills of the Altay Mountains, which ran in a long line from west to east, providing something of a northern boundary to the Gobi. The desert beyond the hills was huge: it stretched away to the southern, western and eastern horizons, flatter than flat, vaster than vast. Jack could see a narrow, dirt road heading east for thirty miles without a bend or a turn.

Everything—mountain, road, plain—was covered in permafrost.

But then he spotted something in the distance . . . on the dirt road . . . something moving.

A large white-grey dustcloud.

And it was advancing toward them.

Zoe saw it, too. 'What is that . . . ?'

Jack was about to say something about a sandstorm when he zoomed in with his binoculars and saw what lay at the head of the dustcloud.

Two main battle tanks.

Chinese Type-90s. Behind the lead tanks were two long columns of more tanks and armoured vehicles, vehicles that were no doubt filled with Chinese infantry troops.

Jack couldn't guess how many troops were coming toward him: it might have been as many as fifteen hundred men. With 1.6 million soldiers, China had the largest land army in the world. Deploying a battalion of them to the Gobi Desert was not a major challenge.

Was Wolf, with his Chinese ally, Colonel Mao Gongli, leading that massive force?

For a moment, Jack felt elated at the thought that he might have leapfrogged Wolf and would get to the Arsenal of Genghis Khan first.

From his hilltop position, Jack could see down a long narrow valley flanked by low mountains and bearing perfectly-formed meteor craters all the way along its length, every one of them covered in a layer of the white-grey frost. Interspersed among the remarkable craters were conical earthen mounds—primitive burial mounds, some eight feet tall, others fifty or even a hundred feet high.

Jack scanned the isolated valley through his high-tech binoculars.

Beside one of the larger mounds—a towering frost-covered mass nestled close to a mountain—he saw a cluster of military vehicles, troop trucks and jeeps, all bearing red stars on their sides. They were parked beside a very narrow tunnel that appeared to burrow into the base of the giant mound.

An advance team, he thought. *Damn. Wolf did get here first. He must have led a smaller, lighter team here, to be joined by the larger Chinese force later—*

But then, panning over the scene through his binoculars, Jack saw that nobody was moving near these parked vehicles, not even sentries standing guard. In fact, there appeared to be no-one at all stationed with the cars.

Curious, Jack increased his magnification and a horrific image appeared in his viewfinder.

Beside the Chinese Army vehicles were bodies, about ten of them, all lying with their heads face-down in star-shaped pools of blood.

'Uh-oh,' he breathed. 'Wolf *is* here, but I think our Japanese friends have already arrived as well.'

Jack, Lily, Wizard, Zoe and Sky Monster stood beside the parked Chinese vehicles in front of the gigantic burial mound. It towered above them, wide and massive, at least a hundred feet tall.

'Lily, stay back, okay,' Jack said as he checked the bloodied bodies on the ground.

They'd all been shot in the head, executed.

'Chinese special forces, plus a couple of Wolf's CIEF guys,' he said. 'And they were slaughtered.'

'Jack,' Zoe called. 'Look at this.'

She was standing at the top of the narrow tunnel that burrowed into the base of the mound.

Joining her, Jack now saw that it was more than just a tunnel. It was a thin chasm, open at the top and barely a metre wide, that descended via a series of about one hundred stone steps *into* the ground beneath the mound.

Jack frowned, threw Zoe a questioning look.

'Search me,' she replied.

'Wizard?'

'I have a feeling,' he said, 'that this mound is no mound at all.'

'Sky Monster, you're our lookout. Stay up here and maintain radio contact. Zoe, Wizard and Lily, follow me,' Jack said, lifting his MP-7 to his shoulder, assault-style, before he headed down the stairs, descending into the earth.

Jack hustled down the narrow flight of stone steps, the chasm's earthen walls pressing tight against his shoulders. If he looked up, he would have seen the sky, but right now his eyes were locked dead ahead, fixed down the barrel of his gun.

Down the stone steps he flew, when all of a sudden the stairway stopped abruptly and Jack skidded to a halt and beheld a stunning, stunning sight.

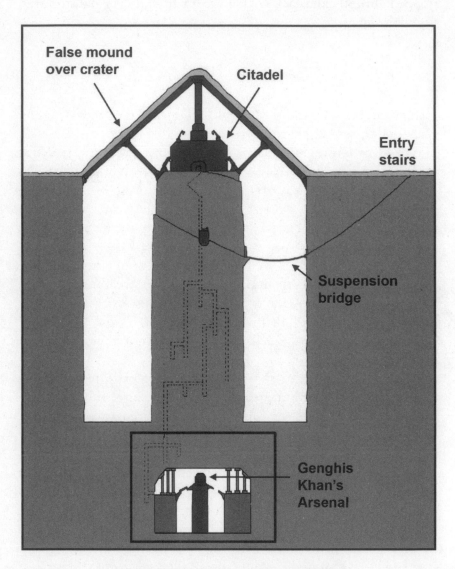

THE TOWER IN THE CRATER

Jack found himself staring at what had once been a meteor crater. Only this crater had been *roofed over*.

And in its centre, mounted in a high upthrust of rock, stood an imposing black structure that appeared to be made entirely of cast-iron.

The overall effect was of a tower the size of an office building built in the middle of a deep circular hole. But it was beautiful; it was a genuine work of art.

The whole tower structure must have been fifteen storeys tall. Its vertical rocky flanks were lined in a cladding of cast-iron plates (some of them had fallen off), but the defensive structure at its summit seemed to be wrought wholly of cast-iron—thick and strong, with the consistency of an anvil.

Wizard appeared behind Jack. 'Like I said, not a mound.'

'Indeed . . .'

Jack scanned the 'roof' that encased the meteor crater. A chunky iron column rose above the black tower like a spire, only it was not decorative—it was the central support for a circular conical 'roof' that fanned out from the column's uppermost point, reaching down to the rim of the crater.

Four mighty iron support-beams branched out from the tower, forming the skeleton of this roof—hundreds of wooden beams filled in the gaps so that from the outside the conical structure would take the shape of a primitive burial mound.

'Clever,' Zoe said. 'There are thousands of mounds like these all over China and Mongolia. And most of them have nothing beneath them except a single body. So you make your secret arsenal look like one of them.'

Giving access to the 700-year-old citadel in the middle of the crater was a far more modern creation: a steel-cable suspension bridge. It spanned the hundred-foot void between Jack's group and the black tower.

Jack instantly recognised it as a standard US Army model.

'Wolf,' he said.

They crossed the long swooping suspension bridge.

Leading the way, Jack arrived at a platform on the outer flank of the iron-clad tower. From there, a steep staircase spiralled up and around the four sides of the tower, leading to the squat black citadel at its summit.

The bridge, the platform and the outer spiral staircase were all covered by aggressive archer-stations, so that—at least in ancient times—no intruder could enter the great citadel easily.

More bloodied bodies lay here—plus numerous shell casings indicating a fierce firefight—only this time the bodies were Chinese *and* American . . . plus at least one dead Japanese trooper dressed in black combat gear.

'God, I hate arriving last,' Jack muttered.

He, Lily, Zoe and Wizard pressed on, moving to the summit structure, where a great black cast-iron door yawned before them, recently blasted open by modern explosives. Two more dead CIEF troops lay on the floor here, their blood still warm.

'NVGs,' Jack ordered.

If two groups of bad guys were already here, he wasn't going to reveal his presence by using flashlights or glowsticks. Everyone donned their night-vision goggles.

'All right, in we go.'

Inside the citadel tower was a complex network of vertical shafts. Each shaft was square-sided with walls clad in smooth cast-iron plating, offering no handholds. All of them plummeted to ominous black depths.

Every now and then, however, low horizontal cross-tunnels would link the vertical shafts to others—but always leaving a further section of vertical darkness *below* the cross-tunnel: creating hardwalled pits from which unwary tomb robbers could not escape, unless they had ropes going back up to the upper levels.

Wizard marvelled at the engineering of it all. 'The false roof, the iron plating, the pits. Genghis didn't want anyone finding this place, or if they did find it, getting out of it alive.'

Some of the cross-tunnels, Jack noted, were filled with rubble and dust. By the look of it, Wolf's people had had to jackhammer through rubble that had blocked up the tunnels. That would have taken time.

Arriving last on this occasion, Jack figured, had actually been beneficial: for a change, his predecessors had done the time-consuming guesswork and gruntwork for him.

Ropes hanging from A-frames revealed the shafts Wolf had taken successfully and the occasional row of glowsticks showed the correct horizontal cross-tunnel to follow.

It made for an unusually quick descent through the trap system.

And so after twenty minutes of roping and crab-crawling through the dark network of shafts and cross-tunnels, Jack, Lily, Wizard and Zoe arrived at a final tunnel: one that was not only filled with dust and rubble, but which also contained the three industrial jackhammers that had created the mess.

This final tunnel ended at an ornate iron doorway where two more American corpses lay in pools of—

A sudden explosion.

Short and sharp.

Jack snapped up.

It had come from beyond the iron doorway.

Then he heard a voice—Wolf's voice—yelling, 'You fucking suicidal bastards—!'

Jack raced through the doorway.

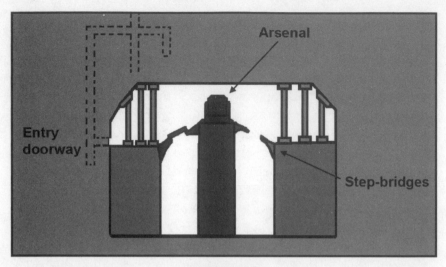

SIDE VIEW

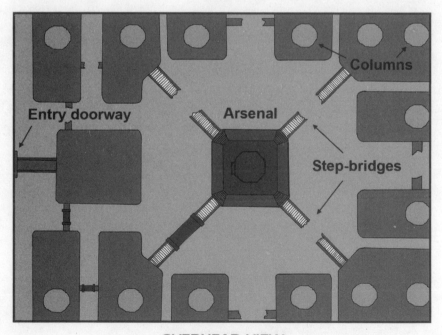

OVERHEAD VIEW

THE ARSENAL OF GENGHIS KHAN

THE SECRET ARSENAL OF GENGHIS KHAN
MONGOLIA, 0700 HOURS
ONE HOUR EARLIER

Sixty minutes earlier, stepping through the same doorway Jack now stood in, Wolf had gazed in grim satisfaction at the sight.

After spending nine hours painfully navigating his way through the vertical shaft system—doubling back at dead-ends, using jackhammers to cut through the densely-packed rubble that filled several of the cross-tunnels—he had finally arrived at the Great Khan's fabled arsenal.

It was set in the middle of a glorious man-made cave hewn out of the earth beneath the crater.

And what a cave it was.

Black iron columns supported a high ceiling, while deep man-made ravines cut across the floor, forming an irregular network of moats that were spanned by narrow stone bridges.

The only problem, every single one of the stone bridges had been destroyed—there were gaping voids in their middles, preventing access to the centrepiece of the cave:

The Arsenal.

A box-shaped garage-sized structure made of dense black iron, it looked like a colossal Chubb safe.

It was set atop a high pinnacle of rock so that it stood thirty feet above the rest of the vast room, encircled by the widest ravine of all. Four stepped bridges swooped up toward it in an X-formation, spanning this moat—but like all the other bridges in this cave, they had been broken in the middle.

Entranced, Wolf looked down into the moat.

Hundreds of thousands of human bones lay at its base, two hundred feet below him. The moat's walls, he noticed, were clad in smooth cast-iron, just like the vertical shafts. Once you fell in, you couldn't climb out.

'Sacrificial victims?' Rapier asked, arriving at Wolf's side.

'No. The bones of the Kwarezmi slaves who built this place. Twenty-five thousand of them. When it was finished, they probably just threw the slaves into the moat and shut them inside, leaving those who didn't die from the fall to starve in the darkness and kill and eat each other.'

He turned to his son and shrugged. 'It's never good to be on the losing side in a war, but back then it was really fucking bad. Come on.'

Lightweight bridging planks were laid over the destroyed ancient bridges, allowing Wolf to cross the ravine network and arrive at the south-west step-bridge leading up to the Arsenal.

As this was being done, he keyed his radio. 'Guard teams, report.'

'*Sir. This is Surface Team, with the vehicles. All clear up here. The only thing on our scopes is our Chinese back-up coming from their base over the border.*'

'*Sir. This is Tower Team, at the suspension bridge. All clear.*'

A special bridging plank with footholds was set over the step-bridge leading up to the Arsenal, spanning the gap in its middle.

When it was in place and tested, Wolf paused, gazing up at the squat black structure sitting on its rock-tower above him.

He nodded, pleased.

Then he strode up the bridging plank, crossing the wide central moat, and became the first man in over seven hundred years to enter the Lost Arsenal of Genghis Khan.

★ ★ ★

Holding an amber glowstick above his head, he entered a compact, black-walled room.

Treasures and trophies lined the walls in large unruly piles: crowns of gold, glittering jewels; goblets and chalices; swords and shields; bronze helmets and greaves.

It was plunder taken from vanquished kings and defeated armies, the colossal booty of wars waged by one of the greatest warriors of all time.

But it was the object taking pride of place in the very centre of the room that seized Wolf's attention.

There stood a magnificent stone altar, carved from a single block of black marble. Deeply etched symbols covered it, all of them painted gold. In and of itself, this altar was an artefact beyond value, but here it was merely a pedestal for what sat proudly on top of it.

Sitting upright in a bowl-shaped indentation on top of the altar was a large egg-like object the size of a football.

No, Wolf corrected himself.

Not egg-*like*. It was an actual egg.

A petrified dinosaur Egg.

Illuminating it with his glowstick, Wolf beheld fine carvings and drawings on its curved glass-like outer shell. Carvings in the Word of Thoth, and gorgeous drawings of landscapes and coastlines, mountains and waterfalls.

The drawings reminded Wolf of medieval Japanese art: they were surprisingly lifelike, with strong lines and three-dimensional *depth*, and Wolf suddenly realised that maybe medieval Japanese art owed a lot to the discovery of this Egg by the Shogun.

Like his first-born son, Jack West Sr could still be awed by discoveries such as this. His wide eyes and sweat-covered face glistened in the light of his glowstick as he gazed upon the marvellous Egg.

Then Wolf saw two images on the Egg that made him start: some pyramidal rock formations in a desert, which he recognised as the pyramid-shaped rock islands at Abu Simbel in Egypt; and a great flat-topped mountain overlooking a bushy coastline that could only be Table Mountain in Cape Town.

'The first two Vertices . . .' he breathed. He also saw four other landscapes on the Egg—showing the locations of the remaining four Vertices.

'Jesus, this thing really is the mother lode. Rapier! Get the cameras and that laser scanner over here and scan this room now!'

Rapier arrived a minute later, carrying a digital camera and the laser scanner. With him was Dr Felix Bonaventura, Wolf's archaeological advisor from M.I.T., who along with Max Epper was one of the world's leading experts on the lore of the Machine.

Bonaventura gazed in awe at the Egg through his round wire-rimmed glasses. 'Abu Simbel and Cape Town. This thing would have been very useful last year.'

'No shit. Photos and scans of the room, with everything in place, then take everything,' Wolf said, stepping away, lifting his radio to his lips. 'Guard teams, report.'

There was a crackle over his radio.

No reply.

Wolf frowned. 'Guard Teams. Report.'

Still no reply.

'What the . . .'

Shwap!

The head of the CIEF trooper standing in the doorway next to Wolf exploded. The man fell like a rag doll, dropping to the floor.

Shwap-shwap-shwap-shwap-shwap!

A volley of silenced automatic gunfire assaulted the cast-iron structure around Wolf, pinging off it, kicking up a thousand sparks. Two more of his men fell, riddled with bullets.

Wolf dived to the ground, ducking behind the doorframe.

Beside him, Rapier quickly drew a SIG Sauer, only to have it shot clear out of his hand, the bullet narrowly missing his fingers.

Losing the gun probably saved his life. The CIEF trooper beside him raised his rifle to fire, just as two black-clad figures appeared in the doorway of the Arsenal bearing silenced Steyr-AUG assault rifles. They blasted the trooper to kingdom come, but merely covered the weaponless Rapier, Wolf and Bonaventura.

This in itself said something to Wolf: these men were disciplined enough to distinguish between threats and non-threats in the heat of combat.

As they entered the chamber with measured strides and guns up, Wolf got a better look at his two attackers: they were dressed completely in black combat gear, including hockey helmets and black jawguards that concealed their mouths. Glock pistols and steel throwing stars lined their belts, while compact but lethal crossbows were fastened to their wristguards. Only their eyes were visible: and they were deadly eyes.

Japanese eyes.

The Steyrs, the jawguards, the ninja stars on their belts and the crossbows on their wristguards all betrayed them as members of the Japanese Defence Force's crack 1st Airborne Brigade: special forces troops, modern ninja.

An older Japanese man entered the chamber behind the two lead assassins, and Wolf recognised him instantly.

'Tank Tanaka,' he said.

Tank Tanaka hardly even glanced at the glittering treasure trove around him.

'Their scanner and hard drive,' he said to one of his men. 'Destroy them.'

The scanner and its drive were promptly shot to shit.

'The digital camera, too,' Tank said, seeing the camera that Bonaventura had been trying to hide.

It was seized and blasted to a million pieces as well. Bonaventura winced.

Tank then stood before the magnificent ancient Egg on the stone altar, assessing it.

'It really is quite beautiful,' he said. 'And filled with so much knowledge.'

Then, with a triumphant glance at Wolf, he attached a small explosive device to the top of the Egg and flicked the detonate switch on it.

He stepped back. 'Feel free to watch, Colonel West, the explosive is not a large one. Although watch out for shards.'

The device on the Egg issued a shrill *beep*. Then—

—*bam!*—

The blast was short and sharp. In a momentary flash the Egg just disappeared, blasting outward in a million glassy fragments that sprayed across the chamber, slamming into every wall before tinkling to the floor.

The Egg, fashioned by an advanced ancient civilisation, with all its priceless world-saving information, was no more.

'You fucking suicidal bastards—!' Wolf yelled.

Tank was unmoved. 'Honour is a far more pure motivation than greed, Colonel. It motivated that young man we slipped into your unit.'

'Who was last seen screaming all the way to his death,' Wolf spat.

'It motivates the entire nation of Japan,' Tank said. 'We know about the Third Vertex on the Hokkaido coast. We have known about it for centuries. It is sacred to our people, the most holy place in our country. A blockade of Japanese naval vessels guards it as I speak. You will not enter the Third Vertex, let alone find the Third Pillar inside it.'

'Are you gonna kill me or what?' Wolf said.

'Yes, I am,' Tank said, whipping up a pistol and firing it in one swift fluid movement.

Blam!

Wolf was hit square in the chest and he went flying backwards, arms and legs flailing. He crashed into a collection of golden chalices and urns, and lay still on the floor of the Arsenal.

Rapier roared in protest, only to find himself staring down the barrel of Tank's gun and—

'Yobu, what are you doing?' A soft voice broke the moment.

Tank spun—startled at hearing his real name—to see a very unlikely figure standing in the doorway behind him.

Wizard.

Beside Wizard stood Jack West Jr, with an MP-7 in his hands, covering the two Japanese special forces troopers in the Arsenal with Tank. The other two ninjas who had escorted Tank down here lay unconscious on the stairs immediately outside the Arsenal, immobilised by Jack. When Rapier saw Jack—alive—his eyes sprang wide.

'Max?' Tank said.

'Where's the Egg, Yobu?'

'It is no more. I destroyed it.'

'Destroyed it? No . . .'

'I'm sorry I never told you my true purpose for studying the Machine with you, Max.'

'And I'm sorry I never saw the hate in you, Yobu.'

'We fight on different sides now, my old friend.'

'I don't think I'm your friend anymore.'

Jack whispered to Wizard: 'If the Egg's cactus, we don't need to be here. We've got half the Chinese Army closing in. We have to go . . .'

Wizard scanned the Arsenal, and seemed to see something. 'Not just yet—'

He never finished the sentence.

Because at that moment, Tank yanked a grenade from his belt and pulled the pin, holding the grenade above his head and yelling, '*Banzai!*'—

—at the very same instant that Wolf rose from the ground behind him, his eyes deadly, a black Kevlar vest visible beneath the ragged bullet hole in his jacket, and his own SIG Sauer now gripped in his hands.

He came up firing, taking out the greatest danger first: the two Japanese ninja troopers. Both men dropped, each taking a hit in the forehead, their faces bursting with blood.

His stream of gunfire never stopping, Wolf turned his gun on Tank and hit him in the back three times, causing Tank to fall to his knees . . . and drop the live grenade.

The grenade bounced to the floor with several dull clunks, rolling wildly.

Jack saw it.

Wolf saw it.

Rapier saw it.

And then, in the confined space of the ancient Arsenal, the grenade went off.

The blast rocked the chamber—a concussion wave shook its walls—and a cloud of smoke shot out its doorway.

As the grenade detonated, Jack pushed Wizard out the door before he scooped up an ancient cast-iron Mongol shield leaning against the doorframe and whipped it up between himself and the fiery cloud that came rushing at him.

The force of the blastcloud sent him and the shield rolling back out the doorway, and in a distant corner of his mind, he was glad he'd decided to leave Lily back at the entrance to the cave with Zoe.

Inside the Arsenal, Wolf and Rapier leapt behind the marble altar that until today had held the fabulous Egg, also avoiding the deadly blast. Their comrade, Felix Bonaventura, seeing them move, ducked behind an ancient studded trunk and covered his head.

In the end, it was Tank himself who took the brunt of the grenade's force. He was flung into the cast-iron wall closest to him and hit it with terrible violence. He slumped to the ground, still.

Small fires burned in the corners of the chamber as Wolf and Rapier stood, arming themselves with the dead Japanese troopers' weapons.

'Still got *your* camera?' Wolf called to Rapier.

'Got it!' Rapier held up a second digital camera, a basic Sony model, one that Tank had not seen.

'How many shots of that Egg did you get?' Wolf asked.

'Six or seven. Got every side.'

'That'll do,' Wolf said. 'Felix! Get up! Time to get out of here!'

★ ★ ★

Still lying flat on his back on the stone steps just outside the Arsenal, Jack could see Wolf and Rapier scooping up the Japanese men's Steyr rifles.

He had to think fast.

Wolf and Rapier versus him and Wizard was a totally unfair fight.

And when you can't fight, you run.

He spun and saw the rebuilt bridge behind him—it led back to the cave's entrance, where Zoe and Lily waited, looking very concerned.

'Zoe! Find somewhere to hide!' Jack said into his radio as he assessed his own options.

He could go for the rebuilt bridge, but it would be the first place Wolf would fire at when he emerged from the Arsenal. He and Wizard would be shot in their backs as they fled.

And so Jack dragged Wizard the other way, around the squat Arsenal structure atop the rocky mount, still gripping his gun and his newfound iron shield.

Coming around the cast-iron building, he saw the broken step-bridge leading to the north-east corner, the one directly opposite the repaired bridge to the south-west.

If they could jump the gap, they could take refuge among the columns on the island-like platform over there.

Wizard seemed to see what he was thinking. He eyed the gap in the middle of the step-bridge: it was about twelve feet across.

'Jack, I can't possibly jump that far—'

'We're higher, which makes the gap smaller.'

'I still don't think—'

'You have to, old buddy, or you die.'

They hit the steps at the top of the broken bridge, hurried down them.

Gripping his shield and his gun, Jack jumped first, without breaking his stride.

He soared through the air—leaping across the void—before he landed with a dusty thump safely on the lower section of the step-bridge.

He turned to wave Wizard on. 'Come on, Max!'

Wizard seemed to hesitate, but then he bit his lip, increased his speed and jumped.

The older man's flight through the air was not as graceful as Jack's, nor as athletic.

He thudded chest-first into the top step of the lower section, his fingers scrabbling and clutching desperately for a handhold, his legs dangling over the two-hundred-foot drop to the bone-filled base of the moat.

He had just got a decent grip when Jack grabbed his wrist and started helping him up. 'Told you you could make it.'

'I should know by now not to doubt you, Jack—'

'Yes, he should, Jack,' another voice said, making them both look up. 'Yes, he should.'

There, standing above them at the upper end of the broken step-bridge, with a Japanese crossbow levelled at them, was Wolf.

Jack and Wizard were totally exposed: Jack lay flat on the steps, gripping Wizard, who dangled awkwardly from the broken bridge with his back to Wolf.

Wolf gazed down at them. 'Twice now you've returned from the dead, my son. Seems the huntsman is a tough spider to crush.'

Jack didn't reply. He'd holstered his gun to help Wizard, and his shield was now slung across his back, offering no protection. He just remained frozen where he lay, hanging onto Wizard, his eyes searching the upper platform for Rapier, but from this low angle, he couldn't see him anywhere.

Wolf grinned. 'Sadly, time is of the essence and I have to go. But if I can't crush your life, Jack, maybe I can crush your spirit.

Wolf raised his crossbow and Jack waited for the end, for the sharp pain of the arrow-bolt hitting him in the head—

Wolf fired.

Jack saw the blur of the bolt come rushing out from it, but it was too fast to follow and he waited for the impact—

Wizard jolted violently, his grip weakening around Jack's wrist, and in an instant Jack realised that Wolf hadn't been aiming at him at all. He'd been aiming at Wizard, at his back.

Wizard's watery eyes locked onto his. 'Jack . . .'

'Oh, God, *no* . . .' Jack breathed, tears forming in his eyes.

Wizard's weight became heavier as the old man's grip slackened and Jack had to take all his weight himself.

Above them, Wolf turned to go, taking one last look at the pathetic sight of his son grappling with the dead weight of the old man.

As Wolf stepped aside, he revealed Rapier standing behind him, gripping a silenced Steyr assault rifle.

Jack saw the gun and his eyes boggled and as Rapier shucked the safety, Jack summoned all his strength and swung Wizard up onto the remains of the step-bridge and hurled him down the steps. Then he dived down them after him.

Rapier opened fire.

A brutal barrage of bullets hammered against Jack's cast-iron shield as he crouch-ran down the step-bridge, trying to cover Wizard with the shield.

With rounds banging against the shield on his back, Jack joined Wizard at the base of the step-bridge, scooped him up, and—sliding on his knees—dragged him behind the nearest column.

A wave of bullets pummelled the massive column, but Jack just held Wizard close to him, tears rolling down his cheeks, huddling up against the column while the bullets struck it.

Then abruptly the bullet-storm stopped and the cave was silent, ominously silent.

At which point, Jack heard Wolf call: 'Here's some free advice, son! You can't win this. You can't win this because *you* are not good enough! You are resilient but you are not brilliant. You keep surviving by your wits, but eventually that sort of luck runs out.'

Taking cover behind the column, Jack said nothing. But he was listening.

Wolf kept calling: 'You fight for your pussy friends. I fight to win. And as you are finding out at this very moment, *you are out of your league here*! A hero you are not, so stop trying to be one! Consider your spirit broken, my son!'

Wolf's voice was replaced by rapid footfalls.

Jack could only remain huddled behind the column, gripping Wizard and staring into space as Wolf's footfalls grew ever more distant, until at last he could hear them no more, and the great cavern, filled with the cordite smell of spent rounds and exploded grenades, was completely and utterly silent.

★ ★ ★

Wolf, Rapier and Bonaventura would emerge from the great tower above the Arsenal thirty minutes later—passing but not seeing Zoe and Lily as they hid in the darkened lower section of the vertical shaft outside the doorway to the Arsenal's cave.

The three Americans crossed the suspension bridge, leaving the concealed crater, and emerged on the Mongolian plain. They joined Mao Gongli about a mile away at the head of his huge Chinese force.

'Did you get the Egg?' Mao asked.

'No, but we got photos of it,' Wolf said. 'Mao, my errant first-born son is inside that Arsenal. Consider this a gift: I leave him to you to do with as you please.'

Mao smiled. 'Thank you. I will make a trophy of his head.'

'So be it,' Wolf said. 'I have to get to Hokkaido.'

A lone figure watched this exchange from the top of the steps that led down into the crater: Sky Monster.

As Wolf had emerged from the crater, alerted by a quick radio message from Zoe, Sky Monster had hidden underneath one of the abandoned vehicles there.

He'd then watched as Wolf and his men departed while Mao's massive force continued on toward the disguised crater.

'Oh, crap.' Sky Monster hurried down the steps, heading into the crater.

Down in the underground cave, Jack knelt behind a column, holding the shivering figure of Wizard in his arms.

The bloody tip of Wolf's arrow-bolt protruded from Wizard's chest, a ragged chunk of flesh hanging from it. It had almost gone right through his body.

Wizard was hyperventilating, speaking rapidly: 'Oh, Jack, Jack . . . his shield . . . his shield . . . and the altar . . . did you see . . . it's not, it's not an—' but then he seemed to snap out of his delirium. 'Oh, Jack, I'd hoped it wouldn't end like this.'

'It's not going to end,' Jack said. 'I'm going to get you out of here.'

'Not this time, my friend. Not this time . . .'

The old man coughed, a convulsive heaving hack that produced blood. The arrow had pierced his lung.

'Max, you gotta stay with me, you gotta fight this. This is your life's work—'

'No, Jack,' Wizard's voice was oddly calm. 'This is your quest now. Yours and Zoe's and Lily's.'

Tears streaked down Jack's face. Through all his adventures, Wizard had been his loyal friend and mentor: from finding Lily as a newborn baby in a volcano in Uganda, to Wizard constructing Jack's extraordinary artificial left arm following his injuries in that volcano; to raising Lily with their international team in Kenya; to the time Wizard, a terrible driver, had sped the unconscious Lily to safety from Abu Simbel, chasing after the *Halicarnassus* while outrunning dozens of enemy vehicles; to the aftermath of the horrific execution of Wizard's wife, Doris, at the hands of Marshall Judah.

'I can't do this without you,' Jack blurted.

'Yes you can. You always could. And your father is wrong about you—you are so much better than he is, not because you are brilliant or resilient, *but because you care.* You care about people and that's what makes you a hero to me. Jack, it was my privilege to be by your side all these years.'

At that moment, Zoe and Lily appeared beside them, having traversed the Arsenal's cave.

'Oh, God, Max . . .' Zoe breathed, seeing the arrow and the blood.

'Wizard!' Lily squealed. 'No!'

'Lily,' Wizard's voice was serene. 'Sweet Lily. You're like the granddaughter I never had. I love you.'

Lily held him tightly, sobbing.

'And Zoe,' Wizard smiled through his bloody teeth. 'Brave Zoe. You have to look after Jack here . . . and Lily . . .'

'I will, Max.'

'You know,' Wizard winced, 'Jack was . . . Jack was going to ask you to marry him once.'

'Hey—' Jack began.

Zoe spun from Wizard to Jack, her eyes widening.

'It was'—another hacking cough—'soon after the Capstone mission. But you got called back to Ireland while he was away in Perth. And when he lost the moment, he lost his nerve. I've never seen it before: Jack West Jr losing his nerve.'

Zoe looked at Jack.

Wizard chuckled. 'It's the only time I've ever seen it happen. And I'm glad. It proves he's human—'

Three gut-wrenching coughs hit Wizard. More blood dribbled from his mouth.

He looked up at the three of them, his eyes sad but also calm, peaceful.

'Jack, Lily, Zoe. Do this. Win this. Save this terrible, awful world. I have to . . . I have to go now and see my lovely Doris again . . .'

And with those words, his eyes closed and his body went limp and in that dark subterranean cavern, Jack, Lily and Zoe could only kneel beside their fallen friend and bow their heads.

Jack closed his eyes to hold back the tears.

Thoughts of Wizard swirled through his mind: of his gentle smile, his patient way of teaching, his thirst for knowledge. He saw a world without Wizard and a profound sadness struck him.

Then anger stirred—a deep fury at Wolf who knew exactly how deeply Wizard's death would cut Jack. Wolf had done many awful things to Jack, but this went beyond them all.

Jack was kneeling there in the underground cavern with his head bent and his eyes closed when a voice came in through his earpiece.

'*Huntsman . . .*' It was Sky Monster. '*I don't know what's going on down there, but we got a rapidly deteriorating situation up here.*'

Jack blinked, snapping out of his reverie as if roused from a dream. The soldier in him was back. 'What?'

Sky Monster stood on the tower-side of the suspension bridge that spanned the meteor crater. He was hurriedly unscrewing its fasteners. The final screw came loose and the great swooping bridge dropped down into the crater, swinging limply up against the opposite side.

'Our crater is about to be invaded by a small army,' he said plainly.

Seconds after the bridge hit the outer wall of the crater, the first Chinese troops arrived at the platform down there and began firing.

'*Cut the suspension bridge,*' Jack ordered.

'Already done that.' Sky Monster hustled up the stairs that spiralled up the outer flanks of the tower. 'Now what do we—'

He never finished the sentence, because right then a shell of some kind hit the roof above the crater and a gigantic explosion rang out.

The roof shuddered violently . . .

. . . and then it began to fall apart.

Great tree-sized lengths of wood and cast-iron rained down into the crater, one of them narrowly missing Sky Monster. Huge drifts of snow followed.

Shafts of grey daylight lanced into the crater, illuminating it majestically.

Then a second—and a third and a fourth—shell hit the conical roof, destroying it entirely. The whole structure plummeted into the crater, exposing the tower to the sky for the first time in seven hundred years.

As the roof rained down around him, Sky Monster hauled ass up the spiral stairs. By the time he reached the cast-iron citadel at the top of the tower—coming slightly higher than the rim of the crater—he saw the full horror of his predicament.

Mao's fifteen-hundred-strong army—rank upon rank of men, tanks, artillery, troop carriers and snowmobiles—stood poised around the rim of the crater, completely surrounding it.

'Fuck me . . .' Sky Monster gasped. 'We've never been in this much trouble before.'

Jack draped Wizard's jacket over his lifeless face. Lily sobbed softly nearby.

Zoe said gently, 'Jack, come on, we have to move.'

'I want to take him with us.'

'You can't, we can't. If we survive all this, we can come back for him. And truthfully, I think he'd be happy resting here with Genghis Khan.'

At her words, Jack turned suddenly.

'What did you say?'

'I said, he'd be happy knowing that he was buried here with Genghis Khan.'

'This isn't Genghis Khan's *tomb*,' Jack said. 'That's never been found. This is his arsenal, his treasure chest.'

Zoe shrugged. 'That sarcophagus up there would suggest otherwise.'

'What sarcophagus?' Jack frowned.

'The big marble one smack bang in the middle of the Arsenal. How could you not see it?'

Jack recalled seeing a solid marble altar in the middle of the Arsenal, on which had sat the ancient Egg. But Zoe had not seen it as an altar: she had seen it as a—

And suddenly Jack recalled Wizard's rant from before: '*his shield . . . his shield . . . and the altar . . . did you see . . . it's not, it's not an . . .*'

'It's not an altar,' Jack said flatly. 'It's a coffin. Zoe, you're a genius.'

Showing even greater genius, when she and Lily had jumped across the broken step-bridge earlier to join Jack and Wizard in the corner of the hall, Zoe had tied a rope to herself. Now, she, Jack and Lily used that rope to get back across to the Arsenal.

Jack hurried into the cast-iron structure.

'"Attack with aggression, but always have a plan of retreat,"' he said, repeating Genghis Khan's great military maxim.

He stood before the solid marble altar in the centre of the Arsenal, only now he was looking at it in a completely different way . . .

. . . and suddenly the 'altar' looked like something else entirely: a great stone sarcophagus.

The sarcophagus of Genghis Khan.

'*Jack,*' Sky Monster's voice called. '*What are you doing down there?*'

Jack gazed at the great stone coffin. 'Maybe finding a way out of here, Monster. What's happening up there?'

Sky Monster stared in horror as Mao's small army moved three huge 155mm artillery guns to the rim of the crater, aiming them directly at the cast-iron citadel.

'We're about to be blown to hell.'

Lifting together, Jack and Zoe raised the great stone altar/sarcophagus slowly to reveal that it was indeed hollow.

Careful not to damage it or what lay beneath it, they tilted the big hollow piece of marble backwards, so that it leaned back at a 45-degree angle against a couple of treasure-filled wooden chests, in the process revealing—

—a crumbling skeleton, clad in full Mongolian armour: helmet, shoulderplates and greaves. A decorated pentagonal shield and a sword lay over the skeleton's chest.

'Genghis Khan . . .' Lily whispered.

Awe gripped them. This was Genghis, the great Khan, arguably the greatest military commander in history. For a moment his remains, lying there in perfect repose, held them completely transfixed.

Jack's eyes fell upon the shield resting on the skeleton's chest.

Unlike most Mongolian shields, which were circular, this one was pentagonal and constructed of iron. Moulded into the iron were some beautifully crafted raised images, all of which had been painted over in lustrous gold and silver:

Jack recognised two of the images instantly, the two at the very bottom of the shield: the pyramid-shaped hills in the desert at Abu Simbel and Table Mountain in Cape Town.

The locations of the First and Second Vertices.

But this shield had six images on it.

It showed the entrances to *all six Vertices*.

'Genghis had the images on the Egg carved onto his shield . . .' Jack said, realising.

He reached down and took the pentagonal shield from the

skeleton. 'He won't be needing it anymore, and as a guy who always had a plan of retreat, he also might have provided us with a way out of here.'

Jack then gently pulled the skeleton of Genghis Khan off its slab, to reveal something beneath it: a round pipe-like shaft that appeared to bore right through the slab and into the floor beneath it.

The shaft, however, was filled with densely-packed rubble right up to the rim.

'This place was a fortress before it became a tomb,' Jack said, 'a fortress designed specifically for use in a siege. So it would have had escape tunnels built into it, like this one. I imagine when Genghis had this place converted into his future tomb, he ordered all the tunnels to be sealed up, filled with rubble. This shaft was once an escape tunnel. And now it's going to be ours.'

'Jack,' Zoe said, 'we're about to be invaded by half the Chinese People's Liberation Army. How can we possibly excavate all that rubble before they arrive?'

Jack stood, a fire in his eyes once again.

He moved to the doorway of the Arsenal and spotted Wolf's jackhammers over by the entrance to the cave.

'I'll defend this castle,' he said, 'and while I do that, I'm going to send Sky Monster down here to help you excavate that escape tunnel.'

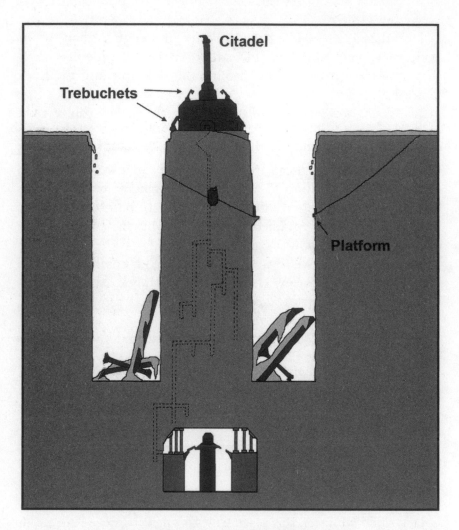

**THE TOWER IN THE CRATER
(WITHOUT ROOF)**

Jack raced out of the Arsenal and up through the shaft system until he arrived at the summit of the tower and to his surprise burst out into cold daylight.

With its false roof blasted away, the cast-iron citadel atop the tower was now exposed to the elements. A chill wind blew, snow fell, the sky was a glaring grey.

From his position atop the citadel, Jack beheld the angry Chinese army surrounding the crater. He saw over a thousand troops, many tanks, three howitzers. In this age of aerial warfare, it was an awesome amount of force to bring to bear on one location.

Jack came alongside Sky Monster, gazing out at the frightening sight.

'This is a whole new world of bad,' Sky Monster said.

'You can say that again,' Jack agreed. 'We're lucky it's too cold for an aerial assault.'

'So what's the plan, fearless leader?'

'You go below and help Zoe dig out an ancient tunnel which will hopefully open a back door for us while I stay up here and hold off these guys.'

'How are you going to do that? One man against a thousand?'

Jack said, 'Monster, this place was designed for siege warfare. It can't hold them out forever, not with their modern weapons, but hopefully it *can* hold them out just long enough for us to dig out that tunnel and get away. Now, go downstairs and help Zoe.'

★ ★ ★

As Sky Monster headed below, Jack hustled around the battlements on the topmost level of the citadel.

Fizz-ping!

Bullets started whizzing past him, pinging off the cast-iron crenellations. Jack looked down to see some Chinese infantrymen standing at the rim of the crater, firing their crude Type-56s as if they were sniper rifles.

Jack came to a trebuchet at one corner of the citadel's roof. Four corners, four iron trebuchets. On the citadel's lower level, there were four more.

A trebuchet is like a catapult, only with greater range, thanks to its heavy counterweight and to the hammock-like sling that flings its ordnance.

Behind each corner-mounted trebuchet, Jack found a cast-iron ordnance dome inside each of which was a clever system of ramps, levers and stacked-up projectiles: huge round boulders, clusters of smaller iron cannonballs that were loosely pasted together, and even some iron balls surrounded by a wooden latticework filled with kindling.

Jack pulled on a lever, and one of the 700-year-old cannonball-clusters rumbled down a ramp and plonked into the trebuchet's waiting sling.

'Nice . . .' he nodded.

Suddenly, three thunderous artillery shots rang out in the valley. Jack dived inside the ordnance dome as the modern shells impacted against the cast-iron citadel and exploded.

Fireclouds erupted all over the citadel. A wave of superheated air rushed around Jack's little dome. But the citadel took the blows like an anvil being hit by a hammer. When the smoke cleared, the squat black fortress was, impressively, completely undamaged.

Jack leapt into action, turning cogwheels and pulling levers— actions that simultaneously readied his trebuchet and turned it on its base so that it was aimed at the nearest Chinese artillery unit.

Jack grabbed the launch lever. 'Okay, Genghis, you old son of a bitch. Let's see if you were as good as they say you were.'

Jack yanked on the lever.

To his amazement, the ancient trebuchet worked. It groaned loudly as its sling swung through and flung its load. The tightly bound cluster of cannonballs soared through the thin Mongolian air . . . missing the artillery unit Jack had been aiming for by a full twenty metres . . . only to smash down on a Chinese tank, denting it, at which point the cluster broke apart, sending 100-kilogram iron cannonballs spraying out in every direction.

Men dived for cover. A jeep was hit and knocked completely over. Windshields shattered.

Jack gasped. 'Thank you, Genghis.'

On the other side of the chasm, Mao Gongli swore. 'Artillery! Target those catapults!'

And so the most bizarre modern skirmish was fought: a surrounding Chinese force firing shells upon an ancient Mongolian citadel, while Jack West Jr fired back from the citadel with its medieval weapons.

Each of his trebuchets would unleash a few shots before the Chinese nailed them with modern artillery fire. But every shot from the catapults did some damage—mainly to the Chinese vehicles approaching the narrow stairway that gave access to the crater.

Racing from one damaged trebuchet to another, with bullets and artillery shells sizzling all around him, Jack centred his fire on that stairway.

On one occasion, he scored a direct hit on a tracked vehicle parked beside the stairway, nailing it with a massive boulder, causing the vehicle to flip and land, upside-down, right on top of the stairway, temporarily blocking access to it.

Then he loaded one of the lattice-shrouded cannonballs into the trebuchet's sling and as Genghis Khan's catapulters would have done seven hundred years previously, he pulled out a lighter, lit the wooden kindling inside it and fired.

This flaming projectile crashed down to earth, *slamming* right into the upturned vehicle lying over the stairway's entrance. The vehicle's gas tanks ignited instantly and it exploded, sending tentacles of fire spraying out all over the entrance to the tight stairway, and causing the Chinese troops near it to pull back.

A few moments later that trebuchet was hit by an incoming shell but by then Jack had already run to the next one to inflict more damage and soak up more time.

'Zoe!' he yelled into his radio. 'How're you doing down there!'

Down in the cave, Zoe was busily jackhammering at the densely-packed rubble choking the escape tunnel beneath Genghis Khan's upturned sarcophagus.

It was a tight vertical tunnel, so she would have to jackhammer for a few minutes, then step away while Lily and Sky Monster hauled out the broken rocks on an ancient—and probably priceless—golden bowl hanging from the end of a rope.

It was slow going, and after thirty minutes of this, they were all covered in a grimy layer of sweat and dust.

'We're sixty feet down!' Zoe called back to Jack. 'It's dense. Really dense. And who knows how far it goes!'

'*Just keep digging!*' Jack ordered. '*Hopefully, you'll break through before these guys break in.*'

Despite Jack's efforts with the trebuchets, the Chinese forces kept advancing.

They used tanks to push the smouldering snow-vehicle off the entrance to the narrow stairway. Then those same tanks covered the stairway while two dozen Chinese infantrymen hustled down it, heading for the crater.

At the same time, the vast numbers of troops on the rim of the crater kept firing up at the citadel—from their slightly lower position, they had little chance of hitting Jack, but their constant fire kept him perpetually crouched as he moved about.

But then, from among their ranks, grappling hooks trailing ropes soared across the sky and landed on the citadel itself. When a grappling hook caught hold, the rope behind it would go taut—creating an upwardly slanted zipline up which Chinese stormtroopers quickly began to climb.

Ducking the incessant gunfire, Jack ran back and forth around the top level of the citadel, slashing at the ziplines with his knife.

Every now and then, he'd check on the Chinese infantry team down at the spot where the suspension bridge had been. They were in the process of a bridging operation themselves: trying to fire some ziplines over the chasm, get across on them, and then pull a ropebridge over after them. Once they had a ropebridge in place, Jack knew, covered by strategic fire, the Chinese force would come flooding in and his last stand would be over—

Abruptly, the shelling stopped. Silence hung over the icy landscape.

'*Captain West! Captain Jack West Jr!*'

A voice came in over a megaphone.

Jack spun and saw Mao Gongli standing at the rim of the crater beside a huge Type-90 main battle tank, holding a loudhailer to his mouth.

'*Captain, know this: we are not coming to capture you, we are coming to kill you! But the more you resist now, the more painful I will make your death! If you surrender now, I promise you a quick clean bullet through the head!*'

'That's some offer . . .' Jack said to himself.

He tried to shoot at the Chinese infantrymen down at the bridge platform, but a renewed wave of cover fire from the troops on the rim forced him back.

Then he glimpsed the bridging team secure two ziplines and start shimmying across the chasm on the ropes.

'Damn it, shit!'

He was now officially out of time.

They'd be across within ten minutes.

Down in the cave, deep in her pipe-like vertical tunnel, Zoe was jackhammering away when suddenly the chisel of her jackhammer popped through the rubble at her feet and the ground gave way and she fell six feet, landing clumsily in a dark horizontal tunnel.

She switched off the jackhammer and by the light of her helmet flashlight, peered down the tunnel. It appeared to lead westward, disappearing into black infinity.

'Jack!' she called into her radio. 'I'm through! I'm in a tunnel of some kind. Looks like it heads west.'

'*Go!*' Jack replied. '*Follow it! And take the shield! The bad guys are about to break into the tower up here! I'll be right behind you!*'

'Roger that.'

And so with Lily and Sky Monster behind her and with Genghis Khan's shield slung across her back, Zoe charged down the horizontal escape tunnel.

She guessed they'd run for about eight hundred metres when—
damn—they came up against a wall of densely-packed rubble,
completely filling the tunnel.

'No . . .' she breathed.

'A dead-end,' Sky Monster said. 'We're fish in a barrel.'

Zoe bit her lip. 'Maybe . . .'

'Maybe what?'

'The vertical escape shaft under Genghis's sarcophagus was
entirely filled with rubble. But not this tunnel. Maybe Genghis's
people only filled both *ends* of the escape system with rubble. We
might be only a hundred feet away from salvation . . .'

Sky Monster started running back up the tunnel. 'I'll get the
jackhammer!'

Another Chinese shell exploded against the ancient black citadel. Fires blazed everywhere. Smoke billowed into the sky.

Jack peered out from the reinforced doorway of the citadel and to his dismay saw a suspension bridge being lifted into place by the Chinese infantrymen down in the crater.

They were in.

His rearguard action was over.

It was time to go below.

Into the shaft system he flew, sliding down the ropes still hanging there.

He left timer-delayed grenades beside the A-frames at the top of each shaft—which he detonated after he was safely down that particular shaft. If Mao was coming in here to kill him, he was going to delay the bastard as long as possible.

He came to the cave containing the Arsenal, ran across the repaired bridges—also blowing them apart behind him—until he came to the Arsenal structure itself.

He paused only once: to gaze out at Wizard's covered body in the far corner of the cave, partially hidden by a thick column.

'See ya, Max,' he whispered. 'Rest in peace.'

Then Jack entered the Arsenal and went over to the small round hole that had been hidden for centuries beneath the body of Genghis Khan.

He looked at the skeleton of Genghis: gifted leader, enlightened ruler, unparalleled warrior.

'Nice to meet you, old man.'

A groan answered him.

Jack spun.

To see the slumped and bloody figure of Tank Tanaka lying face-down on the floor, groaning painfully. Shot and scorched from the grenade blast, Tank was still alive, just.

In the nanoseconds of time in which the mind operates, Jack weighed up his options: he thought about Tank and the knowledge he possessed (a lot), about the threat he would pose to them (not much), and about the trouble it might cause to take him with them . . .

'Okay, Tank,' Jack whispered. 'But if we have to hot-foot it, I'm dropping you like a stone and leaving you to face the Chinese by yourself.'

Jack hurried over to the semi-conscious Japanese professor, hoisted him onto his shoulders and hustled over to the escape shaft.

With Tank slumped over him, Jack then climbed into the escape shaft underneath the carefully balanced stone sarcophagus, still standing poised at a 45-degree angle on one of its sides. Then Jack released it, allowing the big box-shaped coffin to drop back into place over the top of them: concealing him, Tank, the skeleton, and the escape hole in the floor.

To anyone entering the Arsenal now, the sarcophagus would look almost exactly the way Wolf had found it earlier that day, a great stone tomb in the middle of the ornate subterranean chamber, surrounded by grenade-scorched treasures. The only thing missing: the Egg that had long sat on top of it.

Back on the surface, the Chinese force stormed the citadel.

They swarmed onto it, crossing the suspension bridge and whizzing across ziplines from the rim of the crater.

Into the citadel they charged, setting up ropes and A-frames inside the vertical shaft system, aided by a map of the system Wolf had left with them.

It slowed them down a little, but onward they came, hunting Jack West Jr.

Jack raced headlong down the horizontal escape tunnel with Tank on his shoulders, following the sounds of the jackhammer, until he arrived behind Zoe, Lily and Sky Monster.

Zoe was jackhammering away at the wall of rubble, with Genghis Khan's ancient shield still on her back, while Lily and Sky Monster flung dislodged rubble back down the tunnel, out of the way.

'What's the story?' Jack shouted.

Zoe said, 'We've cut through fifty feet of hardpacked rubble. There's no knowing how far it goes.'

Jack looked behind him, half expecting to see the flashlights of Mao's men charging down the dark tunnel.

'Either we strike daylight or we die when they catch up with us,' he said grimly.

Exactly forty-five minutes later, Mao's men entered the Arsenal. It didn't take them long to overturn the marble sarcophagus and spot the escape tunnel beneath it.

'Go! Get down there! Now!' Mao roared.

His troops dropped into the escape shaft. They then hurried down the long horizontal tunnel at its base, flashlights bouncing, submachine-guns pressed to their shoulders.

Gradually the tunnel morphed from a slick sharp-edged passageway into a rough-walled rubble-strewn one, as though their quarry had been forced to dig through the very earth.

Then the Chinese troops turned a final bend in the tunnel and stopped.

They'd come to the end of the tunnel, and there in the glare of their flashlight beams, they saw—

—a gaping hole in the rock, with a jackhammer lying abandoned beside it. Beyond the hole was a natural cave of some sort through which the dim glow of daylight could be seen.

Jack West and his team were gone.

While all this was happening in Mongolia, other things were taking place around the world:

NASA scientists reported unprecedented events in the outer regions of the solar system.

Gargantuan storms in the atmospheres of the four gas giants—Jupiter, Neptune, Uranus and Saturn—had produced the wildest celestial images since the comet Shoemaker-Levy 9 had plunged into Jupiter's atmosphere in 1994.

Great roiling spirals of gas could be seen on each of the four massive planets. It was as if all four planets were being assailed by some invisible violent force.

None of the scientists who appeared on all the morning TV shows could explain this sudden onset of planetary storms.

At the same time, the National Weather Service reported unusual weather patterns all over the world: fierce flooding in Brazil; sandstorms in China; cyclones in the Pacific; even a weeklong rainstorm in the Sahara Desert.

Meteorologists were confounded.

It was as if the world had gone mad.

On the military front, China unveiled the latest additions to its burgeoning navy: two colossal aircraft carriers.

For a decade, Western nations had watched nervously as China had steadily modernised her navy, adding nuclear ballistic and attack submarines plus high-tech Luzhou-class destroyers to it. Three years previously, US satellites had spotted the first carrier being constructed in a shipyard at Dalian. A modern Chinese carrier battle group had thus been expected for some time.

But the appearance of a *second* carrier had come as a complete and embarrassing surprise.

No-one had known the Chinese were building two of them.

At the same time, a major diplomatic announcement was made, with China pledging enormous aid payments to various countries. While the inclusion of the usual rogue regimes—Sudan, Zimbabwe—made the news, the largest payment, oddly, went to Chile.

In any case, when the two carriers took to sea on February 22, it rocked governments from Washington to Moscow and London.

They were numbered 001 and 002 and simply named the *China* and the *Mao Zedong*.

Lastly, on February 28—the day Jack West Jr was waging his war against Mao Gongli's Chinese forces in Mongolia—in the midst of a violent ocean storm, a small tsunami struck the north-eastern tip of Japan's largest island, Honshu.

The tsunami comprised four waves, each about three metres high. Damage was minimal, due to the quick detection of the tsunami by Japan's ocean-based early warning systems and the region's concrete 'tsunami walls'.

Seismologists in Hawaii attributed the wave to an undersea volcanic eruption approximately three hundred miles off the coast of Honshu.

What was unusual in this case, they said, was that the undersea eruption had *not* been preceded by the 'warning tremors' that usually came before such an eruption.

This eruption had been oddly spontaneous—as if, in one commentator's words, 'The floor of the Pacific Ocean just had a sudden jerking spasm.'

★ ★ ★

All of this—the unstable weather patterns, the Chinese warships, the tsunami—was observed by a lone man sitting in his remote headquarters.

He was a man of patience, great patience. He could wait-out even the most stubborn opponent.

He was a man who understood pain—the exposed steel plates that stood in place of his left jawbone, an example of the backward surgery of his homeland, caused him chronic pain, but it was an agony he endured as a daily test of his fortitude.

But most of all, he was a man who prized information, because information gave him power.

By virtue of his previous position in his country's state security organisation, he had access to the systems it had used for years to acquire information: taps on American and British undersea communications cables, spy satellites long thought to have been decommissioned, access codes to the secure military radio channels used by every nation from China to Japan to America and Israel.

For a long time now he had watched the travails of Jack West Jr. He knew all about Jack's previous missions, just as he knew all about Jack's rivals—from Wolf and Vulture and Mao, to Iolanthe and even the Japanese blood order—and their tangled web of two-faced allegiances.

He even knew of Jack's two daring rescues, one at Guantanamo Bay and the more recent one from the Old Master's trophy room in the Negev Desert. The Old Master, with whom this man competed in a gruesome competition, had been most upset by that.

But most of all, this man—this man with the exposed steel jaw—knew about the Dark Star, the Pillars, the Vertices and the Machine.

And now as he saw the world begin to tremble, he knew it was time to make his move.

PERTH, AUSTRALIA
28 FEBRUARY, 2008
12 DAYS BEFORE THE 3RD DEADLINE

While tsunamis struck Japan and Jack fought Mao's siege army in the Gobi Desert, Alby Calvin worked quietly away in his bedroom at his home in Perth.

Like the rooms of most twelve-year-old boys, it was filled with posters and toys, only this bedroom bore posters of the planets and the solar system, a telescope, and taking pride of place above Alby's desk, a print of Albert Einstein and his famous quote:

> **Great spirits have always encountered**
> **violent opposition from mediocre minds.**

Since the conference call with the team in Zanzibar, Alby had been busy doing research. He missed Lily and the others—missed the constant thrill of their adventures—but he'd always known that at some point he'd have to return to his ordinary life back home. Keeping busy doing research, however, made him feel like he was still part of the team.

And the work he was doing today was important.

He was calculating the exact times the Titanic Rising would occur on the days that the final Pillars had to be set in place at their Vertices.

It took a while but eventually Alby figured out all the times, adding them to the list of Pillar-laying *dates* Wizard had taken from the Mayan Killing Stone:

3RD PILLAR – MARCH 11 (0005 HOURS – JAPAN)
4TH PILLAR – MARCH 18 (0231 HOURS – GMT)
5TH PILLAR – MARCH 18 (0231 HOURS – GMT)
6TH PILLAR – MARCH 20 (1800 HOURS – MAYA/
MEXICO) [THE DUAL
EQUINOX]

Since Alby now knew that the Third Vertex was somewhere in Japan, he calculated the local time in Japan for that Titanic Rising. For the next two Vertices, since he didn't know their locations, he just used Greenwich Mean Time. And for the last one, which wasn't a Titanic Rising but rather the rare Dual Equinox, he just used the Mayans' own timezone: that of modern Mexico.

Once that was done, he immersed himself in Japanese history, in particular history related to its northernmost island, Hokkaido, and any reference that could, on a second reading, indicate the location of a Vertex there.

The more he read about Japan and its warrior culture, the more he recalled the words of Iolanthe: that the Japanese were an intensely *proud* people.

But it was a pride that presented itself in forms that Westerners found confusing and grim.

From the death-dives of kamikaze pilots to the ritual suicide of Japanese troops on Okinawa and Iwo Jima during World War II.

Or the way modern Japanese schoolbooks did not mention Japan's attack on Pearl Harbor. They stated that America had been the aggressor in that war.

Death before dishonour.

Anything before dishonour.

Tank had once told the twins that it was Japan's humiliation at losing World War II that drove him to destroy the world now.

Alby shook his head. People were strange.

He was surrounded by printouts and notes, including a bunch of Thoth carvings that Wizard had photographed at the First Vertex and which Lily had decoded.

He glanced at Lily's translation of one of Wizard's photos of the First Vertex.

He sat bolt upright, and read the translation aloud:

> *'Approach the last four temple-shrines with great care.*
> *For in the days before the Return,*
> *Called forth by Ra's Dark Twin himself,*
> *The very waters of the Earth shall rise to their defence.*

'"The very waters of the Earth shall rise to their defence . . ."' he repeated.

'Did you say something?' his mother Lois asked, stopping in the doorway, holding a laundry basket.

'What has Japan had a lot more of than any other country in the world?' Alby asked her.

'What?'

'Tsunamis. Tidal waves.'

'That's nice, dear.' His mom wandered off.

Alby pondered the translation.

The very waters of the Earth shall rise to their defence.

Was it possible that the return of the Dark Sun could trigger a tsunami? Like the one that had hit Japan?

Most tsunamis were thought to be caused by underwater earthquakes or volcanic eruptions. But there was one other theory . . .

He began typing an email to Lily, outlining his theory:

Hi Lily,

Got something for Jack to consider if he makes a run at the Third Vertex.

I think the Vertex on Hokkaido might be protected by a tsunami or a series of tsunamis.

Here's my theory: we all know how the moon affects the Earth's tides by moving close to and away from the Earth.

What fewer people know is that this lunar movement is also thought to affect volcanic eruptions by 'bulging' the surface of the Earth.

The moon comes close to one side of the Earth, and so by virtue of its gravitational pull, that side of the Earth *bulges* toward the moon. Not only do the waters in the nearest ocean rise, but *the very crust of the Earth* also rises. If the Earth's crust bulged near a weak spot in that crust, you would certainly get volcanic activity.

Now imagine this on the scale of the Dark Sun.

It's a great big body of anti-matter, the most powerful force known to science. If it set off a tsunami or two here, that'd be a small side-effect of its presence. It's probably what's causing the mega gas-storms in the atmospheres of Jupiter, Neptune, Uranus and Saturn right now.

By arriving at the outer reaches of our solar system, the Dark Sun is creating a bulging effect on the Earth, thus triggering tsunamis and the unusual weather phenomena.

Anyway, it's just a theory.

Alby

Alby fired off the email and sat back in his chair. It was dark now, the house quiet. His dad and his older brother, Josh, had gone out to see a movie or something. He heard his mom shuffling about in the kitchen.

'The solar system is starting to fall apart as the Dark Star approaches,' he said to no-one, 'and it'll only get worse—'

A banging noise and a scream made him spin. It sounded like his mom in the kitchen.

Alby stood up from his desk, only to see a dark figure appear in the doorway.

The man wore a ski-mask and gripped a silenced MP-5

submachine-gun. A second trooper materialised behind him, holding Alby's struggling mother in a tight grip.

Alby froze.

But then two more men stepped into the doorway, men he knew. Both were Arabian. The first, tall and handsome; the second, hunched and rat-nosed.

Scimitar and Vulture.

'Hello, Albert,' Vulture said with a malevolent grin. 'It's so nice to see you again.'

Within an hour, Alby and his mother were bundled out of the country on a private jet owned by the Saudi Royal Family, a jet that so far as Alby could tell, was heading out over the Indian Ocean.

Naturally, Lois was hysterical with both fear and outrage, so Scimitar injected her with a sedative. As she slumped into a deep sleep, Alby sat beside her, holding her hand.

The sleek private jet zoomed over the Indian Ocean.

But it did not leave completely unnoticed.

High above the Earth, a spy satellite long thought to have been decommissioned was watching it.

A GIRL NAMED LILY PART IV

Ireland

Australia

AUSTRALIA & IRELAND
JUNE 2007 – JANUARY 2008

DUBLIN, IRELAND
JUNE 2007

In that blissfully peaceful period between the Tartarus Rotation of 2006 and the day Chinese forces attacked her remote farm in late 2007, Lily had travelled a lot.

To Dubai with Pooh Bear, to Canada with Wizard, and to New Zealand with Sky Monster (where in Dunedin she stayed with Sky Monster's sweet but somewhat wacky parents; they pestered their son incessantly for a grandchild, which Lily found hilarious).

But her favourite destination of all was Ireland, and going there with Zoe.

To Lily, Ireland was the exact opposite of Australia: where Australia was dry, harsh and sandy, Ireland was green, moist and leafy. And the people were so friendly and she loved their accents.

On a few occasions Zoe took Lily with her when she returned to Ireland to brief her military and political superiors—the officials who had backed the initial mission to locate the Seven Wonders of the Ancient World. Given her integral role in that mission, Lily enjoyed a kind of star status when she met with those people, which of course she loved.

She particularly enjoyed meeting General Colin O'Hara, the silver-haired Irish general who had convened that fateful meeting of nations way back in 1996, shortly after Lily's birth. O'Hara had always acted as something of a grandfather to Lily, and he spoiled her terribly with chocolates and gifts when she came to Ireland.

So it was something of a surprise to Lily when, in June 2007, she and Zoe travelled to Ireland and entered O'Hara's office in the Irish Special Department of State to find O'Hara not there.

A much younger man met them instead.

They found him sitting lazily on O'Hara's desk, waiting for them. He was very handsome, Lily saw, in a slick, city kind of way. He was about Zoe's age and he had dreamy blue eyes, a square jaw and sand-coloured hair that flopped down over his eyes.

'Cieran?' Zoe said in surprise. She pronounced it with a hard 'C': Kieran.

'Hello, Zoe,' the man replied. 'And this must be Lily. Hello there, I'm Cieran Kincaid, Captain Cieran Kincaid, from the Army, but now on secondment to the Special Department of State.'

'Hi,' Lily said softly.

There was something about him that she didn't like. He seemed too smooth, too eager to be seen as easygoing, too oily in his confidence. *Slippery* was the adjective that came to Lily's mind.

Zoe looked flummoxed and, to Lily, a little embarrassed. 'Cieran, what are you—what are you doing here?'

'I'm sorry to be the one to inform you, Zoe, but General O'Hara passed away three weeks ago. Heart attack. He was sixty-five.'

'Oh dear . . .' Zoe said.

Lily's face fell. Zoe put a comforting hand on her shoulder.

Cieran said, 'I've been asked to take his place as case officer for several special missions, including yours.'

'Asked or volunteered?' Zoe said.

'Perhaps a bit of both,' Cieran smiled. 'You know me, Zoe.'

At which point, Cieran Kincaid did something that took Lily by surprise.

He smiled at Zoe, but in a way that Lily had never seen before.

It wasn't a lecherous smile, but there was definitely something sleazy in it—nor was it triumphant, but there was still something condescending about it. Whatever it was, Lily decided she didn't like anyone smiling at Zoe like that.

'So why were you chosen to take over from Colin?' Lily asked

Cieran curtly. 'You're a *lot* younger than he was.'

Cieran nodded evenly. 'I have some experience in special projects and covert intelligence work, and even more in political liaising. You can't imagine how much political liaising you've inspired over the last ten years, my little friend.'

'I'm sure I can't.'

'Rest assured'—Cieran either ignored or did not sense her sarcasm—'I've gone through all of General O'Hara's files and I'm up to speed on everything related to your case. Tell me, Lily, how is life with the great Captain West?'

'It's cool. He's an awesome dad.'

'I saw in the file that he formally adopted you.'

'Like I said, awesome.'

'Do you go to Mass regularly, Lily?'

'Huh?' What did that have to do with anything? 'Er, no.'

Cieran threw a sideways glance at Zoe. 'She doesn't go to church?'

Zoe said, 'Let's just say that my faith isn't what it used to be, Cieran. Along with Jack and Lily, I've seen things that have given me cause to doubt the Catholic Church's true principles.'

'The Church is the way and the light.'

'Yeah, because it's a sun-cul—' Lily retorted, but Zoe delicately cut her off.

'It might be for you, Cieran. But not for everyone.'

Cieran let it go with a shrug that was, again, a little too casual. Transitioning smoothly he said: 'So, Zoe, can I tempt you to join me for dinner this evening? To further discuss the loose ends of this mission. Perhaps we could go to Flaherty's and try the pinot noir again?'

Again? Lily thought, and then, just for an instant, she saw an emotion flash across Zoe's face, an emotion she'd not seen Zoe show before, but it was gone before Lily could process it.

'Thank you but no thank you,' Zoe smiled tightly. 'I think Lily and I will make our report to the operations committee and be on our way.'

'Another time, then,' he said, never losing his smile. 'Since we'll be meeting a lot more often now.'

Lily tried to avoid formal meetings in Ireland after that, but occasionally she would hear Zoe report to Cieran over the phone, always looking somewhat uncomfortable.

PINE GAP COMMUNICATIONS FACILITY
ALICE SPRINGS, CENTRAL AUSTRALIA
SEPTEMBER 2007

In similar fashion, Lily would sometimes travel with Jack to check in with his Australian superiors.

Usually, he met them in Fremantle at the SAS base there, but on one occasion (which Lily had particularly enjoyed) they had met Jack's bosses at the Pine Gap facility outside Alice Springs, in the barren heart of the Australian desert.

It was an ultra-high-security US–Australian communications installation with dozens of antennas, many low buildings half-buried in the earth, an electrified fence and armed perimeter guards. Lily was told that, officially, Pine Gap performed routine satellite links to and from US military satellites.

'Yeah,' Sky Monster had scoffed, 'so what does the five-hundred-foot iridium antenna that plunges into the earth *underneath* Pine Gap do, then? And why do they guard it so intensely?'

Unfortunately for her, Lily never got to see any gigantic underground antennas during her visit to Pine Gap.

What she did see was a whiteboard covered with grainy 8x10 photographs: surveillance photographs of men and women whom she was instructed to avoid at all costs if she ever saw them.

Next to a photo of Father Francisco del Piero (his photo had a red 'X' slashed across it) was one of a severe-looking black-haired Catholic cardinal. It was captioned:

CARDINAL RICARDO MENDOZA
VATICAN CITY; UNDER SECRETARY FOR THE
CONGREGATION FOR THE DOCTRINE OF
THE FAITH (CDF).
EXPERT ON THE 'TRISMAGI'.
SUSPECTED MEMBER OF 'THE OMEGA
GROUP' WITHIN THE VATICAN.

'The Vatican's replacement for del Piero,' the intelligence man giving the briefing said. 'The Congregation for the Doctrine of the Faith is the most powerful curial group in the Vatican. Oversees Catholic doctrine. It was once called the—'

'The Holy Inquisition,' Jack said.

'That's right.'

'Wasn't the new pope, Benedict XVI, the head of the Congregation for the Doctrine of the Faith before he was elected pope?'

'He was,' the briefer said. 'And since Benedict's election, Cardinal Mendoza has been very busy, personally visiting Vatican embassies all over the globe: in the US, India, Brazil and Cambodia.'

'Cambodia?' Jack frowned.

'Yes. Just last month, the new pope himself called the Cambodian president to arrange an audience between the president and Mendoza. The Church is mobilising again.'

'Hmmm,' Jack said, concerned.

There was one other photo on the whiteboard that seized Lily's attention; a photo she would never forget.

It depicted a man with half a face. He was utterly grotesque: with short shaved black hair that receded in a stubbly widow's peak, sickly yellow-rimmed eyes and—yes—the lower left half of his jaw was missing. It looked as if a wild animal had bitten a chunk of it out, ripping it clean off, leaving an ugly void that had been filled with a crude steel replacement jaw.

His caption read:

GENERAL VLADIMIR KARNOV
CALL-SIGN: 'CARNIVORE'
NATIONALITY: RUSSIAN
EX-KGB; FSB; RETIRED 2006
IMPLICATED IN 9 ASSASSINATIONS OF RUSSIAN
JOURNALISTS BY RADIATION POISONING IN
WESTERN COUNTRIES 1997–2006.
WHEREABOUTS UNKNOWN.

Lily stared at the man's horrific face.

'We recently intercepted an encrypted phone call from Balmoral to Windsor Castle,' the briefer told Jack. 'A partial decryption uncovered the words "... *before Carnivore gets involved* ..." in the conversation.'

'A new player?' Jack said.

'If he is, he's a dangerous one. He's got a serious reputation,' the briefer said.

'Only who is he working with?' Jack asked. 'Or is he in this on his own?'

Lily couldn't help but remember Carnivore. His hideous face invaded her dreams for weeks after that meeting.

DECEMBER 2007 – JANUARY 2008
AFTER THE LAYING OF THE 2ND PILLAR

But there were happier times, too, like when Jack taught her self-defence, when she and Zoe did girly things, and when she hung out with the twins.

In the short time she'd spent at Little MacDonald Island after the laying of the Second Pillar, before she had been whisked off to Perth with Alby, Lily had enjoyed getting to know Lachlan and Julius Adamson.

She found them hilarious: always finishing each other's sentences or talking enthusiastically about some new cheat code they'd found in *World of Warcraft* or some ancient palaeolithic site they'd been studying. They were like kids in adults' bodies.

Lily remembered first meeting the two freckle-faced redheaded twins on the way to Stonehenge in early December 2007, when they had performed the light ceremony there.

Scottish by birth, Lachlan and Julius had been grad students at Trinity College writing separate PhD papers on the various neolithic civilisations of the world; Wizard had been their supervisor and this had been why he'd brought them along to Stonehenge.

Their desire to learn new things seemed boundless. One day at Little MacDonald Island, Lily mentioned it to Jack.

'Lachlan and Julius are pretty special guys,' Jack said. 'They just love finding stuff out. It's as if they have to learn something new every day. They're also, I should add, great friends.'

'How do you mean? They're brothers.'

'Yes, they're brothers, but they're best friends, too—and that's not always the case. Look at Pooh Bear and Scimitar. Lachlan and Julius always look out for each other.'

'But they squabble all the time!'

'Sure they squabble, but they always settle their differences, because they're such good friends. Lily, if I can teach you anything in life, let me teach you this: *a friend's loyalty lasts longer than their memory*.'

'I don't understand.'

'You might not have experienced this yet, but over the course of a long friendship, you might fight with your friend, even get angry with them, like Lachlan and Julius do. But a true friend will forget that anger after a while, because their loyalty to their friend out-weighs the memory of the disagreement.'

'So what happened with Pooh Bear and Scimitar?' Lily asked. 'Why aren't they friends anymore?'

'They chose different paths a long time ago,' Jack said softly. 'Unfortunately, those paths intersected recently.'

'In that mine in Ethiopia. What happened there, Daddy? How could Scimitar leave his own brother to die?'

'Scimitar and Pooh Bear are very different men, kiddo. Pooh Bear sees the world in a broad way, like we do, as a place for everyone; Scimitar sees it in a very narrow way, as a place only for people like him. As for brotherhood, sadly, Scimitar doesn't see Pooh Bear as his brother anymore.'

'What about Pooh Bear? Does he still love Scimitar?'

'You should ask him. But you know our Pooh Bear: he's two hundred pounds of walking, talking loyalty. Look at what he did for Stretch in Israel. I reckon he'll always think of Scimitar as his brother, even if Scimitar doesn't think the same way about him.'

Lily paused for a moment, thinking—about her own brother, Alexander, who, raised to rule from an early age, was unlikely to ever be her friend. Then she thought about Alby, her best friend, ever loyal.

'Alby and I never fight,' she said. 'We're great friends.'

Jack nodded. 'I agree. I think you two will be best friends for life.'

Beyond that, it had to be said that Lily's life was pretty good.

During that Christmas at Little MacDonald Island, Jack had given her a pair of Heelys 'roller sneakers'—they looked like regular sneakers, only each shoe had a roller-skate wheel in the heel, allowing you to roll down hills. Of course, Lily's were pink and she wore them everywhere. For the first week, she even wore them to bed at night.

Then in early January 2008, while Jack and the others had gone to Israel to rescue Stretch, she had stayed at Alby's home in Perth— and while she would never admit it, staying with Alby had given her a nice taste of suburban normality.

Except for one thing: the time Lily discovered that not all dads were as awesome as Jack.

While Lois was an attentive mother, Alby's dad was a different story. A mining engineer from America working in Perth, he preferred to spend time with Alby's older brother, Josh. Josh was taller and more sporty than the smaller and bespectacled Alby. Josh was a top athlete at school.

Lily noticed that on weekends Alby's dad would always prefer to throw a football at the park with Josh than sit with Alby at his telescope. And she saw how it saddened Alby.

If only his dad knew the truth, Lily thought as she sat in the main cabin of the *Halicarnassus*, wearing her scuffed pink roller sneakers and flying eastward out of Mongolia in the predawn light.

Alby had been indispensable in all this. After all, it was he who had discovered the location of the sixth sacred stone, the Basin of Rameses II, in England. That discovery had resulted in Pooh Bear, Stretch and the twins flying to the UK while Jack, Zoe and Lily had gone to Mongolia.

At the thought of him, Lily decided to send Alby a message via the net. She got no reply. He mustn't have been at his computer.

She tried calling him, but no-one answered.

That was weird. There was no reply from Alby's home at all.

A MISSION IN BRITAIN

THE SIXTH SACRED STONE

England

ENGLAND

28 FEBRUARY, 2008

12 DAYS BEFORE THE 3RD DEADLINE

THE BASIN OF RAMESES II
(BRITISH MUSEUM)

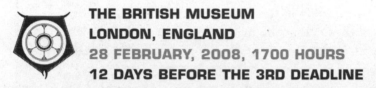

THE BRITISH MUSEUM
LONDON, ENGLAND
28 FEBRUARY, 2008, 1700 HOURS
12 DAYS BEFORE THE 3RD DEADLINE

The security staff had been watching him from the moment he'd set foot inside the British Museum.

It wasn't that they were racist, it was just that Pooh Bear perfectly matched the description of a 'man of Middle Eastern appearance'. And in these fearful times—especially after the public transport bombings in 2005—whether it was racist or not, men of such appearance were watched closely when they entered public places wearing bulging backpacks.

And even though his backpack had successfully passed through the metal detectors, they watched him anyway.

Which meant they hardly noticed the other two members of Pooh's team entering the British Museum behind him—a pair of red-haired Scottish twins wearing *Transformers* T-shirts (one bearing the Autobot symbol, the other the Decepticon symbol) underneath khaki gardeners' overalls and carrying plastic lunch-boxes filled with a mossy green salad-like substance.

It was Alby's late discovery—made just as Jack had been leaving for Mongolia and just before Alby himself had been kidnapped by Vulture and Scimitar—that had seen Pooh Bear, Stretch and the twins sent to the British Museum, tasked with finding the sixth and last Ramesean Stone: the Basin of Rameses II.

Alby had made the crucial connection that revealed the Basin's whereabouts: a link between Egyptian artefacts and one of the five warriors, Napoleon.

This had occurred when Alby had pondered why the Rosetta Stone, perhaps the most famous Egyptian artefact ever found, stood proudly in the *British* Museum when it had been discovered in 1799 by *French* soldiers serving under Napoleon. Why, he asked, was it not on display in the Louvre?

The answer was that the British had defeated Napoleon's forces two years after the Stone's discovery and relieved Napoleon of all of his Egyptian finds.

So Alby had embarked on a mission to learn just what other artefacts Britain had taken from Napoleon's forces.

It was a long and tortuous history, filled with accusations of dishonesty and theft on the part of both nations and in which the only apparently true statement was that 'the incredible stone from Rosetta and sixteen other crates of the most varied Aegyptian antiquities' arrived in London aboard the captured French warship *L'Egyptienne* in 1802.

Among the information about those sixteen other crates, Alby found a reference to a small stone basin called 'The Basin of Montuemhat'.

So he had looked up Montuemhat.

Montuemhat was a colourful character from Egyptian history. Around 660 BC, he had been the 'Mayor' of Thebes and the regional governor of all of southern Egypt.

Importantly, he had held court in the Ramesseum, the former palace of Rameses II, living and ruling in the very same rooms that Rameses the Great had occupied 600 years before him. It was entirely possible that a long-lost basin Montuemhat had used in the Ramesseum could have actually belonged to Rameses.

Studies of the Basin of Montuemhat had revealed that, while damaged, it actually contained not a single reference to Montuemhat at all. The name, it seemed, had been given to it by a lazy French curator, lumping it in with some other finds. And then Alby saw a picture of it on the Web . . .

. . . and saw some carvings in the Word of Thoth cut into its rim. Translated later by Lily, they read:

THE CLEANSING BASIN

He had found the sixth sacred stone.

And where was it now?

In the British Museum, sitting quietly in a corner of the Egyptian wing, ignored and unnoticed by the thronging crowds, eighty feet from the spotlit glass case that housed the museum's greatest prize: the Rosetta Stone.

And that was why Pooh Bear and his sub-team had been dispatched to Britain now: to steal the Basin of Montuemhat.

Pooh Bear strolled around the great museum's magnificent fully-enclosed concourse, all the while watched by Museum Security.

He stopped at the museum's café, where he ate lunch under the watchful gaze of an enormous Easter Island statue. The statue, or *moai*, had been in the news recently: stolen by the British from Easter Island in 1868, the Easter Islanders had been petitioning the British government to give it back—which of course the British refused to do. When the statue was recently repositioned as a decoration in the museum's cafeteria, the Easter Islanders were outraged and renewed their demands for repatriation of the *moai*.

At one point during his lunch, Pooh Bear made a phone call on his cell, looking around cautiously as he did so, knowing he was being watched.

Then—also according to plan—he went to the men's room, leaving his backpack unattended in the concourse café. It took the nearest security guard exactly twelve seconds to hear the soft '*beep-beep . . . beep-beep*' coming from the unattended bag.

The museum went into bomb-scare mode.

A single-tone warning siren blared out and a courteous but firm announcement was made for all patrons to evacuate the museum.

A heaving stream of people converged on the exits, hundreds of school children, tourists, museum staff and members of the public.

Pooh Bear—emerging from the men's room—was immediately detained by four security guards and hauled away.

Among the throng of people who gathered in the wide courtyard out in front of the British Museum were two red-haired men wearing gardeners' overalls over *Transformers* T-shirts.

They pushed between them a wheeled cart, on which was a small stone basin of some sort. It looked like an ornament from one of the museum's many water fountains, all the more so since it was covered in a green moss.

By all appearances, the two gardeners had been wheeling it out for cleaning when the alarm had been raised and the museum evacuated.

Fifty minutes later, a British Army bomb squad would discover that the beeping object in Pooh Bear's backpack was a Nintendo DS handheld game unit that he'd accidentally left switched on. The DS had been asking him if he wanted to continue playing.

Naturally, Pooh Bear was released to a chorus of bashful apologies, although he was warned not to leave his backpack lying around in a public place again.

The British Museum was re-opened shortly after.

Strangely, however, the two red-haired gardeners and the mossy stone basin were nowhere to be found. They'd last been seen heading away from the crowd massed in front of the museum, toward a parked van driven by a tall thin Israeli.

EASTERN RUSSIA—LONDON, ENGLAND
9 MARCH, 2008, 0145 HOURS
2 DAYS BEFORE THE 3RD DEADLINE

The *Halicarnassus* sat parked on the runway of an abandoned Soviet airbase deep in the mountains north of the Russian Pacific seaport of Vladivostok.

After escaping from Genghis Khan's Arsenal in the Gobi Desert and hiking their way back to the *Hali*, Jack, Lily, Zoe and Sky Monster—along with their prisoner, the wounded Tank—had flown eastward, arriving here only a few hundred miles from the Japanese island of Hokkaido.

It was late. A full moon illuminated the grim mountain peaks around the *Halicarnassus*. And it was cold, twenty below. In fifteen minutes, Jack was scheduled to check in with Pooh Bear's team in London.

Still reeling from the loss of Wizard—Lily had hardly spoken in the days since the dreadful confrontation at the Arsenal—Jack tried to keep them all busy.

They attempted to contact Alby again in Perth but got no response.

'Odd,' Jack said.

'Yeah. Usually, he answers on the first ring, he's so keen to be involved,' Lily said.

What they did receive, however, was an email from Alby, containing the times of the Titanic Rising on the Pillar-laying dates, plus a theory Alby had about tsunamis caused by the Dark Sun.

'Not a bad theory,' Jack observed. 'That kid's smarter than half the adults I know.'

He checked the list of times Alby had added to the dates taken from the Mayan Killing Stone:

3RD **PILLAR – MARCH 11 (0005 HOURS – JAPAN)**
4TH **PILLAR – MARCH 18 (0231 HOURS – GMT)**
5TH **PILLAR – MARCH 18 (0231 HOURS – GMT)**
6TH **PILLAR – MARCH 20 (1800 HOURS – MAYA/**
MEXICO) [THE DUAL
EQUINOX]

The Third Pillar had to be laid by March 11. Two days from now.

Jack considered what he knew about the Third Vertex: the golden plaque at the First Vertex had called it 'The Fire Maze'; the Third *Pillar* was hidden somewhere in there in its own internal maze; and according to the twins, the whole complex was located somewhere on the north-western coast of Hokkaido.

Jack bit his lip. 'If the maze is as big as the Shogun said it was, it'll take time to get through. We don't want to get there too late. And at the moment, Wolf is the only person who can actually cleanse the Third Pillar and set it in place, since he has the Philosopher's Stone and the Firestone.'

'So what do we do?' Zoe asked.

'The only thing we *can* do right now is watch. Watch from afar. We're only an hour away by air from the coast of Hokkaido. We watch Wolf's progress from a distance, and hope he can find the entrance and negotiate the maze inside.'

'Do you think he can?' Lily asked.

'He's a ratbastard, but he's smart, smart enough to do this,' Jack said. 'And unlike the Japanese Blood Brotherhood, he's not suicidal. My father wants to rule the world and to do that he needs to lay this Pillar.'

Just then, from behind them, Tank groaned, waking.

He was bound to a flight seat with flex cuffs, his face blistered and scorched by the blast of his own grenade inside Genghis's Arsenal. His cheeks and forehead glistened underneath a layer of antiseptic cream Jack had applied to the burns.

The old Japanese professor blinked awake, took in his surroundings. Then, feeling his bonds, he looked up sharply at Jack, Lily and Zoe.

'You failed, Tank,' Jack said.

Tank said nothing.

'You destroyed the Egg, but Genghis copied its images onto his shield.' Jack held up the magnificent pentagonal shield.

Tank still said nothing.

'We've deduced that the Third Vertex is on the coast of Hokkaido. Now thanks to this shield, we know what the entrance looks like. It's only a matter of time till Wolf finds it and, for a change, we have a little time on our hands.'

Tank snorted derisively.

Then he spoke in a hoarse croaking whisper.

'You don't have time.'

'What?'

'You're out of time,' Tank grinned through his burnt face. 'You still don't understand, do you? My blood brothers and I do not act *alone* in our mission to stop you placing the Pillars. We are but the point of a much larger sword.'

Jack frowned at that.

Tank said, 'The imperial rulers of Japan have long known the location of our nation's Vertex. It is our people's most sacred shrine, its location passed down from emperor to emperor since the time of the Great Khan's visit.

'Jack, you foolish man, understand! I do not represent some small group of ageing fanatics bent upon destroying the world out of simple vengeance. I represent *the entire nation of Japan* bent upon righting the most profound insult to our honour.

'If you venture toward Hokkaido now, you will find the coast guarded by warships of the Japanese Imperial Navy. You will find the landward approach guarded by our finest special forces troops. Throughout this mission, I have acted *on the express authority* of my government and my emperor. You are not doing battle against just me and my brethren, Jack West, you are fighting the entire nation of Japan.'

Jack's face fell.

Zoe turned to him. 'A naval blockade of the coastline? How is Wolf going to get past that?'

Jack was thinking fast. 'I don't know, I hadn't—'

'Jack,' Sky Monster said from the top of the stairs. 'Pooh Bear's on the line from England.'

Stunned, Jack, Zoe and Lily headed to the upper deck to take the call.

On a monitor in the *Hali*'s upper deck, Jack saw Pooh Bear in London.

Pooh Bear, Stretch and the twins were sitting in a cheap hotel room not far from Waterloo Station.

Jack informed them of Wizard's death in Mongolia.

'Oh, no . . .' Pooh Bear breathed.

'It was a disaster,' Jack said. 'The Japanese Blood Brotherhood were there, Wolf, too, and a massive Chinese contingent. My father killed Wizard.'

'Jack, I'm sorry,' Stretch said.

'And the mission?' Pooh asked gently.

'We got what we needed,' Jack said. 'We didn't get the Egg, but we have the images from it: pictures of the entrances to all six vertices. Genghis Khan had them inscribed on his shield. Zoe's emailing you a digital photo of it right now.'

'Got it,' Julius said from his computer nearby, eyeing the jpeg of the shield. 'Sheesh, that's beautiful . . .'

'How about you guys?' Jack asked. 'Did you get the Basin?'

'We got it,' Pooh said.

Stretch added, 'But we were hoping to talk with Wizard about our next step. Lily said that the last three Pillars must be cleansed twice: in the Philosopher's Stone and in the Basin *in the pure waters of the Spring of the Black Poplar*. We have the Basin, now we need to find the Spring of the Black Poplar, whatever that is.'

Julius said, 'We also need the Fourth Pillar, which we cleansed at that base on Mortimer Island, back when we cleansed the First Pillar, when that royal chick, Iolanthe, was on our side. I assume she still has it.'

'But how will we find her?' Lachlan asked.

'Maybe the answer is to get her to find you,' Jack said. 'Sorry guys, you're gonna have to figure out the rest of this by yourselves, because we're about to get very busy over here. The Third Vertex is more heavily defended than we anticipated. We're watching Wolf now: he's got to get past a massive Japanese naval blockade of Hokkaido just to get into the maze protecting the Vertex.'

'Right, then,' Zoe said, 'we'd all better get cracking . . .'

At that moment, her laptop pinged. The videolink window was flashing with an icon that read: 'RON'.

'It's Alby!' Lily exclaimed, immediately clicking on the icon. At the same time in London, Pooh Bear did likewise, making it a conference call.

Jack and Lily huddled around the screen, eager to see—

—the dark beak-like face of Vulture appeared.

'Hello, minnows,' the Saudi intelligence agent said. He stepped aside to reveal—

Alby and Lois gagged and bound behind him, covered by Scimitar. They were in a beige cabin of some sort: the interior of a private jet. Lois was slumped in her seat, unconscious. Alby's eyes were wide with fear.

'Look what I found,' Vulture hissed. Then he noticed Pooh Bear: 'Why, Zahir, you escaped from that mine in Ethiopia. You might not be as useless as I first thought.'

'What do you want, Vulture?' Jack demanded.

Vulture shrugged carelessly. 'You know, Huntsman, they say children can withstand a considerable amount of pain. I've often wondered how much torture a small boy could tolerate—torture exacted upon him, or perhaps witnessed by him when it is exacted on his mother. What do I want? I want your attention, Huntsman, and I think I just got it.'

The screen cut to hash.

Lily burst into tears. Zoe spun to face Jack.

Jack closed his eyes.

Vulture and Scimitar had Alby and his mother. It was one thing to take a hostage dear to Jack. It was another to take someone dear to his daughter.

Goddamn it . . .

'Jack.' Sky Monster emerged from the cockpit. 'Wolf just launched his attack on Hokkaido and it sounds like World War III just started. If you want to keep an eye on it, we have to go now.'

Jack sat up straight, collected himself, and said, 'Pooh Bear, find that Spring. We gotta move.'

AIRSPACE OVER THE ARABIAN SEA

In the plush cabin of his Gulfstream-IV private jet, Vulture turned from the computer, smiled at Alby and removed the boy's gag.

'Thank you, Albert. Part of every battle is the psychological war, and you've proven to be quite useful, again.'

'Again?' Alby frowned. Beside him, his sedated mother groaned in her restless drug-induced sleep.

'But of course, you don't know . . .' Vulture said, sliding into a wide leather chair. 'You will recall that last year, Captain West experienced an unfortunate invasion at his farm in the Australian desert.'

'I was there.'

'We know you were,' Vulture grinned over at Scimitar, who knocked back a slug of whiskey. 'It was you who led us to the Huntsman's farm, Albert.'

'*What?*' Alby sat upright.

'The Huntsman is a skilled operator, a man who makes few mistakes. We watched the girl, of course, but he ensured she was well protected when at school. And he never returned to his farm via the same route, even when he picked her up from that school of yours in Perth. So we could never find his farm and the Firestone it contained.

'But then you befriended the girl. So we started watching *you*, and suddenly the Huntsman made a rare error. For you, young man, do not possess the fieldcraft of a professional. When you went to their farm for a holiday, you were being watched the whole way there. It was you who led our associates—Wolf and Mao and Mao's Chinese force—to Jack West's home in the desert. Yes, Albert, you were his biggest mistake.'

Alby was horrified that this might be true. Could he really have led Lily's enemies right to her secret home?

'We know a lot about you, Albert,' Vulture said, clearly enjoying Alby's discomfort. 'We know how your mother dotes on you, how your brother ignores you and how your father distances himself from you, appalled by your bookishness, your softness.'

Tears began to well in Alby's eyes.

Scimitar glanced over at him. 'Oh, cut that out. You remind me of my own worthless brother.'

Scimitar extracted a glistening knife from his belt. It was an extraordinary blade, long and sharp, with an exquisite gold and jewel-encrusted hilt.

'See this?' he grunted. 'A gift from my father, given to me on my thirteenth birthday. A gift from a man to a man. To this day, my father has not given a similar one to Zahir, because Zahir is not a man, because Zahir has not proven himself worthy of such a gift.'

'Pooh Bear is twice the man you'll ever be—'

Scimitar crossed the cabin with surprising speed and before Alby knew it, the ornate knife's blade was pressed against his throat and Scimitar's hot whiskey-flavoured breath was right in his face.

'Say that again,' Scimitar hissed softly. 'Just say that again . . .'

'Scimitar!' Vulture barked. 'Not now—'

A pair of thunderous noises from outside made everyone spin.

To Alby, they sounded like sonic-booms . . .

He peered out the windows of the Gulfstream and suddenly saw two MiG fighters with Russian markings swing into formation on either side of the private jet, paralleling it, flanking it. They were so close, Alby could see the visors of their Russian pilots glinting in the sun.

'They're ordering us to follow them or they'll shoot us down!' the Saudi pilot called back from the cockpit.

Vulture seemed both enraged and perplexed at the same time.

'What the hell is this . . . ?' he breathed as he moved from window to window.

Abruptly, one of the MiGs fired a burst of tracers across the bow of the Gulfstream.

'What do you want me to do!' the pilot asked urgently.

'There's nothing we can do,' Vulture said, his mind whirring at this unexpected turn of events. 'We go where they tell us to go.'

And so the Gulfstream banked away to the right, departing from its intended course, escorted by the two Russian fighters.

THIRD BATTLE

THE BATTLE FOR THE THIRD VERTEX

Hokkaido,
Japan

HOKKAIDO, JAPAN
9 MARCH, 2008
2 DAYS BEFORE THE 3RD DEADLINE

**THE THIRD VERTEX
AS DEPICTED ON GENGHIS'S SHIELD**

**THE NORTH-WESTERN COAST
OF HOKKAIDO, JAPAN
9 MARCH, 2008, 0730 HOURS
2 DAYS BEFORE THE 3RD DEADLINE**

The fierce ocean storm that assailed the north-western coast of Hokkaido on the 9th of March, 2008, would break records. Never once in 1,300 years of precise Japanese record-keeping had a storm of such ferocious intensity been encountered.

Huge fifty-foot waves crashed against the coastal cliffs. Sleet lashed down from low stormclouds. Icy gusts of snow swirled down from the mountains bordering the strife-torn sea.

And that was all before one beheld the four gigantic tsunami waves that were approaching the coast from the west, each one the equivalent of the devastating Boxing Day Tsunami of 2004.

Local fisherman knew the perils of this strip of coastline and so kept well away from it even at the best of times. It was notoriously dangerous. Submerged rocks tore through hulls with ease. Powerful offshore currents dragged even the largest boats toward the jagged shore.

And so it was here, in an already dangerous channel, in a record-breaking storm, that Wolf's full-frontal military shore landing would take place.

As the raging sea pounded the coast of Hokkaido—*boom!-boom!-boom!*—equally thunderous booms sounded in the sky above it.

Twenty-three vessels from the Japanese Navy were gathered in a semi-circular formation, all facing outward from the snow-covered coast, and all engaged in a vicious firefight with a force of incoming American aircraft.

Every kind of warship short of an aircraft carrier was there: destroyers, frigates, cruisers, all of them determined to defend Hokkaido to the bitter end.

A wave of American UAVs—unmanned aerial vehicles or 'drones'—led the way for Wolf's assault force.

Despite the fact they had no pilots, the drones were heavily armed and they soared down from the sky at the same angle as the sleeting rain, plunging into a dense storm of upward-firing tracers.

A dozen drones were blasted out of the sky in sudden flashing explosions, but another dozen punched through the bombardment, including three important drones: those carrying ALQ-9 tactical jamming systems and LDS laser-blinding systems.

These were important because they formed a safe aerial entry corridor for the second wave of assault vehicles that was coming in behind them: a collection of bullet-shaped armoured pods, holding four men each.

The aerial assault had been precisely timed to coincide with the incoming tsunamis, or rather a peculiar phenomenon associated with tsumanis.

Before a tsunami strikes, it is always preceded by a 'sucking back' of the coastal waters. The ocean literally recedes from the shore as the approaching wave runs up over shallower ground and crests, folding over on itself before crashing into the coastal land formation.

During the famous Lisbon Tsunami of 1755, the ocean receded, revealing many shipwrecks and cargo crates on the floor of Lisbon's harbour. Curious and greedy onlookers ran out across the exposed seabed to plunder the wrecks, only for the tsunami to arrive twenty minutes later, drowning them all.

The size and duration of a 'tsunami recession' depends solely on the size and power of the incoming wave. The bigger the wave, the longer the recession.

The Japanese naval vessels defending Hokkaido that day were well aware of the concept of tsunami recession, and so set their perimeter a full two kilometres out from the coast.

It would prove to be their only weak point.

Soaring down through the sky inside one of his armoured pods, high above the Hokkaido coast and the Japanese fleet defending it, Wolf watched the ocean pull back from the north-western coast of Hokkaido on a monitor.

It was a stunning sight to behold from this angle.

A vast semi-circle of water swept back from the shoreline in a gigantic curving arc, revealing the flat seabed. It looked like an enormous beach, and on it Wolf discerned several rust-covered shipwrecks: fishing trawlers, two ancient Chinese junks, and dominating the exposed seabed, one massive modern supertanker, lying on its side close to the shore.

He could also see a series of sharply-pointed black objects on this newly formed 'beach', but he couldn't tell what they were from this height.

Most importantly, however, perfectly replicating the image he had photographed on the Dragon's Egg, he saw a semi-frozen waterfall dropping into the sea from a triangular fissure in the coastal clifftop. On the landward side of this waterfall loomed an extinct volcano.

And directly beneath the waterfall, exactly as it was depicted on the Egg, at the now-exposed base of the coastal cliff, he saw an enormous rectangular stone doorway the size of an aeroplane hangar.

It was the entrance to the Third Vertex.

Covered by the squadron of drones, Wolf's armoured pods—they were PA-27 Airborne Assault Pods, used exclusively by the CIEF—zoomed down toward the entrance to the Vertex.

Waves of anti-aircraft fire from the Japanese warships on the ocean surface—as well as from a dozen land-positions on the cliffs— lanced up toward the incoming pods. Ordinary rounds just bounced off the assault pods' tungsten armour, while RPGs and missiles were nullified by their advanced laser-blinding system.

When the pods' altimeters sensed that they were two hundred feet above the exposed seabed, a pair of rotors flipped out laterally above each pod and instantly began rotating in opposite directions, arresting their falls.

Wolf's pod landed lightly on the seabed, helicopter-style, only a hundred yards from the entrance to the Vertex, not far from the wreck of the supertanker.

Its armoured door hissed open and Wolf emerged, flanked by two CIEF troops and the Neetha warlock.

On his back Wolf wore a Samsonite pack containing the Fire-stone. Out of another pod nearby stepped Rapier—he carried the Philosopher's Stone in a similar backpack.

It was only now that he was on the ground that Wolf saw what the pointed black objects on the seabed were: they were towering black rocks, all of which had been sharpened to jagged points by the hand of man, their edges deliberately serrated.

'They're designed to sink any ship that comes too close to the entrance . . .' a CIEF trooper observed.

'Indeed,' Wolf said.

There must have been thirty of the things, arrayed in a random pattern around the coastal cliffs. Good protection for a secret place.

All around Wolf, forty CIEF troopers were hustling out of the ten other PA-27 pods that had landed on the seabed.

It was then that gunfire began to rain down on them from Japanese troops positioned on the clifftops overlooking the exposed beach.

'All units!' Wolf yelled. 'Return fire! And get to the entrance before the wave comes in!'

Circling in the *Halicarnassus* in clear skies high above the stormclouds fifty miles to the west, Jack listened in on Wolf's communications—at the same time watching the battle via a live satellite infra-red feed beamed to him from Pine Gap.

He saw the entire battle from a black-and-white overhead view: saw the Japanese warships firing tracers skyward; saw the American armoured pods raining down; and most bizarrely, he saw the waters of the Sea of Japan retreat in a wide semi-circle away from the coastal cliffs, revealing the seabed, the shipwrecks and the jagged rocks.

'—*All units! Return fire! And get to the entrance before the wave comes in!*'

Gunfire. Orders. Whizzing bullets.

And then came the screams.

'—*Thompson's hit!*'

'—*Fuck!*'

'—*Team One is inside the entrance! Come on, people! Move it!*'

'—*Sir, this is Rapier! I'm experiencing heavy fire from those fuckers on the cliffs—we're pinned down at the supertanker!*'

'—*Well, you better get fucking unpinned, because that tsunami is nine minutes away! All units, provide cover fire for Rapier. I need him inside! He's carrying the Philosopher's Stone—*'

Jack snapped upright.

Wolf had timed his forced insertion perfectly, coinciding it with the outflow of the tsunami wave. But now the tidal wave was coming in and one of his units—the one carrying the all-important Philosopher's Stone—was stuck out on the exposed seabed under heavy fire from the Japanese forces on the cliffs.

Then, to his surprise, Jack heard a familiar voice over the radio.

'—*Sir, this is Astro*'—the puncture-like whump of a rocket launcher rang out—'*We're targeting those guys up on the cliffs with RPGs. Rapier! Go!*'

Rapier: '—*Can't! That fire is still too strong!*'

Astro: '—*Hang tight! We're coming to you!*'

Astro, Jack thought. He'd last seen him inside that mine in Ethiopia, standing beside Wolf. *Had Astro really betrayed Jack's group? Had he been working for Wolf all along?*

More gunfire. More RPG explosions. It sounded like total battle-field hell.

Astro's voice came in again. '—*Sir! That cover fire from the cliffs ain't stopping! We can't get to Rapier! Oh shit, do you see that . . . ?*'

Gun in hand, Lieutenant Sean Miller—'Astro'—stood on the most bizarre battlefield he had ever seen.

He was crouched behind a high triangular boulder out on the exposed seabed beneath the cliffs of the Hokkaido coast, pelted by sleet and ducking a seemingly unending fusillade of bullets and rocket-propelled grenades coming from the Japanese troops on the clifftops above him.

The Japanese were annihilating them.

Astro had landed with a force of forty CIEF men, at least fifteen of whom were now dead. This was a nightmare.

'—We can't get to Rapier!' he yelled into his radio, seeing Rapi-er's team pinned down behind the upturned supertanker a hundred yards from the Vertex's entrance. Some of them lay dead on the wet sand. Rapier himself was huddled behind the massive rusted propeller of the wreck, bullet-sparks impacting all around him.

It was then that Astro saw the wave on the horizon. 'Oh shit, do you see that . . . ?'

It looked like a thin line of dark-blue superimposed on the grey ocean, stretching across the width of the horizon, a great rolling wave that had not yet crested.

A wall of water.

And it was advancing fast.

The exposed section of seabed wasn't going to be exposed for much longer.

Wolf's voice exploded in his ear: '*Team Four, do whatever you have to do to get Rapier out of there! We need that Stone!*'

'Sir,' Astro saw Wolf taking shelter inside the hangar-like entrance cut into the cliff's base, 'those Japanese guys on the clifftops are dug in! They've had years to prepare this place for a defence like this!'

'*Get—That—Fucking—Stone!*'

Astro spun, wondering how he was possibly going to get out of this alive, when he again saw the wave . . .

. . . only now he saw something in the air above it, a small fast-moving aircraft flying incredibly low over the advancing sea, also incoming.

What the hell . . . ?

The sleek black glider skimmed over the surface of the Sea of Japan, flying at phenomenal speed low over the waves.

It shot between two Japanese warships—ships whose radar crews hadn't even noticed the tiny attack plane until their gunners saw it whiz by the deck.

Designed by Wizard, it was a very small Light Attack Glider, christened by him the 'Black Bee'. Based on the dual-tailfin airframe of the highly manoeuvrable ARES light attack fighter, the Bee had no engine to weigh it down. All it had was an advanced stealth bodykit and a super-lightweight carbon-fibre cockpit that seated two people.

Without the heat signature of an engine, its stealth profile was tiny, smaller than that of a seagull. Indeed, the Bee was so physically small, Jack had long kept it in pieces in a single Ziploc bag in the hold of the *Hali*.

Of course, being a bee it still possessed a vicious sting: two Sidewinder missiles hung from its swept-back wings, weighing more than the plane itself.

As the Black Bee sped toward the Hokkaido coast, it overtook the fast-moving tsunami wave, zooming out over the expanse of bare seabed in front of the coastal cliffs.

In the cockpit, Jack flew, while Zoe sat in the rear navigator's seat with Lily on her lap. 'Would you look at that wave . . .' Zoe gasped.

Jack, however, was looking intently forward.

Hokkaido loomed before him.

It was covered in snow, almost totally white. Its endless mountain ranges were covered in drifts, while directly ahead of him, just as it was depicted on Genghis Khan's shield, he saw an immense extinct volcano towering above a frozen coastal waterfall.

At the base of the waterfall, he could just make out the rectangular hangar-sized Vertex entrance and the shipwrecks on the seabed before it.

'Hang on,' he said as he fired both Sidewinders and brought the Bee even lower over the seabed, extending its ski-like landing struts as he did so.

The two missiles lanced out toward the Japanese positions on the clifftops, smashing into them simultaneously, sending twin geysers of snow, dirt and men flying into the air.

The Bee's struts touched down on the exposed seabed and the little glider slid across the hardpacked sand like a car on a wet road.

It skidded to a stop right alongside the rusty wreck of the supertanker and Rapier's CIEF team trapped behind it.

Jack flung open the Bee's canopy and leapt out, with Zoe providing cover and Lily running between them.

Despite the barrage of Japanese fire raining down at them, not a single round struck them.

The reason: Jack and Zoe carried activated Warblers in their jacket pockets.

Jack hadn't used Warblers since that time at Hamilcar's Refuge in Tunisia. Designed for frontal assaults just like this, the Warbler was another invention of Wizard's: a grenade-sized Closed Atmospheric Field Destabiliser that created a powerful electromagnetic field which disrupted the flight of high-subsonic projectiles like bullets. They had only one drawback: their superstrong electromagnetic fields also disrupted radio signals.

And so the wave of Japanese bullets just fanned out, left and right, away from them as they ran across the open ground of the sea floor.

Jack, Zoe and Lily came to Rapier—hunched behind the enormous propeller of the beached supertanker and now out of ammo. Only one other member of his team had survived the assault from the cliffs, and he lay on the ground with wounds to his chest. Dead men lay all around them.

'Get up, you're coming with us,' Jack said roughly, ripping the Samsonite pack off Rapier's back and slinging it over his shoulder while dragging his half-brother toward the cliffs, firing with his spare hand.

Zoe covered them as they went, firing measured bursts. The two Sidewinder hits had been very effective, blowing apart the Japanese nests closest to the Vertex's entrance, while the Warblers took care of the rest.

Jack saw the entrance before him.

It was absolutely huge—high and rectangular with sharp edges, it was an intricately-crafted yet massive stone doorway cut into the uneven natural stone of the cliff.

He was reminded of the underwater entrance to the Second Vertex near Cape Town. It had been easily large enough for an entire submarine to pass through it. This one was just as big. It looked like the biggest aeroplane hangar in the world.

Jack saw Wolf and his remaining men—twenty-two of them, plus Astro and the Neetha warlock—huddled at the base of the gigantic entrance, waving them over.

Jack, Zoe, Lily and Rapier joined Wolf at the entrance, but didn't stop. Wolf and his men—including Astro and the warlock—fell into step beside them, hurrying inside the cave.

'I'm getting tired of watching over you,' Jack said. 'Didn't expect this many Japanese defenders?'

'We suspected the Brotherhood was acting with the tacit approval of the Japanese government. We didn't know it *was* the government,' Wolf said.

'Let's just get through this, 'cause while I'm pretty fucking angry with you right now, I'd rather save the world first. How you doing, Astro?' Jack said as he passed the astonished young Marine. 'Long time, no see.'

Astro just hurried to keep up, momentarily speechless.

The cave inside the entrance was broad and high-ceilinged, with a polished floor and smooth stone walls, all covered in Thoth hieroglyphs; a long and broad avenue of thick columns supported the soaring ceiling.

About five hundred yards in, Jack saw a small mountain of steps rising into a wide void in the ceiling.

Just like at Cape Town, he thought.

He and Zoe both grabbed Lily by the hand, and with Wolf's team around them, they started climbing the hill of stone stairs at speed.

Then a chilling rush of air billowed in through the entrance and a great roar filled the cavern. Jack spun as he climbed the stairs to see a terrible sight filling the entrance doorway.

The tsunami had arrived.

Through the rectangular frame of the entrance, Jack saw the massive tsunami rush across the exposed seabed, easily travelling at 100 kilometres an hour.

Then, in a kind of majestic slow motion, it crested—rising and rising and rising—before it crashed down—*smashed* down—right on top of the wreck of the supertanker. The 600-foot-long supertanker just vanished in an instant, swallowed by the immense wave.

As the leading edge of the tsunami crunched down on the seabed, it made a *boom* that was beyond deafening.

But it wasn't done yet.

Now the mighty tsunami rushed toward the shore as a ten-storey-tall body of deadly foaming whitewater.

It swept in through the Vertex's entrance at outrageous speed, blasting through the entry hall, rampaging down the avenue of columns, heading for the base of the step-mountain that Jack and the others were still ascending.

Jack hustled up the hill of steps as fast as his legs would carry him.

'Keep running!' he yelled to Lily and Zoe, eyeing the eerie red glow leaking over the summit of the step-mountain above them.

Moments later, Jack leapt up onto the topmost step and beheld the space beyond the step-mountain.

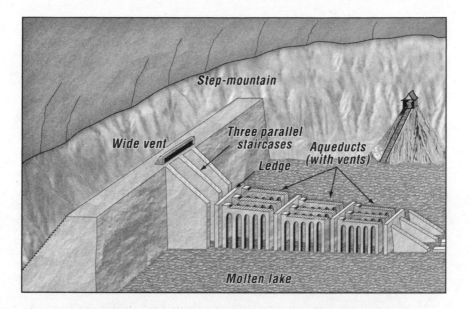

Step-mountain

Wide vent

Three parallel
staircases   Aqueducts
(with vents)

Ledge

Molten lake

THE STAIRCASES AND THE AQUEDUCTS

He glimpsed a vast cavern and a fantastical landscape—a wide lake of molten lava that was dotted with towers, bridges and even a stepped pyramid—but the first thing he saw before him were three parallel descending staircases, all leading down to a series of multi-arched aqueducts that rose above the lava lake.

Next to Jack, a wide rectangular vent opened onto the three descending staircases, as if designed to spurt some kind of liquid down them.

An ominous gurgling sound echoed from within the vent . . . and Jack saw a reddish glow rising up from it.

'Something's coming up that vent . . .'

The roar of the tsunami blasting into the entry hall behind them was as loud as ten jet engines.

The glow inside the vent grew brighter.

Things were happening too fast.

'We have to choose a staircase!' Zoe yelled.

'But which one!' Astro called, staring at the three staircases. Each descended for about fifty metres before ending at a small horizontal ledge that separated each staircase from its matching aqueduct.

'Screw this!' a CIEF man yelled as he and two other members of Wolf's team bolted down the nearest staircase, the right-hand one.

'Get back here!' Wolf called after them, but they didn't hear him.

'Damn it,' Jack said. 'Which one . . . ?'

'The left one!' a voice called firmly from beside him.

Lily. She held something in her hand.

Out of the corner of his eye, Jack saw Wolf glance at the Neetha warlock. The warlock shook his head in an 'I don't know' gesture.

'Okay, kiddo!' Jack shouted. 'We follow your lead! No time for explanations! Let's move!'

Jack, Lily and Zoe raced for the left-hand staircase and hurried down its steep stone steps. As he charged down it, Jack noticed that the stairway was guttered.

That was a bad sign. It usually meant some kind of deadly liquid flowed down it . . .

Wolf followed them, accompanied by the warlock.

Astro, Rapier and the rest of Wolf's CIEF force raced after them, taking the same downward staircase.

Two CIEF men hesitated, unsure, and remained atop the summit of the step-mountain.

Their hesitation killed them—for a moment later, the tsunami came crashing over the summit in a furious explosion of whitewater.

Like an ocean wave smashing against a coastal rock, the tsunami exploded over the stair-mountain in a starburst of spray, spray that hurled the two hesitant CIEF men off it and out into the lava lake beyond it.

As the initial spray of the tsunami rained back down to earth, a huge body of frothing water came surging over the summit, *carrying the carcass of the supertanker within its mass* and hurling the great ship *clear over* the top of the step-mountain!

The great rusted hulk of the supertanker groaned as it rolled over the summit of the step-mountain and dropped into the lava on the other side, landing to the right of the three parallel staircases with a massive glooping thud.

The rest of the tsunami came to rest a few feet below the summit of the step-mountain, swirling and roiling on the ocean side, contained for now.

'Holy moly . . .' Lily gasped as she hustled down the left-hand staircase, which—like the other two staircases—had been protected from the tsunami by the wide vent at the summit.

The reason why became clear a moment later.

They came bursting forth from the vent at frightening speed: twin bodies of knee-deep molten lava that surged down the middle and right-hand staircases, contained by their gutters and descending fast.

The left-hand staircase, however, remained clear.

Agonised shrieks rang out as the lava caught up with the three CIEF men who had taken the right-hand staircase.

The pouring lava *melted* their shins, causing them to drop into the superheated fluid. Their clothes caught fire; their skin bubbled; then their hands and forearms liquefied, becoming grotesque mixes of skin, bone and blood; they died screaming, watching their own bodies deform horrifically.

Everyone on the left-hand staircase had the same realisation at once: if they'd taken either of the other two staircases, the lava would have got them. There was no way they could have outrun it.

Somehow, Lily had made the right choice.

In any case, they were finally inside the Third Vertex—and thanks to the waters of the tsunami, they were sealed inside it, safe from their enemies outside.

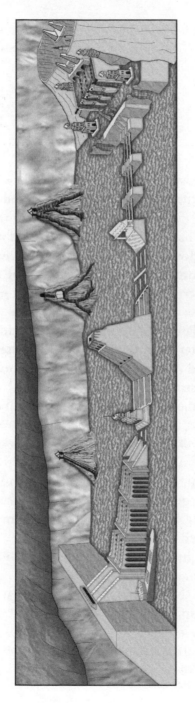

THE THIRD VERTEX AT HOKKAIDO

At the bottom of the steep guttered staircase they all leapt over a narrow gap onto the next horizontal ledge—a kind of intermediate platform between the three staircases and the next three aqueducts.

Jack spun to look back at the staircases behind him.

Long fingers of glowing-hot lava oozed down the other two staircases, dropping off their ends in thin lavafalls.

Lily had made a crucial choice, literally a choice between life and death.

Jack turned to take in the motley crew around him. It hadn't escaped his notice that he was now inside a Vertex with his enemies, people who had tried to kill him on several occasions.

It was certainly a strange situation.

On the one hand, there was himself, Zoe and Lily, looking something like a family.

On the other was what remained of Wolf's assault force: Wolf himself, the warlock of the Neetha, Rapier, Astro and seventeen other CIEF troops, all of whom were covered in sand and blood after the disastrous frontal assault out on the seabed.

'Nice choice, young lady,' Wolf said to Lily. 'I'm very curious to know how you figured that out.'

Lily just glared at him. 'Don't *speak* to me. You killed Wizard. You're a horrible man and I hope you die.'

Wolf feigned hurt. 'Now, now, don't be like that . . .'

Rapier whipped up a gun and aimed it at Jack. 'Father, we should kill them now—'

The head of the CIEF trooper standing beside Wolf exploded. There was no sound of a gunshot.

Shot in the back of the head from long range, the man's face just blew apart, spraying blood all over Wolf, before his body fell off the high aqueduct and sailed down into the molten lake below.

Shwap! Shwap! Shwap!

More bullets slammed into the aqueduct all around the gathered group. Another CIEF man was hit and fell to the platform at Lily's and Zoe's feet.

Someone was firing on them!

And they were completely exposed out on this high platform.

'There!' Jack called, spotting two snipers on the peak of a huge step-pyramid in the middle of the cavern.

A pair of black-clad Japanese snipers.

'They've got people *in here* . . .' Astro said in disbelief.

'Return fire!' Jack called, ignoring Rapier and loosing a burst from his MP-7 at the snipers. 'We can all kill each other later, but right now we've got to get off these bridges! Go! *Go!* Get to that tower up ahead!'

A five-storey-tall tower rose out of the lava lake about a hundred yards ahead of them, between them and the snipers' pyramid. It appeared to be built entirely of stone in the ornate style of a Japanese palace. And so far as Jack could see, it was the only source of cover from the Japanese snipers on the pyramid.

Another CIEF trooper snapped backward, his head spraying blood. As he spun with the impact, Jack saw that the man had been trying to raise a long-barrelled Barrett sniper rifle. Then Jack saw the other dead trooper at Zoe's feet . . . and noticed the long rifle on *his* back.

'They're taking out our snipers!' he yelled. 'Zoe! Get that gun before it falls!'

As bullets impacted all around them, Zoe dived to the ground and snatched the dead man's Barrett just before it fell over the edge.

'Cover fire!' Jack called to the remaining CIEF men. But they all baulked, confused at following the orders of their enemy.

All except Astro.

He obeyed immediately and joined Jack in firing up at the Japanese snipers.

Now covered, Zoe knelt, taking careful aim through the Barrett's telescopic sight, and . . .

Bam—!

She fired, and one of the Japanese snipers on top of the pyramid was thrown backwards in a puff of red.

'Gotcha.'

Wolf was yelling at his men: '*Stephens! Whitfield!* Do as he says! Get a laser on that sniper position! Rapier! RPG!'

'Lily!' Jack turned. 'Which bridge do we take from here!'

Now he saw the object she was holding: Zoe's Canon digital camera.

It was the same digital camera Zoe had used to take photos at the First Vertex and which she'd later used in Africa to solve the circular maze of the Neetha.

Lily was looking closely at a certain photo, and after analysing it, called, 'The right-hand one, then the middle one, then the left-hand one!'

'Right, middle, left—okay!' Jack called, leading the way, racing out onto the right-hand aqueduct-bridge.

Like the descending staircases earlier, each aqueduct-bridge featured guttered edges and downward-sloping steps, only they were not as steep.

The first step of each aqueduct-bridge, however, concealed within it a knee-high vent that opened onto the guttered bridge itself; a vent, Jack figured, that spewed forth molten magma like the big one at the top of the descending staircases had.

He was right.

As soon as he'd taken a few steps down the right-hand aqueduct-bridge—at some point stepping on a concealed trigger stone—blazing-hot lava vomited out from the step-vents on the other two bridges.

Running down the high rail-less bridge, he looked out at the sets of bridges and stairways ahead of him—always in groups of three, always parallel—and suddenly it all became clear to him.

This place is one big series of booby-trapped bridges and stair-cases. You get three choices every time, but only one choice is safe. The other two get flooded with lava when you're a few steps down them.

The name of this Vertex suddenly took on real meaning: *the Fire Maze.*

Following Lily's directions, the combined force hustled along the aqueduct-bridges, with Zoe exchanging fire with the remaining Japanese sniper atop the pyramid.

Each time they raced down one bridge, the other two bridges would flood with fast-flowing knee-deep lava.

Without Lily's predictions, there was no way they could have negotiated the booby-trapped bridges. How she was doing it—or more precisely, which photo on the camera she was using—Jack didn't care, so long as she kept choosing correctly.

As they ran across the high narrow bridges under heavy fire, he was also glad that he and Zoe had Warblers. The CIEF men didn't and two more of them got hit and fell to their deaths.

At the end of the last aqueduct-bridge, the combined group came to three more parallel descending staircases.

'The right-hand one!' Lily called.

At the same time, the CIEF man named Whitfield called out, 'Sniper position is lased!' He was aiming a handheld laser unit up at the summit of the step-pyramid.

'Got it!' Rapier answered, hefting a lightweight Predator rocket launcher onto his shoulder and firing it.

The RPG shoomed into the air, trailing a finger of smoke. It banked at wicked speed *around* the tower in between their posi-tion on the staircase and the sniper on the step-pyramid, before it thundered into the sniper's nest and detonated in a billowing

explosion, blasting the Japanese soldier to kingdom come.

Safe now from sniper fire, the group rushed down the stairs and stepped over onto the base of the tower—where the first thing Wolf's people did was turn their guns on Jack, Zoe and Lily.

'Stand down!' Wolf called, stepping forward. 'They're not here to threaten us. On this occasion, we actually have the same goal they do: finding the Third Pillar and laying it.'

His men slowly lowered their weapons.

The two sides gazed at each other, standing awkwardly apart.

Wolf appraised Lily closely. 'The famous Miss Lily. We haven't met in person till now, but we did speak on the phone once, when you were in Africa. How did you know which bridges were safe?'

'Lucky guesses,' Lily said curtly.

'Indeed.' Wolf smiled ruefully, seeing the situation for what it was: he needed Lily and the knowledge she possessed to successfully navigate the maze system. 'Dare I propose a truce—a temporary one, naturally—at least while we find ourselves in this maze together? Since our goals are identical and our enemy is the same.'

Lily frowned, unconvinced.

Wolf said, 'If I kill you, I effectively kill myself. And I'm not into mutually assured destruction.'

'All right . . .' Lily said.

Wolf glanced at Jack.

'A *very* temporary truce,' Jack said evenly. 'Kiddo, a word.'

He took Lily aside, huddling with her and Zoe.

'Care to let us in on the secret?' he said.

She held up the digital camera and clicked on one particular photo. It was the shot Zoe had taken of the golden plaque inside the First Vertex at Abu Simbel, the plaque that listed the names of all six Vertices:

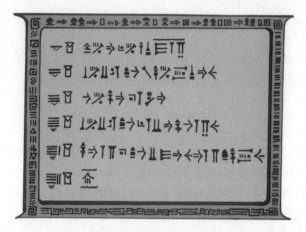

Without saying a word, Lily subtly pointed at the bottom edge of the plaque's frame. It depicted an odd series of lines that were clustered *in parallel groups of three*, and through which a single line safely threaded its way.

'Well, I'll be,' Zoe breathed.

'Clever girl,' Jack said.

Lily said, 'When I saw the parallel stairways and bridges from the entrance to this place, all in groups of three, I knew I'd seen a pattern like it before. This pattern.'

Lily abruptly clicked off the photo. Wolf was approaching.

'You can keep your secrets, little one,' he said. 'But we can't afford to linger. The clock is ticking and we have a Pillar to lay. Lead the way.'

And so, flanked by their armed rivals, Jack, Lily and Zoe made their way through the deadly network of bridges and walkways that guarded the Third Vertex of the Machine.

At every step, they were presented with a triple choice of

parallel paths, a choice that Lily made correctly.

Through the tower, over the step-pyramid, even down through a set of sunken trenches buried *below* the waterline of the lake.

Whenever they came close to the surface of the lava lake, they had to cover their eyes with goggles or anti-flash glasses and wrap wet cloths or bandanas over their mouths—the simmering heat of the lava was enough to cause their skin to peel. If they stayed too close to it for too long, it would sear their skin, essentially cooking them in their own bodies.

'Why doesn't this lava solidify and crust over?' Zoe asked, wiping sweat off her brow as she walked.

'We must be near a volcanic rift,' Jack said. 'The heat from below is keeping the lava in a semi-liquid state.'

'Why doesn't the lava eat away at these bridges?' Lily said. 'I thought lava ate through everything.'

'That's the ultimate mystery in all this,' Jack said. 'Whoever built this place, built the Machine. We're talking about a super-ancient civilisation, one that was advanced enough to see the Dark Sun coming and create the Machine to repel it. These bridges and towers and whatever "stone" material they're made of, were built by that civilisation, too, and they were clearly able to make them lava-proof.'

Lily was silent for a moment.

'And yet that civilisation was still wiped out,' she said as they walked. 'By something.'

Jack nodded. 'Every empire comes to an end eventually, kiddo. Nothing lasts forever. Nothing we build can ever outlast the relentless march of space and time. Whether it's a Dark Sun, a rogue asteroid or a shift in the Earth's orbit around the Sun, this planet is still just a small rock in the vastness of space. And space and time always win eventually.'

'So if these ancient people were smart enough to survive the coming of the Dark Sun, what killed them?'

'I don't know.' Jack turned to face her as he walked. 'Hey, I'm finding this Dark Sun thing hard enough.'

★ ★ ★

At length, the group came to what appeared to be the centrepiece of the mighty cavern: a huge volcano cone.

Into the face of this cone had been carved a stupendous multi-levelled castle-like structure. Flowing freely over its fortifications were several waterfalls of magma.

Traversing the structure, however, still meant choosing one of three paths or stairways, and this took a whole hour by itself—but eventually the group arrived at the uppermost level of the massive castle, where a cleft had been cut into the rim of the cone and two soaring stone buttresses formed a gateway leading into it.

As he arrived at the gateway, Jack beheld the inside of the crater beyond it, and caught his breath.

'Mother of mercy . . .' he said in disbelief.

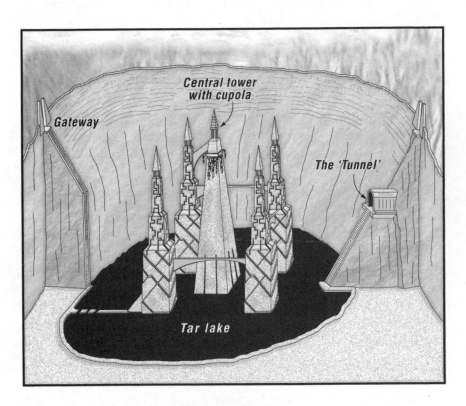

THE CRATER
(THE RESTING PLACE OF THE 3RD PILLAR)

Jack looked down on five magnificent spires: four pinnacle-like towers surrounding a taller fifth one.

The four outer towers were all made of a pale grey igneous rock and they all bore complex winding channels cut into their flanks. The central tower was made of darker stone and it had sheer polished sides. Its sole defence was an encircling gutter four-fifths of the way up its body. All five buildings rose up out of a foul black lake of bubbling tar.

Then Jack saw it.

There, mounted on a pedestal inside a cupola at the lofty summit of the central tower, looking like a cloudy glass brick, was the Third Pillar.

It was actually quite close to him—so high was the tower, it was almost level with his gateway. But to get to the Pillar, Jack saw, one had to negotiate a series of narrow swooping bridges that connected the four outer towers in an anti-clockwise sequence before a final bridge sprang up at a frightening angle from the fourth tower to the cupola on the central pinnacle.

It was dizzying just to look at.

Beyond the Pillar in the cupola, directly across from his position on the rim of the crater, Jack saw the opposite rim—and beyond that, glimpsed a now-familiar shape.

The upper reaches of an immense inverted bronze pyramid.

The Third Vertex itself.

Wolf gazed at the five towers nestled in the crater.

'The Shogun's maze-within-the-maze,' he said. 'The rest of

this place was built by the ancient makers of the Machine, but these towers were built by the Japanese at the time of Genghis Khan.'

'The smaller maze they built to protect the Third Pillar,' Zoe said.

'So how does it work?' Rapier asked.

Jack took in the towers and bridges. 'Looks like a time-and-speed trap . . .'

'Hey,' Lily said from behind him. She was standing near a statue of a dragon at the edge of the gateway platform. She pointed to a Japanese inscription carved into the dragon's podium. 'It says:

> A simple test,
> Held at the birth and death of Ra each day.
> The brave warrior ascends while the fire liquid descends.
> He who beats the deadly fluid to the summit, will keep
> the Great Khan's gift;
> He who beats it back, will keep his life.'

Jack assessed the twisting channels cut into the flanks of the four surrounding towers. At the top of each tower was a chimney-like opening in which bubbled a level pool of lava. At some trigger, he guessed, the lava overflowed from the chimney-opening and made its way down the channels. If you wanted the Pillar, you had to negotiate the maze of zig-zagging stairways on the towers' flanks and get to the cupola—*and then you had to get back down again* before the descending lava cut off your retreat.

Jack looked out across the seventy metres of air separating his platform from the central tower.

'It's at times like this, I wish I'd brought Horus along,' he said. He'd left her with Sky Monster in the *Halicarnassus*.

'Too far for a Maghook to reach,' Zoe said.

'The birth and death of Ra . . .' Astro said. 'Sunrise and sunset. So at sunrise and sunset every day, the tower system becomes accessible?'

Jack jerked his chin at a couple of broad stepping stones down at lake-level giving access to the first tower. There was a wide gap between the stones, a gap that could not be jumped. 'I imagine twice a day, at dawn and dusk, a stepping stone rises up out of the tar, allowing you to get across to the first tower. Then you race the lava coming down the towers.'

'What time is it now?' Wolf asked.

'Eleven in the morning,' Rapier said.

'When's sunset?'

'Around 5:50 p.m.'

'And when is tomorrow's Titanic Rising?'

'0005 hours. Five past midnight,' Jack said.

Wolf took a deep breath and sat down against the wall of the high gateway. 'Almost seven hours till we can make a run for this Pillar. Another six after that before the Pillar has to be set in place. Looks like we're stuck here for a while.'

He smiled at Lily.

'How delightful. It will give us a chance to get to know each other.'

The hours ticked by.

The members of the mismatched group slumped around the gateway platform, variously resting against its walls or pacing to stretch their legs.

Lily slept in Zoe's lap. Wolf sat across from them, staring at Lily intently—as if he were pondering exactly how she worked.

At Jack's insistence, Wolf sent two men ahead to scout the terrain on the far side of the volcano's crater—to make sure there were no surprises there, especially more Japanese ones, and that laying the Pillar could be done inside the seven hours after sunset.

The two men crossed the crater without incident and disappeared inside a long tunnel-like structure on the other side, sending back images on a digital video camera. At first, interference from the Warblers affected the signal, so Jack had them switched off.

The dark tunnel was about fifty yards long and two storeys high, roughly the size of a train tunnel. After passing through it, the two scouts emerged on the other side of the crater.

Here their camera showed the massive inverted pyramid of the Vertex surrounded by another lake of lava and suspended above a great abyss like at the other Vertices. No mazes or labyrinths protected it. Seven hours would be more than enough time to get to it.

The two scouts returned.

Astro was standing at the edge of the gateway platform, gazing out over the five towers in the crater, when Jack joined him.

'It's been a while, Astro.'

Astro didn't reply.

'What did they tell you about me?' Jack asked.

Astro was silent for a long moment, then he said, 'They said you were planning to kill me as soon as we got out of Egypt.'

Jack had wondered what had happened to Astro. The young Marine had joined their team during the first meeting in Dubai, at the request of Paul Robertson of the CIA, just before a plane had smashed into the Burj al Arab tower.

From there, Astro had accompanied Jack through Laozi's trap system in China, been at a second meeting at Mortimer Island in the Bristol Channel, and then gone with Jack to Abu Simbel—during which time Jack had felt he had become a loyal team member.

But then after the wild chase on the desert highway involving the *Halicarnassus* and several dozen Egyptian Army vehicles, Astro, Jack, Pooh Bear and Stretch had all been captured. At the time, Jack was knocked out and had woken up crucified inside Wolf's mine in Ethiopia . . .

. . . where he had seen Astro standing loyally beside Wolf.

Jack had felt betrayed, and had said so to Pooh Bear. But Pooh Bear had advised him not to rush to judgement on Astro.

'Do you seriously think I wanted to kill you, after all we'd been through? Does that match up with what you've seen me do?' Jack asked.

Astro said nothing.

'Do you remember seeing me in that mine?' Jack said.

Astro frowned, as if trying to recall. 'I don't remember much after Abu Simbel, and certainly not any mine. I woke up at the airbase on Diego Garcia, in a hospital bed. They said I'd fallen to the road during an armed pursuit and been airlifted out. I was unconscious for two whole days, they said.'

'You don't remember the Ethiopian mine at all?'

'No.'

This was unexpected. Pooh Bear's advice might have been very wise.

'You didn't fall to the road,' Jack explained. 'We all survived that episode just fine. They must have drugged you after they pistol-whipped me.'

'They told me you're actually working against America. And that by helping you, so was I. Wolf said Robertson should never have assigned me to your team. After Abu Simbel, because of my experience with all this ancient stuff, I was reassigned to Wolf's team.'

It was then that Jack realised that Astro had *not* been present when Jack had become aware of the complex network of clandestine international alliances surrounding this mission: that Wolf was working not for America but for the rich and powerful Caldwell Group—with its network of rogue elements in the American armed forces and completely outside American oversight—alongside China and Saudi Arabia.

'Astro,' he said, 'I represent a group of concerned small nations who don't want to see the world get destroyed, that's all. As for you, I think you're a pawn in someone's larger game. I think Wolf and Robertson are working together and that they used you because you're an honest soldier who follows orders. But what if the people giving those orders are morally bankrupt? They put you into my team *not* so America could join our coalition, but so they could watch me.'

'Easy to say, hard to prove,' Astro said.

'Not so hard. I imagine you'll discover the truth soon enough.'

Jack turned to go.

'Jack.' Astro stared off into the distance. 'After the Pillar is found and set in place, I have orders to kill you. So does every member of this CIEF team.'

Jack paused. 'I'm sorry to hear that. I sincerely hope you're not the one who has to do it.'

Jack returned to Lily and Zoe just as Lily awoke. She smiled up at him.

'Hi Daddy.'

'Hey kiddo.'

'Ah, the model family,' Wolf said from across the platform. 'So touching.'

'You got a problem with families?' Lily said.

Wolf toyed with his thick Annapolis graduation ring as he spoke. 'The concept of "family" is a human invention and a flawed one at that. There is only procreation for the male, there's no such thing as family. I always loved my offspring more than their mothers.'

Lily said, 'A strong family is greater than the sum of its parts.'

'Oh, really? Do you believe, then, that your little family here is strong?' Wolf asked, eyeing Lily closely.

'Yes,' Lily said firmly.

'Loyal?'

'Absolutely.'

Wolf nodded slowly.

Then he glanced enigmatically in Zoe's direction. 'They haven't always been so.'

Lily frowned, so did Zoe.

Lily turned to face Jack questioningly.

'My father,' Jack said to her, 'thinks about families differently to me. He thinks men just want to sire children and women are merely vessels to supply those children. He doesn't believe in the family that is created when two people have a child.'

'And what is your theory then?' Wolf said to him. 'Please. Enlighten me.'

Jack looked back at him evenly. 'Family members are like the ultimate best friends. Their loyalty *always* lasts longer than their memory.'

A few hours later, most of the combined group were sleeping, including Wolf.

Jack was keeping watch while Lily and Zoe dozed. To keep himself alert, he stood on the edge of the platform and stared out at the towers in the crater, trying to figure out the best path through the stairmazes on their flanks—

A voice in his ear made him start.

'I'm going to kill you, you know.'

Rapier stood right behind Jack, his face close behind Jack's left ear.

Jack said nothing. He was very aware of how close he was to the precipice.

Rapier nodded over at the sleeping figure of Wolf. 'While you're alive, I'll always be the second son, and in his eyes, the *second best* son. He respects you, you know, in a way he doesn't respect me. And while you live and breathe and carry his name, I will always be number two. But if I kill you, then I prove that I'm the better soldier, the better man, the better son—'

'Get away from him.'

Both men spun to see Zoe awake and on her feet with her Glock pistol raised at Rapier.

With a casual shrug, Rapier stepped away from Jack. 'The better son,' he said.

Only when he was a safe distance away did Jack release the breath he'd been holding and unclench every muscle in his body.

In the hour before sunset, the combined force made their way to the base of the crater via a set of extremely steep stairs and a high wall-ladder.

They stepped out onto a low stone path that ran around one side of the tar lake. The simmering black lake smelled disgusting, like rotten eggs; the odd slow-forming bubble popped wetly on its surface. It was hotter down here in the crater, so Jack and Zoe took off their jackets.

A nearby CIEF man stared at Jack's now-visible left arm: while Jack still wore a leather glove on that hand, his left forearm could now be seen to be made of glistening silver steel: this was the high-tech artificial arm Wizard had made for him many years ago.

'What?' Lily said to the gawking man. 'You never seen a bionic arm before?'

As they walked, Jack and Zoe gazed up at the nearest tower, trying to figure out the labyrinth of criss-crossing stone stairways on the flanks of its lower half.

'Looks like you have to go down to go up,' Zoe observed. 'Those upper stairways all arrive at dead-ends just short of the bridge to the second tower. It's a trap. You're so keen to get to the bridge, you rush straight up, but in reality you have to go all the way down to the lake level, run along that low path, and then up the other side.'

'All while the lava is coming down from the top,' Jack said. 'Not only do you have to move fast, you can't make too many mistakes. Every mistake you make on the way up gives the lava a better chance to cut you off on the way down, and if you go too slow, you're stranded. Then all you can do is wait to die.'

★ ★ ★

A few minutes before sunset, they stood on the low stone ledge facing the first tower, separated from it by the lake of bubbling black tar.

Five CIEF men, including Rapier and Astro, stepped forward. They wore the lightweight plastic-polymer armour of Delta specialists and they carried climbing gear—pitons, ropes, carabiners. They'd discarded their heavy weapons and now only carried Glock pistols in thigh-holsters.

'This is the team that will retrieve the Pillar,' Wolf said. 'My fastest men. Do you approve?'

Jack raised his palms and sat down by the wall. 'I'm happy to leave this one to you and your All Stars. I hate time-and-speed traps.'

'I've sent two men back up the wall-ladder,' Wolf said to his tower team. 'They'll act as spotters for you, giving you guidance via radio from the higher vantage point. The rest of us will wait down here.'

'Roger that,' Rapier said.

Astro just nodded.

'All right, get ready . . .' Wolf said.

A few minutes later, on a horizon they could not see, the Sun set, and as it had done every night and every morning for the last seven hundred years, a broad stepping stone rose from beneath the tar lake to allow whoever might dare to cross it access to the five-towered fire maze.

Drinking water was thrown onto the superhot stepping stone to cool it. It sizzled loudly.

Rapier leapt out onto the stone, a full striding jump. He landed with a thump . . .

. . . and the stepping stone sank ever so slightly, the trigger for the maze's elaborate defence system.

And the system came spectacularly alive.

The first tower vomited a bubbling mass of glowing-hot lava from its chimney-like peak, lava that immediately began to ooze down the zig-zagging channels carved into its sides.

'Go!' Wolf yelled to Rapier.

Rapier, Astro and the other three CIEF men took off, bolting out across the stepping stone and ascending a narrow stairway that gave access to the first tower.

Astro charged up the stairs behind Rapier, breathing hard and fast.

'*Rapier! Go right and down!*' one of the spotters called in his ear.

They went right and down, skirting the lower half of the tower. Looking up as he ran, Astro glimpsed the oozing red lava trickling down the channels of the upper half, travelling slowly downward. Where he couldn't actually see it, the telltale yellow glow of the superheated liquid told him where it was.

Guided by their two elevated spotters, the five-man team did a full circuit of the tower, clambering up and down its stairways—and Astro quickly realised that without the guides' instructions, they would have got hopelessly lost very quickly.

He also noticed something else—something that you could see only when you encountered the tower's walls up close.

The walls of the tower were *not* made of sheer stone. Rather the surface of the wall was comprised of a superfine mesh of tiny upwardly-pointed spikes. Touching the micro-spikes, Astro found they were viciously sharp. Just brushing your hand against them drew blood.

Then, abruptly, his group rounded a corner and arrived at the long stone bridge that led to the second tower.

They dashed out across it, Astro running close behind Rapier. As he ran, he saw that a bubbling body of lava was now oozing from the peak of the *second* tower.

They were being set off in sequence—giving you a chance to reach the summit, but also giving the lava four chances to catch you on the way back.

A spotter called, '*Okay, cross the bridge and take the stairway leading—shwap!-shwap!*'

Standing out on the bridge, Astro spun to look back up at the gateway just in time to see both of his spotters snap backwards, their heads vanishing in matching bursts of red, their bodies tumbling off their perch and freefalling all the way down to the tar lake.

'What the—?' the CIEF man behind Astro said a split second before he too was shot and hurled off the narrow bridge. He landed in the tar lake, emitting a half-scream before the simmering black goo melted the skin off his face and sucked him under.

Slit-fzzzzzz!

Astro ducked as a bullet intended for his head nicked his sleeve and fizzed away. He caught a glimpse of muzzle-flash—maybe two muzzle-flashes—high up near the gateway on the opposite side of the crater.

Two more Japanese snipers.

Snipers who had *waited* for them to get this far before opening fire . . .

'We're under fire!' Rapier yelled into his throatmike. 'We need cover! Give us some goddamn cover!'

Down on the path at lake-level, Jack stood and watched in horror as the tower team walked right into the trap.

The full extent of their situation unfolded in his mind:

The Japanese had more people in here.

They'd waited patiently until Wolf's men had triggered the tower system's trap. Then they'd taken out the spotters and were now nailing the tower team itself.

Then came the bigger realisation.

This was their only *chance to get the Pillar.*

It had to be set in place before *dawn tomorrow morning. If they didn't get it now—during this sunset opening—the Japanese forces would win and the world would be doomed.*

This was their one, only and last chance.

Jack snapped back to the present, to the scene on the towers.

Bullets were flying.

Men were being hit. Another fell into the foul tar lake.

Lava was still oozing from the tops of the first two towers, running in rivulets down their convoluted channel systems.

Rapier was shouting over the radio '—*us some goddamn cover!*'

'There!' Zoe pointed, and Jack saw two Japanese snipers up on the far gateway, on the Vertex-side of the crater, just as one of them fired in his direction.

Beside him, Wolf's right ear exploded in a starburst of blood, while the man beside him fell, shot through the eye.

Wolf yelled, '*Return fire!*'

And in the midst of all this, amid all the bullets and the shouting and the falling lava, Jack West Jr sprang into action.

Jack scooped up his MP-7 plus the MP-5 of the dead man near him, and called, 'Zoe! Grab the Barrett and come with me! Lily, get behind something and *stay down*!'

Then he was off, wearing just his white T-shirt, cargo pants and fireman's helmet, his artificial left forearm glinting, racing across the stepping stone and charging for the first tower with Zoe hurrying to catch up behind him.

More gunfire rang out as they pounded up and down the first tower's labyrinth of external stairways.

They came to a corner—the next stairway ran around it and underneath the narrow bridge to the next tower.

On the bridge, Jack saw Astro's team getting annihilated by the gunmen on the far gateway—two more CIEF men were shot. Taking cover behind their dead teammates, Astro and Rapier, outgunned and woefully exposed, were firing their pistols uselessly up at the shooters.

'Zoe!' Jack called. 'One shot then we move!'

Pressed against the corner, Jack waited while Zoe crouched behind him, levelling her Barrett sniper rifle up at the men on the distant gateway.

She fired.

One sniper was thrown backward.

'Great shot, now go!' Jack shouted.

And off they went again, racing up and down the stairways of the first tower, now a target of the lone remaining sniper, whose bullets slammed into the walls inches behind them—and suddenly Jack realised that both he and Zoe had taken off their jackets,

jackets which had contained their Warblers. They were out here unprotected.

There was also one other thing to worry about: high above them, the lava kept oozing downward, slithering like a glowing snake down its channels.

They came to the last corner before the bridge, just out of the line of fire.

'Okay,' Jack said to Zoe. 'You got one shot again. When I run out onto that bridge, he'll take about two seconds to get a bead on me. In that time, you take him out.'

'But Jack, what if I miss?'

'It's a one-shot contest, Zoe. Either you shoot him or he shoots me. Ready, *now!*'

Jack broke cover, bolting out into the open, charging onto the bridge, both his guns blazing.

The tiny figure of the Japanese sniper could be seen spotting him and adjusting his aim through his sights and—

Blam!

Gunshot.

Who had fired it, Jack couldn't tell.

To his horror, he glimpsed a muzzle-flash up at the gateway and for a terrifying moment, he thought that maybe Zoe hadn't got her shot off in time, but a split second after the muzzle flashed, he saw the back of the sniper's head blow outwards in a grisly spray of blood and brains—just as the sniper's bullet sheared through the chinstrap of Jack's fireman's helmet.

Zoe had got her shot off perhaps a hundredth of a second faster than the Japanese sniper.

'Thanks, Zoe! I gotta run!'

He bolted out across the narrow bridge, stepping over the dead bodies of the CIEF team before hurdling Rapier and Astro, and charging for the second tower, now racing on his own against the lava descending from above.

★ ★ ★

As soon as Jack set foot on the first step of the second tower, lava began oozing out the top of the *third* one, so that now three separate rivers of lava were pouring down from the peaks of the first three towers, all at different stages in their descents.

Jack didn't stop running.

Legs pumping, he negotiated the maze of stairways, working from memory, bounding up them, dancing down them, trying not to touch the wall of the tower—at one point, he brushed against one wall and its skin of tiny razor-sharp teeth sliced through the sleeve of his T-shirt as if it were tissue paper, drawing a large gash in his shoulder that seeped blood down his right arm.

The short sleeve dangled uselessly as he ran, so Jack ripped it off, revealing a totally bloodsoaked arm.

Running hard and fast, Jack came to the bridge leading to the third tower—this one stretched upward and was fitted with stairs.

Jack surmounted the bridge and arrived at the middle tier of the third tower. He was higher up now and he could see this tower's snake-like lava flow much more closely. It glowed fiercely as it descended steadily through its channels.

It was almost at the halfway point between the peak of the tower and the bridge Jack had just crossed.

If he didn't grab the Pillar and start his return journey before it reached that halfway point, he'd be screwed, stranded, stuck up here and sentenced to wait for his own painful death.

Can't stop now.

He ran along a path that cut through the third tower and pounded up a stairway that ran up its far flank, leading to another long bridge that gave access to the fourth tower—across that bridge and up the fourth tower, now dizzyingly high, clambering up rung ladders cut into the flank of that tower's uppermost tier—within feet of the simmering lava that now oozed down *its* channels—before he mounted the final super-steep rockbridge, a soaring ultra-narrow piece of stone that sprang up and across to

the summit of the central pinnacle, and suddenly Jack found himself standing at the highest point in the crater, inside the glorious cupola housing the Third Pillar.

Had he time to marvel, Jack would have gawked at the cupola atop the central tower. It featured golden columns, a gold pedestal and gold-leafed tiles.

But he didn't have time.

Instead, he just snatched the cloudy oblong Pillar from its pedestal and commenced the desperate return journey.

Down the rockbridge he flew, stepping onto the fourth tower two metres ahead of its lava flow.

Across the bridge to the third tower, down its steps and then running into the cutaway tunnel in it, dashing through the tunnel just as the molten lava above him split into three channels and came splashing down into the tunnel a bare metre behind his fleeing feet.

Down to the second tower, whose upper half was now positively riddled with glowing lava channels—they looked like iridescent red veins. Here Jack had to navigate three sides and the lava fell from more chutes and in more places—and once it landed on a stairway it sizzled fiercely and chased you further down *that* stairway: take the wrong stairway and there was no way to retrace your steps. No margin for error.

Over to the first tower he flew, trying desperately to remember the correct stairways to take, hurdling an oozing finger of lava that had edged across his path. The lava was closing around him.

Rapier had already gone all the way back to the safety of the path at the crater's base and was watching Jack with furious eyes.

Zoe and Astro had lingered at the last set of stairs, waiting anxiously for Jack.

Jack was exhausted. He could only hear the throb of his own heart inside his head mixed with his own breathing.

He tried to concentrate:

Must watch each step . . .

Don't trip, don't slip . . .

Lava dripped all round him now, falling in a steady rain of fat drops, but at every turn he was a few inches ahead of it.

Then the final staircase came into view, and he risked a smile—a moment before he slipped on a slick step and went sprawling awkwardly onto his chest, gripping the Pillar for dear life, bouncing face-first down the penultimate stairway, with the ravenous lava still chasing him.

Jack tried to stand, fell, looked back . . . and saw the lava about to touch his feet—when two sets of hands suddenly gripped his shoulders and yanked him away from it.

Zoe and Astro.

They carried him down the last staircase just as the oozing lava flowed onto it. Then they hurled him onto the broad stepping stone, leaping across after him, just as the entire final staircase was completely enveloped by lava.

By this time, all four of the surrounding towers of the labyrinth were glowing red, spectacularly lit by the lava coursing through their channel-mazes.

Jack slumped against the wall of the crater, safely on the path, panting and gasping and holding in his hand the Third Pillar of the Machine.

'Got the little sucker.'

About ten minutes later, having caught his breath, Jack stood up, put on his jacket and threw the Third Pillar to Wolf. 'Cleanse it. That thing has to be laid at five minutes past midnight.'

Without waiting for a reply, Jack joined Lily and Zoe and started for the far side of the crater. 'Let's go see what laying this Pillar will involve.'

After the Pillar had been cleansed in the Philosopher's Stone, Wolf's force—now down to eleven men in total: seven CIEF men plus Wolf, Rapier, Astro and the warlock—caught up with them.

They all followed the path that skirted the base of the crater. It ended at a steep staircase that led to the dark tunnel-like structure that bored through the crater's far wall.

Jack, Lily and Zoe stepped up onto the summit of the staircase and beheld the tunnel.

Through it, in the distance, they could see the immense bulk of the inverted bronze pyramid that was the Vertex.

The tunnel itself was dark and silent, roughly the size of a subway tunnel. Its stone walls and high ceiling were irregularly shaped, bulging in places. Nooks and dark recesses were everywhere; a balcony level overlooked the main passageway.

'That bulging is not natural,' Jack observed. 'It's been cut that way . . .'

Evenly spaced along the length of the tunnel was a series of carved stone dragon heads. Beautifully crafted, each one was large, about five feet tall, and they jutted out from the walls as if frozen in mid-lunge, their huge jaws bared in fierce snarls.

'Dragons?' Wolf frowned, coming alongside them.

'Look more like snakes to me,' Lily said. 'Serpents. See the bulging of the walls? It's their bodies.'

'You're right . . .' Rapier seemed surprised that Lily could be so observant.

She was right. The tunnel had been carved so that it seemed as if the snakes' bodies coiled and wound around the entire two-storey passageway, constricting it, creating all the nooks and crannies.

Jack stopped in mid-stride.

He counted the heads.

There were eight in total.

'Eight heads . . .' he whispered. 'An eight-headed serpent. Orochi . . . the Hall of Orochi in Yomi . . . Oh, *shit*. Lily, Zoe, take cover! Now!'

Without waiting for a reply, he snatched up Lily and pulled Zoe with him, covering them both with his body as he hurled them behind one of the dragon heads, a bare moment before the entire tunnel erupted in gunfire from over a dozen of the dark recesses in its upper level.

Three members of Wolf's eleven-strong CIEF force were cut down where they stood, shot to bits, killed instantly.

Two more convulsed violently as they were hit by a second hailstorm of gunfire from above—gunfire from a garrison of Japanese special forces troops stationed inside this tunnel, this bottleneck, this perfect place for an ambush.

In a distant corner of his mind, Jack recalled the intercepted Japanese transmission he'd seen several days previously:

TELL THE GARRISON FORCE AT YOMI
TO MAINTAIN THEIR POSITION INSIDE
THE HALL OF OROCHI.

This tunnel, with its massive carving of an eight-headed serpent, was the Hall of Orochi, and this hellish underground landscape was Yomi.

Damn it.

Jack also realised it must have taken great restraint for the Japanese soldiers here *not* to kill the two scouts he'd sent out earlier. To do so would've given away their presence, and they'd been tasked with a larger goal: to ambush Jack's force if it got this far and finish them once and for all.

As the bullets flew and their CIEF companions fell all around them, Rapier, Wolf and Astro fired several grenades from M-60 launchers. Explosions blasted out from the upper level of the tunnel.

Jack and Zoe joined the fight, standing back to back and

once again protected by their Warblers, firing up into the shadowy recesses created by the massive spiral-shaped carving of the serpent.

As his eyes grew accustomed to the darkness, Jack made out figures in the gloom: Japanese special forces troops, all wearing mantis-like night-vision goggles.

Abruptly, a flaring yellow light illuminated the entire tunnel as Rapier let rip with a flamethrower—the fountain of liquid fire sprayed across one whole side of the upper level, engulfing the men up there in fire and blinding the others in their NVGs.

Flaming men fell from their perches.

As the battle raged, Wolf was shot in the forearm, which only seemed to enrage him more, and he unleashed some withering fire upon the Japanese ambush force, nailing every exposed enemy soldier he saw.

It was a bitter fight, with bullets flying, men falling and Rapier's flamethrower blazing, but in the end the more powerful and accurate shooting of Wolf and Jack's people plus the added protection of the Warblers overcame the Japanese advantage of surprise.

When the last Japanese man fell wounded from his perch, Rapier finished him off *by hand* with two brutal blows—the first vicious punch stunned him into silence, the second to the nose killed him.

Wolf's team had been reduced from eleven to six by the ambush, and all the survivors bar one bore bullet wounds of some kind: Rapier alone was miraculously unhit and unhurt in the melee.

The corpses of twelve Japanese soldiers were found, all dressed in black, all wearing night-vision goggles. Scuba equipment, Defence Force ration packs, water kits and sleeping gear were found up on the second level.

During the fracas, Jack had been hit in his right hand by some ricocheting shards of rock: it bled a lot and when combined with the blood already caked on that arm from the gash to his shoulder from the mini-spikes, Jack's right arm looked like it had been dipped in a bloodbath.

Zoe, also protected from bullets by her Warbler, had taken a similar ricocheting nick to her right calf. It hurt like hell, but with some painkillers she could still limp along. Lily, thankfully, had ridden out the battle unscathed, huddled behind Jack and Zoe.

She and Rapier were the only ones in the group of survivors somehow not smeared in their own blood.

As the fires petered out and the smoke settled, Jack trudged to the far end of the tunnel, and beheld the third and last stage of this Vertex.

'The last test,' he breathed.

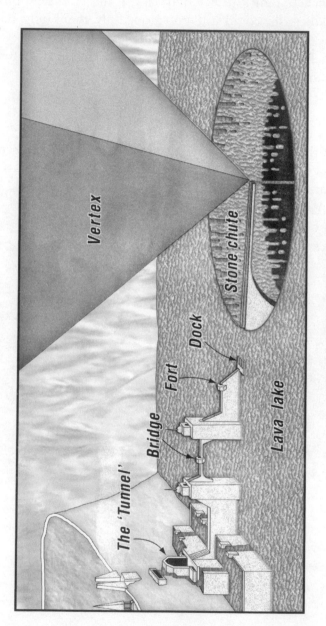

THE THIRD VERTEX

Jack stood on a wide balcony cut into the flank of the volcano, looking out over an incredible sight.

The image he'd seen from the digital camera earlier hadn't done the Third Vertex justice.

The Vertex's inverted bronze pyramid lorded over the space before him, looming above the scene like a gigantic hovering spacecraft. As had been the case at the two previous Vertices, it hung from the ceiling of the cavern, suspended above a dark abyss.

But with one key difference.

This pyramid was surrounded by a seething lake of molten lava that flowed over the rim of the abyss in a completely circular lavafall. (A similarly circular tray a short way below the main rim caught the overflowing lava and presumably pumped it back up into the system above.)

The only means of access to the pyramid's peak was a long tongue-like stone chute that leapt out across the abyss like a half-completed bridge. A small river of lava ran down this chute like a sluice, ending right at the pyramid's peak, where it plunged in a tiny waterfall into the bottomless abyss.

To get to the chute and the pyramid, Jack saw, required negotiating a high stone walkway and a pair of towers connected by a narrow bridge—all of which stood high above the lake of molten lava.

But it was the object at the very end of this extended pathway, down at lake-level, that captured his attention: a stone dock of some sort.

★ ★ ★

Twenty minutes later, Jack stood on that dock, barely a foot above the glowing lava lake.

The heat from the lake was intense; it burned his throat. Once again he covered his mouth with a moist bandana. The others did the same.

'You've got to be kidding me . . .' Zoe said, looking out at the chute.

'It's a suicide voyage . . .' Rapier said.

'The Japanese don't have the same view of suicide that we have in the West,' Jack said. 'Never have.'

Two ornate stone canoes sat nestled in separate niches of the dock. Each canoe bore two seats and they appeared to be made of the same lava-resistant stone as the dock; only these stone canoes were clearly designed to float *on* the lava.

If you pushed one away from the dock, the flow of the lava lake would take you straight into the chute and down its length to the pyramid's peak.

The only problem: there was no way to guide your canoe *back up* the sluice-like chute against the flow of lava. The idea was obvious: you floated down the chute, set the Pillar in place, and then you went over the edge into the abyss.

It was a one-way trip.

The Neetha warlock said something in Greek. Lily translated: 'He says the greatest death of all is one given in honour of Nepthys, the Dark Sun. One of us, he says, should be honoured to die laying this Pillar.'

'So who's going to make the ultimate sacrifice, then?' Rapier snorted.

Jack was staring at the chute and the thin ribbon of lava flowing down it, when someone answered Rapier's question.

'I will,' Wolf said.

The strange thing was, he wasn't looking at the pyramid when he said it, but rather back the way they had come.

★ ★ ★

It took the group three hours to get them—an hour to hike back to the entrance of the cave system, an hour of searching in the wreck, and an hour to return to the dock—but it was worth it.

As Wolf had hoped they would, in the wreck of the supertanker—now resting in the lava lake, sinking inch by painful inch—they had found a pair of winches, equipped with long spools of steel cable.

'Not a bad idea,' Jack said, as they tied a cable to each of the two stone canoes.

'Time check?' Wolf asked.

Lily checked her watch. '11:30. We have thirty-five minutes.'

The two canoes edged out from the dock, floating on the steady current of lava, travelling end-on-end, trailing two steel cables behind them.

Wolf and Jack were in the first boat and nobody was in the second—it was tied to the stern of their canoe with some rope and was there at Jack's insistence, as a back-up in case of emergency. Each canoe trailed its own separate steel cable, another safety precaution.

Rapier, Astro and Zoe had moved to a little fort-like structure at the top of the staircase immediately behind the dock, and from there they managed the two winches, unspooling the cables that would prevent the canoes from going over the edge—always careful to keep the long swooping cables above the lava. Rapier and Astro held the winch connected to the first canoe; Zoe held the back-up.

Lily remained on the dock, watching Jack intently.

The canoes drifted away from the dock, gliding slowly toward the mouth of the chute at the lip of the massive circular lavafall.

With the aid of the current, the cables, and a pair of stone chunks that Jack and Wolf were using as paddles, they guided their boats in toward the chute. The two men looked like Wild West bandits, with wet bandanas covering their mouths and anti-flash glasses protecting their eyes from the fierce heat all around them.

The canoes entered the chute, their flanks brushing against its guttered sides, a perfect fit.

As the two connected boats glided slowly down the chute, Jack saw the great bronze pyramid looming above him. It was utterly huge. He saw its peak at the very end of the chute, squared-off, waiting for its Pillar to be set in place.

Jack also peered out over the side of his canoe—over the rail of the narrow chute—and saw the fathomless abyss beneath the Vertex.

Jesus.

Their canoes approached the end of the chute.

'Careful now,' Wolf said into his radio. 'Ease us close to the edge.'

Rapier and Astro responded by unspooling their winch very slowly, a few inches at a time, until the lead canoe was poised at the very lip of the chute, just above its tiny lavafall and directly underneath the pyramid's squared-off peak.

During the whole delicate operation that followed, Jack watched his father closely.

Wolf was literally covered in blood—a glistening trickle of the stuff ran from his wounded ear down his neck, and his hands were red from wiping it.

But Wolf didn't seem to either notice or care about his gruesome appearance, so intently was he focused on the pyramid and the laying of the clear diamond Pillar—which, of course, was now smeared with his bloody fingerprints.

Jack looked at his own dirty body. He was covered in grime and soot and his right hand was slick with blood, too.

What a totally messed up mission this is, he thought.

'Okay, hold it there!' Wolf called. 'We're in position. What time is it?'

'*11:56,*' Lily said over the radio.

'Okay. I'm going to set the Pillar in place . . .'

★ ★ ★

Up at the fort-like structure, Zoe watched as the tiny figure of Wolf stood in his canoe and reached up toward the inverted pyramid's peak.

Beside her, anchoring his winch lazily against a battlement, Rapier smirked. 'Plenty of time.'

Which was precisely when he was shot in the back.

With a powerful *shwap!* Rapier was thrown violently into the battlement and he lost his grip on the winch. Astro was yanked forward by the sudden extra weight in his hands, but after losing a foot of cable, he managed to regain his grip.

Down at the pyramid's peak, the first canoe jerked forward, causing Wolf—in the process of laying the Pillar—to lurch toward the abyss, but he threw out a hand and propped himself up against the pyramid itself, at the same moment that Astro regathered control of the winch cable.

'What the fu—?' Wolf growled, only to be cut off by a sizzling burst of automatic gunfire that peppered the pyramid, the canoes and the chute all around him. He dived onto his belly, behind the low stone flanks of the first canoe.

Beside him, Jack whirled, crouched on one knee, searching for the source of the gunfire.

He found it: repeated muzzle-flash up at the rim of the volcano crater. One last lone Japanese sniper.

Jack fired back, his big Desert Eagle booming, but he knew that accurate pistol-fire was not really possible at this distance.

'Zoe!' he called into the radio. 'Sniper rifle!'

'*On it!*' came the reply.

Up at the fort, two of the three remaining CIEF troopers behind Zoe fell in matching fountains of blood. Ducking the barrage, Zoe wedged her winch against the battlement, swept up her Barrett and tried to locate the sniper.

She found him and unleashed a spray that forced him to take cover, thus giving Jack and Wolf some respite. It also gave Astro, gripping the cable attached to their canoe all by himself, some much-needed cover.

Jack's watch ticked over to 12:03.

He yelled to Wolf, 'We have to place the Pillar!'

Wolf raised his head—as a Japanese bullet ricocheted off his stone canoe inches away from his face. He ducked again.

They were pinned down.

'We need to co-ordinate this.' Jack keyed his radio: 'Zoe! We need a sustained burst of cover fire so we can plant this Pillar. In three, two, one . . . *Now!'*

Right on cue, Zoe rose and unleashed some heavy suppressing fire, forcing the Japanese sniper to duck—allowing Wolf a moment to leap up and, with Jack gripping the back of his belt, lean out over the bow of their canoe, out over the end of the chute and the yawning black abyss of the Vertex, and reach up with the cleansed Pillar, stretching, stretching, stretching, and . . .

. . . the Japanese sniper popped up again and loosed another burst of gunfire. Bullets sizzled all around the pyramid, one of them ripping into Wolf's left shoulder in a sudden burst of blood.

Wolf roared in pain, but as Zoe provided more cover fire from the fort and Jack held him upright, he reached out and jammed the cleansed Pillar up into its matching slot in the peak of the pyramid.

No sooner had Wolf laid the Pillar than Jack yanked him back into the lead canoe and the clock struck 12:05 and the great pyramid began to thrum ominously before—*whap!*—it sent forth a blinding laser-beam of light down into the abyss. Blazing white light filled the supercavern and then in an instant, it was over.

Jack felt a sense of relief flood over him. They'd survived another Vertex and now all he wanted to do was get out of here.

Wolf, however, wanted to get the Pillar and its reward. Jack vaguely recalled what this Vertex's reward was—*sight*, or something like that—but he really didn't care about that right now.

Their Japanese attacker, having failed to stop them laying the Pillar, was now firing on full-auto both on them and at the others in the fort, more out of frustration than any other reason.

And that was precisely when the sniper hit Astro—twice.

The bullets slammed into his forearm and his leg and he shouted out just as Zoe loosed a brilliantly aimed shot that sent a round driving up into the Japanese sniper's mouth and out the back of his head, ending his last stand.

Beside her, Astro slumped to the ground, *dropping the winch* that held the first canoe in place.

With its support cable lost, the lead canoe, already poised precariously at the end of the chute, lurched abruptly.

Jack felt it move beneath him and he saw the future: the canoe was going to tip over the waterfall of lava and plummet into the abyss!

Quick as a cat, he leapt back into the stationary second canoe, turning as he did so to see Wolf snatch the charged Pillar from the pyramid's peak, and glance down in horror to see that his canoe was moving.

'Jump!' Jack called.

With the canoe beneath him only inches from tipping over the lavafall, Wolf took two steps along its length and leapt, arms outstretched . . .

. . . at the same time as Jack reached out from the second canoe, leaning his upper body over its forward edge . . .

. . . and his bloodied hands caught, of all things, the Pillar in Wolf's right hand.

They ended up in a most unusual position: Jack in the secured second canoe, Wolf in the unsecured first one, his thighs wedged against its stern, both leaning out over the lava in between their boats, joined by their mutual grip on the Pillar.

It was then that something very strange happened to Jack.

A flash of light exploded in his mind's eye and in a single split second, he went to another place, another time.

It was like a dream, and in it he was falling, falling in slow motion through the air beneath an inverted bronze pyramid.

At first, Jack thought he was reliving his fall from the pyramid at the Second Vertex, but this was different, this Vertex was different.

And this time, an entire aeroplane was falling with him, a huge black 747 that looked like the Halicarnassus, *but it only had one wing, not two. The big free-falling 747 obscured Jack's view of the pyramid above him, a pyramid that grew smaller and smaller as he fell deeper and deeper into the abyss, plummeting to his death—*

Jack blinked back to the present, not knowing what the bizarre vision had been, and again found himself clutching the same Pillar as his father, joining them in their separate canoes.

Zoe's voice shouted in his ear: '*Hang on, Jack! We're going to haul you in!*'

A moment later, the two canoes began to move back up the chute, winched in by the second canoe's cable. Zoe and Rapier wound the winch; the gunshot to Rapier's back had hit him squarely in his Kevlar spinal guard and so had only felled him.

The two canoes arrived back at the dock and there both Jack Wests, Senior and Junior, fell onto solid ground, the clear diamond Pillar in their grasp, its internal liquid core pulsing, its glass-like flanks smeared with their bloody fingerprints.

Lily hurried to Jack's side as Zoe and Rapier came down from the fort.

'Daddy! You did it!' Lily hugged him.

Rapier lifted Wolf to his feet, the older man still clutching the charged Pillar. Then Rapier levelled his pistol at the back of Jack's head, coldly cocked the hammer and—

'No!' Wolf barked at him.

'He's no more use to us! We should have killed him before!'

'No, Rapier,' Wolf said in a tone that surprised Jack. It was a tone he'd never heard from his father before—one of quiet respect. To Jack: 'You just . . . saved my life . . . Why?'

Jack actually didn't know why. It had been instinctive. He didn't respond. Lily and Zoe watched this exchange, frozen in horror.

Wolf seemed genuinely confused. 'You could easily have let me go, let me fall off the bottom of that chute, and yet even after everything I've done to you, you didn't.'

Jack was silent for a long moment. Then he said:

'I'm not like you.'

Wolf looked at Jack.

'You most certainly are not,' he said. 'I'm not given to acts of gratitude or mercy, my son, but today I will make a once-only exception. I'm not going to kill you. Rapier.'

He turned and left, leaving Rapier glaring at Jack, before he reluctantly followed their father.

Wolf, Rapier and the Neetha warlock swept back up the stairs behind the dock, taking the charged Pillar with them, leaving Jack, Lily and Zoe there.

They paused briefly at the fort where Astro lay wounded, looking pale and clutching his new wounds. Rapier checked the damage and shook his head.

'He's alive, but he'll be a bitch to carry back through this place. He'll slow us down.'

'Leave him,' Wolf said. 'We have to catch our sub.'

Thus with only the Neetha warlock and one of the forty CIEF men they had brought with them to the Third Vertex, Wolf and Rapier headed back toward the flooded entrance to the cave system.

Wolf led the way, striding purposefully across the high narrow bridge that led back to the volcano.

Rapier followed—the only person to escape this terrible place unscathed, unwounded—and with a sly look back at Jack, unseen by Wolf, he casually dropped a grenade inside the small watch-house in the centre of the narrow bridge.

Moments later, as Rapier stepped off that bridge, the grenade detonated and in a great blast of stonedust, the middle section of the bridge blew apart. The bridge tumbled down into the lava lake, leaving a wide void between the two towers that gave access to the dock . . .

. . . leaving Jack and the others stranded in the dark heart of the Third Vertex of the Machine.

Wolf turned at the unexpected explosion, saw the destroyed bridge. He glanced at Rapier but said nothing.

He just moved on.

After the bridge had crashed down into the lake of lava, Jack just shook his head.

'Never saw that coming,' he said wryly.

With the immense bronze pyramid looming above him, he went up to the little fort to check on Astro.

'How are we going to get out of here?' Lily asked.

'We'll find a way, kiddo.' Jack grabbed a syringe from his first-aid pouch and jabbed it into Astro's leg. 'This'll numb your leg a little while I extract the bullet.'

Astro grimaced.

'But it's still gonna hurt like hell.' Jack grabbed some tweezers and set about finding the bullet in Astro's calf. Despite the anaesthetic, Astro grunted in agony until Jack finally extracted the bloodstained round.

Astro lay back, gasping. Jack started bandaging the wound.

'Why did you save Wolf?' Lily asked, an edge to her voice. 'He murdered Wizard.'

Jack didn't look up. 'Like I said, I'm not like him.'

'But he's a bad man. I think you should have let him fall and die.'

Jack stopped bandaging for a moment and looked up at her. 'Killing someone is a terrible thing, Lily, and not something to wish on anyone lightly. I've killed quite a few people in my life—and then only when they were trying to kill me or someone I loved. But even then, not once has it made me happy or satisfied. Trust me, killing someone is not something you ever want to do.'

'But he—'

'I know. Listen, you're angry right now and I understand that.

But if we're going to win this thing, we have to win it being true to ourselves, being *who we are*.'

'What do you mean?'

Jack sighed. 'My father doesn't care about anyone but himself—he takes what he wants and doesn't care who gets hurt in the process. He kills people who oppose him. I don't. And if I ever do, then I'll be no better than him.

'Yes, I'd like to see him get what's coming to him for what he did to Wizard but my first instinct is always to save someone, to not let them fall. That's who I am. If I'd let him fall when I could have saved him, I'd have *become* him. And I don't ever want to be like him.'

'Hmm,' Lily frowned, not really satisfied.

'Zoe,' Jack said, resuming his dressing of Astro's leg, 'what's the reward for laying the Third Pillar? *Sight*?'

'Yes. But I'm not sure if we ever figured out what that meant.'

'Well, I certainly saw something when I touched that Pillar.'

He described to the others the flashing vision he'd had when he'd gripped the charged Pillar with his bloodied hands, a fantastical vision of falling beneath a Vertex with a one-winged black 747 falling with him.

'Wizard and I once talked about it,' Jack said. 'He never got a definitive answer as to what *sight* meant, but he had a theory.'

'And what was that?' Lily asked.

'He said the reward *sight* was the ability to see one's own death.'

Neither Zoe nor Lily had a reply for that.

Jack finished Astro's leg and hoisted the young Marine to his feet, slinging one arm over his own shoulder. Astro hopped on his good leg.

'How's that feel?'

'Hurts like hell, but I can make it. And hey, at least you didn't leave me to die like my asshole commanding officer just did. How can you help me after what I did to you?'

'It wasn't you who did it. You thought you were following

legitimate orders,' Jack said, shrugging. He glanced at Lily. 'Beyond that, same reasons I gave her.'

He looked up at the volcano cone and the exploded bridge leading back to it. 'Now. How about we figure a way out of this godforsaken place?'

Two hours after Wolf had abandoned them on the dock, a second explosion rang out in the underground cavern.

This one came from a bunch of grenades—the entire collection of Jack, Zoe and Astro—that Jack had lowered by winch-cable to the base of their tower.

He had lowered the cluster of grenades down the side of the tower, pulled the pin on one via a second cable and then raced back down to the fort near the dock.

The grenades detonated—a huge blast at the base of the tower—and a second later, the great tower fell, tipping over from its blasted-open base like a slow-falling tree, tilting away from the dock and across the void left by Rapier, landing with a colossal *bang* up against the second tower, coming to rest at a precarious thirty-degree angle, awkwardly bridging the gap.

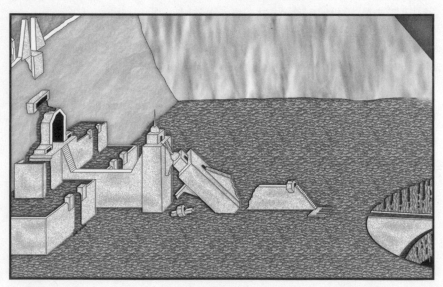

'Go! Before it slips!' Jack called, supporting Astro on his shoulder and running up the slope of the semi-fallen tower . . . as the whole structure began to groan ominously.

Lily ran out in front, and the small group of tiny figures hustled up the fallen tower, arriving at its pointed summit and jumping across a short gap onto the flat upper ledge of the still-standing second tower.

'Keep going!' Jack called to Lily. 'Get to the volcano!'

Lily obeyed and together they all ran across the narrow elevated pathway that led back to the volcano, arriving at the safety of the tunnel there just as the fallen tower brought down the standing one and amid the deafening groan of rending stone, the two towers fell sideways into the molten lake, creating a tremendous lava splash and taking half the elevated pathway with them.

Like some living breathing predator, the lava lake proceeded to swallow the two towers whole and soon all that remained between the volcano and the pyramid of the Third Vertex was the low stone dock and a section of the path behind it, now an island out on the simmering molten lake.

It would take Jack several hours to get back to the entrance to the Vertex. It was very slow going: Lily and the limping Zoe walked out in front, while he trailed behind with Astro draped over his shoulder, all the while negotiating the booby-trapped triple-pathways.

On the way, they had rummaged through the Japanese ambush station inside the tunnel and grabbed food and water . . . and the scuba gear the Japanese soldiers had used to penetrate the Vertex's submerged ocean entrance.

At last, standing at the flooded entrance to the Vertex, with a lake of glowing lava behind him and a lake of sloshing ocean water before him, Jack saw no sign of Wolf.

Astro mentioned Wolf saying something about catching a retrieval sub, but it must have been and gone.

'What are we going to do when we get outside?' Lily asked. 'The Japanese ships will still be out there, plus the shooters on the cliffs.'

Jack helped the wounded pair of Zoe and Astro get into the scuba gear. 'I'm hoping Wolf had a plan for that which might allow us to get ashore somehow and call Sky Monster. All I know for certain is we can't stay in here.'

So out they went, wearing the scuba gear of the Japanese garrison.

Jack pulled Astro through the deep blue haze while Lily helped Zoe—the four of them gliding past the gargantuan pillars of the entry hall.

At length they emerged from the hangar-like doorway to the Vertex, feeling the rhythmic tug of the ocean as they ascended.

Then they surfaced.

Hovering in the seething ocean, Jack spat out his mouthpiece, looked around, and said, 'Oh, shit.'

Driving ocean rain slammed down on Jack's face as he took in the scene off the Hokkaido coast.

It was not as he had left it a day before.

The ships of the Japanese Navy had backed off, and were now distant specks on the horizon.

Wolf's retrieval sub—a small American Sturgeon-class boat—lay immobile on the waves, surrounded by six heavily armed Russian Mi-48 Chinook-clone helicopters and five Hind gunships.

A gang of twelve MiG fighters boomed across the sky, keeping the Japanese Navy at bay.

'Who the hell are these guys?' Jack asked. '*Russians?*'

The four of them were spotted quickly and with no possible escape were winched up into one of the big double-rotored Chinooks.

A moment after he dropped to the deck of the chopper's hold, wet and exhausted, Jack was surrounded by six Spetsnaz commandos wearing oversized helmets and brandishing VZ-61 Skorpion machine pistols.

'Captain West?' the leader yelled over the din of the rotor blades. 'Captain Jack West Jr, no?'

'Yes!' Jack nodded.

Whack.

The blow came from the side, from one of the other Russian commandos, and Jack dropped to the steel floor of the hold, hearing Lily scream a moment before everything went black.

A MISSION IN SCOTLAND

THE SPRING OF THE BLACK POPLAR

Scotland

SCOTLAND
12 MARCH, 2008
6 DAYS BEFORE THE 4TH AND 5TH DEADLINES

NORTHERN SCOTLAND
12 MARCH, 2008, 0700 HOURS

The high-speed train zoomed through the highlands of northern Scotland. A grim sky touched grim mountains which towered over grim snow-filled valleys. It was two degrees Celsius but the wind-chill made it seem colder.

The train thundered into a tunnel bored into the base of a mountain, enveloping it in noisy darkness.

In a private first-class cabin at the front of the train, Lachlan Adamson shook his head. 'I don't know, Julius. First we moved some 5,000-year-old stones at Stonehenge. Now we've stolen an ancient Egyptian basin from the British Museum. What's next? Taking the Scottish Crown Jewels?'

'Hey, we're saving the world here,' Julius said. 'Besides, the British Museum has no idea how important that Basin is. At least we're *using* it. Seriously, that museum has no clue as to how special some of its items are. Like that Easter Island statue in the cafeteria, it's one of only four *moai* carved from basalt, and they have it on display *in the cafeteria*. You remember when we went to Easter Island—'

'You guys have been to Easter Island?' Stretch said.

'Sure, back in '02. Awesome place,' Julius said.

'What *is* the story with the statues there?' Stretch asked.

'*Well . . .*' Julius rubbed his hands. 'For over 700 years, the Easter Islanders built their huge statues, called *moai*. They made over 1200 of them, ranging from little six-foot-tall ones to absolute monsters that are eleven metres tall and weigh eighty tons. But nearly all of those 1200 statues were carved from tufa, a soft volcanic rock. Only four were fashioned from basalt, a much harder stone, so they would have taken a lot longer to carve.'

Lachlan said, 'And when the British came in 1868, they stole only two *moai* and both of them were made of basalt. They knew exactly what they were after: the rare basalt ones. They knew they were special, unlike today.'

'That island is way cool,' Julius said to Stretch. 'Seriously, if we survive this, you should go sometime. We backpacked there with a couple of hottie American anthropology students, Penny and Stacy Baker. God, I had such a thing for Stacy. You remember her, Lachie? Stacy Baker?'

A momentary look of shock spread across Lachlan's face. 'What, oh, yeah, sure . . . she was . . . nice.'

Julius saw it. His eyes narrowed. 'Nice or *nice*, brother?'

Lachlan's face went red. 'Julius, I always meant to tell you about Stacy, but I never got the chance . . .'

Julius's jaw dropped. 'You hooked up with Stacy Baker? On Easter Island?'

'Yeah . . . one night after you fell asleep—'

'You knew I liked her!'

'It sort of . . . well . . . just happened, Julius—'

Julius was furious. 'These things don't *just happen*! You lying, sneaking traitor. I'll give you a new call-sign: Judas—'

'Boys!' Pooh called from his laptop nearby. 'Some quiet, please! I just got a message from Sky Monster. He says he's somewhere near Vladivostok. He's lost contact with Jack on Hokkaido, but since the time for laying the Third Pillar is past and the world is still turning, he thinks Jack must have laid it successfully.'

'Or someone else did,' Stretch said. 'So let me get our mission straight: before the last three Pillars are placed at their Vertices, they must be cleansed twice, in the Philosopher's Stone *and* in the Basin "in the pure waters of the Spring of the Black Poplar"?'

'Correct,' Lachlan said.

'And we have the Basin,' Julius said, still scowling at his brother.

'So all we need to do now is find this mysterious Spring.' Stretch looked at the twins. 'And you think it's up here?'

'Not us,' Julius said, 'Wizard. It was on his summary sheet all along. We just verified it through some of Isaac Newton's writings.'

At that moment, right on cue, the train burst out of the tunnel, revealing a dramatic landscape ahead of it: a long almost eerily flat lake, veiled in fog and flanked on both sides by mountains that plunged directly into it.

It was perhaps the most famous lake in the world.

Loch Ness.

After Jack had tasked the twins with finding the Spring of the Black Poplar, it had been Julius who had provided the breakthrough.

His starting point had been the initial reference to the Spring, the inscription at Saqqara:

> *Cleanse the last three also in my basin,*
> *In the pure waters of the Spring of the Black Poplar.*
> *Do this and Ra's Twin will be satisfied and*
> *Upon you he will confer his bounties.*

While the others had been looking up references to black poplars in the historic and scientific literature, Julius had glanced at Wizard's summary sheet for the millionth time and noticed something:

REWARDS
(according to Rameses II at Abydos)

1. KNOWLEDGE
2. HEAT
3. SIGHT
4. LIFE
5. DEATH
6. POWER

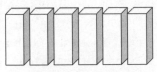

THE GREAT MACHINE

Pillars???

But what are the TRIANGLES then?

THE SIX PILLARS

- Oblong uncut diamonds;
- Must be '*cleansed*' by the Ph's Stone before they can be placed in the Machine;
- Whereabouts? The Great Houses of Europe; Perhaps the 'Five Warriors'???

MUST HAVE BOTH
THE SA-BENBEN
AND
THE PHILOSOPHER'S
STONE! THEY ARE
CENTRAL TO
EVERYTHING!!

The Sa-Benben (a.k.a. 'The Firestone')

**Interacts uniquely with each of
the Six Ramesean Stones:**

1. <u>Philosopher's</u>: cleanses Pillars.
2. <u>Stonehenge</u>: gives location of vertices of the Great Machine.
3. <u>Delphi</u>: allows one to see the Dark Sun.
4. <u>Tablets</u>: contain the final incantation.
5. <u>Killing</u>: gives dates by which Pillars must be laid.
6. <u>Basin</u>: unknown.

Rate of approach must be calculated. Call the Twins!

16,467 X 365.25
Mean V = 125,445 km/s
Max output in 1962 was 10.57
But in 1991 was 10.72. Growing.

**TITANIC SINKING
& RISING (DEC 2007)
CONNECTION? POSSIBLE
SIGHTING OPPORTUNITY?**

WRONG!

Faberge Egg - Newton's alchemical work
The Ness spring...?
Equinox/Easter '08

There it was, at the very bottom of the sheet.

'The Ness spring . . . ?' written in Wizard's own hand, right under 'Faberge Egg—Newton's alchemical work' and 'Equinox/Easter '08'.

That reference had defied explanation till now—till they had been searching for a special spring.

Cross-references were made.

First the twins deduced that black poplars grew only in northern latitude countries like Scotland. They also searched for any links between the only warrior of 'The Five' who could realistically have had contact with Loch Ness—Napoleon—and found none.

But they also looked up links to Isaac Newton and his alchemical work, since it appeared so close to 'The Ness spring' on Wizard's sheet, and it was Julius who found a reference to the Loch in one of Isaac Newton's handwritten letters to Christopher Wren, helpfully scanned and archived on the Internet:

> *'Dear Edmund has found an old well in those dreadful ruins of his at Loch Ness, with a strange black poplar growing through the stones—'*

Julius explained: '"Dear Edmund" is Sir Edmund Halley, Newton's close friend and the famous astronomer after whom the comet is named. Halley was very wealthy and owned large estates across the UK, including one on the eastern shore of Loch Ness. It's now public land.'

And so they had jumped on the first train north, heading for the highlands of Scotland and the famous monster-infested lake.

Located in the rugged north of Scotland, Loch Ness is a deep freshwater lake, superlong yet extremely thin. It is roughly 23 miles in length but barely a mile wide.

Its western shore is serviced by the A82 road and so it is on that side, up near the north of the lake, that one finds the guesthouses and hotels for the tourists who come to see the monster.

The eastern shore, however, is a different story.

In an area already thinly populated, it is not serviced by any major road. And in the southern stretches, it is still in many ways an untouched highland wilderness—with forests that run all the way down to the Loch, the odd isolated farm, and rugged cliffs and hills. It is a harsh land and not many people go there.

Using records that dated from the 1680s, the team located the land that was once Edmund Halley's Scottish estate and ventured there in a rented four-wheel-drive Toyota Land Cruiser.

A thick fog lay over the Loch. Drizzle fell. A chill wind had everyone dressed in boots and high-collared parkas.

For four days, the twins, Pooh Bear and Stretch searched on foot and in a motorised dinghy for signs of ruins or an ancient spring among the thick forest near the Loch's edge.

Julius sulked, still aggrieved by his brother's revelation about scoring with Stacy Baker at Easter Island six years previously.

Ignoring him, Lachlan said, 'Most ruins in this area are actually built on older ruins—strategic locations didn't really change much in the Middle Ages. What was a strategic spot for some ancient tribe was also strategic for Robert the Bruce. We're looking for something older within an existing ruin.'

He also explained that there were springs and holy wells all over the British Isles. Primitive tribes like the Celts had marvelled at the mineral-rich waters that rose from within the Earth and the curative properties they sometimes possessed. The Romans used the springs as baths, while monks in the Middle Ages built churches on top of them, like at St Oswald's in Cumbria.

Pooh Bear said, 'There are several revered springs in the deserts of Arabia, where we call them *ein*s. My father once told me that aside from simply quenching one's thirst in a desert, the mystique of a spring is related to the *energy* in the water that comes from under the ground: people die, they are buried, then their souls rise again within the waters of springs.'

For four days they searched. In the evenings, seated in the boot of the Land Cruiser, the twins would work away on their computers, trying to figure out their other task: the location of the Fourth Vertex. Working from their original photos of Stonehenge during the lightshow, it was somewhere in the British Isles.

Then, late on the fourth day, as he sat in the dinghy with Lachlan, Pooh Bear saw something.

'Hey!'

They'd been cruising up a narrow inlet shrouded by moss-covered crags and thick overhanging trees when a small cave at its farthest extremity, veiled by vines, had caught his eye.

Just inside the cave's mouth, behind the veil of vines, Pooh Bear saw a low ankle-high wall constructed of square stone bricks. It was worn down by centuries of moisture, to the point where it was almost perfectly camouflaged against the natural walls of the cave.

Barely a foot high, it was the remains of a very old man-made structure—a barrier, Pooh Bear thought as he stepped over it—but in a land of magnificent castle ruins and mythical monsters, this little cave had clearly been dismissed as small-time and ignored.

A trickle of water ran out through a cleft in the low wall, coming from inside the cave itself, before dropping in a weak dribble into the black waters of the Loch.

Venturing inside the cave, climbing steadily into darkness, Pooh Bear found the source of the trickle.

A circular stone well, not even twelve inches in diameter, ringed by a man-made rim of ancient bricks, all covered in slimy green moss.

Shining his flashlight onto the rim, Pooh Bear brushed away the moss—

—and immediately saw a pattern carved into the stones.

It was an image of a tree, with many flowing branches, branches that continued from brick to brick—or, as Newton had put it, 'growing' through them.

It was an image of a black tree.

A poplar.

Pooh Bear, Stretch and the twins gathered in the cave and stared at the little ancient well. The only sound was that of the soft trickle of springwater issuing from it.

'From the humblest of origins come the mightiest of things,' Pooh Bear said softly.

'*That* trickle is going to save the planet?' Julius said.

'It's certainly not much to look at,' Lachlan said.

'I wasn't talking to you, traitor—'

'There's writing cut into the brickwork, alongside the branches of the tree,' Stretch said, peering closely at the well with his flashlight. 'Looks like it's written in Thoth.'

'We have to show this to Lily,' Pooh Bear said. 'Lachlan, can you get a shot of that?'

Lachlan had been taking digital photos of the cave for their records. He took several close-ups of the well's circular rim.

Pooh Bear asked, 'Can you see any symbols that refer to the Vertices, especially the Fourth one?'

'I don't see any,' Lachlan said as he took his shots.

'Like you didn't see my love for Stacy Baker,' Julius muttered.

'So what do we do now?' Stretch asked.

Pooh Bear shrugged. 'We collect as much of the springwater as we can carry.'

An hour later, they'd filled ten two-litre plastic bottles with springwater from the well, enough to fill the Basin many times over.

'That should be enough,' Pooh Bear said.

As they made to leave the cave, Julius ducked back to the well

and filled his empty Gatorade bottle with the sacred water of the Spring.

'Julius!' Lachlan said, aghast.

'Hey, it's still water and I'm thirsty. Might also give me super-human powers. And given your recent revelations, brother dearest, I'll not be lectured by you on what is or is not decent!'

'Come on, you two. Let's go,' Stretch said.

That night, they were once again on an express train, only this time they were heading south, back toward England, their ten bottles of the precious water stowed in large hikers' backpacks.

'Oh my God, I think I've got it . . .' Julius said from the fold-down desk of his first-class cabin.

Stretch leaned in from the adjoining cabin. 'Got what?'

Julius looked up at him. 'The location of the Fourth Vertex.'

As the others gathered around him, Julius explained.

'Here is our starting point, the lightshow at Stonehenge and the fourth pinprick of light up near the top of the stone, marked "4":

'As we know, the dots marked "1" and "2" represent the Vertices at Abu Simbel and Cape Town. "4" is clearly somewhere in the British Isles, but the detail is poor. Using high magnification and digital image intensifiers, Lachlan and I were able to narrow it down to the west coast of Great Britain.

'Now, the golden plaque from the First Vertex said that the Fourth Vertex was "The City of Waterfalls". At first I thought this could mean one of the many waterfalls in Wales. But then I thought: what if they're *ocean* waterfalls. What if this Vertex is built underneath a small island somewhere off the west coast of England or Wales and water pours *into* it?'

'But there must be hundreds of—' Stretch began.

Julius smiled. 'Yes, but sometimes what you're looking for is not only right under your nose, you've actually *seen it before*.'

'What do you mean?'

With a flourish, Julius pulled out a sheet of paper: it was a map of the UK, over which someone had drawn a right-angled triangle.

'This is a picture Lachlan drew for Lily last year, back when we went to Stonehenge to perform the lightshow. We were showing her the link between the Preseli Hills in Wales—where the bluestones for Stonehenge were mined—and Stonehenge itself and that if you extend the line connecting the Preseli Hills to Stonehenge, you end up at the Great Pyramid in Giza.

'The thing is, we were so caught up in the link between Stonehenge and the Great Pyramid, we never noticed the *third* corner of the triangle, the right-angled corner. Look at its location: in an area full of water, it lands *precisely* on an island in the Bristol Channel. I looked it up. It's Lundy Island. Although the ancient Welsh knew it by another name, *Ynys Elen*, "the Island of the Goddess of the Dying Sun".'

'The Dying Sun,' Stretch said. 'How appropriate.'

Julius said, 'These days only thirty-odd people live there, but Lundy has a colourful history: it was once owned by the Knights Templar; 13th-century pirates used it as a base because it has very dangerous hidden shoals. And since it's in the Bristol Channel, it's subject to the Channel's huge ten-metre tides, the second largest in the world.

'According to local fishermen, when the tide is low, some reefs and rocks on the western coast of Lundy Island are revealed. One such rock formation is known as "The Well" because the weathered rocks resemble the shape of a brick well.'

'So?' Stretch frowned.

Julius smiled, and turned his laptop around: on it was the jpeg of Genghis Khan's shield:

'Look at the picture at the top right-hand corner,' Julius said. 'It shows the entrance to the Fourth Vertex, and it looks to me a lot like a well. Gentlemen, I propose to you that Lundy Island is the location of the Fourth Vertex.'

As Julius spoke, Pooh Bear stared out the window of the speeding train, only half paying attention.

He was on edge. Something didn't feel right. It was as if things were going *too* well lately.

His eyes followed two pairs of blinking red lights hovering in the night-time sky to the east, moving parallel to their train and moving fast.

They looked like aircraft lights, but they were flying too low to be planes.

The train had emerged from the northern highlands and was now racing through the rolling fields of the lowlands. It was nearing midnight when it zoomed out onto a long high bridge over a particularly wide valley gorge.

The cluster of blinking red lights kept following.

'Pooh Bear, relax,' Lachlan grinned, sitting beside him. 'For the first time in our lives we've found something first and made a clean getaway. Quite a rarity, really. And much more pleasant than the usual running, shooting and screaming.'

'Don't speak too—' Pooh Bear said.

At that moment, a soft droning alarm began to sound and the train's brakes started squealing.

They were slowing down, out in the middle of the long high bridge.

Pooh Bear gazed out at the blinking red lights, and as they came closer, he swore.

They were helicopters, military helicopters, four of them: AW-101 Merlins capable of holding thirty Royal Marines each.

Two of the massive choppers fell into identical hovers on either side of the stopped train. They switched on their spotlights, illuminating the stationary train in blinding white light.

The other two hovered just out of Pooh's sight directly over the train—but from the muffled thumps coming from above him, Pooh knew they were unloading Royal Marines onto the roof.

Pooh Bear shook his head. 'Our getaway wasn't clean at all. They've been following us all along.'

As a pleasant Scottish voice asked all passengers on the train to evacuate to the rear in a calm and orderly manner, black-clad Royal Marines brandishing MP-5SNs secured the first-class carriage, zeroing in on the team's two cabins.

Pooh Bear turned to the twins: 'Do you have anything in writing that mentions the location of the Fourth Vertex on Lundy Island?'

Julius said, 'No, it's just a conclusion I drew from various stuff, pictures, research. It's not written down anywhere—'

'Good, because in about fifteen seconds we're going to have a bunch of men with guns in here and the only thing that will keep us alive is the location of that Vertex—'

'*Freeze! Hands where we can see them!*'

Six Royal Marines appeared in the doorway, guns up. As one, the team all raised their hands.

A moment later, gliding casually into the cabin, sliding past the armed Royal Marines, came a smiling female figure.

Iolanthe Compton-Jones.

'Hello, boys,' she said lightly. 'From the British Museum to the wilds of Loch Ness. My, you have been busy.'

'We have the Basin, the springwater and we know the location of the Fourth Vertex,' Pooh Bear said.

Iolanthe's eyes narrowed. 'How clever of you, Sergeant Abbas. I can take the Basin from you, and I might even already have my own supply of the sacred springwater, but I imagine getting the location of the Vertex out of you won't be quite as easy.' She shrugged. 'All in good time. In any case, I'm not here to take any-thing from you just yet, or even kill you for that matter.'

With a loud thunk, she placed a reinforced military-spec communications laptop onto the cabin's fold-out desk. The markings on it, curiously, were in Cyrillic text.

It was *Russian*-made . . .

'No,' Iolanthe said, 'I'm here tonight as a messenger, because someone wants to talk to you.'

FOURTH BATTLE

THE LAIR OF THE CARNIVORE

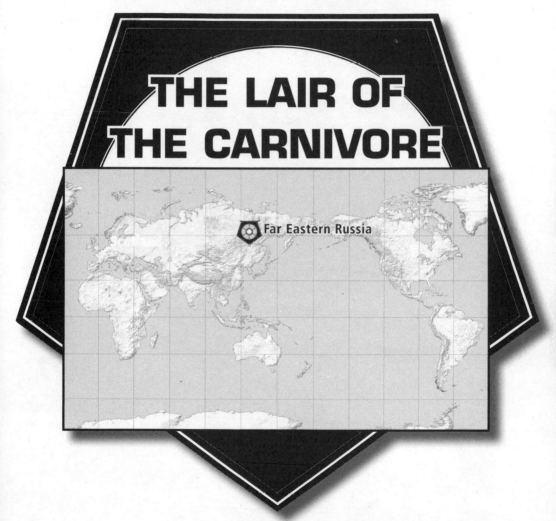

Far Eastern Russia

FAR EASTERN RUSSIA
16 MARCH, 2008
2 DAYS BEFORE THE 4TH AND 5TH DEADLINES

SOMEWHERE IN FAR EASTERN RUSSIA
16 MARCH, 2008
2 DAYS BEFORE THE 4TH AND 5TH DEADLINES

A bucketload of icy water splashed onto Jack's face, waking him with a start.

He sat up. He was in a dank cell with sickly-white ceramic walls and a drainage grate in the floor.

Not a good sign: the Soviets had built cells this way because it made cleaning them easier. You just hosed the blood off the ceramic walls and it drained away through the grate.

'Get up!' the Spetsnaz soldier holding the bucket barked. 'The general desires a word with you.'

'Where are my friends?'

'Move!'

His hands cuffed, Jack was escorted from the cell up through a labyrinth of concrete stairways and tunnels. Their common feature: pipes, dozens of them, lined the ceiling of every passageway.

At one point, he crossed an enormous concrete hall via an elevated steel catwalk. The wide grey hall was lined with sixteen huge turbines fed by pipes as big as buses. It looked like the inside of a—

Another windowless concrete stairwell led up for many storeys until Jack came to a door, which the Spetsnaz guard flung open.

Blinding winter sunshine assaulted Jack's eyes as he emerged to find himself standing atop a colossal mountain dam, nestled between two snow-covered peaks. On one side, the dam held back a modest lake; on the other it plummeted for five hundred feet all the way down to a rocky gorge. The landscape around it was bleak and bare. Wind whistled. He was in the middle *of the middle* of nowhere.

The guard shoved Jack along the top of the dam, around its long sweeping curve. They were heading, Jack saw, for a dome-shaped building that overlooked the dam, sitting proudly on one of the mountain peaks that bookended the immense concrete barrier.

As he came closer to it, Jack frowned, realising the true nature of the dome-shaped building.

It was an observatory.

Jack stepped inside a huge hemispherical space.

It was old and grimy and built mainly of concrete, another classic product of the Soviet era. And it smelled like an old hospital, stale yet sterile at the same time. A gigantic silver telescope dominated the space, pointing up and out through a gap in the top of the dome. Unlike everything else here, it was modern and new, state-of-the-art.

'Ah-ha, here he is! West the Younger,' a voice intoned, echoing in the space. It spoke in English, but the accent was Russian.

A lone man, older, around sixty, stepped out from behind the telescope, stopping in front of Jack as if he were the host of a dinner party greeting a guest.

Jack recognised him instantly. It was hard not to.

The exposed silver mass of steel that formed the man's left lower jaw was both horrifying and unique. His eyes were grey orbs that moved constantly: they took in Jack entirely, as if they were evaluating every part of him, every muscle, every muscle's potential.

Then the man with the steel jaw looked deep into Jack's eyes, and it was as if he were assessing the potential *inside* Jack—his brains, his resolve, his courage.

Only then did the man with the steel jaw blink.

'Welcome to my humble facility, West the Younger,' he said. 'My name is General Vladimir Karnov of the *Federalnaya Sluzhba Bezopasnosti*, the FSB, but you probably know me by a different name: Carnivore.'

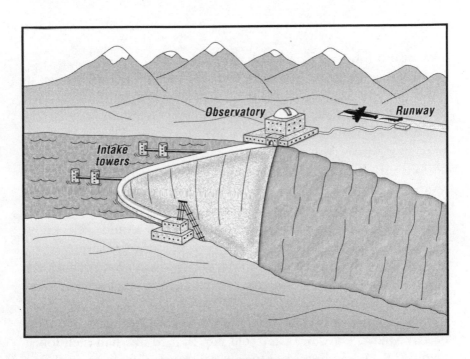

THE RUSSIAN DAM

'Where are Lily and Zoe?' Jack demanded.

'Patience, West the Younger. You will be reunited with them in good time. Please, come this way.' Carnivore began guiding Jack around the great telescope.

'I've been watching you for some time, you know. You're a brave one; smart, too, like your father. But unlike him, you have a curious propensity for *loyalty*, which leads you to perform reckless and unnecessary acts. Like your assault a month ago on my friend Mordechai Muniz's little lair in Israel.'

Jack glanced sharply at Carnivore. 'How could you know about—?'

'Oh, how you angered old Mordechai,' Carnivore chuckled. 'Didn't your father ever tell you: never anger a man who collects men for pleasure.'

Jack caught his breath. After they'd rescued Stretch from Mordechai Muniz, Pooh Bear had told him that Muniz had mentioned he'd learned his technique of 'live-imprisonment' from an ex-Soviet general, a man with whom Muniz had 'a friendly competition going' in the collection of human beings.

Jack breathed. 'You're—'

'Yes, I am,' Carnivore smiled like a crocodile as they walked around the telescope. 'I am the one who taught the Old Master his technique of collecting people; I like to call such tanks "living tombs". But that is not my only interest. I have also been a keen observer of your exploits over the years—from re-erecting the Capstone of the Great Pyramid to your efforts in recent months to rebuild the mythic Machine. As I said, I've been watching you for a long time.'

With those words, Carnivore led Jack fully around the massive telescope—

—and Jack stopped dead in his tracks.

Arrayed around the long curving wall of the old observatory were no less than *fifteen* reinforced water tanks filled with murky green liquid and the shadowy outlines of human beings shackled inside them.

'Mother of . . .' Jack breathed.

Only that wasn't the end of it.

Further along the curved wall, Jack saw a collection of more prisoners, all standing wearily against the ceramic wall, manacled to it by sturdy ringbolts:

Zoe.

Astro.

Wolf, Rapier and the Neetha warlock.

Lily stood off to one side, unchained, but not going anywhere.

All nabbed at Hokkaido, just like Jack himself.

But it didn't stop there.

Carnivore had been busy indeed. The veterans of the Vertex at Hokkaido weren't the only prisoners he had gathered here. There were more, also chained to the wall:

Mao Gongli from China—last seen in Mongolia.

Agent Paul Robertson of the CIA, who had been at the meeting in Dubai when Astro had been planted in Jack's team; Robertson had last been seen at Mortimer Island.

Sky Monster and Tank Tanaka—Carnivore must have found them in the *Halicarnassus* near Vladivostok.

Vulture, the Saudi spy.

And Scimitar, Pooh Bear's treacherous older brother who was in league with Vulture.

Jack recalled when he'd last seen them. They'd video-called him, claiming to have abducted—

Carnivore seemed to enjoy the look of shock on Jack's face. He went over to a workbench set up near the prisoners.

On it was the Philosopher's Stone, taken from Wolf at Hokkaido. The Firestone, however, which had also been in Wolf's possession, was not with it.

Carnivore turned to one of his guards, who sat at a communications console. 'Do we have contact with Young West's cohorts in the United Kingdom?'

'Yes, sir.' The guard flicked on a larger screen, allowing Jack to see Pooh Bear, Stretch and the twins on it, all facing the camera and all covered by armed Royal Marines. Iolanthe sat with them.

'Miss Iolanthe,' Carnivore bowed. 'How do you do?'

'I am very well, thank you, cousin,' Iolanthe replied.

Cousin? Jack thought.

'Has the Firestone arrived there yet?' Carnivore asked Iolanthe.

'I'm told that it just landed at Stansted. I'll be collecting it shortly,' Iolanthe said.

'Very good,' Carnivore turned back to Jack. 'Long have I known about the mission to rebuild the Machine. Long have I lived in secret, working for a vile regime while disguising my royal roots, waiting for precisely this moment. My family is old and noble, older than those communist brutes who stole Russia from my grandfather, the last tsar. My name is not Karnov, but Romanov, and like Miss Iolanthe, my heritage derives from *the* most noble source, the Deus Rex.'

With a look at Jack, Carnivore pulled something from inside his coat.

It was a Pillar.

Jack saw five horizontal lines inscribed on it: the Fifth one. It was also clear, not hazy. Carnivore must have already cleansed it with the Philosopher's Stone and the Firestone, before dispatching the Firestone to Iolanthe. Carnivore placed it on the workbench beside the Philosopher's Stone.

Jack's mind raced to keep up. He recalled the briefing he and Lily had received at Pine Gap about Carnivore.

Vladimir Karnov—no, Romanov—had been a high-ranking

member of the KGB. He had come to prominence in the West when he'd blown the whistle on the KGB's plot in 1991 to overthrow Gorbachev in the dying days of the USSR, a move that had cemented his future in the FSB when it replaced the KGB after the demise of the Soviet Union.

For all that time, Jack guessed, no-one in Russia had known of Carnivore's Romanov blood. Duping the KGB—the same force that under another name, the Cheka, had hunted down his royal ancestors—must have given him great pleasure.

Carnivore said, 'But now, people, this great quest has reached a critical juncture, a point at which I must intervene.'

Carnivore gazed at them all: at Jack and his people, at Wolf, Rapier and Robertson, at Mao, Vulture and Scimitar.

'You all work for me now,' he said. 'And mark my words, you will give me what I want.'

Jack was manacled to the wall alongside the others.

Carnivore strolled lazily in front of them.

'So here you are, the great nations of the world, the players in this grand game.'

He paused before Mao Gongli. 'Power-hungry China.'

Then Vulture: 'The wealthy but worthless Saudis.'

To Scimitar: 'The robber-barons of Dubai.'

To Wolf, Rapier and Robertson: 'The Freemasons of America and their leaders, the illustrious Caldwell Group.'

To Tank: 'The pride-wounded Japanese, the ones who performed the counter-ceremony with the second Capstone and thus undid Tartarus. So filled with hate. But since you *want* to see the world destroyed, I fear I have no use for you—'

The gunshot made everyone jump. Carnivore had raised a pistol quickly and a grisly star of blood splattered the wall behind Tank's head. The old Japanese professor slumped, hanging from his manacles, dead.

Carnivore holstered the gun and kept strolling, hardly even blinking.

He resumed his casual tone as he addressed Jack and Zoe: 'And let us not forget the dogged coalition of small nations that fights to protect the world from succumbing to a single tyrannical overlord.

'Finally, there is my bloodline, the royal families of Europe, the Deus Rex, our ruling status bequeathed to us by the Lord God himself, our connection to these Pillars perhaps the longest standing of all.'

Carnivore walked over to his collection of water tanks.

Jack found himself glancing at some of the figures inside the tanks: men and women of various ages, their heads bowed, their hair floating in aqueous slow motion, all still alive.

Most of them Jack didn't recognise. But some he did.

A female Russian journalist who had been critical of the Putin regime and who had gone missing in 2001. Her flame-red hair was unmistakable.

The Chechen separatist leader Nikolai Golgov: his famous black dragon tattoo was visible on his chest.

Jack grimaced in revulsion at the horrific series of display cases.

Carnivore stopped at the end of the line of tanks, beside a pair of large sliding doors. He turned. 'You know, West the Younger, I really ought to thank you.'

'What for?'

'Our royal records regarding the Machine only go so far. But our tentacles spread wide and deep. Under the guise of university endowments and scholarships, over the years my family has employed numerous academics and historians to unearth information and evidence concerning the Machine. Our best researcher actually disappeared a few years ago in Africa, and we thought her dead. But then late last year, *your* people rescued her from the fabled Neetha tribe.'

Jack breathed, 'No way . . .'

Carnivore grinned as he opened one of the doors and Diane Cassidy walked into the observatory.

Diane nodded at Jack. 'Hello, Jack.'

'Son of a bitch . . .'

'There is nothing you have done this last month that I have not been aware of,' Carnivore said. 'Dr Cassidy here has kept me informed of everything you have seen, heard and discovered since the Second Vertex.

'Once she informed us that she was with you, I told her to help you, knowing that it was not yet time for me to enter this quest. I mean, why should I waste my energies when you can waste yours for me?'

Jack glared at Diane Cassidy. It had never occurred to him that his people might have rescued one of their *rivals* from the Neetha.

'We all work for someone,' Diane said to him.

'Lily may be right. We should be more careful about who we rescue,' he replied.

Diane jerked her chin at the Neetha warlock, now addressing Carnivore. 'This one is like the Japanese: he desires the end of the Earth. He should be eliminated.'

Carnivore nodded. 'I know. I also know what his people did to you. But he would make such an exotic addition to my collection. I think I'll entomb him.'

Diane glared at the warlock. 'Good enough.'

Carnivore stopped beside the other large sliding door. 'Now you're all probably wondering how I will coerce you into acting on my behalf. Wonder no more.'

With a thin smile, he slid the big door open to reveal several more imprisonment-tanks, half-filled with formaldehyde and filling quickly.

Already spreadeagled inside those tanks were more prisoners.

Jack caught his breath. 'Jesus H. Christ . . .'

In the first tank, waist-deep in the foul green liquid, naked and handcuffed, with a half-face mouthpiece covering his mouth and nose, his eyes wide with fear, was the rotund figure of Sheik Anzar al Abbas, Pooh Bear and Scimitar's father.

In the next pair of tanks was a small Chinese child and his mother. At the sight of them, Mao Gongli gasped.

And in the final pair of half-filled tanks were—

Alby Calvin and his mother, Lois.

'No . . .' Jack said. 'No, no, no . . .'

Jack just stared at Alby and Lois.

Above the breathing regulators covering the lower halves of their faces, their eyes met his, pleading with him to save them.

Jack flashed a look at Carnivore. 'You son of a—'

'Don't blame me, Young West.' Carnivore nodded at Vulture and Scimitar: 'It was *they* who kidnapped the boy and his mother, presumably to blackmail you. I merely acquired them later when I grabbed the Arabs.'

Jack's deadly glare turned to Vulture and Scimitar.

'When this is over,' he said to them, 'we're going to have words.'

'*Take a number, Jack,*' Pooh Bear said from the screen. '*Hello, brother,*' he said to Scimitar. '*It's been a while since you betrayed our father and our mission and left me to die in that mine.*'

Scimitar glanced over at their father, imprisoned in his tank. At first he seemed shocked, but then shock morphed into boldness. 'I know better than both of you.'

Carnivore chuckled. 'Ah, infighting, I love it! Love it!'

Then he got back to business, addressing the group of prisoners manacled to the wall: Jack, Zoe, Wolf, Robertson, Rapier, Mao, Scimitar and Vulture.

'My proposed bargain is this. You will give to me *all* the Pillars that you already possess: the Pillar of Knowledge from the First Vertex, and that of Heat from the Second—'

The CIA man, Robertson, snorted. 'Not a chance.'

Carnivore sighed . . .

. . . and just drew his pistol again and shot Robertson in the forehead at close range. Robertson's head exploded as it slammed back against the wall, showering Rapier beside him in blood and brain matter.

Carnivore holstered the gun and continued speaking as if a cold-blooded murder had not just taken place.

'As I was saying, you will give me the first two Pillars . . .'

Wolf nodded. So did Vulture.

'Good. I have already taken the Pillar of Sight from West the Elder, after he emerged from the Third Vertex in Japan with it. Its reward is most interesting to those who know its full potential.

'Plus, you will lay for me the next two Pillars: the Fourth and the Fifth . . .'

'But you already possess those two,' Jack said. 'Iolanthe has the Fourth and you have the Fifth.'

'Yes,' Carnivore said, 'but I do not possess the locations of their corresponding Vertices.'

Carnivore turned to Wolf: 'The United States controls the Fifth Vertex, do they not? You have held it since 1973 on the island of Diego Garcia in the Indian Ocean.'

Wolf clenched his jaw. 'We do.'

'And all you need is the Pillar.'

'That's right.'

Carnivore turned to the video screen, addressing the twins, Pooh Bear and Stretch. 'And you, loyal footsoldiers of West the Younger. You found the Basin in the British Museum and uncovered the Spring of the Black Poplar, did you not? Have you also found the location of the Fourth Vertex, long lost to history, even to our extensive royal records?'

Lachlan said evenly, 'We know where it is, yes.'

'Then this is what you will do,' Carnivore said. 'You will cleanse Iolanthe's Fourth Pillar in the sacred springwater in the Basin and take it to the Fourth Vertex, where you shall overcome that Vertex's deadly protections and plant the Pillar. Then you will return the charged Pillar to my royal relatives in Britain. When this is done, and only when this is done, Sheik Abbas will be released from his imprisonment. If it is not, he spends the rest of his days floating in my presence.'

On the screen, Pooh Bear swallowed.

Carnivore said, 'After the Fourth Pillar is cleansed in the Basin, the Basin itself and some springwater will be dispatched to meet my Fifth Pillar at Diego Garcia, where West the Elder will use his influence in the US military to warrant its safe passage into and out of the American base there.'

Wolf snorted. 'What makes you think I'll help you? You hold nothing of value to me.'

Carnivore smiled at him. 'Oh, but I will soon. I have a special bargain in store for you, West the Elder.'

'What about the Sixth Pillar?' Jack asked. 'The last one? We don't even know where it is yet or where its Vertex is located.'

Carnivore waved at Alby and Lois Calvin in their tanks. 'Their fate depends on *you* finding the last Pillar, Young West. If it is found and returned to me, they emerge from their living tombs. If not, then they do not.'

At the old man's words, Jack saw Lily's horrified face. Her eyes pleaded: *Don't let that happen. Not to Alby.*

'So I'm your bitch, then,' Jack said to Carnivore. 'I now have to do all this for you.'

Again, Carnivore smiled, that mean silver-jawed crocodile smile. 'Why, West the Younger, I never said that. You see, as your father pointed out, I currently have no leverage over him. You may indeed go and do these things on my behalf . . . but then, so might he. I fear you're going to have to fight for the privilege of doing so.'

With those words, Carnivore pushed the large sliding door open a little further to reveal one last imprisonment tank. Like the others, this tank was half-filled with green formaldehyde solution, but unlike the others, its handcuffs hung open.

It did not yet contain a prisoner.

Carnivore turned to face Jack. 'Only one Jack West will continue in this adventure. Having two of you on the loose is far too dangerous even for me. No. You, West the Younger, will fight your half-brother here'—a nod at Rapier, whose eyes jerked up—'for my amusement and titillation. A fight to the death between rival siblings.

'If you win, Huntsman, your half-brother will be dead, your father will be imprisoned in this tank and you will go free to continue on this quest on my behalf.'

He turned to Rapier. 'And if you win, second son of the Wolf, you not only get the pleasure of killing the brother you so despise, you will win for your father the right to continue on this quest. You will then remain here as my hostage to guarantee your father's future performance of this bargain—although I will reward you with confinement in a cell and not a tank; victory must have its privileges, after all. But as I'm sure you'll understand, I still need my leverage. In the end, though, only one Jack West will continue on this quest. Is this satisfactory?'

'Abso-fuckin-lutely,' Rapier said quickly, glaring at Jack.

Wolf nodded.

Jack swallowed, sizing up his huge half-brother. He glanced over at Zoe and Lily. They both looked horrified.

A fight to the death.

With Rapier.

'Do I have a choice?' he said.

Led by Carnivore, Jack and Rapier were marched at gunpoint out of the observatory and onto the curving upper rim of the enormous dam.

From there they were directed across a long straight concrete bridge that extended out over the dam's lake to a pair of cylindrical intake towers, also made of concrete, that jutted up from the lake.

The two towers seemed to rise only about fifty feet above the surface of the man-made reservoir, but in truth they plummeted all the way down to the lakebed some five hundred feet below.

Their job was twofold: to draw water from the reservoir into the dam's power-generating turbines deep in the bowels of the structure and to regulate the level of the lake itself.

Valves positioned all the way up the intake towers' flanks could allow water into their cylindrical bodies, water that would then flow either down through the huge turbines or into a spillway that delivered it to the gorge on the low-side of the dam.

Jack entered the second intake tower, just as one of Carnivore's men lifted the lid on the tower's central well. Jack looked down into the well: about thirty feet in diameter, its smooth concrete walls disappeared into darkness. Rusty intake vents could be seen at regular intervals along its length.

About sixty feet below Jack's feet, a large grated basket made of interlocking steel struts stretched across the width of the tower. It looked like a large sieve—

'A catching tray,' Carnivore said, 'for collecting debris before it reaches the turbines. Tree branches, roots, animal carcasses that fall into the lake. Today, it will serve as your arena.' To his guards: 'Put them in.'

Jack and Rapier were shoved over the rim of the well and clambered down some handrungs cut into the concrete wall.

Soon they were standing sixty feet below Carnivore, balancing on the thin steel struts of the catching tray. The struts intersected in a grid formation, at right angles; the square gaps formed between them were roughly two feet wide—wide enough for a man to fall through if he didn't keep careful footing. Jack also noticed a small hinged gate in the very centre of the floor, also made of steel struts.

It wouldn't be so bad if you dropped through a gap, Jack thought, you'd probably still land in water—

'Start the turbines!' Carnivore called. A moment later, an immense mechanical roar came echoing up the shaft beneath Jack— it sounded like a jet engine had been switched on down there.

That *was* bad, he thought. Now if he or Rapier fell through the grating of the tray, they'd be sucked into the dam's turbines and diced into a million pieces.

'Release the water!' Carnivore shouted above the din and instantly a pair of shockingly powerful water-blasts came spraying into the catching tray from two intake vents on opposite sides of it. The blasting water hammered into both Jack and Rapier, drenching them, almost knocking them off their feet.

Difficult footing. The deafening roar of the turbines below. The blasting sprays of water up here. It was the arena from hell, and Carnivore knew it.

He smiled. 'Now, gentlemen. If you would be so kind, fight.'

The unexpected blast of whitewater gushing into the tray had momentarily caused Jack to lose sight of Rapier—which was why he was taken by surprise when Rapier came rushing out of the mist, fists clenched and flying.

Jack ducked, avoiding the first blow by millimetres. He

crab-walked sideways, through the spray of the horizontal white-water geysers, losing his footing briefly as one of his boots dropped through the grating.

Jack recalled Rapier at the Vertex in Japan, in the Hall of Orochi, where he had killed the last Japanese soldier with a vicious one-two combination: the first punch stunned you, the second killed you.

Don't let him land a solid first hit, Jack's mind screamed. *If he stuns you, it's over.*

Having seized the initiative in this battle, Rapier didn't let it go—he pursued Jack across the tray, moving surely while Jack slipped and tripped backwards on the lattice of wet struts.

And then Jack stumbled through the powerful incoming spray and he tripped again, looking up in time to see Rapier rush at him and unload two swift punches to his face. Jack fell to the grating.

They were good hits, but not stunning blows and Jack rolled just as Rapier tried to stomp on his backbone, his boot missing and going through a gap in the tray, allowing Jack to spring to his feet, grab Rapier by the collar and jam his face into one of the incoming water-geysers.

But Rapier shook himself free and in a rapid series of moves, elbowed Jack hard in the face and—*bam!*—landed a withering blow on Jack's nose, breaking it, and suddenly Jack's vision blurred and he knew immediately Rapier had landed one of his stunning blows.

Jack swayed on his feet, willing himself to move, to swing a fist, to run, to do anything. But he couldn't. His brain was slowing, his vision hazing over.

All he saw was Rapier towering over him, advancing toward him, his right fist drawn back ready to deliver the final killing blow and then—

—Jack dropped through the air and Rapier's killer blow swished above his head.

Unable to move quickly or whip up a defensive forearm, Jack had done the only thing he could think of to avoid the death blow: he had stepped off the steel struts and allowed himself to drop *through* the two-foot gap beneath him.

As he fell through the square gap, Jack allowed his right armpit to loop over one of the steel struts and it stopped his fall abruptly and painfully.

But his mind was working again now, and hanging half through the tray's floor, Jack lashed out at Rapier's left boot, punching it, knocking Rapier's foot off the slippery strut and suddenly Rapier fell awkwardly through the lattice-like floor too and found himself hanging alongside Jack.

The roar from the turbines was deafening. The spray from the intake vents still rained down on them.

Rapier yelled at Jack: 'I was always better than you! I was always loyal to our father! And yet he still thinks you're better!'

Hanging one-handed, Rapier loosed a big punch that caused Jack to jolt from his awkward position. His armpit came free of its strut and now Jack hung from the tray's floor by his fingertips, arms outstretched above him, his face bloody, completely at Rapier's mercy.

'Goodbye, *brother*!' Rapier yelled, drawing back his huge fist for the blow that would knock Jack off the tray and down into the well, into the grinding turbines somewhere down in the darkness.

'Yes, goodbye . . .' Jack replied.

Rapier swung, roaring with anger—

Just as Jack unlatched something near his fingertips—

With startling suddenness the small but heavy steel gate in the floor of the catching tray came swinging downward on its hinges, swinging *right into* Rapier's face, smashing into it with frightening force. The leading edge of the gate swung directly into Rapier's nose—not just breaking it, but exploding it—and in a grotesque instant, Rapier's face was completely splattered with his own blood, his eyes springing open in shock, in perhaps the last conscious thought of his life.

He may have already been dead, Jack couldn't tell, but a full two seconds after the horrific blow, Rapier's grip on the floor of the tray came free, and with his eyes staring balefully into Jack's, he fell.

Jack watched as the body of his half-brother dropped into the shaft beneath him, falling with the rain of water toward the roar of the turbines.

A brief crunching noise followed as the turbines chewed Rapier's body, before they resumed their regular droning and Jack—hanging from the floor of the tray, exhausted, bleeding and soaked to the bone—looked up to see Carnivore peering into the well, and although Jack couldn't hear it, he could see that the bastard was clapping.

'Daddy!' Lily ran into Jack's arms as he re-entered the observatory. Soaked and limping, his cracked nose leaking blood, he still managed to hold her tight.

His happiness was shortlived. While he'd been fighting Rapier in the intake tower, Carnivore's guards had been busy.

Alby and Lois were now fully immersed in their formaldehyde tanks, suspended in the green haze, their eyes wide with terror. Sheik Anzar al Abbas was also fully submerged in his living tomb, as was the Neetha warlock, his robes billowing in the haze.

Astro and Zoe had also been placed into tanks of their own.

Astro hung limply in his, completely submerged, his energy sapped by his wounds.

Zoe hung spreadeagled in her tank, which was in the process of being filled with the green solution—it was half-full now and rising. When she saw Jack re-enter the observatory, she tried to shout to him, but her mouth and nose were covered by a tightly fitted scuba regulator.

When Wolf saw Jack re-enter the wide space, walking beside Carnivore, his face just went white with shock.

'I know!' Carnivore exclaimed. 'Unexpected isn't it? I thought the brawny one would win, too! But the fight was won fairly by this West. Your other boy was turned into chum by the turbines.' Carnivore nodded to his guards. 'Entomb West the Elder.'

And so as Jack watched, Wolf was secured inside a tank and the tank began to fill with the green preservative fluid.

After all he'd done, perhaps this was the fate Wolf truly deserved, Jack thought, to spend the remainder of his life in a state of total powerlessness.

Nearby, Vulture and Scimitar also watched in silence.

As the green liquid in Zoe's tank sloshed up around her throat, Jack called to her: 'Stay strong, Zoe. I'll be back for you. I promise.'

Carnivore eyed Jack sideways.

He strolled up to Zoe's tank and addressed her. 'What heroic words. Pledging to return for you. If only he knew of *your* betrayal of him, Miss Kissane, two years ago in Dublin . . .'

Zoe's eyes bulged, flashing to Jack.

Jack frowned, not understanding.

Lily swung from Zoe to Jack to Carnivore, also perplexed.

Carnivore turned to Jack, his eyes narrowing. 'I'm so sorry, hero. Over the years, your love for her has grown. But in the months after your mission to replace the Capstone, while she was back in Dublin, your loved one betrayed you and gave her body to another.'

Jack felt his face flush red. 'What—?'

He snapped to face Zoe . . .

. . . only to see her close her eyes and bow her head.

It was true.

Jack was floored. Zoe with another man. He couldn't believe it. She wouldn't . . . she couldn't . . .

And then he thought, *With who?*

Carnivore was loving it. 'Will you still be rushing back for her, West the Younger?'

At first, Jack said nothing. Then he turned to face the Russian. 'I'll be back for all of my people after I go and do your dirty work and bring you back the last Pillar. And when I do come back, I'm going to rip your heart out through your throat.'

Carnivore smiled again. 'And at last we see it: the raw anger of the famously noble Huntsman. Doesn't that feel *good*, Young West? I shall look forward to your return.'

★ ★ ★

Thirty minutes later, Jack, Lily and Sky Monster were standing on an exposed runway a kilometre away from the remote dam, braced against the wind. The *Halicarnassus*, flown here from Vladivostok by Carnivore's forces, stood proudly on the tarmac. Twenty yards away, a massive twin-rotored Russian Chinook helicopter was powering up.

Vulture, Scimitar and Mao Gongli were also there, as were Carnivore and some of his Spetsnaz guards.

'Captain West!' Carnivore called above the din. 'Accompanied by some of my guards, you will make your way to the Vertex at Diego Garcia with the Fifth Pillar. You may take your daughter, as you will no doubt need her skills. I will ensure that by the time you get to the American base, the Basin will be waiting there for you, and your father will have forewarned the American forces there of your arrival. Place the Pillar by the due date, then return it to me, charged with its reward. I have already taken the Twin Tablets of Thuthmosis from your plane, as I will be needing them at the last Vertex.'

He turned to Vulture, Scimitar and Mao. 'You, Saudi. You know the whereabouts of the tomb of the Christ, do you not?'

Vulture blinked, surprised Carnivore would know this. Then, slowly, he nodded. 'By repute, yes. My people have heard whispers of its location for over a thousand years.'

'My helicopter will take the three of you to a Chinese airbase four hundred miles from here. From there, also under the watchful eyes of my guards, you are to get to the tomb and find the Sixth and last Pillar inside it. You will return that Pillar to me for cleansing since by then I will have all three of the cleansing stones: the Philosopher's Stone, the Firestone and the Basin of Rameses.'

Carnivore stepped away, leaving the two groups to board their respective aircraft.

'Godspeed to you all on your missions,' he called. 'I look forward to seeing you again.'

Vulture, Scimitar and Mao headed for their Chinook, but Jack hesitated. Something Carnivore had just said had triggered something in his brain.

He went over to Carnivore. 'Why are you letting me take Lily? She's far too valuable to risk. You need her to read from the Twin Tablets at the last Vertex, to recite the final Thoth incantation written on them.'

A thin smile appeared on Carnivore's deformed face.

'I don't *need* anything, Young West. The girl is valuable but not invaluable. Nor is she unique. I already have someone to read the Twin Tablets at the final Vertex.'

'You already have—?' Jack began, confused.

Carnivore nodded toward the observatory. Jack followed his gaze, and saw a small figure standing on a balcony up there, watching the scene on the runway with cool detachment.

It was a small boy of eleven.

Jack's eyes widened in surprise. Of course, he knew the boy, but he hadn't seen him in a long time.

It was Alexander, Lily's twin brother—and the only other person in the world born with the ability to read the Word of Thoth.

Two years ago, Alexander—a proud, pretentious boy—had been sent to live in a top secret safehouse in County Kerry, Ireland. But in December last year, on the very day Jack's farm had been attacked by Mao's Chinese forces, the boy had been broken out of there in a bloody raid by a crack force of persons unknown.

'You were the ones who grabbed him . . .' Jack breathed.

'Like I said, Young West, I have been watching you for a long time,' Carnivore said. 'Now, if you would be so kind . . .' he indicated the waiting *Halicarnassus*.

Jack and Lily boarded the plane, looking back up at Alexander as they did so.

Minutes later, the big Chinook helicopter carrying Vulture, Scimitar and Mao lifted off, pivoted in mid-air, and powered away to the south, toward China—while the *Halicarnassus* rumbled down the runway, took to the air, and banked south-west, in the direction of the Indian Ocean.

Both were watched by Carnivore, his cold eyes squinting.

FIFTH BATTLE

TWO VERTICES

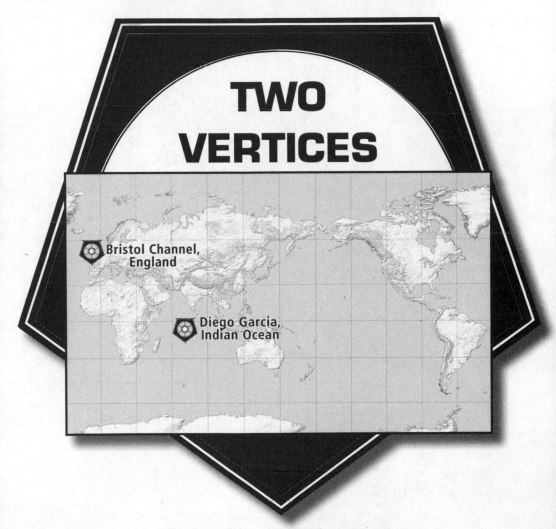

ENGLAND – DIEGO GARCIA
18 MARCH, 2008
THE DAY OF THE 4TH AND 5TH DEADLINES

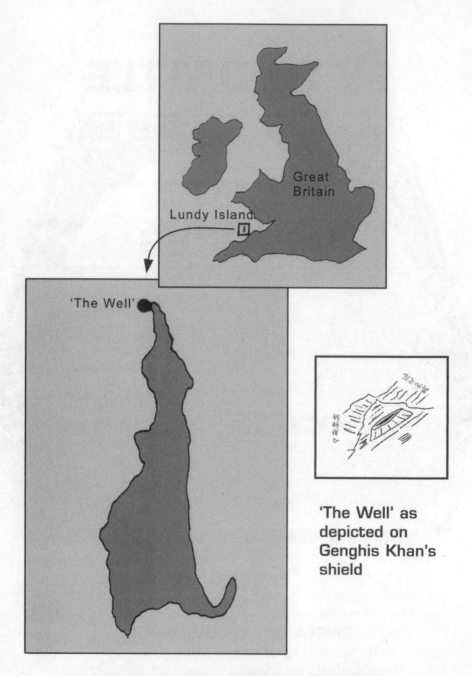

Great
Britain

Lundy Island

'The Well'

'The Well' as
depicted on
Genghis Khan's
shield

LUNDY ISLAND, BRISTOL CHANNEL

The waters of the Bristol Channel heaved and churned as if acted upon by some unearthly force. Powerful forty-foot waves crashed against the rocky coast of Lundy Island. The moon was veiled by clouds and a hard rain fell.

A lone Lynx helicopter flew low over the waves, a spotlight on its underbelly slicing through the rain, trained on the shoreline.

Inside the chopper, looking intently down at the shore, were the twins, Pooh Bear and Stretch, flanked by four of Iolanthe's Royal Marines.

In a pack on Pooh Bear's chest was the Fourth Pillar, long held by the British Royal Family. Last year, at Mortimer Island, it had been cleansed by the Philosopher's Stone and the Firestone.

Late yesterday, in a hangar at Stansted airport, it had undergone a second ritual cleansing: first, the Basin of Rameses had been joined with the all-powerful Firestone—as with Stonehenge and the Philosopher's Stone, the Basin needed the power of the Firestone to activate its special properties.

The pyramidal Firestone had slotted perfectly into a matching pyramidal indentation in the Basin's chunky stem. Then the Basin had been filled with water from the Spring of the Black Poplar. After that, the Pillar was immersed in the Basin's pool . . .

. . . and the second cleansing took place.

The water flashed momentarily, as if it were deflecting a passing light, and suddenly the Fourth Pillar took on a lustrous glassy sheen. If indeed it were possible, now it looked even more crystalline, more beautiful than before.

It was now ready to be placed at its Vertex.

After that second cleansing Iolanthe had departed immediately, boarding a waiting private jet—taking the Basin, some springwater, and the Firestone with her—while Pooh Bear and his team were pushed onto this military helicopter with orders to find the Fourth Vertex and plant the Pillar there.

Which was how they came to be here, flying in the midst of a night-time storm above the furious Bristol Channel.

After a time, they came to that part of the coast where the rock formation known as 'The Well' could be found. It was low tide and the formation was visible, and it looked just like the image on Genghis Khan's shield.

The chopper swung into a hover above the rock formation. Pooh Bear was lowered by winch-cable down to it.

It was certainly peculiar, Pooh thought as he dangled from the chopper in the pouring rain. It was cylindrical in shape but the single piece of rock that formed it—whether by an accident of nature or by the hand of an ancient culture—had been fashioned into the shape of a brick well. The waves of the Channel sloshed over the unusual formation, draining away through the joins between the 'bricks'.

Hanging from the helicopter, with the cleansed Fourth Pillar in his chest-pack, Pooh Bear touched down on the Well and he peered into it.

It wasn't very deep. The shaft of the Well ended with solid rock a short way down, barely a few feet. This added weight to the conclusion that its formation was merely a fluke of nature.

But then as Pooh leaned further down, bringing the Pillar closer to the rock formation, a curious thing happened.

That solid rock base of the Well suddenly *rotated* and retreated back into the rock, leaving a deep black void plunging into darkness.

Pooh Bear's eyes went wide.

'Open Sesame,' he breathed. 'The twins were right. We found it . . .'

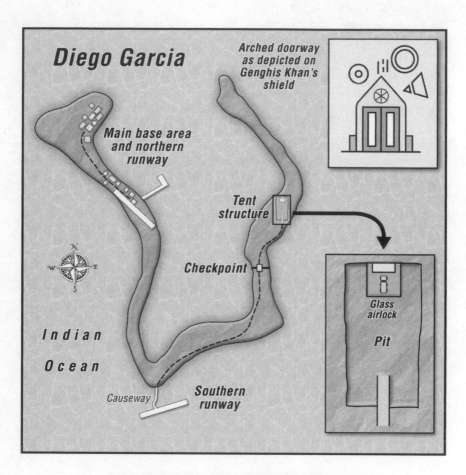

THE ISLAND OF DIEGO GARCIA

DIEGO GARCIA, INDIAN OCEAN
18 MARCH, 2008, 0500 HOURS
2 HOURS BEFORE THE 4TH AND 5TH DEADLINES

At the same time, Jack and Lily were arriving at the remote island of Diego Garcia in the Indian Ocean.

While it was just after midnight in the UK, it was five in the morning here; the eastern sky glowed purple, announcing the coming dawn.

As they began their descent, Jack was sitting at his laptop, examining one of the digital pictures of Stonehenge taken during the lightshow, specifically the shaft of light marked '5':

It all made sense now. As with Hokkaido, the coastline had changed a lot over the millennia—Sri Lanka had been completely detached from mainland India—which was why Jack's team hadn't been able to pinpoint the Fifth Vertex. But Wolf had, either through good research, good contacts or prior secret knowledge.

And there it was, in the middle of the Indian Ocean: Diego Garcia.

On the way to the remote atoll, Jack had looked into its history. It was certainly intriguing.

Lying a thousand kilometres south of India, technically it is owned by Britain—although, like the Rosetta Stone and the Basin of Rameses, it was actually owned by Napoleon's France before the British seized it from the French in 1814.

In 1971, however, an eager British minister—perhaps unaware of the island's importance—allowed the atoll to be used as a military base by the US. It is still the launching point for all of America's military activities in the nearby Persian Gulf.

Its *other* activities, however, are highly classified.

What is known is this: Diego Garcia supports a standing squadron of B-2 Stealth Bombers; it is technically part of US Space Command; and perhaps most curiously of all: no family dependents of service personnel are allowed to live on the island. This is most unusual for an offshore US base.

For the last 37 years—and perhaps the 200 years before that—activity at Diego Garcia had taken place under the tightest of security, unobserved by the rest of the world.

Jack shook his head. *Napoleon, the British, and now America.* They had all known about Diego Garcia's importance for some time.

'Why am I always the last to know?' he said aloud as the *Halicarnassus* touched down on a long island-runway at the southern tip of Diego Garcia.

The big black 747 taxied to the end of the runway, coming to a halt between a pair of semi-trailer-sized MIM-104 Patriot missile launchers.

A motorcade of Humvees, jeeps and motorcycles was waiting for it, plus about thirty Army Rangers.

And there, standing at the head of this welcoming party, leaning lazily on the bonnet of the first Humvee in her hiking boots and cargo pants, was Miss Iolanthe Compton-Jones of the British Royal Family.

Jack emerged from the *Halicarnassus* with Lily close behind him and two Spetsnaz guards flanking him. They stepped cautiously down some airstairs onto the tarmac, where they were met by Iolanthe.

'Isn't it wonderful to be met at the airport?' Iolanthe said lightly. 'So nice to see you, Jack. I hear you might be single.' She winked suggestively.

Jack just glanced at the Army Rangers flanking the line of Humvees. They looked pissed as hell. Clearly Jack and Iolanthe were not welcome guests, but Wolf—no doubt unhappily—had made the call to allow them total access before being imprisoned completely in his tank.

Iolanthe guided Jack to the most senior American, a grey-haired three-star general. 'Captain Jack West Jr, this is Lieutenant-General Jackson T. Dyer, commander of the base here at Diego Garcia.'

'So this is Wolf's prodigal son,' Dyer said, assessing Jack. 'I've known your father a long time. He's a great patriot.'

'Are all you Caldwell Group guys "great patriots"?' Jack asked.

'Yes,' Dyer snorted. 'Yes, we are. Welcome to Garcia.'

Standing with the general was a hunched, bespectacled man Jack hadn't seen since Genghis Khan's Arsenal: Felix Bonaventura, Wolf's archaeology expert from MIT. Bonaventura's little black eyes peered at Jack through John Lennon glasses.

'This is Dr Bonaventura,' Iolanthe said. 'He's been based at Diego Garcia for many years now. He'll be taking us to see America's hidden jewel here.'

'The site is remarkable. Beyond anything you will have seen so far,' Bonaventura said.

'You'd be amazed at what I've seen,' Jack said.

General Dyer said, 'I have instructions to allow West, the girl and the woman inside, but those two Russian assholes are going to have to wait out here.'

'Fine by me,' Jack said. 'They're not travelling with me by choice.'

'That's okay,' Iolanthe said calmly. She spoke quickly to the Spetsnaz guards in Russian. They nodded obediently, although clearly not entirely comfortable with waiting on a US military airfield.

'You ready, then?' General Dyer said.

Iolanthe turned to Jack: 'I have the Firestone, the Basin and the springwater. Did you bring the Fifth Pillar?'

'I did.'

Iolanthe smiled. 'Then, yes, we're ready. After you, General.'

Leaving Sky Monster and the Spetsnaz guards with the *Halicarnassus*, Jack, Lily and Iolanthe were driven from the runway onto the atoll proper via a sweeping mile-long causeway not unlike those found in southern Florida.

In shape, Diego Garcia resembles a warped 'V'—with a sheltered lagoon in the middle and most of the main military facilities on the left-hand western arm of the V. Jack's motorcade joined the V at its base and zoomed up the right-hand arm.

After passing through several checkpoints, they arrived at a twelve-foot-high chain-link fence covered with opaque black material. Here their Ranger escorts were left behind, and only Jack, Lily, Iolanthe, Bonaventura and the general progressed.

It was 5:31 a.m.

They had two hours till the Fourth and Fifth Pillars had to be laid simultaneously.

Jack keyed his radio. 'Pooh Bear? You read me?'

A moment later, his earpiece crackled. '*Loud and clear, Huntsman.*'

'Are you in position?'

'*We're at the entrance to the Fourth Vertex! I'm entering it now with Stretch and the twins!*' Pooh Bear had to shout over the roar of his helicopter.

'We just arrived at the Fifth Vertex and are about to go in,' Jack said. 'Stay in voice contact because we have to plant these Pillars at exactly the same time, two hours from now.'

'*Good luck, Huntsman.*'

'Same to you.'

As he said this, Jack's Humvee emerged from the final check-point and Jack saw what lay beyond the high black fence.

A superlong hangar-like building stretched away from him. Apart from its size, it was actually a pretty simple structure: just a peaked tent-like roof mounted on steel supports, open to the air at the sides.

'Daddy?' Lily asked, confused.

'It's an awning,' Jack said, 'to conceal whatever's underneath it from satellite observation.'

Their car sped into the hangar-like tent and Jack and Lily got to see what lay beneath it.

'Wow . . .' Lily gasped.

An enormous rectangular pit yawned before them, completely covered by the massive temporary roof. It resembled an open-cut mine, at least seven storeys deep, with a broad earthen ramp running down into it.

Parked around the great pit were many eight-wheeled HEMTTs—Heavy Expanded Mobility Tactical Trucks, the workhorses of the US military. The size of a semi-trailer, a HEMTT is a versatile eight-wheel-drive that can be adapted for many uses: most of the HEMTTs here had been configured as dumptrucks and bore trays on their backs filled with earth. Others, however, towed mobile Patriot missile launchers. They guarded the rim of the pit.

At the far end of the pit—in total contrast to its tent-like roof and dirt walls—was a sparkling modern structure, a cube made entirely of glass that butted up against the northern wall of the pit.

An airlock, Jack realised.

As their Humvee zoomed down the earthen ramp into the pit, Jack discerned an object inside the glittering glass cube.

Built into the face of the brown earthen wall, not unlike the famous rock-cut buildings at Petra in Jordan, was a beautiful arched stone doorway.

LUNDY ISLAND

Pooh Bear, Stretch and the twins entered the Well, abseiling down its tight vertical shaft. Two of Iolanthe's Royal Marines accompanied them to make sure they did what they were supposed to.

Rain fell on them as they roped down the shaft. The harsh white spotlight of the chopper danced overhead.

After about a hundred feet they emerged in a wide tunnel that led downward at a gentle angle. Glowsticks were cracked, flares ignited. The four of them, plus their two armed Royal Marine guards, walked cautiously down the tunnel, before they came to an ornate arched doorway that opened onto a larger space.

'Whoa . . .' Julius breathed.

DIEGO GARCIA

Jack, Lily and Iolanthe were driven into the big glass cube at the end of the enormous pit.

The cube itself was three storeys tall, an airlock that could hold within its clear walls an entire semi-trailer rig.

Their Humvee stopped briefly at the towering ancient doorway cut into the dirt wall of the pit. It must have been sixty feet high. Hieroglyphs covered it. The circular symbol for the Machine was carved above its great stone doors.

Jack pulled out a printout of Genghis Khan's shield, and noted the image at the upper left corner:

It was the same door, perfectly replicated on the shield.

But it was far more impressive in real life: it was utterly huge and impossibly ancient. The dirt path passing through it was wide enough for HEMTTs to fit and easily big enough for their Humvee.

The Humvee drove through the massive ancient archway, looking positively tiny, then headed down a long sloping passageway beyond it, before it arrived at a larger space and stopped.

Jack, Lily and Iolanthe stepped out of the car, their jaws dropping.

'Whoa . . .' Lily said, just as Julius had done on the other side of the world.

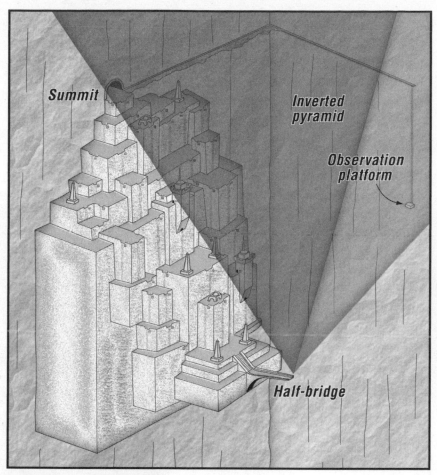

Summit

Inverted pyramid

Observation platform

Half-bridge

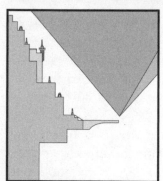

SIDE VIEW

THE 4TH VERTEX
LUNDY ISLAND, BRISTOL CHANNEL

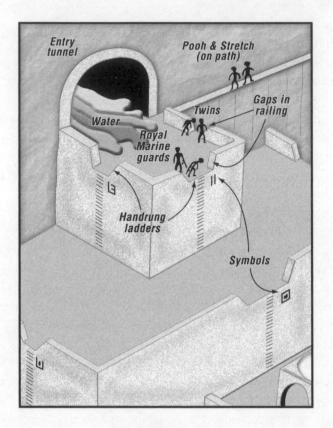

THE SUMMIT

LUNDY ISLAND (4TH VERTEX)

Pooh Bear, Stretch and the twins stood at the summit of a vast and complex box-like structure mounted on the wall of an enormous abyss.

Directly in front of the wall-mounted structure, dwarfing it, was the inverted bronze pyramid that was the Fourth Vertex.

But unlike the other Vertices so far—where a pyramid had been suspended above a narrower abyss, or where the abyss itself had been surrounded by a viewing hall or a model city or a lava lake—at this Vertex *the entire cavern* was the abyss, one giant four-sided shaft.

'This is beyond vertiginous,' Lachlan said, peering out at the bottomless darkness.

The box-like structure was a complicated tangle of interconnected towers, all clustered in a descending pattern one on top of each other, like a miniature *city* mounted on a wall, until at the very bottom of the irregular structure there appeared a long half-bridge of stone that stretched out to meet the peak of the inverted pyramid.

'What are these gaps?' Stretch nodded at some curious voids built into the waist-high stone walls on the summits of all the towers. They looked like open gates. Every rooftop bore at least one such void, while some, like their current one, bore as many as three.

Julius looked at the three gaps on their rooftop. 'There's a handrung ladder cut into the wall below each gap. It's a pathway down the structure, but you have to choose the correct ladder. The question is how?'

'Lily said the golden plaque from the First Vertex called this place "The City of Waterfalls",' Lachlan said. 'I don't see any waterfalls.'

'The plaque!' Julius said. 'That's where the answer is. Jack said the *frame* of that plaque contains clues to getting safely through each of the last four Vertices.'

While the other three hurried to check Julius's laptop for an image of the golden plaque, Pooh Bear stood on his own, gazing far to the left of their position, looking out at another odd feature of this already very odd place.

An ultra-narrow path led around two walls of the square-sided abyss, a quarter of the way around the pyramid itself, before arriving at a terrifying wall-ladder that led down to a tiny stone platform.

'What about that?' he said.

The twins looked up from the computer.

'Looks like an observation platform of some kind . . .' Julius offered absently.

'But to observe what?' Pooh Bear asked.

'Here's the plaque.' Julius brought it up on his screen:

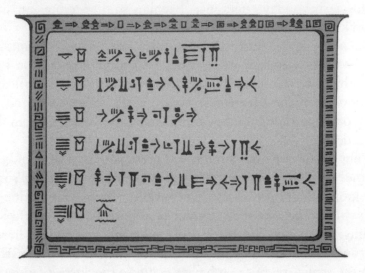

'Jack said the bottom edge of the frame solved the maze protecting the Third Vertex,' Julius said.

'So which edge solves this one?' Lachlan asked.

'Don't know—' Julius said.

'It's the left side,' Stretch said. Taking the laptop from Julius, he walked a short way out onto the ultra-narrow path and pointed back at the wall of their tower, just below the gap cut into its rail.

'There's a symbol cut into the wall beneath the gap,' he said. 'Three diagonal lines. Just like the symbol here, at the top of the left side of the plaque's frame.'

Pooh Bear joined him on the path and saw the carving. 'You're absolutely right, that must be the—'

A deep rumbling noise cut him off.

Everybody spun.

It had come from the tunnel through which they had entered the Vertex.

A sudden blast of wind hit them, rustling their clothes. It was closely followed by a fast-moving trickle of seawater that came sweeping round the final bend in the tunnel, bouncing against its outer wall.

'Something's coming down that tunnel . . .' Julius said softly.

'Run!' Pooh Bear called. 'Now!'

But the group was standing in three clearly defined sub-groups: Pooh Bear and Stretch out on the narrow path; the twins on the rooftop, near the gap in its rail, and the two Royal Marine guards a short distance further away.

'Which wa—' Lachlan began, but then he saw it.

A huge foaming body of seawater came rampaging around the bend in the tunnel. It roared as it moved—violent, charging, blasting. It would be on them in seconds. Not enough time for the twins to get to the safety of the path.

Lachlan froze.

'Lachie! This way!' Julius yanked his brother to the left side of the rooftop and pushed him over the gap on that side, where they found another wall-ladder cut into the tower's flank.

Following behind Lachlan, Julius ducked below the rim of the gap *just as* the surging torrent of seawater hit the rooftop, picked up the two Royal Marines within its surging mass and flung them like a pair of ragdolls into the stone rail ringing the rooftop.

The rest of the great body of water swirled on the summit rooftop, as if it were a living, thinking creature searching for a way down.

It found it in the *other* two gaps on the towertop, which were marginally lower than the left-hand one, and a moment later the two Royal Marines were swept over one of those gaps—looking like two small objects disappearing down a kitchen sink—dropping from view with matching horrified looks on their faces, doomed to die somewhere down below.

From his position on the narrow path, Pooh Bear saw it all happen. He also realised that he could never cross the fast-flowing stream of seawater now gushing out onto the rooftop.

Below him, the twins were clambering down their wall-ladder. In moments, the water would flow over the gap above them . . . and pour down on them hard.

Pooh Bear's eyes searched the space for an answer—and he found it in the form of the tiny platform over to the side.

'It's an observation platform . . .' he breathed. 'What does it observe? *It observes the correct path through this maze.*'

He snapped up.

'Boys!' he called into his radio. 'Wait on the next rooftop down! I understand this place now! We have to *guide* you through this maze from over there!' He pointed to the faraway platform.

'*What!*' Julius looked up at him from the rooftop fifty feet below.

Pooh Bear just threw him the Pillar, underhand.

Julius caught the priceless diamond brick on a reflex, surprised and shocked. He looked up. 'You want *us* to do this?'

'You *have* to do this! Now go!'

As they hustled down the narrow path, Stretch called to Pooh Bear: 'You can't be serious? The fate of the world depends on those two geekboys successfully navigating a rapidly flooding maze and planting that Pillar? Lachlan loses his breath walking to the cupboard to get a donut.'

'That's the way it is,' Pooh Bear said grimly, 'and the fate of the world depends on us helping them!'

A minute later, Pooh Bear and Stretch were out on the section of the narrow path that ran along the adjoining wall of the great abyss.

From here they could see more symbols carved into the walls of the towers—each symbol was positioned a short way below the gaps in each tower's waist-high stone guardrail. Wall-ladders were carved everywhere, giving anyone brave enough to challenge the maze a dizzying array of choices.

Pooh Bear raised some night-vision binoculars to his eyes. 'Stretch! What's the second symbol on the plaque?'

'Three horizontal lines, if you read it upward. A box with a single diagonal line if you read it downward.'

'I see two ladders that the boys can take, and the choices are three horizontal lines or three vertical lines. It reads upward.' Then, into his radio he yelled: 'Boys! Take the gap to the left, that's the safe one!'

On the exposed rooftop below the summit, the twins were awaiting instructions when a thick torrent of water came surging through the gap above them and gushed down on top of them with tremendous force.

Both of them were thrown off their feet, the water now pouring over the lip of the summit in a thick unbroken stream.

Instantly drenched, they struggled to their feet, sloshing in ankle-deep water. Now *this* rooftop was rapidly filling up.

Pooh Bear's voice called in their earpieces: '*Take the gap to the left, that's the safe one!*'

Julius plunged toward that gap, pushing his way through the churning seawater.

A quick glance behind him revealed that at least two spectacular waterfalls were now launching themselves off the summit of the vertical city. He assumed a third one was flowing off the other side, but it was out of his sight.

'See any waterfalls now?' he yelled to Lachlan.

'Mother of Mercy!' Lachlan shouted back. 'This is not the kind of study that I'm used to!'

'Move!'

Through the next gap they went, climbing down the wall-ladder below it, while the incoming seawater behind them rose and rose . . . until it flowed out through the *other* gaps in the stone guardrail as magnificent cascading waterfalls.

After a hasty dash, Pooh Bear and Stretch reached the observation platform.

From here they had a clear view of the entire collection of towers. It was a stunning sight—an enormous miniature city attached to the sheer cliff, suspended above the abyss; and now, adding to

the spectacle, it featured some glittering waterfalls tumbling over its uppermost levels.

More importantly, however, from here they could make out the series of symbols cut into the towers' sides that showed the safe path down through the maze.

From this angle Pooh and Stretch could only see two of the three sides of each tower, but that was enough. If they didn't see the symbol they were looking for, they assumed it was on the unsighted side and sent the twins that way.

It was 1:50 a.m.

They had forty-one minutes to get to the bottom of the maze.

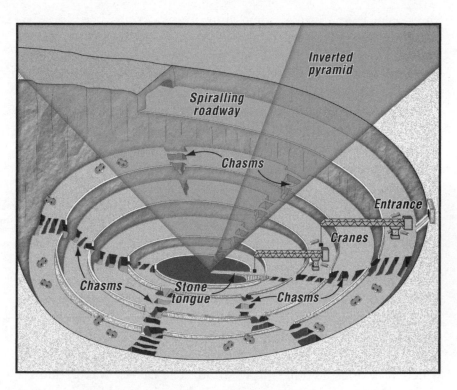

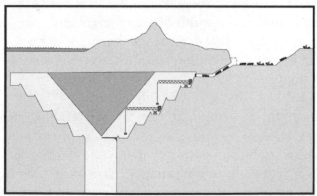

SIDE VIEW

THE 5TH VERTEX
DIEGO GARCIA, INDIAN OCEAN

DIEGO GARCIA (5TH VERTEX)

It was like standing in the back row of a football stadium, Jack thought.

The Fifth Vertex lay before him, and it was completely different from any of the Vertices he'd seen so far. Indeed, the only familiar thing about it was the immense bronze pyramid hanging over the gigantic underground space.

A huge bowl-shaped cavern dropped away from the archway in which Jack and the others now stood. The cavern was perhaps a thousand feet across and roughly circular in shape. A broad curving roadway—it was the width of a city street and guarded on the inner side by a seven-foot-high stone barrier—swept around the cavern in a smooth descending spiral that converged on the peak of the pyramid.

'It's shaped like a big seashell,' Lily gasped.

She was right, Jack thought. The great spiralling road began with a long straight section, like the horn of a seashell. Then it wound in on itself, plunging downward as it spiralled inward, the roadway gradually diminishing in size as it did so, until it reached the epicentre of the cavern, the peak of the pyramid, as a thin path.

The final feature of the cavern that caught Jack's eye was *not* part of the Vertex: over the years, the various owners of this island had been busy.

The spiralling roadway was strewn with vehicles and odd constructions.

Jeeps and motorcycles lay on their sides, rusted over; several large tracked bridging vehicles had been upturned near the entrance; and bizarrely, some horse-drawn cannons lay overturned further down the curving road.

The most prominent man-made additions to the space, however, were two very modern hammerhead construction cranes, enormous T-shaped cranes that had been erected at strategic points along the road: one near the entrance archway, another halfway down the spiralling road.

Both cranes were fitted with steel baskets that could hold several people. The baskets could then be drawn out along each crane's arm and lowered vertically to a lower level of the spiral.

The two cranes stood on solid concrete bases that were themselves guarded on the high side of the road by thick A-shaped concrete barriers.

The presence of the cranes and their curiously shaped protective barriers told Jack a lot.

'Let me guess,' he said. 'Every time you venture down that roadway, you trip some unseen mechanism and a gush of—I don't know—seawater floods down the roadway, sweeping away any person or vehicle in its path, until the water ultimately flows down into the abyss at the bottom.'

Bonaventura was surprised. 'How could you know—?'

'The overturned bridging vehicles are the first clue—only a big wave of water could knock over one of those brutes—but the concrete barriers protecting your cranes are a bigger clue. The A-shape of the barriers sends any oncoming wave *around* the crane. I just guessed it was seawater, since we're on an atoll in the middle of a fucking ocean, you dolt.'

'Swear jar,' Lily whispered.

Bonaventura took the insult in his stride. 'Those cranes have allowed us to make detailed observations of this site. Scans of the pyramid, of the ancient glyphs cut into its sides and the road.

I myself have spent countless hours in the basket of the lower crane inspecting the pyramid at close range. It's given us crucial information about the locations of the other Vertices and the nature of some of the rewards.'

'But it all counts for nothing without the Pillar,' Jack said. 'As the French and British found out before you.'

'The knowledge we found here enabled us to find a few things before *you*,' Bonaventura shot back.

Jack checked his watch.

It was 4:50 a.m.

They had forty-one minutes.

He keyed his radio. 'Pooh Bear? How're you doing up there?'

His earpiece crackled sharply before a hashing roar came through it, followed by Pooh Bear's shouting voice.

'*It's all happening here, Huntsman! Sorry! Can't talk! Gotta guide the twins through the maze! Will call you back!*'

The signal cut off.

Jack looked at Lily, then turned to General Dyer.

'I'm gonna need a motorbike.'

A military motorcycle was brought down the entry tunnel and handed over to Jack.

Jack straddled the bike. Lily jumped on behind him, riding pillion, gripping the double-cleansed Pillar.

Bonaventura was shocked. 'You're not going to use the cranes?' He looked to Iolanthe for support. 'But they're the safest way down . . .'

The first hammerhead crane was indeed level with them, its counterbalanced rear arm only a few feet away.

Jack shook his head. 'You just don't get it, do you? In a place like this, you can't cheat, you can't bypass the traps. Did it ever occur to you that the Vertex might *reward* the person who can figure out its trap system?'

'Well, I—'

Jack said, 'These trap systems are just like those of the Egyptians, the Chinese and the Maya: they're designed to keep the *unknowledgeable* out. Which means they're designed to allow the right people in. If you have the Pillar in your hands, this system will let you pass through it safely. But if you try to cheat it, it'll attack you.'

Bonaventura and General Dyer turned to Iolanthe, as if she were the ultimate judge.

She just shrugged. 'Let him do it his way. He knows what he's doing.'

'Thanks,' Jack said drily.

'You'll be dead before you reach the second ring,' Bonaventura snorted. 'And then we'll have to clean up what's left of you and plant the Pillar ourselves.'

'Then it's been nice knowing you,' Jack said, gunning the motor-bike and bouncing it down the short set of stairs that gave access to the roadway.

Then he hit the bottom of the stairway near the base of the crane, and swung left, zooming down the outermost ring of the deadly spiralling roadway.

A hundred yards into their journey, Jack and Lily came to a jagged chasm that sliced across the roadway.

Three stone bridges spanned it.

Two red crosses had been crudely spray-painted across the two outer bridges, while a green arrow indicated that the middle bridge was the safe one.

Jack, however, ignored the painted markings. Instead, he gazed at a smaller and far more ancient marking carved neatly into the stone bridge beneath the green-painted arrow:

'Plaque?' he asked Lily.

'Plaque.' Lily pulled out her digital camera and brought up the photo of the golden plaque from the First Vertex.

They both saw that along the top edge of the frame, the same symbol appeared as the first in a sequence:

Looking out over the stadium-like space, Jack counted several more chasms cutting across the spiralling road. Over each of the chasms were two or sometimes three bridges. As at Hokkaido, you had to choose the correct bridge or else you set off the trap mechanism.

He turned to Lily. 'What do you say, kiddo?'

'Let's kick some ass.'

'Couldn't have said it better myself.'

And so guided by the symbols depicted on their camera, they took off down the wide spiralling avenue, speeding toward the heart of the Fifth Vertex.

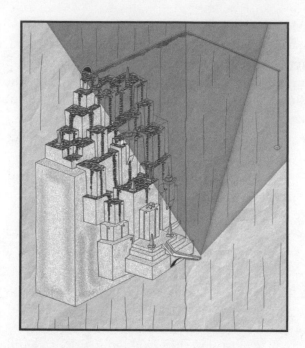

THE CITY OF WATERFALLS

LUNDY ISLAND (4TH VERTEX)

The silence at the Fifth Vertex could not have been more unlike the chaos at the Fourth.

From his position on the observation platform, Pooh Bear looked out at the miniature city mounted on the wall of the abyss.

By now, the entire upper half of the city was overflowing with waterfalls—dozens of them, all cascading in glorious vertical streams down the many levels of the structure, before they hit the next rooftop and separated, left or right or straight ahead, ever forced by gravity to search for the path of least resistance downward.

Pooh Bear was amazed. It looked like the world's biggest water feature.

And there, clambering down the wall-ladders cut into the

towers of the mini-city, running across rooftops, sloshing through knee-deep water, microscopic specks against the grandeur of the structure, were the two tiny figures of Lachlan and Julius Adamson running for their lives in a desperate race against the ravenous streams of water tumbling down the system above and behind them.

They were about halfway down the enormous structure and it was already 2:11 a.m.

It had taken them twenty minutes to get this far, and now they only had twenty minutes to get through the bottom half. It was going to be close.

'Go left!' Stretch yelled into his radio. 'No! Left! Left!'

Out on the rooftops, the twins spun, disoriented.

If they hadn't had Pooh Bear and Stretch to guide them, they would have got hopelessly lost by now and been swept to their deaths by the cascading torrents of water coming down behind them.

Instead, they were still in the game, only saturated and shivering, their red hair plastered flat against their scalps, rivulets of water running down their faces and off their chins.

Julius hurried to the left-hand gap in the guardrail of their current rooftop.

'*Yes! That one!*' Stretch's voice yelled over the radio.

Julius stopped at the precipice, turned.

Behind him, Lachlan was struggling. Although they were identical in looks—and in many tastes, hobbies and other things—they were not identical in fitness. Julius was far fitter than Lachlan. He ate better and sometimes he even joined Jack and Zoe on their morning runs. Lachlan ate a lot of junk food and did little exercise.

And now it was showing.

Lachlan was lagging behind, heaving for breath.

'*Boys! Look out—!*' they heard Pooh Bear shout.

With startling suddenness, a drenching waterfall came slamming down on top of the twins, engulfing them completely.

Both were hurled against the guardrail and Lachlan almost fell down the newly created waterfall beside it, but Julius threw out a hand and clutched his wrist at the last moment. He hauled him back to safety and they straggled over to the correct gap.

'Thanks, brother!' Lachlan shouted.

Julius didn't answer.

'You know, this may not be the right time, but I'm really sorry about Stacy Baker!'

Julius just said, 'Come on, we have to keep going!'

Down the side of that tower they went, clinging to the wall-ladder cut into its side.

DIEGO GARCIA (5TH VERTEX)

Jack and Lily zoomed round the enormous spiralling roadway of the Fifth Vertex on their motorbike.

As they rode, they swept past the remains of a variety of vehicles strewn across the road: evidence of the violence this trap system could unleash.

Using the symbols on the upper edge of the golden plaque, they'd successfully crossed five of the chasms cutting across the roadway without setting off the master trap.

It was 5:11 a.m. and, with twenty minutes to go, they'd barely made one full circle of the giant descending spiral. It was slow going. *Too slow,* Jack thought. *We need to get cracking.*

To this point, the green arrows and red Xs spray-painted onto the bridges had been correct; the result, Jack guessed, of deadly trial and error by his French, British and American predecessors over the years. He noticed, however, that the spray-painted advice ceased at the next chasm.

He and Lily came to it and stopped. Two bridges spanned this one.

While there were a couple of wrecks *in* this chasm, Jack suddenly noticed that there were no more vehicle-wrecks on the road *beyond* it. 'This is where all our predecessors lost their way. Until the Americans started using cranes, no-one ever got past here—'

Oddly, *neither* of the two symbols carved into the ground before this chasm's bridges matched the next symbol from the golden plaque. The next symbol on the plaque was:

whereas the two symbols on the ground were:

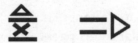

Suddenly, an ominous rumble echoed out from somewhere above him.

'Uh-oh . . .' Jack snapped to look up.

It had come from the uppermost section of the spiral, from the large tunnel up there.

'Oh, damn,' Jack said.

Bonaventura's voice came over the radio: '*You fool! You've set it off! The master trap is about to go off!*'

'We didn't set anything off,' Jack said. 'We didn't *do* anything.'

'That symbol looks like a pillar . . .' Lily said.

Jack was really worried now.

'We've missed something,' he said softly.

The rumbling from above grew louder.

'*I told you to use the cranes!*' Bonaventura was panicking.

But Jack wasn't.

He spun, looking back up the curving road behind them, his eyes searching—

—and he spotted something on the ground underneath an upturned 1930s British jeep back there.

He swung the motorbike around and gunned it back to the overturned jeep, where he jumped off, slid to the ground and peered at the roadway.

Carved into the stone roadway was the familiar image of the Machine:

And it was lifesized, its rectangular depictions of the Pillars were the same size as the Pillar in his pack. And while five of them were simple carvings, one was fully indented into the road.

Jack had seen this before, back at the First Vertex at Abu Simbel. He snatched the Pillar from his pack and jammed it into the indented rectangle in the carving.

The rumbling from above stopped instantly.

Silence enveloped the cavern once again.

'*You did it . . .*' Bonaventura said, amazed. '*No-one's got past there before.*'

'What can I say, we're specialists,' Jack replied. But in his mind, he was thinking about the advanced technology at work within this place: technology that worked in concert with the Pillar.

'Now the symbols on the golden plaque make much more sense,' Lily said.

"See, there's a Pillar-symbol every so often. At those times, we have to place the Pillar in a carving like this. Otherwise, the system's master trap goes off. No wonder no-one could get past this bridge. They would always set off the big trap.'

'Like I said,' Jack turned to her, 'you're not allowed to cheat in a place like this. If you can figure it out, the system lets you pass.

That's why it was built: to allow the knowledgeable to enter and keep the pretenders out.'

Armed with this knowledge, Jack and Lily made rapid progress through the lower half of the spiral.

Travelling in this way, they encountered no more difficulties and ten minutes later, arrived at the lowest and innermost ring.

Coming to that ring, they saw a long tongue of stone stretching out to the peak of the inverted pyramid. Cut into the ground near its starting point was one last carving of the Machine.

By Lily's count, they had used all but two of the symbols from the plaque. After they placed the Pillar in that carving of the Machine, there must be one more choice to make.

As Jack rounded the final ring, still twenty yards away from the tongue of stone, the basket from the second crane slowly lowered itself into view.

Felix Bonaventura and Iolanthe were in it, along with General Dyer.

Bonaventura was ecstatic. Stepping out of the basket onto the last few feet of the spiralling roadway, he opened his arms and smiled broadly. 'Well done! No-one's managed to tame this place the way you have!' He took a step onto the long tongue of stone leading to the pyramid's peak. 'Now all we have to do is—'

'No!' Jack skidded to a halt and leapt off the motorcycle. 'Wait! Not yet, stop—!'

But it was too late.

By virtue of its advanced sensory mechanism, the Vertex knew that someone had crossed that last carving of the Machine *without* the Pillar in their possession.

From the upper regions of the cavern, the ominous rumbling echoed again.

It sounded like thunder.

Jack snapped up, so did Lily and Iolanthe.

Both Bonaventura and General Dyer looked upward in horror,

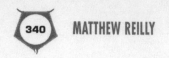

since they knew what this place looked like when its master trap went off.

'Dear me, no . . .' Bonaventura whispered a moment before the Vertex was plunged into absolute mayhem.

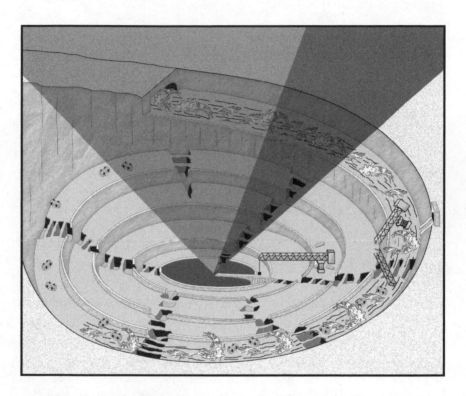

THE 5TH VERTEX'S MASTER TRAP GOES OFF

It came *exploding* out from the wide tunnel in the uppermost section of the spiral: a huge whitewater wave, seven feet high and sixty feet wide, taking up the full breadth of the roadway.

It thundered down the descending roadway, sweeping around its curve, bounded on the inside by the stone guardrail, galloping forward like a stampede of buffalos.

The rampaging wave blasted past the entry archway, shooting by it, before it smashed into the concrete barrier protecting the upper crane. Unexpectedly, the wave completely collected the barrier within its mass and hurled it into the crane itself, knocking the crane over!

As he watched the crane topple, Jack wondered if previous occurrences of the massive wave had been weaker. Perhaps, since this wave had been set off by a transgression at the very epicentre of the Vertex, it was bigger, stronger, more deadly.

Either way, Bonaventura's thick protective concrete barrier had been picked up by the wave as if it weighed nothing at all and the upper crane now tumbled along *within* the angry wave.

What followed was as spectacular as it was horrifying.

Jack turned on the spot as he watched the giant wave sweep around the perimeter of the cavern, roaring as it went. It wound quickly downward, a raging foaming river that sped down the descending curve of the spiral, bounding over the chasms as if they were minor inconveniences, charging angrily toward the intruders at the centre of the system.

'You stupid, stupid man!' he yelled at Bonaventura.

They were completely screwed.

When that wave hit the innermost ring of the spiral, it would bounce off a final wall and shoot out across the thin tongue of stone: sweeping away whoever happened to be standing on it at the time.

The second crane was an option, although not a great one, since the upper crane hadn't been able to withstand the rushing body of water.

Bonaventura and General Dyer figured it was better than nothing. Before Jack or Iolanthe could stop them, they scrambled back into the basket and started rising up the crane's vertical cable.

'Hey!' Iolanthe called.

But it didn't save them.

Moments later, the speeding wave slammed into the base of the second crane and ripped it off its mounting, causing the whole crane, still stretched out over the innermost ring, to lurch sickeningly and topple downward—into the abyss! Bonaventura and the general fell into the darkness, screaming, with the entire crane falling after them.

'No-one likes to see that,' Jack observed drily.

He checked his watch: 7:28 a.m.

They had to plant the Pillar at precisely 7:31 a.m. They had three minutes to go. But the rampaging river would be on them in less than one.

He keyed his radio. 'Pooh Bear! How you doing!'

'*The twins are almost at the Vertex! They're going to get there with about thirty seconds to spare! You?*'

'Things just got really nasty here.' The whitewater wave was past halfway now. 'We're at our Vertex, but waiting at the peak is gonna be a problem! Let me know when the twins are in position! We'll only get one shot at this!'

Jack turned to Lily and Iolanthe. 'This way.'

Gripping the Pillar in his hand, he led his two female companions out onto the tongue of stone, to the peak of the great bronze pyramid.

The descending wave was three-quarters of the way down the system now, galloping downward at frightening speed.

At the very end of the tongue of stone, Jack searched for

something, something he couldn't find, completely ignoring the stupendous pyramid two feet in front of him and the chaos all around him.

'What the hell are you looking for!' Iolanthe shouted.

'Lily, there's still one symbol on the plaque we haven't used yet, right?' he said.

'Yes.'

'You're sure?'

'I checked three times.'

Iolanthe saw the incoming wave sweep into the lowest ring of the spiral. It looked incredibly powerful and it was almost on them.

To her complete incomprehension, Jack wasn't even looking at it. He actually lay down on his belly and peered over the very end of the tongue of stone, looking at its *underside*.

'There it is!' he called triumphantly. He sprang up. 'Lily, Iolanthe, over the edge, now. There's a series of handrungs carved into the underside of this half-bridge and they lead to a pair of tunnels cut into the wall of the abyss: the last choice. Go!'

As the charging whitewater wave came round the final curve of the spiral, the three tiny figures of Lily, Iolanthe and Jack lowered themselves over the end of the long tongue of stone.

Then the deadly wave hit the wall at the bottom of the spiral and bounced out over the tongue of stone, spraying across it, all the way down its length, showering off its edges in a spectacular three-sided waterfall.

And there, hanging from the handrungs cut into the underside of the narrow stone tongue, dangling above the bottomless abyss, glistening curtains of water falling all around them, were Jack, Iolanthe and Lily.

LUNDY ISLAND (4TH VERTEX)

Julius Adamson's watch ticked over to 2:30 a.m. as he and Lachlan raced out onto an open forecourt at the base of the Fourth

Vertex's mini-city, passing between two obelisks before dashing down a flight of steps that gave access to this Vertex's half-bridge and pyramid.

The mini-city above and behind them was now literally teeming with waterfalls: a complex network of streams that twisted and turned, at some times diverging, at others converging, on their inexorable journey down the watercourse toward the forecourt that the twins had just crossed. Once the water hit that forecourt, there was no way back for the twins.

From their position on the spotting platform, Pooh Bear and Stretch had guided the twins expertly through the maze, always one step ahead of the water chasing them.

They now watched tensely as the two tiny figures of the twins raced out across the half-bridge at the base of the mini-city, arriving at the peak of the inverted pyramid.

Julius got there first, clutching the Pillar. Huffing and puffing, Lachlan peered back up at the waterfalls chasing them.

'We're here!' Julius yelled into his radio. 'How about you, Jack!'

His watch hit 2:31 a.m.

DIEGO GARCIA (5TH VERTEX)

Jack's watch beeped as it struck 7:31 a.m.

Clear curtains of free-flowing water continued to stream off the tongue of stone from which he hung. Beside him, Iolanthe had looped her belt over a handrung and strapped it round her right wrist to help her hang on. It was a smart move that Lily had copied.

Jack pursed his lips in thought.

There was only one way to do this, he figured, and that required doing something he wasn't so happy doing: trusting Iolanthe.

'I need your help!' he yelled. 'I have to swing up through that water curtain to plant the Pillar—but as soon as I lay the Pillar, the water's gonna take me down into the abyss. I need you to hold my belt and catch me!'

His eyes locked on hers. The beautiful British royal stared back at him with her mesmerising green eyes, water dripping down her face. She was inscrutable. She gave nothing away. He couldn't tell if she would help him or not.

'Okay!' she yelled back.

'Right . . .' Jack said, unsure, but with no other choice. He needed an adult to hold him. Lily wasn't strong enough.

He shuffled to the very end of the stone tongue, directly underneath the pyramid's peak.

Into his radio: 'Okay, Julius! On my mark! In three—'

He glanced at Lily and wondered if this would be the last time he saw her.

'—two—'

LUNDY ISLAND (4TH VERTEX)

Julius brought his Pillar up to within an inch of the peak of his pyramid. Behind him, the roar of the many waterfalls was deafening.

'—one—mark!'

Julius jammed the Pillar into its matching slot in the pyramid.

DIEGO GARCIA (5TH VERTEX)

With a heave that took all his strength, Jack swung himself up through the curtain of water flowing over the tongue of stone above him.

He burst up through the flowing stream, water slamming into his face, opened his eyes and saw the peak of the pyramid right above him. He reached out and thrust his Pillar up into the pyramid's peak.

The Pillar locked into place and Jack released his grip on it—and just as he'd anticipated, he was instantly hurled by the flowing water over the edge and thrown down into the abyss . . .

. . . where Iolanthe caught him!

She was hanging by one hand from her belt, still looped over a handrung, while gripping his waistband with the other.

She could easily have let him fall—and given their rival sides in this quest, could well have been expected to.

But to Jack's surprise she hadn't.

She'd saved his life.

He climbed up her body and grabbed hold of a handrung, just as the Vertex came to life.

A blazing white beam of light shot like a laser down from the peak of the inverted pyramid into the dark abyss beneath them, illuminating the depths of the great shaft, disappearing into infinity.

LUNDY ISLAND (4TH VERTEX)

A similar event was happening at the Fourth Vertex.

Julius and Lachlan Adamson stood in stunned awed as the inverted pyramid at their Vertex loosed its own blinding white beam into the abyss beneath their half-bridge. The great pyramid thrummed loudly as the entire cavern was lit up by the harsh white light.

'Good God!' Julius shouted.

Then abruptly, the mighty shaft of light vanished, plunging the wide abyss back into the pale light of their glowsticks and flares.

The Pillar pulsed in the pyramid's peak, crystal clear, white Thoth glyphs appearing on its sides, glyphs that described its reward, *life*, in detail.

Julius reached out and grabbed it, and the glass-like Pillar came away from the peak, leaving a small pyramidal part of itself there.

'Julius! We have to go!' Lachlan called, eyeing the still-falling series of waterfalls gaining on them.

'Right!' Julius started running.

Guided once again by Pooh Bear and Stretch, they struggled back up the mini-city, following a winding vertical path through the labyrinthine watercourse.

Like Jack, Pooh and Stretch had counted the symbols they'd used to this point: to get to the pyramid, they'd used exactly half the symbols. It was Stretch who'd realised that the remaining symbols provided the safe path *back up* through the mini-city.

Streams of water still flowed off every towertop but on a select few it was shallow and had formed into gentle swirling pools—this was the safe way up.

At one point, the exhausted Lachlan, trudging against the knee-deep flow, lost his footing and was swept backwards, toward the brink of a large fall. Diving back, Julius managed to grab his arm and pull him back to his feet.

But Lachlan had lost it. Lost the will. 'Go, Julius! Get out of here! Don't let me slow you down!'

'Shut up, Lachie . . .'

'I'm sorry, Julius!' Lachlan called. 'I'm sorry I can't keep up! I just can't! And I'm sorry about Stacy Baker, too!'

In the endless spray of the waterfalls, the two brothers stood there, facing each other, wondering what to do.

Some time later, Pooh Bear and Stretch were standing again on the summit of the miniature city, waiting tensely.

At length, Julius's hand appeared above the edge of their tower and he hauled himself over the rim, soaking and breathless.

There was no immediate sign of Lachlan, and Pooh Bear gasped.

Then he saw him. Draped over Julius's back, clinging to him piggyback-style.

Julius had *carried* Lachlan up the last half of the journey.

The two young men rolled to the ground, sucking in air. Pooh and Stretch rushed to their side.

Stretch bent to help Julius, grabbing Lachlan's other arm. 'Here, let me help, he must be heavy.'

Julius smiled grimly, his face dripping with water. 'He's not heavy, he's my brother.'

DIEGO GARCIA (5TH VERTEX)

At the Fifth Vertex, the water kept flowing down the spiral road-way, but after a few minutes it began to lose its intensity and diminished to a trickle.

When the flow was weak enough, Jack again hoisted himself above the water-curtain and snatched the Pillar from the pyramid's peak, then swung back down to his handrung on the underside of the stone tongue. Like the Pillar at Lundy Island, this Pillar now glowed with lines of ancient white text: text that outlined its reward, *death*.

'What now?' Iolanthe asked.

'Well—' Jack began.

'*Captain West!*' a voice over a megaphone called from some-where above them. '*We have just received some new orders . . . from your father. He has informed the entire force here at Diego Garcia that after successfully laying the Pillar, you and the royal are not to be permitted to leave this island alive. The entire American garrison at Diego Garcia has been ordered to kill you.*'

Out on Diego Garcia's southern runway, Sky Monster saw clear evidence of his hosts' change of heart almost immediately.

Six fearsome Avenger-class Humvees came rushing across the causeway, speeding toward the island airstrip. Each Avenger was equipped with two upwardly-pointed pods containing four Stinger surface-to-air missiles. That meant eight missiles per car, forty-eight missiles in total.

A dozen Army Rangers started running on foot toward the 747 from the airstrip's tower, while five pilots in full flight-gear hustled across the runway toward some F-15 Eagle fighter jets.

The timing of all this wasn't lost on Sky Monster. The time for laying the Pillar had just passed. Jack must have set it in place and now the bad guys were doing what bad guys did: fucking you over after you saved their asses.

Diego Garcia had just declared war on Jack and his team.

Closing the exterior door and running for the cockpit—with no objection from his two Spetsnaz minders—Sky Monster decided to declare war right back at them.

Inside the Vertex, Jack, Lily and Iolanthe were still hanging from the stone tongue.

'We can't go out the way we came in,' Jack said. He jerked his chin at the pair of square stone holes at the end of their line of handrungs. 'We make the last choice and see where it takes us.'

The left-hand hole was the correct one and it led into a long upwardly-sloping tunnel that wound higher and higher until it ended abruptly at a dead-end made of a single sandstone block.

As they arrived at the dead-end, Sky Monster's voice came through Jack's earpiece: '*Huntsman! You still alive down there? I just came under attack on the runway and had to take off and launch about a billion countermeasures! It's pandemonium up here!*'

Explosions boomed in the background.

'Can you touch down at all to pick us up?'

'*Er, negative.*'

'What about an aerial option? Is that available?'

'*I can do that. Near the runway's hangar. Hurry, Jack. I can hold them off for another ten, maybe fifteen minutes. After that I'll be a sitting duck up here.*'

'We'll get there as fast as we can. Thanks, Monster.'

★ ★ ★

Outside, explosions boomed and columns of smoke rose as the *Halicarnassus* banked in the sky above the island runway, unleashing tracer bullets and dropping incendiary bombs on the airstrip below.

Sky Monster's first wave had taken out the two Patriot missile launchers at the end of the runway; his second had created deep craters in the runway that prevented the launching of the F-15s.

Stinger missiles lanced into the sky from the Avengers on the ground, but the *Hali*'s electromagnetic countermeasures were way too good for them and they just veered wildly away before ditching into the sea.

The F-15 fighters themselves were Sky Monster's next target. Although they couldn't take off now, they might later—and Sky Monster was just pissed off—so he nailed the first three on the short taxiway outside their hangar, hitting them in their forewheels, so that they crumpled nose-down onto the taxiway, their broken carcasses blocking the way of the two unhit fighters.

He swung in a wide circle over the V-shaped atoll and loosed another pair of missiles at Diego Garcia's main runway on the western arm. High-spraying explosions of asphalt and dirt rose into the air. That runway wouldn't be launching anything either.

'You want a war!' Sky Monster shouted. 'I'll give you a mother-fucking war!!!'

Shwack!

The blast from Jack's C-2 plastic explosive was short and sharp and it cracked the thick sandstone brick blocking their way.

The brick crumbled and Jack threw its pieces behind him, creating a small hole—

—only to see the wheels of a huge HEMTT truck rumble by right in front of his nose.

Enlarging the gap, Jack discovered that they had arrived back at the entry tunnel leading to the spiral cavern; the brick he'd just blasted was part of the tunnel's sandstone wall.

The tunnel was dimly lit and as he pulled the crumbling pieces of the brick away, making the gap wide enough to fit through, Jack saw several Humvees speed by, heading for the Vertex, their headlights bouncing in the darkness.

Heading in the other direction, however, were some of the earth-filled HEMTT dumptrucks Jack had seen on the way in. They were getting them out of the way of the incoming troops.

'Quickly!' Jack whispered to Lily and Iolanthe. 'This way!'

Moments later, one of the fleeing HEMTT dumptrucks emerged from the tent-covered pit into bright daylight, swerving to avoid a bunch of Humvees rushing into the pit complex.

No-one saw the three figures clinging to its underside. Nor did they see them leap into the cab of a HEMTT towing a Patriot missile launcher, immobilise the driver, and rumble off in the direction of the strife-torn southern runway.

Jack's HEMTT sped across the long causeway that gave access to the island runway. Smaller jeeps carrying armed troops overtook it, heading for the battle there.

Jack knew exactly where he was going: the hangar that had housed the base's F-15s. Only he didn't enter it from the front.

Instead, his giant truck blasted through the flimsy rear wall of the hangar, smashing through it and skittling a couple of FA-18 fighters as if they were toys, before Jack brought the big truck to a skidding halt beside one of the semi-destroyed F-15s on the taxiway in front of the hangar.

Of course, the fighter's pilot had long since abandoned the broken jet, its nose tilted down over its destroyed forward landing gear.

'Into the cockpit!' Jack pulled Lily with him, Iolanthe running along behind them. Into his radio: 'Sky Monster! Aerial pick-up! On the next pass! Give us thirty seconds!'

'*You got it, Jack!*' The *Halicarnassus* swept round in a wide arc until it was flying directly toward the taxiway.

Jack clambered into the cockpit of the damaged fighter.

Iolanthe hesitated. 'What are you doing! This thing isn't going to fly!'

Jack hoisted Lily onto his lap and started checking the cockpit. 'It's not but we are. Now you can come or you can stay.'

Iolanthe bit her lip, and decided that whatever Jack West Jr was planning was better than staying at Diego Garcia.

'Where do I sit?'

'On my lap, with Lily in between us and the seatbelt around all three of us.'

Iolanthe did as she was told. She now sat facing Jack, on his lap, with Lily snuggled between them. Jack clicked the seatbelt around them all.

'Is this plan as crazy as I think it is?' Lily asked him softly.

'Pretty much.' Jack looked up at the sky.

Iolanthe saw this and suddenly she got it. 'Oh, you can't be serious—'

'Hang on, princess.'

And with those words, Jack yanked on the F-15's ejection cords.

Whoosh!

The ejection seat of the F-15 rocketed into the sky above the island runway, bearing Jack, Lily and Iolanthe on it.

It shot a full two hundred feet into the air before a parachute blossomed above it and the seat itself fell away, leaving the three of them dangling awkwardly from the chute.

Normally, with such extra weight, the chute wouldn't have been able to hold them for long—but today it didn't have to.

For, a second later, the *Halicarnassus* came roaring by, trailing a long hook from its open rear hold. Designed for snagging weather balloons, Wizard had reconfigured it using the arresting hook from an old F-14 Tomcat. It was kept for occasions just like this: for a hot extraction where no landing was possible.

The hook snagged Jack's parachute perfectly and swept it forward, pulling it along behind the low-flying 747, the arresting hook's elasticised cable taking the brunt of the massive whiplash.

Then the *Halicarnassus* was out of there, a tiny speck soaring off into the lightening sky dragging the parachute behind it, speeding away from the American base at Diego Garcia and the ancient Vertex concealed beneath it.

LUNDY ISLAND (4TH VERTEX)

At length, Pooh Bear, Stretch and the twins emerged from the Fourth Vertex, resigned to being picked up by their Royal Marine helicopter outside.

The four of them climbed out of the Well, stepping up into the rain. Waves crashed all around them.

They signalled to the Royal Marine chopper and held up the charged Pillar, and saw the chopper's co-pilot say something into his radio.

Then the chopper exploded. Suddenly. Unexpectedly. It just burst apart in a billowing ball of flames.

The night sky flared with orange light and the Royal Marine chopper fell into the sea, a flaming smoking wreck—in doing so, revealing *another* helicopter in the sky far behind it.

'What the hell—?' Stretch shouted.

This new helicopter came closer and as he saw it clearly, Pooh sighed with relief: it bore the markings of the Irish Army. It was friendly.

Indeed, sitting in its co-pilot's seat, smiling at them, was their Irish liaison officer, Captain Cieran Kincaid.

CARNIVORE'S LAIR
FAR EASTERN RUSSIA
18 MARCH, 2008, 1133 HOURS LOCAL TIME
(0233 HOURS GMT)
MINUTES AFTER THE 4TH AND 5TH DEADLINES

As soon as he was certain that the Fourth and Fifth Pillars had been laid at their respective Vertices, Carnivore gave the order.

His small personal force of Spetsnaz guards had been busy these last thirty-six hours.

Key equipment had already been gathered and taken on board Carnivore's private jet—a sleek black Tupolev-144. With its delta shape, long slim body and distinctive downturned nose, the Tu-144 looked like the long-lost twin of the famous Aerospatiale Concorde. Indeed, like the Concorde, it was capable of supersonic cruise.

Under Diane Cassidy's direction, all manner of documents, computers and astronomical charts—all of Carnivore's research on the Machine—had been brought onboard the Tu-144.

Then the calls came in: from the Royal Marines hovering in their chopper above Lundy Island and from Diego Garcia. The Pillars had been laid successfully.

It was time to go.

Carnivore was abandoning his lair.

As his men departed, the wily old Russian royal stood for one last time in front of his grisly collection of human trophies encased in their liquid tombs. Diane Cassidy stood by his side.

Carnivore gazed at the formidable Wolf; at the younger soldiers, Zoe and Astro; at Anzar al Abbas, the proud sheik from Dubai; at the Neetha warlock; and last of all, at the very end of the line of tanks, at the little figure of Alby Calvin, the friend of the Oracle, beside his mother.

Carnivore smiled philosophically.

It was a shame to leave behind such a fine collection.

He pressed an intercom button connected to speakers inside all the tanks.

'My guests. Sadly, the time has come for me to leave. I thank you all for the pleasure you have given me—in the cases of some of you, for many years. This base is being abandoned. The consequence for all of you is unfortunately somewhat dire. With no-one manning this base, there will be no-one to replenish the oxygen tanks connected to your mouthpieces. At a guess, I imagine you have about 72 hours of air left, longer if you can breathe shallowly. Goodbye.'

The responses from his captives were varied: Abbas shouted soundlessly; Zoe looked up sharply; Astro just bowed his head wearily; and Alby's eyes boggled. Wolf did nothing but stare evenly back at Carnivore.

'May I?' Diane asked.

'If it will make you feel better,' Carnivore said.

'Oh, it will.' Diane stepped forward and stood before the Neetha warlock's tank. She knocked on the front window and the old man looked up. 'Hey! My return gift for the years of slavery in your tribe.'

Then with a firm hand Diane turned a valve and shut off his oxygen supply. The old man coughed once before he started convulsing violently, gagging, unable to breathe. After a few moments of this, he became still, hovering in the haze, dead.

'Much better.' Diane strode past Carnivore and headed outside.

A few seconds later, Carnivore followed her, sweeping out of his observatory and taking off in his plane, leaving the isolated base behind him, its location known only to a privileged few, its living decorations left there to die.

Nine minutes after Carnivore's departure, the observatory was silent and still.

The massive telescope sat on its mounting, pointed toward the sky. The only movement: the rising bubbles in the tanks lining the walls.

Then abruptly one of the tanks shattered, and stinking green liquid came gushing out of it, washing across the porcelain floor.

It was Wolf's tank.

Inside the shattered, now-empty tank, Wolf hung from his manacles, covered from head to toe in a layer of green fluid, *only now his left hand was hanging free*. He immediately used it to yank off his half-face scuba mask, before he sucked in deep gasps of fresh clean air.

It had taken an incredible effort in patience and concentration to get to this point.

If one looked closely, one would have seen that the false top on Wolf's Annapolis graduation ring had been popped open—a ring that contained a small amount of C-2 plastic explosive. Jack West Jr and Pooh Bear weren't the only soldiers in the world who carried escape gear on their persons.

First, Wolf had very carefully used the fingers of his manacled left hand to pop open the ring and use some of the plastique in it to crack open his left manacle. Then, when that hand was free, he stuck some C-2 to the front wall of his tank and shattered it.

Dripping with green wetness, Wolf slowly unclasped the other three manacles gripping his limbs and dropped to the floor of the empty tank and stood on his own two feet.

Now came the painful part: removing the excretion catheter from his own body. Wolf grabbed the scuba facemask and, biting down hard on its rubber edges, set about the grim task. It took three shockingly painful yanks—he almost fainted with the last one—but he got it out.

A moment later, staggering a little but okay, Jack West Sr stepped down from the semi-destroyed tank.

Free.

For a moment Wolf pondered the other tanks—as the occupants of those tanks stared incredulously back at him. Zoe screamed and shook her bonds, begging him to set her free. Astro also looked up, waiting to see if Wolf would help him.

Wolf didn't set any of them free.

He went over to the radio console on the wall and called his people for a pick-up. He also radioed Diego Garcia and ordered the force there not to let Jack and Iolanthe leave the island alive. After that, he found a shower room in a nearby building and some clothes and cleaned himself up.

Then Wolf returned to the observatory, pulled up a chair and, gazing at the green tanks and the captives within them, waited for his extraction team.

It arrived a few hours later in the form of a pair of F-15s. And then just like Carnivore before him, Wolf left the remote observatory without a word, leaving the other prisoners there to slowly run out of air.

SIXTH BATTLE

THE TOMB OF THE CHRIST

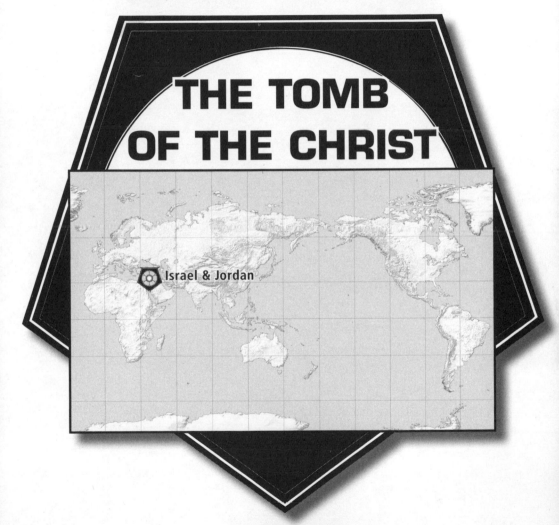

Israel & Jordan

**THE DEAD SEA
ISRAEL–JORDAN BORDER**
18 MARCH, 2008
2 DAYS BEFORE THE FINAL DEADLINE

MILITARY AIRBASE, DUBAI
UNITED ARAB EMIRATES
18 MARCH, 2008, 2200 HOURS

The *Halicarnassus* stood parked on a runway in a remote corner of the U.A.E., a black shadow against the night-time horizon.

Jack sat in his office at the back of the plane, lit by a single lamp, bent over his desk. An array of books, notes and maps lay strewn on the table in front of him. Horus was perched loyally on his chairback, ever watchful, while Lily lay on the floor behind him, fast asleep. One of his two Spetsnaz minders stood guard at the door while the other slept in a bunkroom. Iolanthe was taking a shower in the crew quarters.

Jack was gazing at the James Letter that the twins had found earlier, which purported to reveal the final resting place of Jesus Christ:

> *He lies in peace,*
> *In a place where even the mighty Romans fear to tread.*
> *In a kingdom of white*
> *He does not grow old.*
> *His wisdom lies with him still,*
> *Protected by a twin who meets all thieves first.*

Jack was pondering what it meant when Pooh Bear and the others came in over the videolink.

Jack told them what had happened at Diego Garcia and Pooh

informed him about their mission at Lundy Island, including how Cieran Kincaid had rescued them on the way out. Pooh, Stretch, the twins and Cieran were now in Dublin at a friendly army base with the charged Fourth Pillar in their possession.

'What do we do now?' Pooh Bear asked.

Jack cast a glance at his Spetsnaz guard who showed no outward sign that he understood English.

'I don't see that we have a choice,' he said. 'We have to go for the Sixth Pillar. Carnivore sent Vulture, Scimitar and Mao to get it for him, but we can't allow any of them to find it and lay it. We have to get it first.'

'Which only requires us to find the lost tomb of Jesus Christ . . .' Julius said.

'I'm aware of that.' Jack indicated the mess of books and notes around him.

Cieran Kincaid appeared on the screen beside Pooh Bear. 'Jack . . .'

'Yes, Cieran.' Jack could see what was coming.

'Jack, Jesus Christ rose from the dead and ascended bodily to heaven. This is beyond a question of faith. It is accepted fact. There is no tomb.'

'Cieran, I thank you for saving my guys, but I'm sorry, I can't agree with you. I've seen enough crazy stuff in my travels to say that where religion is concerned, there are no facts, only beliefs. You can believe whatever you want. In the meantime, I'm going to search for that tomb.'

'Crunch time's coming and we're further behind our adversaries than usual, Jack,' Stretch said seriously. 'We have two days to lay that Pillar at the final Vertex and we don't know where either the Pillar *or* the Vertex is.'

'I know, I know,' Jack said. 'But where there's life, there's hope.'

'So this is our plan?' Lachlan said. 'This is it?'

'This is all I've got,' Jack said wearily. 'Just hit the books and help me out. I'll call you if I find something.'

He clicked off, sighed, and went back to work.

★ ★ ★

A few minutes later, Iolanthe appeared in the doorway, freshly showered and now dressed in shorts and a close-fitting white singlet that accentuated her sleek physique. Her usually tied-back hair hung loose around her bare shoulders. She placed a coffee mug on Jack's desk.

'You seriously think you can find the Jesus Pillar?' she asked.

Jack looked up at her. 'I can't let your Russian cousin get that Pillar and plant it at the final Vertex. I have to find it first.'

Iolanthe leaned against the door, eyeing him closely. 'If you find it, I'll have to inform Carnivore. So will they,' she nodded at the guard by the door. 'We *are* here to keep an eye on you, after all.'

'You don't *have* to tell him,' Jack said softly.

Iolanthe smiled, shaking her head. Then she stepped into the room and closed the door behind her, leaving the guard outside. 'You really are something, you know that?'

'I do what I think is right.'

'But you just keep doing it. You never stop. You're the most determined man I've ever met.'

'It's a gift—'

'It's why your people follow you. And,' she stepped closer, whispering, 'it could be why I might be convinced to follow you, too. I suppose I could be *persuaded* not to tell Carnivore . . .'

Jack stopped what he was doing.

'You'd betray the royal families?' he said.

'Like all families, our members have their differences and their petty schemes. Carnivore is the most senior member of the European royals, but some in Britain think him too ruthless, too . . . unseemly. His blood might be blue, but his methods are crude.'

'And what do you think?'

'I think Carnivore looks out for Carnivore. I think I've given my royal relatives far more than they have ever given me.' She licked her lips. 'I think I deserve some reward for my efforts. My family *expects* my loyalty, whereas you *win* people's loyalty. You impress me time and again, and that tends to win a girl over . . .'

She stepped behind Jack, moving smoothly and quietly, leaned over him to look at his notes. He could feel her breasts pressing gently against his shoulder. Her long hair smelled wet; her beautifully scented skin was soft, feminine.

'You saved my life in that Vertex,' he said, not looking at her. 'I wasn't sure you would.'

'Like I said, you inspired me in a way I've not been inspired before.'

Jack said nothing.

Iolanthe looked at him. 'I was sorry to hear about Miss Kissane's betrayal of you. I didn't know about that.'

'Neither did I.' Jack still didn't look her in the eye.

When Iolanthe spoke again, her voice was a whisper, spoken directly into Jack's left ear from millimetres away.

'A girl would have to be crazy to see another man behind your back, Jack West. You're all I'd need.'

Jack swallowed. He looked straight ahead, a flurry of thoughts and images swirling in his mind: of Zoe back at his farm, covered in dust; of Iolanthe here, beautiful and sweet-smelling and pressed against his shoulder in her tight little singlet, practically offering herself to him; the image of Carnivore informing him about Zoe sleeping with another man, and Zoe in her tank, bowing her head in admission.

He turned to answer her—

—only to abruptly feel Iolanthe's lips press against his own. She was kissing him, smoothly, sensuously, with genuine passion.

Jack didn't move. He closed his eyes as he let her kiss him. The touch of her lips was simply electrifying.

Jesus . . .

Iolanthe pulled away slowly, looked him in the eye.

'We needn't be on different sides in all this, Jack. But even if we are, it shouldn't mean we can't enjoy each other. I'm going to my bunkroom now, where I'm going to slip out of these clothes and sleep naked for the first time in days. I'd very much like it if you joined me . . .'

Then she kissed his ear and left the office.

Jack sat face-forward, frozen.

Then he blinked out of it, exhaled, and looked at Horus. The falcon squawked.

'Tell me about it,' he said, before resuming his work.

He never went to her bunkroom.

A few hours later, Lily awoke. Jack was still at his desk, making markings on a map of some sort.

'Hey,' she said sleepily.

'Hey, kiddo.'

'What are you doing?'

'Trying to find in one day what men have been seeking for centuries: the tomb of Jesus Christ.'

'Any luck?'

Jack shrugged. 'Maybe some.'

He showed her the ancient map in front of him. It was a map of Asia Minor: Israel, Palestine, Jordan, Syria and Turkey.

'The twins did a lot of research on Jesus,' he said. 'They canvassed all the myths about what happened to him after the crucifixion. The most persistent theory is that Jesus lived out his days at Masada, while others suggest he headed east, ending up in the Kashmir region of India.'

'I can see a "but" coming,' Lily said.

'But they're just theories. There's no actual proof of either. What I need is a new angle,' Jack said. 'Everybody who's looked for the tomb of Jesus has tried to follow the trail of Jesus himself, which eventually peters out into myth and legend. I think we need to follow *somebody else's* trail, someone who knew Jesus, and I think I just found out who.'

'Who?'

Jack pointed to another sheet on his desk, one Lily had seen before. 'His brother, James.'

Lily looked at the sheet:

Jerusalem	Dibon
Ephraim	Medeba
Jericho	Rabbath Ammon
Gilgal	Damascus
Masada	Aleppo
Ein Gedi	Diyar Bakir
Ein Bokek	Erzurum
Mountain of Sodom	Mountain of Ararat
Ein Aradhim	Yerevan
Kir Moab	Van
Aroer	

'This is the detailed description of James's epic journey from Judea to the Fortress of Van that the twins found earlier,' Jack said. 'It's the journey James made with two of the Pillars in his possession.'

'Okay . . .'

'Well, something about this list always bothered me. Something about it wasn't right. Now I know.'

'What was it?'

'I found this old map of Asia Minor and I plotted James's course on it. Take a look.'

Jack turned the map so Lily could see it:

'See it?' Jack asked.

Lily did.

James had not taken the most direct route from Jerusalem to Van. He'd made a gigantic detour to the south before heading north-east, going almost completely around the Dead Sea. As a list of town-names, the detour wasn't readily apparent, but once you plotted them on a map, it was glaringly obvious.

Jack said, 'James didn't go straight from Jerusalem to the Fortress at Van. He took a big detour to the south, passing through Masada, some desert springs known as Ein Gedi and Ein Bokek— before he came to Mount Sodom and a spring near it, Ein Aradhim. Only then did he resume his trip north-east, going quickly and directly to Van.'

'So what are you thinking?' Lily asked.

'I'm thinking that before he ventured off into exile for the rest of his life, James visited his brother's tomb first. But it wasn't at Masada. James went well beyond Masada.' Jack pointed at the lowest point of James's journey. 'Lily, I think Jesus's tomb is somewhere here, down at the southern tip of the Dead Sea, near the Ein Aradhim spring at the base of the Mount Sodom salt hills.'

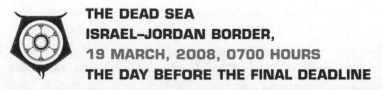

THE DEAD SEA
ISRAEL–JORDAN BORDER,
19 MARCH, 2008, 0700 HOURS
THE DAY BEFORE THE FINAL DEADLINE

The Dead Sea is the lowest point on Earth. It lies a full 400 metres below sea level. It is known mainly for its extreme salinity—a white crust of salt crystallises at its edges. It is also shrinking, due to constant evaporation, losing approximately fifty metres of width every year. True to its name, the Dead Sea is indeed dying.

At the extreme southern end of the sea one will find Mount Sodom, a collection of jagged snow-white spires made of pure salt, sodium chloride. Many ancient salt mines, long abandoned, delve into its base.

'Salt was hugely important in ancient times,' Jack explained to Lily as the *Halicarnassus* rolled to a stop on an empty stretch of desert highway on the Jordanian side of the salt hills. 'Roman soldiers were often paid in salt. Before refrigeration, it was used to preserve meat. The Romans mined it everywhere they ruled: from Germania to Judea.'

They drove out of the hold of the *Hali* in a jeep they'd grabbed in the Emirates. Iolanthe went with them, apparently totally unconcerned that Jack had not taken her up on her offer the night before. Their two Spetsnaz guards—whom Lily had christened Ding and Dong—remained with Sky Monster at the *Halicarnassus*, correctly gauging that the plane was the only way Jack could escape from this place.

Bizarre white hills rose before them, looking more like high snow-mounds than desert hills. The Dead Sea stretched northward, low and flat, glinting in the dawn.

'And salt mines make for excellent tombs,' Jack added, 'because salt crystals seal doorways, keeping oxygen out and thus perfectly preserving anything inside.'

Up the hill from the *Halicarnassus*, they came to a modest fresh-water spring, the Ein Aradhim, the seemingly unnecessary stop James had made on his way to Van.

It was little more than a small bubbling pool that ran in a pathetic trickle in the direction of the inland sea; the trickle was so weak, its water flow evaporated before it reached the Dead Sea.

Cut into a salt mountain near the spring, however, was the entrance to a long-abandoned mine.

The entrance was sealed with dried-out wooden planks and half-a-century's worth of windblown sand. Rail tracks disappeared under the planks and a few iron minecars stood rusted to the tracks. Smashed kerosene lamps lay strewn on the ground.

Weathered signs in English, Hebrew and Arabic warned: 'DANGER: UNSTABLE/FALLING ROCKS', 'DO NOT ENTER' and 'DANGER: FLAMMABLE GASES IN THIS MINE (METHANE): NO LIVE FLAMES'.

'1930s-era mine. British,' Iolanthe said, looking at the build-plates on the minecars. 'These minecars were built in Sheffield in 1922.'

'But it's probably built on top of a much older mine started by the Romans,' Jack said. 'I'd guess it was the modern miners who struck methane, since the Romans would've used live flames.'

'Flammable gas leaks in mines are not pretty when they ignite,' Iolanthe warned.

Jack nodded at a bulky blue canvas bag he'd put in the back of the jeep. 'I've brought some breathing masks along, as well as an inflatable air-seal, just in case it becomes necessary to seal off a nasty section of the mine.'

'Is this the only entrance?' Lily asked.

'I doubt it,' Jack said. 'There could be miles of roadways inside this place. There are probably several entrances dotted along the mountain spur.'

'So what do we do exactly?' Iolanthe asked.

'We go in,' Jack said. 'And see what we find.'

Using a crowbar, Jack dislodged the old wooden planks sealing the entrance. Then, guided by the headlights of their little jeep, the three of them headed into the mine.

It was like a fantasy world: the walls and ceilings were completely white, made entirely of salt. Crystalline and translucent, it looked like the inside of an ice castle. The crusty white roads were as slippery as hell.

It was a world of white, and even though each tunnel was numbered, it was completely disorienting. The only trick Jack could think of to mark their route was the same one used by Theseus in the Minotaur's labyrinth: he laid glowsticks along the way, so at least they'd be able to get back out.

Jack drove carefully through the network of white-walled tunnels, rising and falling, bending and twisting.

As they descended further into the mine, they noticed an unusual progression: near the surface, the mine tunnels were wider and more sharply cut, with the major arteries featuring minecar tracks and cabling for the electric lights; but as they went deeper, the trappings of modern mining gradually disappeared.

The tunnels became rougher, rounder and narrower; the wooden supports holding up the ceiling became thicker and more primitive. And the numbers above each tunnel were now carved as long-faded Roman numerals.

Jack pulled the jeep to a halt.

'We're now in the original Roman salt mine.' He eyed the ancient timber supports warily. 'Hope those beams hold up for a little while longer. Still, it's too narrow for the jeep. We go on foot from here.'

He grabbed the canvas bag from the back of the jeep and slung it over his shoulder.

They walked for thirty minutes.

'Captain,' Iolanthe said wearily, 'do you have a plan here? Are we actually looking for something?'

'Yes, as a matter of fact . . .'

They stepped out into a tunnel-junction: three tunnels branched off it, but all three had been boarded up with loosely nailed wooden slats.

The usual modern warnings had been painted in glaring red onto the slats but much older warnings had been etched into the salt-encrusted doorways themselves. They were only just readable.

NOLI INTRARE. CANALIS INSTABILIS.

'It's Latin,' Lily said. '"Do not enter. Mine tunnels unstable."'

'Even the Romans had their limits,' Jack said. 'This is what we're looking for.'

'And that is . . . ?' Iolanthe asked.

Jack turned. 'Remember the James Letter, the one James sent to Mary Magdalene in France:

> *He lies in peace,*
> *In a place where even the mighty Romans fear to tread.*
> *In a kingdom of white . . .*

'Scholars assumed James was describing someplace *hostile* to the Romans: Persia or northern Europe. But nobody thought of a place the Romans had barred off themselves. I was looking for this: for the point at which the Romans found this mine to be too dangerous, the point *beyond which they feared to tread.*'

Jack stood before the triple junction, assessing each possible passageway. He stood deathly still.

'What are you looking for—?'

'Shhh,' he said. 'Not looking . . . listening.'

He stepped over to the left-hand tunnel, peered through its slats, listening intently.

'Shit,' he said.

'What?' Iolanthe asked.

'*Listen* . . .'

Iolanthe did so. And suddenly she heard it.

Voices. Distant, echoing voices. Coming from somewhere down in the barred-off section of the mine.

Quickly, quietly and firmly, Jack started pulling the slats free.

'Someone's already here,' he whispered.

Moving with extreme caution, Jack ventured down a steep slippery passageway on foot, followed by Lily and Iolanthe. The passageway appeared to end at a dark precipice up ahead.

'We came in from the north. There must be another entrance from the south—'

A flash of artificial light suddenly slashed across the end of their passageway.

'Flashlights . . .' Jack breathed. 'Stay low.'

The three of them crept toward the end of the passageway.

Jack stopped at the precipice—their passageway ended at a sharp brink overlooking a gallery from up near its ceiling.

And there, down on the floor of the gallery, standing beside a large flat wheel-shaped device, Jack saw several figures carrying flashlights, looking down into a wide salt pit.

Scimitar and Mao Gongli, flanked by four of Carnivore's Russian Spetsnaz guards.

'Son of a bitch,' Jack whispered. 'We found it.'

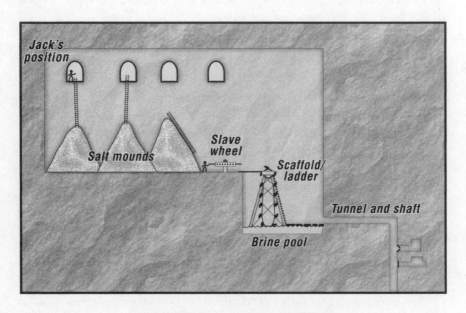

THE ROMAN SALT MINE

Gazing down on the scene from his high position, Jack realised the purpose of this gallery.

It was a collection point: six twenty-foot-high mounds of salt stood in two rows of three, each one positioned directly underneath an elevated passageway like his. Salt gathered by slaves in the depths of the mine would be brought here for co-ordinated delivery to the surface.

The horizontal wheel-like object near Scimitar and Mao, Jack saw, was a slave wheel that drove a conveyor belt that rose from the wide pit. The conveyor belt was attached to a high scaffold structure that stood in the pit—slaves manacled to the wheel would turn it, raising salt in buckets on the belt.

But then as he gazed down at the wide gallery, Jack realised something else.

Where was Vulture?

Carnivore had tasked Mao, Scimitar *and Vulture* with the job of finding the Sixth Pillar.

Then Vulture appeared.

He climbed up into view via the scaffold in the pit . . .

. . . and he held in his hand a cloth-wrapped bundle the size of a football.

Jack gasped.

Vulture stepped up out of the hole and unwrapped the bundle, revealing a translucent diamond brick.

The Sixth and last Pillar.

The Jesus Pillar.

Sound carried well in the cavern. They heard Vulture clearly when he addressed his Russian guards.

'Your master's prize,' the Saudi spat, handing it over to the guards.

The commander of the guards looked pleased. 'We will return to the surface and inform the general of your find.'

Covered by their Russian guards, Vulture, Scimitar and Mao then left the chamber through a doorway to the south.

Lily made to stand. 'Daddy, we have to do something. They're getting away . . .'

But Jack hadn't moved.

He was just staring down at the ancient scaffold rising up from the pit.

Iolanthe watched him closely. 'What is it?'

Jack quoted:

> 'His wisdom lies with him still,
> Protected by a twin who meets all thieves first.

'A twin . . .' he said, still staring intently downward. 'A twin who meets all thieves first . . .'

Then it clicked.

'It's a fake,' he said softly.

'A what?' Iolanthe spun.

'What's a fake?' Lily said.

Jack swallowed. 'The Pillar they just took. It's designed to deceive anyone who comes here: to make them think they found the real Pillar. Mao, Vulture and Scimitar just took a fake Pillar to Carnivore.'

A Roman-era ladder led down from Jack's perch to one of the salt piles on the floor of the abandoned gallery.

Walking slowly and silently by the light of a couple of glow-sticks, followed by Lily and Iolanthe, Jack passed between the high mounds of salt before coming to the edge of the wide rectangular pit at the far end.

The slave wheel was a lot bigger up close, the size of a small car. Rusty manacles dangled from it.

The pit itself dropped a full fifty feet to a floor that was covered in a layer of sickly milk-coloured water.

'Brine,' Jack said. 'They must have struck groundwater and it mixed with the salt.'

Some tied-together wooden planks formed a loose bridge across the brine lake, giving access to four slightly elevated square tunnels on the other side. Vulture had left some glowsticks in the far-right tunnel.

'You, stay here,' Jack said to Iolanthe. 'You'—to Lily—'come with me.'

'Why can't I come?' Iolanthe protested.

'Because I still haven't figured you out. I can't tell when you're going to kill me or save me, so it's better just to keep you out of the equation. You keep watch up here.'

Iolanthe rolled her eyes, completely unruffled. 'Fine.'

Jack climbed down the ladder into the pit. Lily followed.

Then, equally slowly, almost with reverence, they walked across the loosely-tied boards that spanned the brine lake, before disappearing inside the right-hand tunnel.

The white-walled tunnel wasn't long, only about forty feet. It ended at a vertical salt-walled shaft that plunged further downward. An A-frame with a rope hanging from it dangled into the shaft, presumably left by Vulture.

Jack shone his flashlight down the shaft.

Ten feet down, a horizontal cross-shaft bored into the salt wall. Its mouth was heavily salt-encrusted, as if a seal of some kind had been broken. More of Vulture's glowsticks led into it.

'Vulture was too hasty,' Jack said. 'He took the first option, and found the twin who meets all thieves first.'

Jack shone the beam of his flashlight *further* down the shaft, to a part of the salt wall below the cross-shaft Vulture had broken into, to reveal . . .

. . . a translucent section of wall.

Lily caught her breath.

The apparently solid wall of the shaft was not solid at all. There was another cross-shaft down there, whose entrance had been covered over with a layer of—

'Salt seals,' Jack said. 'And that explains the middle part of the letter.

> 'He lies in peace,
> In a place where even the mighty Romans fear to tread.
> In a kingdom of white
> He does not grow old.

'He doesn't grow old because the sealing of the salt protects his body from the corrosive effects of oxygen in the air. Archaeologists have found bodies in salt mines in Romania and Iran that date from over a thousand years *before* Christ and they still have skin, hair and beards. Even their clothes retain their colour because the salt has kept out the air.'

Slinging his canvas bag over his shoulder, Jack grabbed the rope hanging from the A-frame and started to lower himself into the shaft.

Lily was only just starting to grasp what he had said.

'Daddy, wait. Are you saying that lying in a sealed chamber down there, with the last Pillar buried with him, is the perfectly preserved body of Jesus Christ?'

In answer Jack stopped what he was doing, looked Lily in the eye, and gave her a single silent nod.

Then he continued his descent.

Moments later, Jack hung in front of the wall of the salt shaft, staring at the translucent section of it ten feet below Vulture's cross-shaft.

He raised a small handheld pick-axe and then abruptly, for some reason, Jack West Jr paused.

He'd uncovered many ancient things in his time: the scrolls from the Library of Alexandria, most of the Seven Wonders of the Ancient World, the tombs of Alexander the Great and Genghis Khan.

But this was something else.

This was something *more*.

This was the most famous person to ever walk the Earth. A man who inspired religions, whose acts and words were still repeated two thousand years after he had lived, and most of all, this was a man who many believed had risen bodily to heaven after he had been crucified.

'Daddy?' Lily said from twenty feet above him. 'You okay?'

Jack blinked. 'Yeah . . . yeah, I'm okay.'

Then he took a deep breath and hit the false salt wall with his little pick-axe.

It wasn't very thick—barely a centimetre—and it came away easily as Jack chipped at it.

Soon, a round gap the size of a manhole appeared and Jack climbed through it, guided by a fresh glowstick.

After a short crawl down a tight tunnel, he came to a small wooden door, encrusted around the edges with salt crystals.

He paused again. If the chamber beyond that door really was oxygen-sealed, and if it really contained—well, he didn't want to be the one who contaminated it with fresh oxygen.

He extracted the inflatable air-seal unit from his bag. Made of clear plastic, it was designed to inflate across the width of a larger passageway, sealing it. But it would work in this small space just as well. Two Ziploc zippered doors in its middle acted like an airlock.

Jack inflated the air-seal unit behind him and it expanded quickly to fill the tight tunnel. Once it was safely in place, he turned his attention back to the small salt-encrusted wooden door.

It opened with a sharp *crack*, the salt seal breaking free.

Jack passed through it.

He emerged inside a small salt-walled chamber in which he was only just able to stand. The walls were pure white. The air was musty and stale.

A coffin-sized recess was cut into the salt wall at the far end. Nailed to the wall above the recess was a square of faded wood on which four letters had been crudely carved:

'INRI'.

Jack swallowed at the sight of it. *It was the sign.* The *actual* sign . . .

It stood for: IESVS NAZARENVS REX IVDAEORVM.

Jesus the Nazarene, King of the Jews.

Jack lowered his eyes to behold the recess itself.

Lying on it was a man-sized figure, wrapped entirely in loose white cloth, arms folded across its chest in eternal rest.

Where the arms met, Jack could discern a rectangular bulge.

The Pillar.

With a slowness that betrayed the awe he felt, Jack West Jr approached the cloth-wrapped figure.

He stood before it.

He could hear his heart pounding inside his head.

To get the Pillar, he would have to remove the loose cloth over the figure's face.

Slowly, Jack pulled back the cloth.

For some reason that he could not explain, Jack couldn't bring himself to look directly upon the figure's face—in some corner of his mind, he felt that he was *unworthy* to look upon the face of so great an individual.

Alexander the Great, Genghis Khan, they were one thing, but this was different.

This man was different.

He was not a warrior in the usual sense, the military sense. His war had been one of ideas, ideas that had swept the world. His victories had been far more long-lasting than anything Genghis or Alexander or Napoleon had achieved. Their victories had barely outlived them. This man's victories were still going.

Jack gulped.

Taking Jesus Christ's Pillar was sacrilegious enough. He would not look upon the man himself.

And so, keeping his eyes firmly focused on the figure's chest, Jack saw the Pillar clasped in perfectly preserved hands.

Out of the corner of his eye, Jack could see a bearded face—the beard was brown, the eyes were closed, the face serene.

He couldn't look at it directly.

Gently, slowly, reverently, Jack lifted the Pillar from the perfectly preserved hands, for a moment brushing his fingers against those of the Pillar's former owner.

Electricity flowed through him—an electricity unlike anything he had ever felt in his life—an incredible feeling of clarity and lightness. It shot through his body like a lightning bolt of pure—

Jack replaced the cloth over the bearded figure's face, and the feeling immediately went away. He still did not look directly at the face.

He released the breath he'd been holding. In his shaking hand was the Pillar.

Then he backed out of the salt-walled chamber in silence and closed its small wooden door behind him, knowing that the salt crystals at the door's edges would reseal in time.

Then he left, passing through his plastic airlock, not quite believing what he had just seen and done.

Jack rejoined Lily at the top of the salt shaft.

'Got it?' she asked.

'Got it.'

'Was *he* . . . in there?'

'He was, and it was like nothing I've ever experienced,' Jack said softly. 'Come on, let's go.'

They crossed the brine lake and started climbing the scaffold structure that led back to the gallery. Iolanthe was still waiting for them at the top of the scaffold.

Lily climbed in the lead, with Jack behind her in case she slipped or fell, so she reached the top first.

He heard her scream before he saw why.

The short plank-bridge between the scaffold and the lip of the pit fell away, past Jack's disbelieving eyes, leaving a nine-foot gap between them and the lip.

They were stranded out on the scaffold.

Jack joined Lily and Iolanthe on the top of the scaffold and looked out across the gap.

Two men brandishing crossbows stood on the other side.

Vulture and Scimitar.

They'd come back.

'You knew the other Pillar was a fake,' Jack said from his position out on the scaffold.

Vulture smiled. 'Of course. This place has long been known to our people, so too its secrets. Our Chinese colleague is now taking that other Pillar back to the Russian, completely unaware that it is worthless. Deeming us to be of no more use, our guards left us here, which happens to be just fine with us.'

'I thought you and China were in this together,' Jack said.

'As the end approaches, partnerships of convenience will naturally dissolve,' Scimitar said.

'I think the phrase you're looking for is "There's no honour among thieves,"' Jack retorted.

'Throw the Pillar over to me and I might spare the girl. Rest assured, I will not be sparing you or the royal bitch.'

Jack gripped the Pillar, biting his lip.

He was screwed. He couldn't fire a gun in this methane-filled environment. And he, Lily and Iolanthe couldn't possibly jump across the gap. They were trapped, totally out of options.

Vulture sneered, raised his crossbow. 'You've played well, Huntsman, very well. But here your adventure ends.'

Jack closed his eyes . . .

. . . just as another voice echoed out from somewhere else in the cavern.

'*Not yet!*'

Vulture spun. So did Scimitar and Iolanthe and Lily.

Jack didn't need to. He'd know that voice anywhere. Deep and gruff, it belonged to the one man in the world who wanted to stop Vulture and Scimitar more than Jack did.

It belonged to Pooh Bear.

Pooh Bear stood with Stretch at the northern end of the gallery, in between the salt mounds. Jack guessed that they must have entered the mine through the same tunnels he had and followed his trail of glowsticks here.

Pooh and Stretch stood opposite Vulture and Scimitar like gunslingers on a wild west street.

Vulture grinned. 'Well, well, well, Fat Zahir returns.'

Pooh Bear ignored the Saudi, jerked his chin at Scimitar. 'Brother. A simple question. Do you still side with this snake?'

Scimitar hesitated for a second, then raised his nose. 'My way is the right way, Zahir, for our country and for our faith.'

'What about our father in his watery tomb in Russia?' Pooh Bear asked.

'His death is a sacrifice I am prepared to endure,' Scimitar replied evenly.

'You are truly lost, then, aren't you . . .'

'You do not have to die here, Zahir. But if you stand in my way, you most certainly will.'

'I do not wish to fight you, brother,' Pooh Bear said. 'But I will if I must. I cannot let you pass. I am sorry that it has to come to this.'

Pooh Bear drew a long-bladed knife from his weapons belt. Stretch did the same.

An incredulous grin broke out across Scimitar's face. 'You intend to fight me, Zahir? Me! Never even in our childhood wrestling matches could you beat me. And your sickly Jew friend is no match for a blade-handler of Vulture's skill.'

Pooh Bear was unmoved. 'That may be so, brother. But you hold

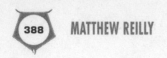

our friends at your mercy, so we will fight you anyway. Only one of us can leave this place alive.'

'So be it,' Scimitar said. 'Fight we shall.'

Quick as a whip, he raised his crossbow and fired it. The bolt thudded directly into Pooh Bear's chest. At the same time, Vulture fired at Stretch, but Stretch was ready—he swerved and the bolt went wide.

Pooh Bear shuddered as Scimitar's crossbow bolt struck him, but he remained standing, the bolt protruding from his chest.

He looked up at Scimitar in apparent disbelief.

Scimitar said, 'I never said I would fight fair.'

Pooh Bear didn't move. Perhaps he was in shock, perhaps he was—

Then he calmly reached down and wrenched the bolt from his chest, revealing a Kevlar vest. He threw the bolt to the ground.

'Neither did I,' he said.

Their crossbows expended, Scimitar and Vulture discarded them and drew their own curving blades. Pooh noticed that Scimitar's knife was the beautiful gold-hilted bejewelled dagger their father had given to Scimitar on his thirteenth birthday—a prized gift from a father to his firstborn son.

Pooh and Stretch raised their own more humble Ka-Bar knives.

Scimitar and Vulture gripped theirs backhanded, special forces style, and suddenly it was on.

And in the darkness of the ancient Roman salt mine, the two pairs engaged.

Jack watched in horror as Pooh Bear and Stretch took on Vulture and Scimitar in hand-to-hand combat—in a battle that was not only for their lives, but for his as well.

If Pooh and Stretch lost, Jack would be killed and Lily taken captive.

Their fates were entirely in Pooh's and Stretch's hands.

★ ★ ★

Blades flashed and clashed as two separate knifefights began near the brink: Pooh Bear vs Scimitar and Stretch vs Vulture.

Scimitar roared as he slashed at his younger brother with great sweeping swipes, and at first Pooh Bear successfully parried each blow away, holding his ground, sparks flying with each impact of their knives.

But then, gradually, Scimitar forced him backwards, and started drawing blood—slashes to the hand, then taunting gashes to the face. Still, Pooh Bear kept fighting, grimly, determinedly.

As for Stretch, he was in trouble from the moment Vulture unsheathed his cutlass. Vulture was indeed a skilled bladesman, extremely skilled. His knife moved with blurring speed and it was all Stretch could do to defend himself.

It soon became apparent that while Stretch was fighting with every ounce of concentration and energy he had, Vulture was toying with him, barely even perspiring.

Vulture was pushing him toward the edge of the pit, forcing him back. Stretch tripped, stumbled, raised his knife again. Then Vulture punched him and he fell against the big wooden slave wheel, his back momentarily turned to his opponent—

—and to his utter horror he felt the cold blade of Vulture's knife plunge into his lower back.

Stretch froze. Bullets of sweat broke out on his forehead.

Vulture pressed himself close to him, hissed in his ear: 'Feel that, Jew? Feel my blade inside you?'

Vulture twisted the knife. Fiery pain shot through Stretch's body. He clenched his teeth in agony, slumped to the ground. His own knife fell from his hand.

'No!' Lily screamed from the scaffold.

Stretch turned and saw her, his eyes pleading, but he was spent. Despite his exhaustion, he reached pathetically for the knife, his bloody hand shaking.

Clink!

He frowned. Looked around.

And saw that Vulture had clasped one of the slave wheel's manacles to his left wrist.

Stretch looked up in horror. He was now bound to the slave wheel.

'Come, watch the death of your friend,' Vulture said. 'Then I shall come back and hack off your fucking head in front of the girl.'

Vulture stood and headed over toward Scimitar and Pooh Bear's fight.

Stretch yanked on the manacle, but it was no use. His strength was gone and the manacle was too strong.

At that same moment, Pooh Bear was struggling in his own battle with Scimitar—he was backed up against a salt mound, desperately deflecting Scimitar's vicious thrusts.

Then he saw Vulture approaching—glimpsed Stretch, slumped and beaten, manacled to the slave wheel—and he realised that this was quickly becoming a disaster—

—when suddenly Scimitar broke through Pooh Bear's defences and slashed him horrifically across the left side of his face.

Pooh roared, his face exploding blood. His whole left eye had been slashed clean in two.

Pooh slumped to the ground, clutching his eye socket with his free hand, blood pouring down his face.

Scimitar stood triumphantly over him as Vulture arrived at his side.

Jack and Lily watched in horror from the scaffold, only fifteen metres away, but helpless to intervene.

The end was coming for Pooh Bear and Jack clutched Lily to his chest, shielding her eyes, not wanting her to see this.

Pooh sat dumbly against the salt mound, legs outstretched, head bowed, blood running out of the grisly maroon hole that was his eye socket, down his beard and onto his lap. He clutched weakly at his beard as if trying to stem the flow of blood down it, still gripping his knife with one hand.

Scimitar crouched before him, shook his head sadly.

'I will never understand you, Zahir. But understand me when I say that you have brought this upon yourself. You have forced this upon me . . .'

Scimitar raised his cutlass—just as Pooh Bear made one last desperate lunge at his throat!

Only for Scimitar to jerk his head expertly away, just far enough for the tip of Pooh's extended blade to fall an inch short of Scimitar's Adam's apple.

Scimitar smiled. 'An impressive final lunge, my brother, but like I said, you can't beat me. You never could. And nothing can save you now.'

His face covered in gashes, salt and sweat, his left eye socket a dark hole of bloody blackness, Pooh Bear glared at his duplicitous brother with his one remaining eye. His knife-arm was still fully extended so that its blade-tip was directly underneath his brother's chin.

When he spoke, his voice was a husky whisper.

'Just one thing . . .'

'Oh *fuck*—' Vulture saw it.

Scimitar didn't. 'Wha—?'

The compact blast of the small wad of C-2 plastic explosive that Pooh had slipped out of his beard-ring and attached to the tip of his knife-blade completely engulfed the lower half of Scimitar's face. A pocket of stale methane in the surrounding air made the blast flash brightly, scorching Pooh Bear's outstretched knife-hand.

A hideous inhuman scream filled the air—a wailing, primal, blood-curdling shriek—and as the smoke from the short sharp blast dissipated, it revealed a horrific version of the once-handsome Scimitar: he now had only half a face, and he was screaming despite his lack of a jaw.

The entire bottom half of his face had been blown away by the blast, and now it was the picture of gore: a foul mix of bone, blood, exposed teeth and dangling flesh. His scream was one of horror, disbelief and total agony.

Scimitar wobbled on his feet, dropping his gold-hilted knife, clutching at Vulture who recoiled from him in disgust—

—but then Vulture regathered himself and turned toward Pooh Bear—

—in time to see Pooh Bear's arm blur with movement—

—and suddenly something lodged deep in Vulture's throat.

He staggered with the impact, reached for his throat, and found Scimitar's gold-hilted knife embedded in it. Pooh Bear had caught it by the blade when Scimitar had dropped it and in one quick movement had flung it directly into Vulture's throat, piercing the windpipe.

Vulture gasped for air, but his windpipe could no longer facilitate breathing. His eyes bulged. He staggered backwards, his face going purple, then he dropped to his knees and toppled face-first to the hard salt floor, driving the knife fully through the back of his neck. His body sagged, never to move again.

Scimitar was still screaming his shrill mouthless scream when he tripped off the edge of the pit and sailed down into it, landing in the milk-coloured brine where he flopped and thrashed for a minute before the water pouring directly into his lungs was too much and his body floated on the surface, limp, unmoving, dead.

And suddenly the salt cave was quiet.

In the silence, Pooh Bear slumped back against the salt mound behind him, bloodied, broken, half-blinded and exhausted.

'Stretch!' he called. 'You still alive?'

'Yeah . . . just . . .' Stretch groaned, still manacled to the slave wheel.

'Jack?' Pooh Bear called, his eyes shut.

Jack was staring in speechless disbelief at Pooh Bear—he had just single-handedly killed both Scimitar and Vulture in perhaps the bloodiest fucking fight Jack had ever witnessed. He released Lily from his grip, and she squealed when she peered out and saw that Pooh Bear was alive and the bad guys were dead.

'Jack . . . !' Pooh Bear called again, opening his good eye.

'I'm here,' Jack said gently. 'We're here.'

'I'm a little . . . wounded . . . over here, Jack,' Pooh gasped. 'Just give me . . . a minute . . . to catch my breath.'

'Buddy, after what you just did, you take all the time you need.'

While it had taken Jack almost an hour to descend to the bottom of the salt mine, it took him three hours to retrace his steps.

First, he had to tend to Pooh Bear's and Stretch's wounds, and they were severe. Beyond their gashes and cuts, Pooh's eye was a gory mess and the stab wound to Stretch's lower back was life-threatening.

Pooh Bear had been able to walk back to the jeep, leaning heavily on Jack's shoulder, but Stretch was a different story. To get him out, Jack had constructed a stretcher from some old wooden ladders and with Lily and Iolanthe holding a corner each, they had slowly and carefully carried Stretch back up to the parked jeep.

Only then could Jack drive them back to the surface, and even then, very slowly so as not to unnecessarily jolt Stretch.

During the long journey up, Pooh Bear had told Jack how, after speaking with him earlier, they had come directly here, guided by the *Halicarnassus*'s transponder beacon over the final stages. Cieran and the twins were right now up on the surface—having overcome the Russian guards, Ding and Dong—with the charged Fourth Pillar in their possession and a helicopter they'd chartered from Amman airport.

'I'm glad you got here when you did,' Jack said. 'You saved our asses.'

They turned a final corner and saw a small square of daylight up ahead, the outside world.

The jeep rumbled out of the mine, bouncing out into glorious desert sunshine.

Jack brought it to a halt and, smiling with relief, looked down the hill at the *Halicarnassus,* expecting to see the twins and Sky Monster with Ding and Dong subdued—

His face fell.

Down by the *Hali,* he saw Sky Monster and the twins slumped on the ground, handcuffed to the cargo ramp's struts. All three sat with their heads bent, unmoving.

A Bell helicopter stood beside the 747—Pooh Bear's chopper from Amman—but so did another aircraft, parked on the desert highway.

It was a sleek black Concorde-like jetliner with a sharp beak-like nose and missiles on its wings.

A Tupolev-144.

And standing there on the dusty turnaround outside the mine, flanked by four of his own Spetsnaz guards *plus* Ding and Dong, waiting for Jack, was Carnivore.

'West the Younger,' Carnivore grinned, his gruesome steel jaw glinting. 'My, what a handy tool you have turned out to be. I'll take that.'

He took the Jesus Pillar from Jack. 'It will go well with the one your friends laid in the Bristol Channel.'

With Jack and the others disarmed and covered by the Spetsnaz troops, Iolanthe stepped out of the jeep and joined Carnivore. 'The Chinese colonel has a fake Pillar and the Saudi spy is dead,' she reported.

'The Blood Vulture is no more?' Carnivore seemed genuinely surprised. 'Killed by West the Younger?'

'No, by Anzar Abbas's second son. He defeated his elder brother too in single combat. It was impressive.'

'Indeed,' Carnivore eyed the terribly wounded Pooh Bear. 'The Blood Vulture was a very dangerous man.'

'Did Mao call you about the Pillar he acquired?' Iolanthe asked.

'He did. He said he was on his way to eastern Russia with it, but the tracker sewn into his skin indicates that he and his forces are heading directly for the Sixth Vertex. The fool probably thought he could get to the Vertex and force me to co-operate with him.'

As they spoke, Jack gazed out at Sky Monster and the twins cuffed to the *Hali*'s rear ramp.

What had happened here? And where was—

'Hello, Jack.' Cieran Kincaid emerged from behind Carnivore. He was unbound, moving freely.

Jack stared at the young Irish captain, at first not comprehending, and then it all made sense: the raid on Alexander's safehouse in County Kerry last year, Cieran's 'rescue' of Stretch, Pooh and the twins (from his own people) at the Fourth Vertex, and the scene here. Cieran had helped Pooh Bear and Stretch 'overcome' Ding and Dong; they had then gone into the mine to help Jack while Cieran had released the two Spetsnaz guards and turned on Sky Monster and the twins.

Carnivore said, 'I told you once before, Young West, that our tentacles spread far and wide.'

But Jack only had eyes for Cieran. 'You goddamn bastard. It was you who gave them the location of the safehouse holding Alexander. Only members of Colin O'Hara's inner circle in Ireland knew where that safehouse was, and you were part of that circle . . .'

Cieran smiled, the airy smile of the true believer. 'My allegiance to God is greater than my allegiance to a mere nation, Jack.'

'What?'

'The Deus Rex, Jack. The God Kings. They were chosen by our Lord. They rule by His decree. Nations are the creation of men; the Deus Rex are the chosen vessels of God Himself. They are as close to Him as you or I shall ever get.'

'Maybe as close as you'll get,' Jack said, thinking about his experience down in the tomb.

'It's my honour to serve them. You don't understand, which is why you are lost,' Cieran said.

'Is that so?' Jack said.

Iolanthe and Carnivore had finished speaking and were now watching this exchange with amusement.

Carnivore gazed at Jack, but when he spoke, it was to Iolanthe: 'Thoughts?'

'He's truly remarkable, cousin,' Iolanthe said. 'It would be a shame. I would prefer we not do so.'

Carnivore seemed to think about that. 'If we take the girl, he'll come after her, and that's far too dangerous. He would have to be immobilised till the final Pillar was laid. I can't have him running around . . .'

'I'll kill him,' Cieran said firmly, turning to face them.

Carnivore glanced at Cieran, considering the offer.

Jack just turned from Cieran to Carnivore to Iolanthe, aware that his life was under judgement. His gaze came to rest on Carnivore, the final arbiter, deep in thought.

As Carnivore deliberated, Cieran stepped close behind Jack.

'You know, Jack, we have more in common than you think,' he whispered. 'Like Zoe Kissane.'

Jack cocked his head sideways.

'Oh yes, she tasted *nice*, that night in Dublin a few years back,' Cieran smirked.

Jack stared forward.

Cieran said, 'Sure, I might have plied her with more alcohol than she was used to, and maybe even slipped some extra shots into her drinks, but it's never just the alcohol, is it? She wanted something to happen. Although you should have seen her the next morning, when she woke up in bed beside me. She was in quite a state, saying, "Oh, God, what have I done! What have I done!"'

Cieran chuckled.

Jack said nothing, but his jaw was grinding.

'You two-faced treacherous pig!' Pooh Bear spat from behind him. 'I thought sex outside of marriage wasn't the done thing for religious fanatics like you.'

Cieran said airily, 'Alas, it is my weakness, and on that occasion, as on similar ones before it, I confessed my sins at church and the Lord in his infinite mercy absolved me.'

Jack still said nothing. But his face was deadly.

It was then that Carnivore made his decision.

To Iolanthe, he said: 'Take the girl. Better to have her with us in case something happens to the boy.'

Covered by the six Spetsnaz guards, Iolanthe pulled Lily away from Jack.

'Daddy . . .' Lily said, clearly more afraid for him than for herself.

Carnivore addressed Jack.

'West the Younger. You're a brave man and you have fought well'—he grabbed a Skorpion machine pistol from one of his body-guards and threw it roughly to Cieran—'but sadly your time has come. I can't risk you being alive any longer.'

To Cieran: 'Shoot him and the others. Then join us at the plane. And Captain Kincaid, no games, no speeches, no gloating, just do it now. Make sure of it.'

Carnivore headed off toward his plane, with his guards, Iolanthe and Lily in tow.

'Farewell, Jack West Jr,' Iolanthe said, looking back. 'My apologies. I didn't think it should end this way for you.'

Lily stared fearfully back at Jack as she walked, and at Pooh Bear and the bedbound Stretch, until she was shoved down the rocky slope, out of sight.

Jack watched as she disappeared down the hill, to be replaced moments later by Cieran, holding the Skorpion machine pistol aimed directly at Jack's eyes.

Weaponless and with absolutely nowhere to run this time, Jack stood tall and closed his eyes.

'Not this way . . .'

Then without so much as a blink Cieran Kincaid pulled the trigger.

Twenty yards down the hill, Lily and Iolanthe heard the rapid-fire clatter of the Skorpion.

Lily turned and saw the distant figure of Cieran blasting away. Jack was out of her line of sight, hidden by the slope of the hill.

Lily burst into tears and shouted, 'Daddy! No . . . !'

Iolanthe just shook her head and pulled Lily along, heading for the Tupolev.

Lily had taken only a few more steps when she heard Cieran yell, 'What the fuck!'

She spun. So did Iolanthe—

—just in time to see Jack crashtackle Cieran—hard—hurling him off the edge of the turnaround and sending them both tumbling out of sight, down the other side of the hill in a cloud of dust and sand.

Carnivore saw them, too.

'Get to the plane! Leave him!' he ordered. Then, to his men: 'Missiles! Disable their plane and destroy that helicopter!'

Flanked by their six Spetsnaz bodyguards, Carnivore, Iolanthe and Lily rushed aboard the Tupolev.

As she was pushed inside the sleek black plane, Lily looked back and said, 'Go Daddy . . .'

Moments later, two missiles shoomed out from the Tupolev's wings—the first smashed through the windshield of Pooh Bear's chartered helicopter and blew it to pieces; the second slammed into the forward landing gear of the *Halicarnassus*.

The big 747's nitrogen-filled forward wheels blasted outward

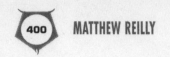

in a gaseous explosion and the great black plane's nose lurched downward, dropping suddenly, its forward landing strut—now wheelless—crunching down onto the bitumen of the desert highway.

The *Halicarnassus* wasn't going anywhere soon.

Then the sleek black Tupolev turned away and taxied down the remote highway, speeding up quickly before lifting off into the sky.

As for Jack, he tumbled and rolled in a dusty heap with Cieran Kincaid.

In the moment before Cieran had fired on him, Jack had done one simple thing.

Pushing through the fabric of his jacket, he had flicked the switch that initiated the grenade-sized Warbler in his pocket.

As such, to Cieran's amazement, all of his bullets had swept apart in a V-shape, fizzing harmlessly past Jack, missing him on either side until the Skorpion started dry-clicking, its magazine spent.

At which point, Jack charged.

He came bounding forward and when he tackled Cieran, it was a crashing hit to the solar plexus that sent the two of them tumbling down the rocky hillside.

When they hit the bottom of the slope, both men leapt to their feet.

Cieran quickly unsheathed a Bowie knife, but what happened next happened way too fast for Cieran Kincaid to comprehend.

No sooner had he extracted the knife than Jack was on him and gripping his knife-hand, their faces inches apart, Jack's face twisted in a fury that chilled Cieran to his very core.

Then with brutal force and a sickening *crack!*, Jack broke Cieran's wrist and Cieran yelled, his knife-hand bent grotesquely round the wrong way, but his scream cut off abruptly as Jack proceeded to slash the knife, still actually gripped by Cieran himself, in a powerful lateral swipe.

Cieran froze, swaying on his feet but still upright, his eyes

boggling. Then the deep horizontal gash across his throat started to leak blood, buckets of it.

His horrified eyes looked directly into Jack's, but he was incapable of speech now.

Jack wasn't.

'See you in Hell,' he said through clenched teeth, 'cause that's the only place you're going, you crazy zealot son of a bitch.'

Cieran dropped to the dusty ground in a heap, his dead eyes staring up into the sky.

With Cieran dead and Carnivore gone, Jack went to check on his battered and injured team.

First he went down to Sky Monster and the twins at the *Halicarnassus*'s rear loading ramp and sawed through their handcuffs.

Sky Monster, it turned out, had been rendered unconscious by some kind of nerve-agent Cieran had unexpectedly sprayed in his face soon after Pooh Bear and Stretch had gone inside the mine. When he came to, he vomited violently.

As for the twins, they'd been drugged by Cieran shortly after they'd arrived at the mine, too—a barbiturate of some sort slipped into their water bottles. When they finally awoke, they looked very pale and had headaches as bad as Sky Monster's.

In the meantime, Jack set about getting Pooh Bear and Stretch into the *Hali*'s infirmary.

Owing to the plane's destroyed forward landing gear, all of its interior cabins were tilted at an extreme angle. But everything was still in workable order, and over the course of two hours, working methodically with Horus perched behind him, Jack West patched up his badly broken team.

It was late in the afternoon of Wednesday, March 19, when Jack emerged from the infirmary, having cleaned up Stretch and Pooh Bear and dosed them up with heavy sedatives. Sky Monster was in his bunkroom, still vomiting into a bucket every fifteen minutes.

The twins greeted Jack as he returned to the main cabin and fell into his seat. They were still pale and sipping Gastrolyte.

'So, where do we stand?' Lachlan asked. 'Is this where our mission ends, one step short of the finish line?'

Jack didn't respond.

His eyes were glued to the floor.

At last he said, 'Carnivore has all the pieces he needs. He has the three cleansing stones—the Philosopher's Stone, the Firestone and the Basin of Rameses—water from the Ness Spring; the last Pillar; the Twin Tablets of Thuthmosis for the incantation; and Lily and Alexander to read from them . . .'

'. . . and, I presume, the location of the Sixth and last Vertex,' Lachlan said.

'Which we never figured out,' Julius added.

Jack said softly, 'I have to get to that Vertex. I have to get Lily back and stop Carnivore before he performs the final ceremony.'

'Jack! Are you listening to us?' Julius said. '*We never found the last Vertex!*'

Jack turned to face them, calm and focused.

'Oh, I know where the last Vertex is.'

'What!' Julius exclaimed. Horus looked up sharply.

'You know where the last Vertex is?' Lachlan said.

'I've known for a while,' Jack said. 'I think Wizard had a good suspicion, too. Your lightshow at Stonehenge wasn't conclusive by itself, but combined with some other factors that have come to light, it helped settle the issue for me.'

'What do you mean?' Lachlan asked. 'What other factors?'

Jack said, 'The Chinese aid payments to the Chilean government two months ago. The inscription in Egypt: "A lone bekhen sentinel stands guard over the entrance to the greatest shrine." Of course, the clincher was the picture from Genghis Khan's shield: of a coastal hill with a single figure standing on it.'

Julius couldn't contain himself. 'Well, come on, Jack! Where the bloody hell is it!'

Jack shrugged sadly. 'You've actually been there before, Julius. You, too, Lachlan. The Sixth Vertex is in the Pacific Ocean, underneath Easter Island.'

'Forgive my slowness,' Lachlan said, 'but how do all those things point to Easter Island?'

Jack flicked on a nearby computer, pulled up one of the twins' photos from Stonehenge:

'See the left-hand upright? It's almost all ocean. Now, I figured this could be the Pacific Ocean and that landmass on the right is the western shore of South America. But that's a pretty big guess to make. Only then I saw a picture on Wizard's summary sheet . . .'

Jack pulled out a photocopy of the summary sheet:

REWARDS
(according to Rameses II at Abydos)

1. KNOWLEDGE
2. HEAT
3. SIGHT
4. LIFE
5. DEATH
6. POWER

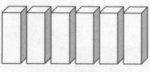

THE SIX PILLARS

- Oblong uncut diamonds;
- Must be '<u>cleansed</u>' by the Ph's Stone before they can be placed in the Machine;
- Whereabouts? The Great Houses of Europe; Perhaps the 'Five Warriors'???

The Sa-Benben (a.k.a. 'The Firestone')

Interacts uniquely with each of the Six Ramesean Stones:

1. <u>Philosopher's</u>: cleanses Pillars.
2. <u>Stonehenge</u>: gives location of vertices of the Great Machine.
3. <u>Delphi</u>: allows one to see the Dark Sun.
4. <u>Tablets</u>: contain the final incantation.
5. <u>Killing</u>: gives dates by which Pillars must be laid.
6. <u>Basin</u>: unknown.

WRONG!

Faberge Egg - Newton's alchemical work
The Ness spring....?
Equinox/Easter '08

THE GREAT MACHINE

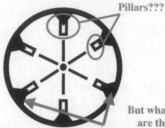

Pillars???

But what are the TRIANGLES then?

MUST HAVE BOTH THE SA-BENBEN **AND** THE PHILOSOPHER'S STONE! THEY ARE CENTRAL TO EVERYTHING!!

Rate of approach must be calculated. Call the Twins!

16,467 X 365.25
Mean v ≡ 125,445 km/s
Max output in 1962 was 10.57
But in 1991 was 10.72. Growing

TITANIC SINKING & RISING (DEC 2007) CONNECTION? POSSIBLE SIGHTING OPPORTUNITY?

'See that picture at the bottom left, over which Wizard scribbled "WRONG!" I didn't recognise it at first, but that's a map of Easter Island. The dots around the edges are the positions of the *moai* statues around the island's coast.

'And see where Wizard wrote "Equinox/Easter '08"? We all thought it was a reference to the special status of Easter this year, occurring on the equinox. But it wasn't. It was a reference to Easter *Island* being the location of the ceremony that must be performed during tomorrow's dual equinox.

'And then came the other factors,' Jack said. 'Easter Island is technically part of Chile. Those Chinese "aid payments" to Chile were more likely bribes to get exclusive use of the island for a few days. I imagine Chinese forces are there now.

'And the "bekhen sentinel" who guards the final shrine is not an *Egyptian* basalt monument as Napoleon thought it was . . .'

'It's one of the four basalt *moai* that have been found on Easter Island,' Julius said, understanding. 'In the 1800s, the British took the two biggest ones—'

'But they were the wrong ones,' Jack said. 'They should have taken the *oldest* one. I've been to Easter Island, too, so I know that the more recent statues, all 1,200 of them, are all cut from volcanic tufa; and while they are certainly impressive to look at, they're of little value to our mission.

'The oldest *moai*, however—which are possibly thousands of years old, which some say predate the arrival of Polynesians to the island—*look nothing like* the famous newer ones. They're smaller, with more rounded heads. They look more like E.T. than human beings. And the oldest basalt, or bekhen, statue is still on the island, standing all by itself on the north-west corner, on a platform called the Ahu Vai Mata. It is the "lone bekhen sentinel" that Napoleon never found.

'Which brings me to the picture on Genghis Khan's shield.' He showed them a jpeg of it:

'See the image on the left-hand side? That sealed the deal for me: it depicts a strip of land that looks to me a lot like the north-west corner of Easter Island. It's a remote corner, far from the main tour-ist sites, and only someone who's been there would know it if they saw it. That little figure on it is the lone basalt statue on the Ahu Vai Mata—'

He cut himself off.

The twins were staring at him, slack-jawed.

'Excuse my language,' Lachlan said, 'but holy fucking shit, Jack. You figured this all out by yourself?'

'I just put the pieces together,' Jack said. 'Oh, and one last thing: Alby's calculations of the Pillar-laying times set the dual equinox at 1800 hours Mexico time. Easter Island's in the same time zone as Mexico, and that time, 6 p.m., has meaning: it's sunset. And on the day of the dual equinox, the moment our sun sets is the exact moment the Dark Sun rises—at exactly 6 p.m. on March 20, the final Vertex will be exposed to *both suns at the same time* and thus hit by the light of each of them.'

Jack grimaced. 'Unfortunately, all this knowledge isn't enough. Now I have to get there and finish this thing once and for all.'

'How are you going to do that?' Julius asked incredulously. 'Look at this plane. Look at all of us.'

Jack did exactly that. He thought about his team and it made him feel ill.

They were broken, wounded and bloodstained. This gigantic mission had taken them all to the very limit and it had torn them to shreds.

Wizard was dead.

Pooh Bear and Stretch were now incapacitated by hideous wounds; indeed, Stretch had never quite recovered fully from his time in Mordechai Muniz's dungeon.

Sky Monster: throwing up due to Cieran's nerve-agent.

The twins: scratched and gashed from their brave run through the Fourth Vertex, both were now sickly pale due to Cieran's drug.

Lily: in Carnivore's hands, heading toward the Sixth Vertex.

That wasn't even mentioning Zoe, Alby and Lois back at Carnivore's lair in eastern Russia, imprisoned in their formaldehyde tanks.

And then there was Jack himself. Bruised and wounded, his nose broken.

This team—this wonderful team of international warriors—had been beaten to a pulp.

And all Jack could think was: *I did this. I did this to them. I didn't lead them well enough and now look at them. Now I have to make it right.*

He clenched his jaw and stood up.

'Julius, Lachlan,' he said. 'I need you two to help me one last time.'

It took them four tries, but eventually they got the jeep in position.

As it was no longer capable of vertical lift-off these days, they had to find another way to get the *Halicarnassus* into the air.

Sitting in the pilot's seat, Jack had reversed the down-tilted plane, scraping its wheelless forward landing strut back along the roadway. Then he had quickly brought the plane forward, making it leap slightly and lurch upward, causing the wheelless landing strut to rise a few feet into the air . . .

. . . at which point the twins had quickly backed the jeep in under the landing strut, just as it came down again . . .

Bam!

The thick vertical strut thunked down onto the bed of the jeep, landing squarely on a big pile of sandbags the twins had positioned just behind the front seats. The jeep's tyres had also been half-deflated, to account for the expansion of the air in them when they heated up later.

Most of a 747's weight is in its middle—mainly due to the engines and fuel in its wings—so the jeep just had to bear the lesser weight of the *Halicarnassus*'s front section. And the *Hali* was also already much lighter than most jumbos, so Jack figured if they could keep the jeep moving, that might disperse the weight a little and maybe they could get the plane into the air.

While the twins had been preparing the jeep, Jack had cleared the *Hali* of any excess weight and all its passengers: Pooh Bear, Stretch and Sky Monster.

Then he boarded the plane, alone. Not even Horus would accompany him on this final mission.

Pooh, Stretch and Sky Monster—with Horus tethered unhappily to his wrist—now sat on the salt hill watching the plane-jeep hybrid like spectators at a football match. They were surrounded by water bottles, guns and as much medical equipment as they could carry.

If Jack got the *Halicarnassus* up and away, the twins would try to get them all to Amman somehow.

With its front strut resting on the jeep, the mighty *Halicarnassus* rolled around on the desert highway.

From the hill, Sky Monster watched sadly. 'That plane has been a goddamn warhorse, as much a part of this team as any of us. If Jack gets her into the air, he won't be able to land her convention-ally. I'm never going to see her again. See you later, *Halicarnassus*.'

The great black 747 was pointed down the highway now. The road stretched away to the horizon.

'Okay, boys,' Jack said into his radio. 'Take-off speed is about 140 miles an hour. Just stay with me as long as you can, then throw the jeep into neutral and, whatever you do, keep her straight.'

'We'll do our best,' Lachlan replied from the jeep.

Jack powered up the *Hali*'s engines.

Lachlan revved the jeep.

Then the big black 747 started moving forward, with the jeep moving with it, acting as its forward landing gear.

Travelling in this way, the two vehicles sped down the highway, getting faster and faster, and for as long as he could, Lachlan kept the gas pedal floored and gripped the steering wheel tightly.

The road sped by beside him, the *Hali*'s nose looming above him and Julius, and then suddenly the twins felt the acceleration of the plane propel them powerfully forward.

'*Neutral!*' Julius yelled above the din. '*Put her into neutral!*'

Lachlan did so and the jeep went into overdrive—shooting along the road at terrific speed, the bitumen streaking by on either side, and Lachlan's knuckles went white on the steering wheel, grappling with it in a desperate effort to keep the jeep moving in a straight line.

'*I'm losing it!*' he yelled. '*I can't hold it straight much long—*'

Then his front left tyre exploded, just as there came an almighty roar from behind him and the jeep spun out, skidding laterally off the highway—round and round and round, kicking up a huge cloud of dust, before it lurched to a halt in the sand beside the

highway, and Lachlan and Julius spun in their seats to see . . .

. . . the *Halicarnassus* soaring into the sky!

Its nose had lifted off their jeep at the exact same moment their tyre had burst.

Jack was away.

And so after all his previous missions with his band of loyal team-mates, in the final confrontation to come, it would just be Jack, alone.

He flew into the night, the last night before the day of the dual equinox, headed for the Sixth and final Vertex.

SEVENTH BATTLE

THE
ARRIVAL OF THE
SECOND SUN

Easter Island

EASTER ISLAND
20 MARCH, 2008
THE DAY OF THE FINAL DEADLINE

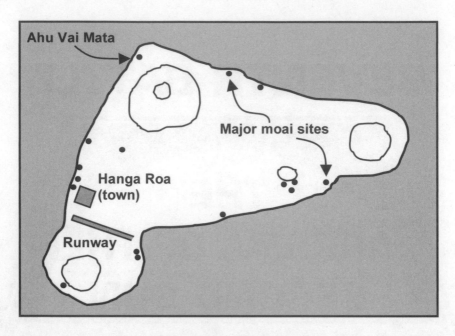

EASTER ISLAND

**BASALT STATUE AT THE AHU VAI MATA
AS IT STANDS TODAY**

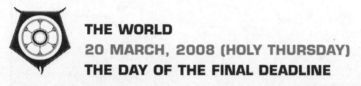

THE WORLD
20 MARCH, 2008 (HOLY THURSDAY)
THE DAY OF THE FINAL DEADLINE

As Thursday, March 20, dawned, weather systems around the world went haywire.

Mountainous waves rolled across the south Atlantic, battering the coast of Africa. In the Indian Ocean, supertankers were thrown around like bath toys. In the Pacific, tsunami warnings had been issued in nine countries.

Tornadoes raged across the American mid-west. Cyclones battered Asia. Active volcanoes from Mount Aetna in Italy to the Cerro Azul in the Galapagos started throwing up fountains of lava while dormant ones started to rumble and smoke, suggesting they wouldn't be dormant for long.

Photos from the International Space Station showed several dozen dramatic cloud formations across the globe, the deep whirlpool-shaped signatures of hurricanes and cyclones.

The world was going mad.

It was as if it were convulsing.

At the same time, astronomers from observatories around the world reported that similar things were happening throughout the solar system: the gaseous atmospheres of Jupiter, Neptune and Saturn were churning and roiling. Volcanoes on Jupiter's geologically active moon, Io, were erupting with such force that their projectiles were escaping the moon's atmosphere.

It wasn't just Earth, the astronomers said. Some silent invisible

force was acting *on the whole solar system.*

Scientists had no answers, governments called for calm, and people across the world flocked to churches, mosques and synagogues. Evangelists and New Agers proclaimed the arrival of the end of the world and for once, they appeared to be right.

The Dark Sun had arrived at the edge of the solar system.

In the midst of this unprecedented weather, two behemoths of the sea powered southward across the storm-ravaged Pacific Ocean.

They were the two newest additions to the Chinese fleet, the mighty aircraft carriers the *Mao Zedong* and the *China*.

Normally the two grey-hulled monsters—and their escort groups of frigates and destroyers—dominated the ocean, but today, lashed by heavy rain and pounded by massive waves, they were making terribly slow progress. Due to the weather, their planes were either stored in their hangars belowdecks or tied down on the flight deck.

On the bridge of the *China* stood Colonel Mao Gongli, alongside Wolf—who a day before had taken one look at Mao's Sixth Pillar and thrown it to the floor, declaring it a crude fake.

Spectral analysis confirmed his opinion. Mao's Pillar was an impressive replica carved from selenite crystal. Vulture and Scimitar had tricked him.

Wolf glared at the horizon, teeth grinding.

They were already a day-and-a-half late and he cursed himself for placing his trust in Mao and his aircraft carriers. After escaping Carnivore's lair, he should have flown directly here, flying above the bad weather, but instead he'd gone directly to Beijing, where he'd been transferred to the Chinese carriers already en route to the final Vertex.

At last, their destination came into view.

It was a tiny barren island in the middle of the largest ocean on the planet. Barely ten miles long and covered with dry grass and low hills, it was famous worldwide for the cult of giant

statue-building that had obsessed its inhabitants for nearly a thousand years.

It was Easter Island.

Wolf thought about Easter Island.

Its mysterious *moai* had long intrigued the world. Reaching heights of over eleven metres—forty feet—they were colossal in every sense of the word. Every statue faced *inland* (except for a unique set of seven which for some reason stared to the south-west), chins raised, gazing forever up at the sky.

Their size, their peculiar elongated faces, and the utter remoteness of the island itself had made the statues a source of mystery and speculation since Europeans found them on Easter Sunday, 1722.

Most experts agreed that the *moai* represented dead chiefs, but over the years, some writers have claimed that they depict extra-terrestrial visitors—an argument that gained credibility from the fact that the earliest statues are *not* elongated. Indeed, the earliest *moai* do not look human at all.

Added to this is the fact that while the first Easter Islanders were Polynesian, *nowhere in Polynesia is there a history of giant statue-building*.

Some scholars have used this information to postulate that the earliest statues on the island were *already there* when the first Polynesians arrived.

This then raised the much bigger question: who built the first statues?

Unfortunately, the arrival of white men severed the historical trail. In the 1800s, Spanish slave ships kidnapped the last of the Easter Islanders en masse, sending them to work and die in the guano mines of Peru, and so any ancestral knowledge of the statues—especially the earliest ones—was lost forever.

★ ★ ★

Wolf gazed at the island before him, covered by low stormclouds, veiled in rain.

If he was angry before, he became positively furious when he arrived at the island thirty minutes later.

A black Tupolev-144 jet was already parked on the island's runway.

EASTER ISLAND, PACIFIC OCEAN
20 MARCH, 2008 (HOLY THURSDAY),
1730 HOURS
30 MINUTES BEFORE THE FINAL DEADLINE

Throughout that afternoon, in the slashing rain and violent seas, the dual-carrier Chinese fleet set about surrounding Easter Island. They anchored the *Mao Zedong* off the north-west corner and the *China* to the south, near the island's sole airport.

The *China* towered above the small town of Hanga Roa, the only town on Easter Island, dwarfing it. Chinese troops poured ashore, ordering the three thousand inhabitants of the island to remain in their homes—it wasn't hard; owing to the drenching rain, most of them were already there.

On Wolf's instructions, the *Mao Zedong* was moved a few kilometres away from the north-west corner—a four-wave tsunami was coming in from the north, and when it arrived, the coastal waters would recede, exposing the seabed. The aircraft carrier needed to be far enough out to avoid being grounded.

Four MiG-26 interceptors and one aerial early-warning plane were launched from the carrier to patrol the skies for intruders.

Finally and most importantly, Wolf led an advance party ashore, landing on the north-west corner of the island above a steep earthen cliff. Sonar scans had revealed a large underwater entrance at the base of the cliff, similar to the entrances at the Second and Third Vertices. On the hill overlooking the cliff, Wolf saw the ruins of a lone *moai* platform known as the Ahu Vai Mata.

The statue—which lay on its side in front of the stage-like platform—was one of the four rare *moai* cut from basalt and one of the oldest statues on the island, from the early period when the statues were shorter, their faces more horizontally aligned; it was one of the statues suspected to have existed before the arrival of the Polynesians.

Had it been standing, Wolf saw, it would have perfectly matched the picture of this Vertex's entrance depicted on the Dragon's Egg.

'The first wave of the tsunami is coming!' Mao yelled to Wolf as they stood on the rainswept cliff.

'I'm counting on it!' Wolf called back above the wind. 'Carnivore's already inside. I assume he used scuba gear to get in. But the sea is too rough for that now! Besides, we're not gonna need scuba gear. When the wave arrives, the ocean will retreat and that's when we'll be going in. Tell your men to get their ziplines ready!'

Minutes later, just as Wolf had predicted, the waters to the north of Easter Island suddenly receded, sweeping dramatically backward a full five hundred metres, retreating in a wide whitewater curve that revealed the sandy ocean floor.

Directly beneath his position on the clifftop, Wolf saw the imposing entrance to the Sixth Vertex. As at Hokkaido, it was rectangular and hangar-sized and cut into the base of the cliff.

Mao gasped, 'Good God . . .'

Wolf just yelled, 'Okay! Go! Down the ziplines!'

Not wasting a moment, their advance party—Wolf, Mao and five Chinese paratroopers—abseiled down the face of the now-exposed cliff, until they eventually landed on wet sand, right in front of the massive stone entry doorway.

Looking inside the doorway, Wolf saw another many-pillared hall that disappeared into darkness, ending at a hill of steps, again just like at Hokkaido.

'Inside! Before the wave arrives!' he yelled.

He had just started to run inside when a frantic voice came in

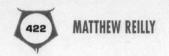

over their radios in Chinese and at first, Wolf couldn't believe what he was hearing.

'*Sir! Hostile aircraft detected! It's a 747, stealth signature! It is incoming at considerable speed, on a dead-straight bearing! It's coming right for us!*'

The *Halicarnassus* dropped out of the cloud layer, flying at a shallow descending angle.

It did not bank. It did not swerve. It flew in an unwavering dead-straight line.

A moment after it appeared on their screens, the Chinese radar operators on the *Mao Zedong* and in their AWACS plane detected a smaller signature zipping away from the 747.

Wolf had warned them about that: his son had a set of carbon-fibre wings called Gullwings that he sometimes used for covert aerial insertions. Predictably, he was using them now.

The MiGs were dispatched with orders to shoot down the *Halicarnassus* and locate-and-destroy the Gullwings.

But when they fired on the steadily-descending *Halicarnassus*, they found it emitting a veritable storm of electromagnetic interference and their missiles veered away from it. They tried guns but had even less luck with them. They couldn't know that inside the plane were some jerry-rigged Warblers, amped up on super-high power levels, so that the *Hali* now had, for a short time at least, its own aeroplane-sized Warbler.

Oddly, though, in the face of all this fire, the plane did not deviate once from its course.

It *still* didn't bank or swerve.

It just kept on flying down through the driving rain.

Either its pilot was crazy or nerveless or—someone realised—there was no-one at the controls at all . . .

While two MiGs chased down the tiny aerial signature that had zipped away from the *Halicarnassus* earlier, the remaining two

MiGs pulled alongside the downward-flying black 747 to visually examine its cockpit.

They flew on either side of it, keeping pace with it. At no time did the *Halicarnassus* fire on them or even seem to notice their presence.

'Mao Zedong, *this is Interceptor One*,' one of the pilots reported. '*I have a visual on the cockpit of that plane. I see no pilot in there. Thing must be flying on autopilot—*'

'Mao Zedong, *this is Interceptor Three. We've located that smaller signal. It's banking in a wide circle to the south, trying to approach the island from the other side!*'

'*The plane is a decoy*,' Mao Gongli's voice came in over the radio. '*Close in on that smaller signal and kill it!*'

As the first tsunami wave rushed toward Easter Island, sweeping in over the section of seabed that had been exposed earlier, the *Halicarnassus* streaked low over its leading edge.

It was going to touch down ahead of the approaching wave, right in front of the ancient hangar-sized doorway to the Vertex. But it did nothing to prepare for landing: it did not alter its angle of approach nor did it lower its landing gear.

The ghost plane just hit the exposed section of seabed roughly and skidded across it, sliding wildly across the wet sand before one of its wings *slammed* into the ancient doorway cut into the cliff-base and the wing was sheared clean off, while the rest of the plane went sliding inside the massive doorway.

The tsunami wave followed it ten seconds later, thundering into the north-western corner of Easter Island, a giant foaming wall of whitewater. It smashed against the cliffs, sending spray showering skyward, while inside the Vertex's multi-pillared entry hall, the great wave just picked up the *Halicarnassus* and hurled it forward, throwing the 747 as if it were a child's plaything onto the hill of steps at the far end, depositing it there only a few minutes after Wolf's entry team had themselves stepped over the hill.

★ ★ ★

Minutes later, as the first wave of the tsunami lost its momentum and curled around the northern side of the island, the Chinese interceptors that had gone south in pursuit of Jack's tiny Gullwing signal caught up with him . . .

. . . and found only the Gullwings, flying by remote, with a smiley-faced sandbag mannequin named George strapped into them.

At the same moment, inside the Vertex, the sorry carcass of the *Halicarnassus* teetered on the top of the step-hill, a sloshing body of water filling the entry hall behind it.

The plane was an absolute wreck: one wing had been ripped off; its underbelly was beyond repair, eviscerated by the slide across the ocean floor; all of its cockpit windows were shattered and clumps of wet sand lined its gun turrets.

For a long moment, the once-great 747 sat silent and still, perched on the summit of the step-hill, when abruptly one of its wing-mounted doors was kicked open from the inside . . .

. . . and out of the destroyed plane stepped Jack West Jr.

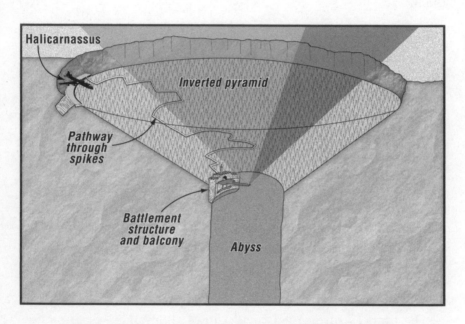

Labels within figure:
- Halicarnassus
- Inverted pyramid
- Pathway through spikes
- Battlement structure and balcony
- Abyss

THE SIXTH VERTEX AT EASTER ISLAND

Jack beheld the Sixth Vertex.

Compared with the other Vertices he'd seen, it seemed a rather simple structure, but its appearance was deceptive.

The Sixth Vertex was fashioned in the shape of an enormous funnel with steeply-sloping sides converging to a round abyss at the bottom. It was perhaps a thousand feet wide at the top, but only two hundred feet across at the base.

Suspended above it all, of course, was a familiar inverted bronze pyramid—which right now bore many pulsing amber flares on two of its sides, no doubt fired by Carnivore on his arrival earlier to illuminate the vast space.

In the dim golden light, Jack assessed the surface of the immense funnel: it appeared to be solid, but on closer examination, he saw that it was not.

Not at all.

The funnel's surface was made up of thousands—perhaps millions—of viciously sharp five-foot-high spikes carved from some kind of slate-coloured stone. Each spike was positioned only a foot from the next one, creating a dense forest of the things—which, when multiplied to cover the surface area of the immense funnel, made it seem solid.

Jack touched the tip of one of the grey spikes. It drew blood, even with a light touch.

Off to his left, a trench of some sort cut through the chest-high forest of supersharp spikes. It looked like a path and Jack saw that it wound irregularly back and forth down the slope of the funnel, providing safe passage through the spike forest before finally arriving at a fortified battlement-like structure mounted at the edge of the abyss. Stretching out from this structure was a long ornate balcony that gave access to the pyramid's peak.

Jack guessed that while the path led you through the spike forest, it also contained this Vertex's traps, to which the golden plaque's frame would provide the solution. Indeed, right now, he saw Wolf and Mao and their team rushing down the path, about a third of the way down its length, their heads bobbing above the spikes.

It was 5:51 p.m.

The last Pillar had to be laid at 6 p.m., at the moment of the dual equinox.

And then Jack saw Carnivore.

He was a long way ahead of Wolf, down on the balcony that stretched out over the abyss to the pyramid. Iolanthe, Diane Cassidy, Lily and Alexander were with him, along with his four Spetsnaz bodyguards.

Mounted on a line of stone pedestals near him were the four Ramesean Stones he needed: the Firestone, the Philosopher's Stone, the Basin of Rameses and the Twin Tablets of Thutmosis.

Also positioned on a pedestal of their own were all five of the previously-charged Pillars, variously taken from the other players in this quest after they had laid them.

And in Carnivore's hand was the Sixth Pillar, the Jesus Pillar, found by Jack in the Roman salt mine. It was dripping wet.

As the *Halicarnassus* had made its spectacular entrance, Carnivore had just finished double-cleansing the Sixth Pillar in the springwater-filled Basin. He spun when he heard the resounding bang of the *Halicarnassus* landing on the summit of the funnel and smiled when he saw it. West the Younger never gave up, even when he was hopelessly lagging behind.

But as Carnivore knew and as Jack now saw, the simple fact of the matter was this: Carnivore was too far in front, his lead was too big.

No-one could get to him in time. Not Wolf, and certainly not Jack. Carnivore was going to lay the Sixth Pillar and save the world from the Dark Star—and in doing so he was going to gain the sixth and final reward: *Power*.

Jack assessed his situation. He was coming last in this three-way race. There was no way to overtake Wolf on the path, not unless he went directly *over* the spike forest—

Jack turned.

The *Halicarnassus*—dented and battered and with only its right wing still attached to it—teetered on the summit of the funnel, held in place by its outer starboard-side jet engine, the engine hooked over the brink of the step-hill.

'It *would* be cheating,' he said aloud, gazing at the plane. 'Screw it.' Jack hurried inside the *Hali*.

Thirty seconds later, he was in the cockpit, sliding into the pilot's seat. He popped a safety cover, revealing four switches: switches that in an emergency disengaged each of the plane's four wing-mounted engines, dropping them from the wings. It was a safety feature on all jet aeroplanes.

Jack patted the plane one last time. 'Thanks for the memories, baby. I'm sorry to do this to you.'

Then he flicked the switch that released the *Halicarnassus*'s outer starboard-side engine.

On the wing, an explosive bolt detonated sharply, and the enormous cylindrical engine hanging from the wing disengaged from it. It didn't fall far, since it was already wedged against the summit of the step-hill.

But the *Halicarnassus* did.

Released from the summit, it began to slide, slowly at first, then faster, down into the gigantic funnel.

The sight of the *Halicarnassus* sliding down into the funnel of the Sixth Vertex was nothing short of astonishing.

The battered black plane, now with only one wing, skidded down the spike-riddled slope, its aluminium belly scraping over the tightly-spaced spikes, emitting an ear-splitting fingernails-on-chalkboard screech.

It picked up speed as it went.

Sparks flew as it slid down the slope, getting faster and faster. The shriek of its underbelly scraping over the spikes ripped the air.

In the trench-path, Wolf saw it—saw the big black plane bypassing the convoluted pathway and taking the direct route to the abyss: straight down.

'Fuck!' he roared.

The plane was rushing down the slope now. Despite its own considerable size, it was dwarfed by the scale of the inverted pyramid and the funnel. It looked like a toy compared with the gargantuan ancient place.

Down on the balcony, Carnivore also turned and his jaw dropped in total surprise.

For the first time in his professional life, something had cracked his unflappable air. For the first time, someone had done something that Carnivore had not anticipated at all.

He watched in frozen horror as the big black *Halicarnassus* rushed down the slope toward him, kicking up sparks.

Then the 747's huge nose blasted *right through* the fortified battlement surrounding the abyss, sending ancient bricks flying every which way, all over the balcony and into the abyss. Carnivore's men dived for cover. Diane Cassidy huddled behind a stone pedestal on the balcony. Iolanthe and the two children did likewise.

When the dust settled, the whole front half of the enormous plane protruded through the smashed fortified wall, the big black 747 tilted precariously downward, its nose almost touching the balcony and for a moment, Carnivore thought it would break through.

But it didn't.

With a groan of straining metal, the big plane stopped, hanging poised over the near end of the balcony at an extreme angle, nose-down, its waist gripped by the semi-destroyed ancient wall.

It was 5:55 p.m.

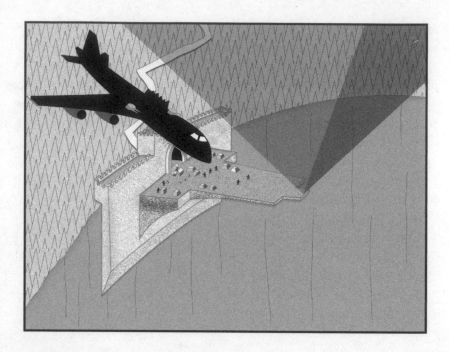

Carnivore stood exposed on the balcony before the *Halicarnassus*. The massive black plane glared down at him like an angry god, its shattered cockpit windows looking remarkably like eyes.

Carnivore searched for a sign of movement in the cockpit, for a glimpse of Jack.

'Gentlemen!' he ordered his troops. 'Guns up! Take out anyone or anything that emerges from that plane!' Then, calling toward the plane: 'West the Younger! I imagine it's you in there! A bold last-ditch move, to be sure, but you cannot win here! You are out-numbered and outgunned!'

Carnivore didn't notice that beside him, Iolanthe had backed away, as had Lily and Alexander.

Then suddenly something moved in the cockpit and the four Spetsnaz guards opened fire on it, pummelling the downtilted cock-pit with hundreds of rounds.

After a moment, they stopped firing, their guns smoking.

There was now no movement from the cockpit.

Carnivore kept watching it, searching for—

Jack's voice came in over a speaker: '*Outnumbered, yes. Outgunned, no . . .*'

Then, startlingly, Carnivore saw movement—not from the cockpit, but from over on the *Halicarnassus*'s sole remaining wing: the 50mm turret-mounted cannon nestled on the shoulder of the wing was revolving . . .

. . . to point its twin barrels directly at Carnivore.

'Oh, Lord . . .' Carnivore breathed as he saw Jack seated at the controls of the turret. 'You win, West the Younger.'

Jack opened fire.

The twin-barrelled 50mm cannon exploded to life, unleashing two long tongues of fire and a withering wave of bullets that would have ripped open a fighter jet.

When it hit a human being, the result was devastating.

The front half of Carnivore's body was instantly turned to pulp, dozens of fist-sized 50mm bullet wounds erupting in violent succession all over his torso. He jolted like a marionette, convulsing with each impact, the fusillade of bullets not allowing him to fall until Jack stopped firing and Carnivore at last collapsed to the ground, motionless, hardly even resembling a human being anymore.

It was the same for the Spetsnaz men beside him. They were blasted away as well, their bodies turned to bloody messes. One man was hurled clear off the balcony by the wave of bullets and he sailed down into the bottomless abyss screaming.

When it was over, Jack clambered out of the turret and down the wing, leaping down onto the balcony with a Desert Eagle pistol in each hand.

Lily rushed to him, embraced him. He let her do so, but did not hug her back—he kept his guns trained on Iolanthe, Alexander and Diane Cassidy. His eyes were like steel.

To Iolanthe: 'You're a strange woman, but you saved my life once so I'm not inclined to kill you now . . . unless you give me a reason to. Now hold the boy and stay out of my way.'

Iolanthe stepped back, gripping Alexander by the hand, and wisely said nothing. Diane Cassidy did the same.

Jack picked up the still-wet Sixth Pillar from the ground beside Carnivore's remains and glanced back at the trench-path, to check on Wolf and Mao's progress—they were still in the trench, but closer now, almost here.

He spun to look over at the inverted pyramid at the far end of the balcony. They had just enough time.

He turned to Lily. 'You know, kiddo, somehow I always knew this would come down to you and me. We do this together.'

5:59 p.m.

Lily grabbed the Twin Tablets and hurried along beside Jack as he strode out across the ornate balcony, high above the dark abyss, toward the upside-down pyramid that was the Sixth Vertex.

They came to the peak of the pyramid . . . where Jack gave Lily the Pillar.

Lily frowned, not understanding.

'You have to read the inscription from one of the tablets when you place the final Pillar,' he said. 'I can't read Thoth. You can.'

Lily nodded nervously. 'What about the reward? *Power.* What if I become, like, all-powerful?'

Jack looked at her closely, sincerely. 'Kiddo. There's no other person on this planet I'd trust with such power.'

Lily smiled a little.

'Okay . . .'

The clock struck 6:00, the moment of sunset.

And so as the dual equinox began and Easter Island became singularly exposed to the rays of the two suns, while Jack guarded her, Lily read from one of the Twin Tablets, speaking aloud a language few had ever heard.

Then, as she uttered the final line, she inserted the Pillar into its matching slot in the peak of the pyramid.

It clicked into place, and as had happened at each of the five Vertices before, a blinding beam of white light lanced out from the ancient inverted pyramid, shooting down into the abyss, plunging into the bowels of the Earth.

Although they couldn't see it, at that moment, a spectacular mechanism within the Earth exploded into action.

At *all five* of the other Vertices—from Abu Simbel to England, to Cape Town, Japan and Diego Garcia—dazzling beams of light also now ignited, lancing down into the centre of the Earth from the diamond-tipped peaks of their inverted pyramids.

The six beams of light converged, striking the Earth's iron core, and a profound planetary resonance began—a vibrating hum that sent an invisible harmonic force out into space, a force that counterbalanced the incoming violence of the Dark Star, nullifying it just as the Dark Star reached the edge of the solar system, the closest it would come to Earth.

The violent weather patterns on the surface of the Earth ceased almost immediately—booming volcanoes fell silent, their showering lava flows becoming calm pools of simmering molten liquid once more; cyclones and hurricanes stopped almost in mid-gust, causing wind-tossed cars and caravans to literally drop to the ground, skidding to shrieking halts; storm-tossed oceans stopped overtopping coastal highways and cliffs, to be replaced immediately by the more benign sounds of regular-sized ocean waves lapping against the shore.

People across the world—previously huddling indoors or battling valiantly against the elements; from the coasts of America to the jungles of Africa, from the snow plains of Norway to the dry plains of India—were left standing amid the destruction, perplexed and confused, as an eerie calm settled over the world and normality returned.

The deadly zero-point force of the Dark Star had been repelled.

At the Sixth Vertex, the funnel-shaped cavern was still bathed in the glare of the unearthly white light plunging into the abyss. Then without warning the laser-like light withdrew up the shaft and all its mighty energy seemed to retreat into the Pillar lodged in the pyramid's peak.

The Pillar glowed brilliantly, pulsing with pure white light.

Then, again as before, the Pillar clicked and came free of the pyramid, and Lily caught it in her hands.

The pulsing white light emanating from the glass-like Pillar shone on her face, and as he watched her, Jack saw Lily's eyes glaze over hypnotically—the whites of her eyes going pitch black—and then they widened as if filled with something . . . some kind of force . . . energy . . . or power . . .

And for a fleeting instant, Jack had an insight into what this final reward, *power*, might actually be and he wondered if in giving it to Lily, he had just made the greatest mistake of his life.

As the cavern returned to relative darkness and silence, Wolf and Mao emerged from the trench-path. Flanked by their five Chinese special forces escorts, they stepped past the stricken *Halicarnassus* and out onto the balcony.

Jack and Lily had moved halfway down the balcony, but were now trapped out on it.

Wolf saw the Pillar in Lily's hands, saw the deadly black stare in her eyes.

'Oh no, *no* . . .' he gasped.

Foolishly, his Chinese special forces guards raised their guns at Jack and Lily.

Lily's black eyes flashed with anger, glaring at them—

—and in that instant, all five of the Chinese soldiers clutched their throats in agony, unable to breathe. They collapsed to their knees, choking, before they all dropped to the ground, dead.

Wolf was stunned. Mao was, too.

Beside Lily, Jack was astonished.

That was the reward power, he realised. *The power to enact your thoughts, to impose your will on others absolutely and without restraint. The ultimate power.*

Jack looked at Lily, at her angry unearthly stare.

She was glaring at Diane Cassidy, still cowering behind a pedestal: 'You. You betrayed us, informed our enemy of everything we were doing. I think you should die.'

Instantly, Diane fell to her knees. Her eyes were locked on Lily's as she began to choke, but then *blood* started to flow from her bulging eyes, an instant before both eyes burst out of her head in twin grisly sprays and she flopped to the ground, dead.

Seeing the hideous deaths of his men and Cassidy, Mao fled.

Her face impassive, Lily just watched him run.

'I imagine you weren't so fearful when you tortured Wizard, Colonel Gongli,' she said, her voice oddly deep.

Breathing in short ragged gasps, Mao hurried off the balcony, running beneath a section of the semi-destroyed battlement above him.

As he did so, Lily casually waved a hand at the battlement—and a great landslide of bricks dropped away from the battlement structure and landed with all their weight *right on top of Mao.*

Mao's body was pulverised in an instant, reduced to a bloody smear on the balcony. The rockfall that killed him lay beside the huddled figures of Iolanthe and Alexander, both scared shitless at what Lily might decide to do to them.

Jack was horrified.

He turned to face Lily. Her face was dark and twisted, shot through with fury. She gripped the glowing Pillar in one tight fist.

The Pillar is giving her these powers, he thought, *feeding her anger . . .*

'Lily, honey—' he said.

She rounded on him, her black eyes blazing . . . and for a fleeting moment, she blinked, recognising him.

And that moment of recognition—that moment of love clashing with all the hate rising within her—was too much for her little girl's brain.

Lily fainted, falling to the balcony, the Pillar dropping from her hand and coming to rest near the edge.

Which left Jack standing there beside her on the balcony: the glowing Pillar at his feet, the immense pyramid above him, the bottomless abyss below him, and one last person blocking his exit: his father.

Wolf's eyes were locked on the Pillar lying on the ground at Jack's feet.

'Jack,' he said, 'think about it. Whoever holds that thing can do *whatever he wants*. He can bend anyone to his will, he can kill with a single thought, he can rule without limit or boundary or—'

'—conscience,' Jack said.

There came a low rumbling sound. Lily's dislodging of the battlement to kill Mao had weakened the wall holding the *Halicarnassus*. The huge 747, already precariously poised above the balcony, was about to drop onto it.

'I could impose peace on the world,' Wolf said. 'Peace through the ultimate threat of force.'

'There's no such thing as a benevolent dictator, Father . . .'

'What about you, then? Go on, pick it up,' Wolf coaxed. 'Feel the power. Feel it flow through you. You know you want to.'

Jack glanced down at the glowing Pillar. It just lay there, all the power in the world . . .

He looked at it, and at Lily beside it, her eyes closed, breathing shallowly, and as he did so, deep in his heart he realised something.

He didn't want to.

He didn't want to pick it up.

He didn't want to rule over anybody.

And in that moment, Jack realised with total clarity that he *wasn't* like his father, wasn't anything like him—

The bullet slammed into Jack's chest armour, taking him completely by surprise, spinning him round, almost throwing him off the side of the balcony.

Jack lay on his belly, halfway down the length of the balcony, his feet dangling over the edge high above the abyss.

He looked up to see Wolf charging down it, going for the Pillar.

All Wolf's talk of power and peace had just been a ruse to get Jack to take his eyes off Wolf for the second he'd needed to draw and fire his gun. It had worked.

The Pillar was a foot from Jack's fingertips. Beside him, Lily was out cold.

Jack's fingers scrabbled against the balcony's polished stone floor, trying to reach the Pillar.

He heard the *Halicarnassus* groan again, saw some stone blocks and mortar crumbling beneath it. The last throes before the fall . . .

Then, just as the charging Wolf was about to get to the glowing Pillar, Jack reached out and with a desperate lunge, didn't grab hold of the Pillar—he didn't want to do that—but instead swiped at it, hitting it hard with the back of his hand, sending it sliding down the balcony, skidding toward the far end.

Wolf took off after it, racing down the balcony.

But Jack knew he'd done enough. He'd hit the Pillar hard enough to send it sliding down the elongated balcony and . . .

. . . off its end, into the abyss.

The glowing Pillar, with all its deadly power, tumbled into the bottomless chasm, disappearing forever.

Wolf chased it to the end, diving in vain, but he was too late.

Jack watched him fall to his knees at the very end of the balcony and roar in frustration—only to be yanked back to harsh reality by a sudden rumble.

Jack snapped round to see the *Halicarnassus,* poised above the balcony, finally lose its purchase on the battlement and drop from its precarious position.

In a dark corner of his mind, Jack realised he'd seen all this before.

At the Third Vertex in Hokkaido, just after he and Wolf had laid the Third Pillar, when they were both gripping it from opposite ends with blood-smeared hands.

At that time, Jack had seen a weird vision: of falling into an abyss beneath a Vertex, with a dark one-winged 747 falling above him.

The reward for laying the Third Pillar, he thought with a chill. *Sight*.

He recalled Wizard's comments about a ritual in ancient Egypt where a priest would grip an object with bloody palms and see visions; and Laozi's postulation that *sight* might be the ability to see one's own death.

So this was it. This was his death.

But that didn't mean he shouldn't try to avoid it.

His chest throbbing, his body aching, Jack summoned his last ounce of strength, scooped up Lily and half-loping, half-staggering, hauled her to the safe end of the balcony just as the full weight of the *Hali* came thundering down on it with a colossal *boom!*

Sliding from its perch, the *Halicarnassus* crashed down onto the elongated balcony about ten feet out from the battlement wall, slicing through it like a colossal axe. Almost the entire balcony was wrenched away from the battlement structure and it dropped into the abyss at the exact moment that Jack and Lily jumped onto the small leftover sliver of balcony that remained.

Jack landed on solid ground and spun, just in time to lock eyes with his father.

Still lying on his belly at the end of the balcony, his hands bunched in frustrated fists, Wolf turned to see the *Halicarnassus* fall and his eyes sprang wide.

And in that fleeting moment, Jack saw horrified understanding on his father's face: Wolf's unbridled quest for the power of the final Pillar had been his undoing. It had put him in this position, this fatal position. His desire for absolute power would kill him.

Hit by the bulk of the *Halicarnassus*, the magnificent balcony was torn from its mount and fell away from the battlement, dropping into the abyss, with Wolf on it.

Wolf fell.

As he did, he looked up and saw the inverted pyramid of the Sixth Vertex receding rapidly, getting smaller and smaller. Then the dark shadow of the one-winged *Halicarnassus* falling above him blocked out the view.

He, too, had seen this image before—at the same time Jack had, when they had simultaneously gripped the Third Pillar with blood-soaked hands; the thing was, it was *Wolf's* blood on the Pillar, not Jack's, so it had been *Wolf's death* that they had both seen.

Thus Jack West Sr, the man known as Wolf, plummeted into the fathomless darkness and, like the all-powerful Pillar that had been hurled into the great abyss before him, he was never seen again.

Getting out of the Vertex took some time and after months of racing the celestial clock, Jack was in no hurry.

Lily woke, dazed and groggy, with no memory at all of her murderous display of power.

Jack held a canteen to her mouth which she sipped gingerly.

Then, with Alexander accompanying them, they carried Carnivore's complete collection of Pillars and Ramesean Stones out of the Vertex.

Iolanthe made no attempt to steal or take them. She seemed to have reached an unspoken understanding with Jack—she would be allowed to leave here alive if she caused no further trouble.

They strapped themselves into the scuba gear Carnivore had used earlier to get through the Vertex's submerged doorway.

'Do you remember how to use all this?' Lily asked Alexander.

The boy didn't say a word. Having seen Lily's display of raw power, he seemed utterly petrified of her.

'Here, I'll show you what to do,' she said.

'How are you going to get past the Chinese warships?' Iolanthe asked Jack a little tentatively.

Jack ignored her, just clicked his radio. 'You out there, J.J.?'

There was a rush of static.

'*Copy that, Jack,*' came the voice of the Sea Ranger. '*Been waiting here a few days now. Wasn't sure you'd turn up.*'

'We turned up, all right,' Jack said wearily. 'We're ready for scuba-assisted extraction. North-west corner.'

'*Swim out and let the current take you eastward across the north shore of the island. I'll be waiting.*'

And so the four of them swam out through the now submerged pillared entry hall, with the two children tethered to Jack for safety. When they emerged from the massive doorway, they felt the tug of a strong ocean current which took them eastward, away from the Chinese naval vessels.

They did not fight it. They just let it carry them away, across the northern coast of Easter Island and several miles to the east, where they were met by J.J. Wickham's submarine, the *Indian Raider*.

They were taken aboard through a hatch and the old Kilo-class submarine sailed away to the south, away from the confused Chinese aircraft carriers still guarding Easter Island.

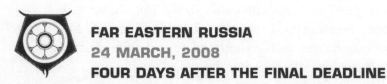

FAR EASTERN RUSSIA
24 MARCH, 2008
FOUR DAYS AFTER THE FINAL DEADLINE

Jack and Lily rushed into the improvised infirmary that had been set up in Carnivore's former lair.

Zoe, Alby and Lois lay in military cots, cleaned up and awake. Next to them, also in a cot, was Astro and beside him, Sheik Anzar al Abbas, who was flanked by Pooh Bear, Stretch, the twins, Sky Monster and a cluster of armed soldiers from Pooh Bear's regiment.

Jack and Lily had flown here as soon as the Sea Ranger had been able to unload them at a friendly nation, in this case New Zealand.

Lily rushed to Alby's side.

Jack went straight to Zoe.

'Are you okay?' Lily hugged Alby tightly.

'We're all right,' he said. 'Pooh and Stretch got here just before our air ran out.'

Lily looked apologetically at Lois, Alby's mother. 'I'm sorry, Mrs Calvin. I'm sorry you got mixed up in all this.'

Lois Calvin smiled warmly at her. 'Over the last few days, Alby has told me everything, Lily. I'm very proud of my little boy, and just as proud to know that he has such a wonderful friend in you.'

★ ★ ★

Jack stood by Zoe's bed a short distance away. For a long moment, they just gazed at each other in silence.

'Hey there,' he said.

'Jack,' Zoe said, 'I'm so sorry about what I did in Dublin and—'

'You don't have to be sorry.'

'I was stupid. I had too much to—'

'It's okay. You never have to say sorry again.'

Lily came over, took Zoe's hand. 'Hi.'

Jack said, 'I once gave Lily some advice about friendship. I told her that a friend's loyalty lasts longer than their memory. Zoe, I don't care what happened, and back then I *was* dragging my feet about us. My loyalty to you is forever. As far as what happened back then is concerned, for me it's already forgotten.'

And Zoe smiled, tears of joy running down her cheeks. Then she threw her arms around Jack's neck and as Lily clapped, kissed him passionately.

Thus the team regathered and for the rest of that day, they celebrated their triumphs, shared stories and compared wounds.

Pooh Bear told his father of his brother's betrayal and death; and of his rescue mission to save Stretch from Mordechai Muniz. The old sheik was horrified and saddened by the reports about Scimitar's actions, but in the end, he put a hand on Pooh Bear's bandaged left eye and said, 'It pleases me to know that I have at least one noble son.'

Jack told them of the *Halicarnassus*'s spectacular entrance at the final Vertex and how he had slid the plane down the slope there.

Lily said, 'I thought you always said you weren't allowed to cheat a trap system?'

Jack shrugged, a little embarrassed. 'I was in a hurry. And the fate of all life on Earth *was* at stake.'

Someone asked about Iolanthe and Alexander.

Jack informed them that he had left the British royal in New Zealand to make her own way home. Her connection with their mission had been complex, at times hostile, at times helpful, and on one occasion at the Fifth Vertex in Diego Garcia, she had saved Jack's life when she could easily have let him die. Jack was sure that they and the world hadn't seen the last of Iolanthe Compton-Jones.

As for Alexander, Jack had left him with some trusted people in New Zealand, a couple unknown to anyone in the world's military and whom Jack knew would look after him as their own: Sky Monster's sweet and grandchild-hungry parents.

'At least they'll stop pestering me for a grandkid now,' Sky Monster said.

At one point in the celebrations, Sky Monster took Jack aside and asked him to explain in more detail what had become of his beloved *Halicarnassus*.

Jack told him the whole story and Sky Monster's face fell. 'She was a good plane . . .'

'She sure was,' Jack agreed. 'But, you know, if you're up for a little break-and-enter in a few weeks' time, I think I might know where we can get you a new one.'

THE SIMPSON DESERT
SOUTH AUSTRALIA
1 MAY, 2008, 1730 HOURS
SIX WEEKS AFTER THE FINAL DEADLINE

The setting sun illuminated Jack West Jr's new farm in a glorious orange glow.

Jack's new place was a huge isolated property in the middle of the vast Australian outback, on the edge of a dry salt lake. It had been given to him by the Australian government as payment for a job well done—and to replace his last one after it had been invaded.

An old Army base, it came with a few of the features of his previous farm: some hills, a small salt mine, a runway with a hangar attached to it and lots of open space; plus some new ones, including satellite, laser and video surveillance systems.

Jack sat on the wraparound verandah of his farmhouse, sipping a cup of coffee with Zoe. In the dusty yard before them, Lily and Alby were playing happily, throwing a fake mouse for Horus to catch in mid-air and return to them.

Jack looked out at the hangar, where he saw Sky Monster doing some work on the black Tupolev-144 they had liberated from an enclosure at Easter Island's airport a few weeks before. It was smaller than the *Hali* had been, but then it was also faster. Sky Monster loved his new plane. He'd christened it the *Sky Warrior*.

As a bonus, they had found inside the Tupolev all of Carnivore's records on the Pillars, the Machine and the Dark Star, including charts, maps and digital photos of the white Thoth writing on the Pillars.

As for the five remaining Pillars themselves, they now resided inside the farm's little salt mine by the lake, in a white-walled chamber sealed with salt crystals, behind a wooden door marked with Thoth symbols carved by Lily.

They glistened, their liquid cores glowing brilliantly, unseen by anyone.

While the Pillars remained here—hidden from the world, far from humanity and the human lust for power—their rewards would remain unused, however powerful, deadly, life-saving or far-reaching they might be.

Jack had told his superiors that *all* of the Pillars had been lost during the confrontation at the final Vertex, that they had fallen with Wolf and the Sixth Pillar into the bottomless abyss there, never to be seen again. This news had been taken with some grumbling, but then, since Jack had saved the world from both destruction and tyrannical rule, it was accepted without much questioning.

In the end, Jack had decided, humanity would just have to make do on its own, without the knowledge and powers of the fabled Pillars.

As they sat together on the deck, Zoe reached out and held Jack's hand. They both now wore matching wedding rings, thanks to a civil ceremony performed the week before.

'And so the world is quiet once more,' she said.

'I have to say, I kinda like it that way,' Jack said.

'It's a good thing that whoever built that Machine built it,' Zoe said. 'They saved our asses. But what bothers me is: they themselves ultimately didn't survive. Somewhere along the way, their civilisation disappeared, despite their obvious technological advancements.'

Jack shrugged. 'The Earth is over two billion years old, Zoe. Yet in a mere 5,000 years, our version of humanity has gone from hunter-gathering to space travel. The builders of the Machine were just a civilisation that rose to a great height and then, well, who knows? Maybe they got a disease. Maybe they fought among themselves. Maybe a rogue asteroid that they never saw coming wiped them out. Civilisations rise then die, and then it all starts over again, That's the way it goes. Our civilisation will end one day—and, yes, we might bring about that end ourselves—only that's not going to happen just yet, not if I have anything to say about it.'

Zoe smiled. She pulled out a notebook. 'You know, there's still one other thing we never figured out.'

'What's that?'

'The identity of the Fifth Greatest Warrior. Let me read three quotes to you.' Zoe held up the notebook:

'"A mortal battle between father and son, one fights for all, the other for one."

'"The Fifth, the Brilliant Warrior, will be there at the Second Coming, and decide the fate of all." And,

'"The Fifth will face the greatest test and decide if all shall live or die."

'As I said, we never found out who the Fifth Warrior was,' Zoe said.

She looked at Jack closely. He just stared out at the horizon, squinting, aware of her gaze.

'You were at the final Vertex during the Second Coming, the return of the Dark Sun,' she said. 'You battled with your father, and from what you've told me, you could have picked up that Pillar and wielded its incredible power. You could have changed the entire nature of life on Earth, you could have ruled it or let Wolf rule it. But by knocking it into the abyss, you determined our fate, you decided if humanity would live or die.'

'I might have,' Jack said innocently.

'Oh, sweet Lord . . .' Zoe said. 'You *know*, don't you?'

'It's occurred to me, yes.'

Zoe shook her head. 'Jesus, Mary and Joseph, we'll never hear the end of it. Jack West Jr . . . *you're* the Fifth Greatest Warrior.'

And as she said it, Jack turned to face her, and he smiled.

THE END

ACKNOWLEDGEMENTS

The greatest thanks, as always, must go to my wonderful wife, Natalie, for indulging all of my creative eccentricities (yes, I have them) and for coming with me on an unforgettable research trip to Easter Island.

I must also send out very special thanks to Ron Cobb, the famous futurist, artist and movie art director, for generously allowing me to use his concept of the PA-27 Airborne Assault Pod in this book. Ron has designed spaceships and DeLoreans for Hollywood movies as well as real-life military applications like the assault pods, so it was a privilege for me to discuss the future of aerial bombardment with him. Thanks, Ron!

Sincere thanks also to all of the guides at the Explora Lodge at Easter Island: Nico, Tito and especially Yoyo who took Natalie and me to the Ahu Vai Mata on the remote north-west coast of the island. If you want to see Easter Island properly, look no further than the Explora Lodge.

At one point in the novel, I mention the Easter Island statue at the British Museum: it *is* indeed one of only four *moai* made of basalt, it *was* taken from Easter Island in 1868 by the British, and, yes, it *was* once erected in the cafeteria of the British Museum!

It was our young Easter Islander guide, Nico, travelling through England, who complained to the Museum's staff about it. Nico, you'll be pleased to know that when I last went there, the basalt moai was on display in a prominent and central position worthy of its historical status.

I am often asked by aspiring writers if they need to visit a location in order to write about it. The answer is: *no, you don't, but it certainly helps*. I had to go to Easter Island to find the really good stuff for this book. That said, I still haven't been to Antarctica (*Ice Station* was researched in my local suburban library!).

To everyone else, family, friends and the good folk at Pan Macmillan, thank you all once again. Never underestimate the power of your encouragement.

Matthew Reilly
Sydney, Australia
September 2009

AN INTERVIEW WITH MATTHEW REILLY

SPOILER WARNING!

The following interview contains SPOILERS from *The Five Greatest Warriors*. Readers who have not yet read the novel are advised to avoid reading this interview as it does give away major plot moments in the book.

After leaving readers falling down the abyss with Jack West Jr at the end of The Six Sacred Stones, *was it good to resume the story in* The Five Greatest Warriors?

It certainly was! Over the past two years, I've received countless emails from readers wanting to know when the next novel is coming out. (I even did a library speaking tour in 2008 and the first question I received at every event was, 'When is the next damn book coming out!')

When I wrote *The Six Sacred Stones* (6SS) way back in 2006, I knew how Jack was going to get out of his situation. Now, while I wasn't planning to start *The Five Greatest Warriors* (5GW) for several months after finishing 6SS, I decided that I would write the first fifty pages of 5GW straight away, so that the flow at the beginning of that book would be exactly the same as the flow at the end of 6SS.

I very much enjoyed finishing 6SS with a huge cliffhanger ending. The only regret I have about it is that my biggest fans (those wonderful readers who bought the book in its first week of release) had to wait the longest to find out what happened to Jack. They

had to wait the full two years between *6SS* and *5GW*, so I apologise to them!

***What did you enjoy most about writing* The Five Greatest Warriors?**

The Five Greatest Warriors was a lot of fun to write, chiefly because it's all action. It's essentially the second half of the story begun in *6SS*. Since I'd done all the set-up work in *6SS*, *5GW* was just going to be one great big rollercoaster ride to the finish.

I got a lot of satisfaction revealing the many plot twists that I'd planted in *6SS*: for instance, all the locations of the remaining Vertices (Hokkaido, Lundy Island, Diego Garcia and Easter Island) had to be figured out when I wrote *6SS*, because they had to be drawn onto the images of Stonehenge.

I particularly enjoyed revealing the location of Lundy Island in the Bristol Sea. As an author, that's one of those twists that you just love writing: the answer is right there in plain sight (the right-angle of the triangle), but readers are hopefully looking at something else that is being talked about (the connection between Stonehenge and the Giza pyramids).

Similarly, planting the solutions to the last four Vertices' protective mazes in the frame of the golden plaque was another twist I took great pleasure in writing. Like the Stonehenge images, I designed that plaque way back in 2006 and it's only now, in 2009, that I get to reveal it as a twist. When you sit on something for such a long time, it's really, really fun to reveal it!

How did you come up with the notion of linking five great historical figures to the story?

I like the idea that 'everything is connected to everything else', that stories or information or treasures travel down through history—and that many of the great individuals throughout history might have been aware of such things.

To work that into my story meant researching some of history's most famous warriors and seeing what connections I could make between them and the story I had started in *Seven Ancient Wonders*. As always, a lot of the most interesting and intriguing stuff is true. Napoleon really did study artillery under Pierre Laplace and he really did bring him to his court as a consultant on Saturn's and Jupiter's movements. Genghis Khan's grandson Kublai Khan really did try to invade Japan twice and failed both times. The Jesus–Moses link via the line of Aaron is legitimate. As for the location of Jesus Christ's tomb, well . . .

How did you come up with the rather gruesome idea of the 'living human tombs' employed by Mordechai Muniz and Carnivore?

In my opinion, one of the key elements of a good thriller is the villain. I think we as readers and moviegoers actually quite enjoy being appalled by great villains: Darth Vader, Hannibal Lecter, Heath Ledger's Joker.

In creating Muniz and Carnivore, the two villains who would make their first appearances in *5GW*, I really wanted readers to fear them. I wanted readers to see that the consequence of crossing these men was beyond terrible. Now, any villain can shoot someone, but that's old. What about a villain who keeps their victims alive for years? That, I thought, would be fearsome. And as Muniz says, just killing his enemies would be too easy; he wants them to suffer for their actions.

As with the twists I mentioned earlier, I determined Stretch's fate way back when I wrote *6SS*, so the idea of the living tombs has been something I've been sitting on for a very long time. It's very satisfying to unleash it now.

Do you ever feel that you're taking too many liberties with history?

Ooh, that's a very interesting question, because it relates not just to authors of historical fiction but also to the very nature of 'history' itself. Do I take liberties? Of course I do, but, then, what is history? Who writes it? What is 'real' history and what is not and who is the judge? Every few years, I see newspaper stories about Japanese school textbooks that claim the US was the aggressor in World War II. Is that history? Is Wikipedia a reliable source of history? The entry for 'Matthew Reilly' on Wikipedia is extraordinarily inaccurate—it contains several basic errors about me, including claims that I went to a high school I've never heard of in a town I've never been to. In China, if you Google 'Tiananmen the Square', you will find no mention of the massacre of 1989. Authors who write history books are often accused of making errors. What I'm saying is that history can be distorted, manipulated and sometimes simply changed—it's often blurry.

And when you're dealing with *ancient* history as I am in the Jack West Jr novels, I think it gets very blurry very quickly. And where the margin for historical error is large, I have no problem taking liberties or making educated guesses. (Can we really know what Khufu was thinking when he built Great Pyramid? Can we know where Genghis Khan is buried? Can we be sure there actually was a Trojan Horse?)

Ultimately, I write to entertain. I do not write textbooks. I will happily state that 85 per cent of the historical statements in my novels are true, but don't go using my books as a source for your high school history assignment because (a) I might have blended the truth with some fiction and (b) I won't tell you when you're reading the 15 per cent which is made up! (And if I've done my job as an author, you won't be able to tell the real from the fake!)

In the end, it's the story that matters to me—a good, fast-paced, fun story. I'll happily use commonly accepted history as a background to my larger story, but where it gets blurry, I'm more than happy to fill in the gaps myself!

You've written Seven Ancient Wonders, The Six Sacred Stones *and* The Five Greatest Warriors. *Will the Jack West Jr series of books count down all the way to* The One . . . ?

I very much enjoy writing about Jack and his team (and I especially like writing about Jack, Lily and Alby). So yes, I'm working on a new idea for Jack, which will be *The Four Something Somethings*.

I'll have to make sure that it's a huge story idea. To my mind, any new Jack West Jr novel will have to be bigger and bolder than the three I've already written. And if I do decide to write it, I will do so with a plan to creating a story that will count down all the way to a seventh and final novel (*The One Something Something*). So it's a good bet that *The Four Something Somethings* will end with a cliffhanger.

What else have you been up to? Any Hollywood news?

I've just finished writing the screenplay for a film adaptation of my novel *Scarecrow*. It was a really challenging project as the producers want *Scarecrow*, if all goes well, to be the first movie in a series of Shane Schofield movies. But as my readers will know, it's the third book in the Schofield series.

So what I set about doing in the *Scarecrow* screenplay was introducing the characters we encounter in the first novel, *Ice Station* (Scarecrow, Mother, Fox, Book etc), but within the story *structure* of *Scarecrow*. I'm really pleased with the result, but as I well know, Hollywood is a fickle place and writing a script is but the first step in a long journey to getting a blockbuster movie made. Fingers crossed.

The TV show I wrote, *Literary Superstars*, tragically bit the dust during the Writers' Guild strike of 2007–2008. I couldn't believe it. We had Jenna Elfman signed to star in it, Darren Star producing it, Sony and the (US) ABC network making it, and I was sitting in casting sessions watching actors read my lines (a real buzz, let me tell you) when the Writers' Guild strike hit. The strike dragged on and by the end of it, the network wanted rewrites and eventually went cold on the project. But that's Hollywood. You come to learn that until your show/movie is up there on a screen in front of an audience, it's still just a dream. But I'm hanging in there! It's always exciting to go to L.A. and 'take meetings', and, hey, *Hover Car Racer* is still at Disney . . .

So what's next? What does the future hold for Matthew Reilly?

Well, I plan to write my next novel over the course of 2010. I'm not sure what it will be about yet, whether it will feature Jack West Jr or the Scarecrow or perhaps a new hero altogether. I've even got a story idea for Aloysius Knight, so who knows?

In the end, I feel extraordinarily fortunate to tell stories for a living. I just keep trying to top myself with each book and come up with the fastest most out-of-control action-adventure stories imaginable, and so long as readers keep enjoying them, I'll keep writing them.

As always, I just hope you liked the book and I'll see you next time!

M.R.
Sydney, Australia
August 2009

Matthew Reilly
Hover Car Racer

NEVER GIVE UP. NEVER SAY DIE.

Meet Jason Chaser, hover car racer. He's won himself a place at the International Race School, where racers either make it onto the Pro Circuit – or they crash and burn.

But he's an outsider. He's younger than the other racers. His car, the *Argonaut*, is older. And on top of that, someone doesn't want him to succeed at the School and will do anything to stop him.

Now Jason isn't just fighting for his place on the starting line, he's racing for his life.

'the fastest book you'll ever read'
SYDNEY MORNING HERALD

'high-octane *Harry Potter*'
THE AGE

'exhilarating . . . fast-action fiction'
CANBERRA TIMES

'fast and furious'
BRISBANE NEWS

Matthew Reilly
Contest

The New York State Library. A brooding labyrinth of towering bookcases, narrow aisles and spiralling staircases. For Doctor Stephen Swain and his daughter, Holly, it is the site of a nightmare. For one night, this historic building is to be the venue for a contest. A contest in which Swain is to compete – whether he likes it or not.

The rules are simple. Seven contestants will enter. Only one will leave. With his daughter in his arms, Swain is plunged into a terrifying fight for survival. He can choose to run, to hide or to fight – but if he wants to live, he has to win. For in this contest, unless you leave as the victor, you do not leave at all.

'edge-of-your-seat suspense'
DAILY TELEGRAPH

'Matt Reilly, genius . . . the arrival of a rare talent'
SYDNEY MORNING HERALD

'A publishing phenomenon'
WEST AUSTRALIAN

Matthew Reilly
Ice Station

At a remote ice station in Antarctica, a team of US scientists has made
an amazing discovery. They have found something buried deep within a
100-million-year-old layer of ice. Something made of METAL.

Led by the enigmatic Lieutenant Shane Schofield, a team of crack
United States marines is sent to the station to secure this discovery for
their country. They are a tight unit, tough and fearless. They would follow
their leader into hell. They just did . . .

'action, action and more action'
DAILY TELEGRAPH

The pace is frantic, the writing snappy, the research thorough.
Unputdownable'
WEST AUSTRALIAN

Matthew Reilly
Temple

Deep in the jungles of Peru, the hunt for a legendary Incan idol in underway – an idol that in the present day could be used as the basis for a terrifying new weapon.

Guiding a US Army team is Professor William Race, a young linguist who must translate an ancient manuscript which contains the location of the idol.

What they find is an ominous stone temple, sealed tight. They open it – and soon discover that some doors are meant to remain unopened . . .

'Matthew Reilly has really arrived'
DAILY TELEGRAPH

'Reilly can be entered with deafening gunfire, in the Crichton/Grisham showcase'
WEEKEND AUSTRALIAN

'The action just keeps on coming . . . Michael Crichton meets Indiana Jones'
KIRKUS REVIEWS

Matthew Reilly
Area 7

It is America's most secret base, a remote installation known only as Area 7.

And today it has a visitor: the President of the United States.

But he's going to get more than he bargained for on this trip. Because hostile forces are waiting inside . . .

Among the President's helicopter crew, however, is a young marine. His name is Schofield. Call-sign: SCARECROW. Rumour has it, he's a good man in a storm.

Judging by what the President has just walked into, he'd better be . . .

'a roller coaster ride'
WEEKEND AUSTRALIAN

'Buckle up, put the seat back, adjust the head-rest and hang on'
THE AGE

'Enjoy, let it shred your mind'
BULLETIN

Matthew Reilly
Scarecrow

IT IS THE GREATEST BOUNTY HUNT IN HISTORY
There are 15 targets. And they must all be dead by 12 noon, today. The
price on their heads: $20 million each.

ONE HERO
Among the names on the target list, one stands out. An enigmatic
marine named Shane Schofield, call-sign: SCARECROW.

NO LIMITS
And so Schofield is hunted by gangs of international bounty hunters,
including the 'Black Knight', a ruthless hunter who seems intent on
eliminating only him.

He led his men into hell in *Ice Station*. He protected the President
against all odds in *Area 7*. This time it's different. Because this time
SCARECROW is the target.

'a metal storm of a book'
WEST AUSTRALIAN

'Reilly is as amazing as his hero . . . a cracking pace'
MELBOURNE WEEKLY

'The pace makes you giddy'
DAILY TELEGRAPH

MOSES

JESUS CHRIST

UNKN